P9-BZN-482

NOVELS BY MERCEDES LACKEY
available from DAW Books:

THE HERALDS OF VALDEMAR

ARROWS OF THE QUEEN
ARROW'S FLIGHT
ARROW'S FALL

THE LAST HERALD-MAGE

MAGIC'S PAWN
MAGIC'S PROMISE
MAGIC'S PRICE

THE MAGE WINDS

WINDS OF FATE
WINDS OF CHANGE
WINDS OF FURY

THE MAGE STORMS

STORM WARNING
STORM RISING
STORM BREAKING

KEROWYN'S TALE

BY THE SWORD

VOWS AND HONOR

THE OATHBOUND
OATHBREAKERS
OATHBLOOD

BRIGHTLY BURNING
TAKE A THIEF
EXILE'S HONOR

DARKOVER NOVEL
(with Marion Zimmer Bradley)
REDISCOVERY

THE BLACK SWAN

THE SERPENT'S SHADOW
THE GATES OF SLEEP
PHOENIX AND ASHES*

Written with **LARRY DIXON:**

THE MAGE WARS

THE BLACK GRYPHON
THE WHITE GRYPHON
THE SILVER GRYPHON

OWLFLIGHT
OWLSIGHT
OWLKNIGHT

*Forthcoming in hardcover from DAW Books

EXILE'S HONOR

A NOVEL OF VALDEMAR

MERCEDES LACKEY

DAW BOOKS, INC.
DONALD A. WOLLHEIM, FOUNDER
375 Hudson Street, New York, NY 10014
ELIZABETH R. WOLLHEIM
SHEILA E. GILBERT
PUBLISHERS
http://www.dawbooks.com

Jacket art by Jody A. Lee

Time Line by Pat Tobin

DAW Books Collectors No. 1235

DAW Books are distributed by Penguin Putnam Inc.

Book designed by Stanley S. Drate/Folio Graphics Co., Inc.

ISBN 0-7564-0085-6

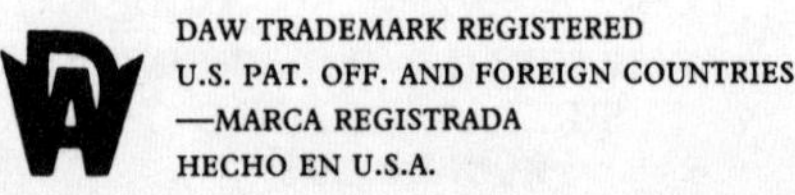

PRINTED IN THE U.S.A.

Dedicated to the memory of NYFD crews lost 9/11/2001:

Squad One:
Brian Bilcher
Gary Box
Thomas Butler
Peter Carroll
Robert Cordice
David Fontana
Matthew Garvey
Stephen Siller
Edward Datri
Michael Esposito
Michael Fodor
James Amato

Squad 18:
Eric Allen
David Halderman
Timothy Haskell
Andrew Fredericks
Lawrence Virgilio
William McGinn

Squad 41:
Thomas Cullen III
Robert Hamilton
Michael Lyons
Gregory Sikorsky
Richard VanHine
Michael Healey

Squad 252:
Tarel Coleman
Thomas Kuveikis
Peter Langone
Patrick Lyons
Kevin Prior

Squad 288:
Ronnie Gies
Joseph Hunter
Jonathon Ielpi
Adam Rand
Ronald Kerwin

Safety Battalion 1:
Robert Crawford

Fire Marshal:
Ronald Bucca

Special Operations:
Timothy Higgins
Michael Russo
Patrick Waters
Raymond Downey

Citywide Tour Commander:
Gerard Barbara
Donald Burns

OFFICIAL TIMELINE FOR THE

by Mercedes Lackey

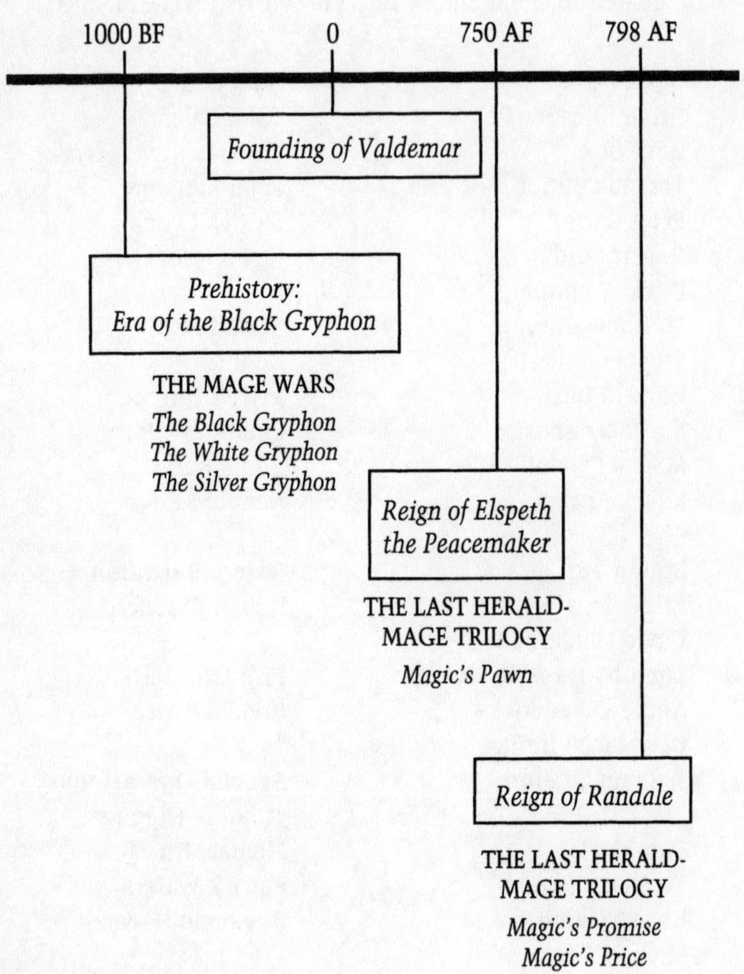

BF Before the Founding
AF After the Founding

HERALDS OF VALDEMAR SERIES

Sequence of events by Valdemar reckoning

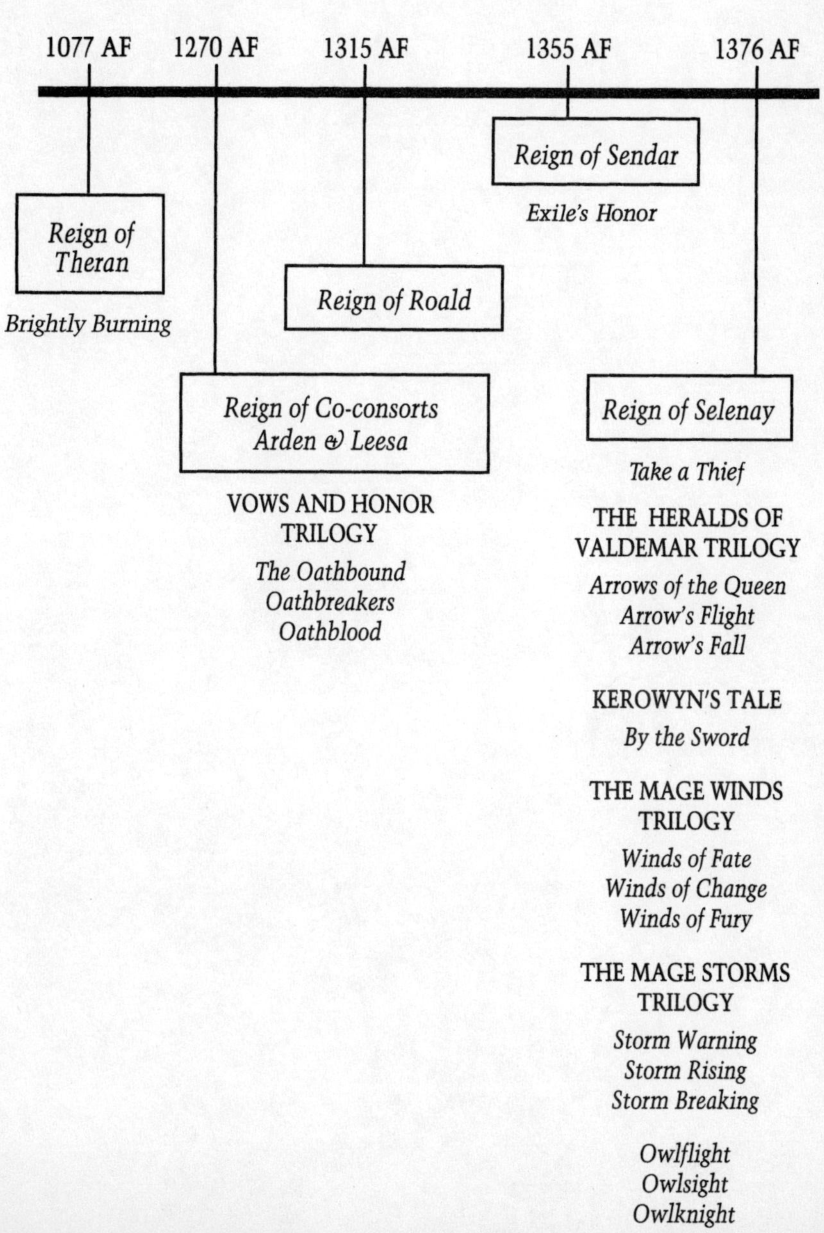

EXILE'S HONOR

PROLOGUE

SILVER stamped restively as another horse on the picket line shifted and blundered into his hindquarters. Alberich clucked to quiet him and patted the stallion's neck; the beast swung his head about to blow softly into the young Captain's hair. Alberich smiled a little, thinking wistfully that the stallion was perhaps the only creature in the entire camp that felt anything like friendship for him.

And possibly the only creature that isn't waiting for me to fail, hoping that I will, and ready to pounce on me and cut me to pieces when I do. Life for an officer of Karsite troops was spent half in defeating the enemies of Karse and half in watching his own back.

Amazingly gentle, for a stallion, Silver had caused no problems either in combat or here, on the picket line. Which was just as well, for if he had, Alberich would have had him gelded or traded off for a more tractable mount, gift of the Voice of Vkandis Sunlord or no. Alberich had enough troubles without worrying about the behavior of his beast.

He wasn't sure where the handsome and muscular creature had come from; Shin'a'in-bred, they'd told him. The Voice had chosen the beast especially for him out of a string of animals "liberated from the enemy." Which meant war booty, of course, from one of the constant conflicts along the borders. Silver hadn't come from one of the bandit nests, that was sure. The only beasts the bandits owned were as disreputable as their owners. Horses "liberated" from the bandits usually weren't worth keeping, they were so run-down and ill-treated. Silver probably came from Menmellith via Rethwellan; the King was rumored to have some kind of connection with the horse-breeding, bloodthirsty Shin'a'in nomads.

Whatever; when Alberich lost his faithful old Smoke a few weeks ago he hadn't expected to get anything better than the obstinate, intractable gelding he'd taken from its bandit owner. But fate ruled otherwise; the Voice chose to "honor" him with a superior replacement along with his commission, the letter that accompanied the paper pointing out that Silver was the perfect mount for a Captain of light cavalry. It was also another evidence of favoritism from above, with the implication that he had earned that favoritism outside of performance in the field.

Talk about a double-edged blade. . . . Both the commission and the horse came with burdens of their own. Not a gift that was likely to increase his popularity with some of the men under his command, and a beast that was going to make him pretty damned conspicuous in any encounter with the enemy. A *white* horse? Might as well paint a target on his back and have done with it.

Plus that's an unlucky color. Those witchy-Heralds of Valdemar ride white horses, and the blue-eyed beasts may be demons or witches, too, for all I know. The priests say they are. The priests call their owners the "Demon-Riders."

The horse nuzzled him again, showing as sweet a temper as any lady's mare. He scratched its nose, and it sighed with content; he wished he could be as contented. Things had been bad enough before getting this commission. Now—

There was an uneasy, prickly sensation between his shoulder blades as he went back to brushing down his new mount. He glanced over his shoulder, to intercept the glare of Leftenant Herdahl; the man dropped his gaze and brushed his horse's flank vigorously, but not quickly enough to prevent Alberich from seeing the hate and anger in the hot blue eyes.

No, indeed, the Voice had done Alberich no favors in rewarding him with the Captaincy and this prize mount, passing over Herdahl and Klaus, both his seniors in years of service, if not in experience. Neither of them had expected that he would be promoted over their heads; during the week's wait for word to come from Headquarters, they had saved their rivalry for each other.

Too bad they didn't murder each other, he thought resentfully, then suppressed the rest of the thought. It was said that some of the priests of Vkandis could pluck the thoughts from a man's head. It could have been thoughts like that one that had led to Herdahl's being passed over for promotion. But it could also be that this was a test, a way of flinging the ambitious young Leftenant Alberich into deep water, to see if he would survive the experience. If he did, well and good; he was of suitable material to continue to advance, perhaps even to the rank of Commander. If he did not—well, that was too bad. If his ambition undid him, or if he wasn't clever enough to see and avoid the machinations of those below him, then he wasn't fit enough for the post.

That was the way of things, in the armies of Karse. You rose by watching your back, and (if the occasion arose) sticking careful knives into the backs of your less-cautious fellows, and ensuring other enemies took the punishment. All the while, the priests of the Sunlord, the ones who were truly in charge, watched and smiled and dispensed favors and punishments with the same dispassionate aloofness displayed by the

One God. Karse was a hard land, and the Sunlord a hard God; the Sunpriests were as hard as both.

But Alberich had given a good account of himself along the border, at the corner where Karse met Menmellith and the witch-nation Valdemar, in the campaign against the bandits there. Frankly, Herdahl and Klaus put together hadn't been half as effective or as energetic as he'd been. He'd earned his rank, he told himself once again, as Silver stamped and shifted his weight beneath the strokes of Alberich's brush.

The spring sun burned down on his head, hotter than he expected without the breeze to cool him, hot as Herdahl's angry glare.

Demons take Herdahl. There was no reason to feel as if he'd cheated to get where he was. He'd led more successful sorties against the bandits in his first year in the field than the other two had achieved in their entire careers. He'd cleared more territory than anyone of leftenant rank ever had in that space of time—and when Captain Anberg had met with one too many arrows, the men had seemed perfectly willing to follow him when the Voice chose him over the other two candidates.

It had been the policy of late to permit the brigands to flourish, provided they confined their attentions to Valdemar and the Menmellith peasantry and left the inhabitants of Karse unmolested. A stupid policy, in Alberich's opinion; you couldn't trust bandits, that was the whole reason why they became bandits in the first place. If they could be trusted, they'd be in the army themselves, or in the Temple Guard, or even have turned mercenary. He'd seen the danger back when he was a youngster in the Academy, in his first tactics classes. He'd even said as much to one of his teachers—phrased as a question, of course, since cadets were not permitted to have opinions. The question had been totally ignored. Perhaps because it wasn't wise to so much as hint that the decisions of the Sunpriests were anything other than divinely inspired.

But, as Alberich had predicted, there had been trouble from

the brigands once they began to multiply; problems that escalated far, far past the point where their use as an irritant to Valdemar was outweighed by their effect as a scourge on Karse. With complete disregard for the unwritten agreements between them and Karse, they struck everyone, and when they finally began attacking villages instead of just robbing solitary travelers or going after single farms, the authorities deemed it time they were disposed of.

Alberich had spent a good part of his young life in the Karsite military schools and had just finished cavalry training as an officer when the troubles broke out. The ultimate authority was in the hands of the Voices, of course. The highest anyone not of the priesthood could expect to rise was to Commander. But officers were never taken from the ranks; many of the rank-and-file were conscripts, and although it was never openly stated, the Voices did not trust their continued loyalty if they were given power.

Alberich, and many others like him, had been selected at the age of thirteen by a Voice sent every year to search out young male children, strong of body and quick of mind, to school into officers. And there was one other qualification—that at least half of them be lowborn, so that they were appropriately grateful to the Voices for their opportunity to rise in rank and station.

Alberich had all those qualities, developing expertise in many weapons with an ease that was the envy of his classmates, picking up his lessons in academic subjects with what seemed to be equal ease.

It wasn't ease; it was the fact that Alberich studied long and hard, knowing that there was no way for the bastard son of a tavern wench to advance in Karse except in the army. There was no place for him to go, no way to get into a trade, no hope for any but the most menial of jobs. The Voices didn't care about a man's parentage once he was chosen as an officer, they cared only about his abilities and whether or not he would use them in service to his God and country. It was a lonely life, though. His mother had loved and cared for him to the best of her abilities, and he'd had friends among the other children of similar circumstances. When he came to the Academy, he had no friends, and his mother was not permitted to contact him, lest she "distract him," or "contaminate his purity of purpose." Alberich had never seen her again, but both of them had known this was the only way for him to live a better life than she had. And there had been a half-promise—which he had no way of knowing was kept—that if he did well at the Academy, his mother would be rewarded, perhaps with a little house of her own, if she could manage to keep herself from further sin. He had trusted in that particular Voice, though. The priest had no reason to lie to him—and every reason to give his mother that reward. After all, Karse needed officers. . . . *willing* officers, and young boys eager to throw themselves into their studies with all the enthusiasm of youth in order to become those willing officers. Knowing that their parents would be taken care of provided plenty of incentive.

And he had done better than well. He had pushed himself harder than any of his classmates pushed themselves.

Friends? When did I have the time for friends? Up before dawn for extra exercise, all my spare time practicing against the older boys, and after dinner studying by the light of Vkandis' lamps in the Temple until the priests came in for midnight prayers.

Alberich had no illusions about the purity of the One God's priesthood. There were as many corrupt and venal priests as there were upright, and more fanatic than there were forgiving. He had seen plenty of the venal kind in the tavern when they passed through his little mountain village on the way to greater places; had hidden from one or two that had come seeking pleasures strictly forbidden by the One God's edicts. He had known they were coming, looking for him, and had managed to make himself scarce long before they arrived. Just as, somehow, he had known when the Voice was coming to look for young male children for the Academy, and had made certain he was noticed and questioned—

And that he had known which customers it was safe to cadge for a penny in return for running errands—

Or that he had known that drunk was going to try to set the stable afire. Oh, that had been a tricky thing to manage—to stay awake despite aching eyes that threatened to close long enough to be able to "stumble out of bed" and into the courtyard in search of a drink from the pump "just in time" to see the first flames. *No matter how much noise is in a tavern, the sound of a child's shrill scream will penetrate it. No matter how drunk the inhabitants, the cry of "Fire!" will get the appropriate response.*

Somehow. That was Alberich's secret. He knew things were going to happen. That was a witch-power, and forbidden by the Voices of the One God. If anyone knew he had it—

The Fires, and the Cleansing. Oh, of course, those whom the One God favors are supposed to be able to endure the Fires and walk from the ashes Cleansed. Not that anyone has ever seen that happen.

But he had also known from the time that the visions first came on him, as surely as he had known all the rest, that he had to conceal the fact that he had this power, even before he knew the law against it.

He'd succeeded fairly well over the years, though it was getting harder and harder all the time. The power struggled inside him, wanting to break free, once or twice overwhelming him with visions so intense that for a moment he was blind and deaf to everything else. It was getting harder to concoct reasons for knowing things he had no business knowing, like the hiding places of the bandits they were chasing, the bolt-holes and escape routes. But it was harder still to ignore them, especially when subsequent visions showed him innocent people suffering because he didn't act on what he knew.

He brushed Silver's neck vigorously, the dust tickling his nose and making him want to sneeze—

—and between one brush stroke and the next, he lost his sense of balance, went light-headed, and the dazzle that heralded a vision-to-come sparkled between his eyes and Silver's neck.

Not here! he thought desperately, clinging to Silver's mane and trying to pretend there was nothing wrong. Not now, not with Herdahl watching—

But the witch-power would not obey him, not this time.

No—Sunlord, help me, not now! He believed in the Sunlord, in His power and goodness, if not in the goodness of those who said they spoke for Him . . .

A flash of blue light, blinding him—

Then came sight again, but not of the picket line, but another place.

Where? Where? Sunlord, where?

The bandits he'd thought were south had slipped behind him, into the north, joining with two more packs of the curs, becoming a group large enough to take on his troops and give them an even fight. But first, they wanted a secure base. They were going to make Alberich meet them on ground of their choosing. Fortified ground.

That this ground was already occupied was only a minor inconvenience, one that would soon be dealt with.

He fought free of the vision for a moment, clinging to Silver's shoulder like a drowning man, both hands full of the beast's silky mane, while the horse curved his head back and looked at him curiously. The big brown eyes flickered blue, briefly, like a half-hidden flash of lightning, reflecting—

—another burst of sapphire. And now, *now* he knew where! The bandits' target was a fortified village, a small one, built on the top of a hill, above the farm fields. Ordinarily, these people would have no difficulty in holding off a score of bandits. But there were three times that number ranged against them, and a recent edict from the High Temple decreed that no one but the Temple Guard and the army could possess anything but the simplest of weapons. Not three weeks ago, a detachment of priests and a Voice had come through here, divesting them of everything but knives, farm implements, and such simple bows and arrows as were suitable for waterfowl and small game. And while they were at it, a third of the able-bodied men had been conscripted for the regular army.

Alberich's own troops had acted as silent guards for the process, to ensure that there were no "incidents" while the conscripts were marched away, while the weapons were taken or destroyed. Yes, he knew this place, knew it too well.

These people didn't have a chance.

The bandits drew closer, under the cover of a brush-filled ravine.

Alberich found himself on Silver's back, without knowing how he'd gotten there, without remembering that he'd flung saddle and bridle back on the beast—

No, not bridle; Silver still wore the halter he'd had on the picket line. Alberich's bugle was in his hand; presumably he'd blown the muster, for his men were running toward him, buckling on swords and slinging quivers over their shoulders.

Blinding flash of sapphire—throwing him back into the vision, showing him what he would rather not see. He *knew* what was coming, so why must he *see* it?

The bandits attacked the village walls, overpowering the poor man who was trying to bar the gate against them, and swarming inside. He couldn't close his eyes to it; the vision came through eyes closed or open. He would look because he had no choice.

It hadn't happened yet, he knew that with the surety with which he knew his own name. It wasn't even going to happen in the next few moments. But it was going to happen soon.

They poured inside, cutting down anyone who resisted them, then throwing off what little restraint they had shown and launching into an orgy of looting and rapine. Alberich gagged as one of them grabbed a pregnant woman and with a single slash of his sword, murdered the child that ran to try and protect her, followed through to her—

The vision released him, and he found himself surrounded by dust and thunder, still on Silver's back—

—but leaning over the stallion's neck as now he led his troops up the road to the village of Sunsdale at full gallop. Hooves pounded the packed earth of the road, making it impossible to hear or speak; the vibration thrummed into his bones as he shifted his weight with the stallion's turns. Silver ran easily, with no sign of distress, though all around him and behind him the other horses streamed saliva from the corners of their mouths, and their flanks ran with sweat and foam, as they strained to keep up.

The lack of a bit didn't seem to make any difference to the stallion; he answered to neck-rein and knee so readily he might have been anticipating Alberich's thoughts.

Alberich dismissed the uneasy feelings that prompted. Better not to think that he might have a second witch-power along with the first. He'd never shown any ability to control beasts by thought before. There was no reason to think he could now. The stallion was just superbly trained, that was all. And he had more important things to worry about.

They topped the crest of a hill; Sunsdale lay atop the next one, just as he had seen in his vision, and the brush-filled ravine beyond it.

There was no sign of trouble.

This time it's been a wild hare, he thought, and his skin crawled at the thought that he'd roused the men and sent them here at the gallop, and there were *sure* to be questions asked for which he had no answers.

And I answer what? That I wanted to see how quick they'd respond to an emergency? That would hardly serve.

He was just about to pull Silver up and bring the rest of

his men to a halt—no point in them running their horses into foundering—

When a flash of sunlight on metal betrayed the bandits' location.

Alberich grabbed for the bugle dangling from his left wrist instead, and pulled his blade with the right. He sounded the charge and led the entire troop down the hill, an unstoppable torrent of hooves and steel, hitting the brigands' hidden line like an avalanche.

Sword in hand, Alberich limped wearily to another body sprawled amid the rocks and trampled weeds of the ravine, and thrust it through to make death certain. His sword felt heavy and unwieldy, his stomach churned, and there was a sour taste in his mouth. He didn't think he was going to lose control of his guts, but he was glad he was almost at the end of the battle line. He hated this part of the fighting—which wasn't fighting at all; it was nothing more than butchery.

But it was necessary. This scum was just as likely to be feigning death as to actually be dead. Other officers hadn't been that thorough—and hadn't lived long enough to regret it.

Silver was being fed and watered along with the rest of the mounts by the youngsters of Sunsdale; the finest fodder and clearest spring water, and a round dozen young boys to brush and curry them clean. And the men were being fed and made much of by the older villagers. Gratitude had made them forgetful of the loss of their weapons and many of their men. Suddenly the army that had conscripted their relatives was no longer their adversary. Or else, since the troops had arrived out of nowhere like Vengeance of the Sunlord Himself, they assumed the One God had a hand in it, and it would be prudent to resign themselves to the sacrifice. And meanwhile, the instrument of their rescue probably ought to be well treated.

Except for the Captain, who was doing a dirty job he refused to assign to anyone else.

Alberich made certain of two more corpses and looked dully around for more.

There weren't any, and he decided, when he spotted a pool of clear rainwater a little farther down the ravine, that he had to wash. He had to get the blood off his hands and the stink of death out of his nostrils.

He picked his way down the rocks to the pool—not rainwater, after all, but fed by a tiny trickle of a spring, a mere thread of clear water that didn't even stir the surface of the pool.

He bent over it, and caught his own reflection staring back at him. A sober fellow, with a face of sharp planes and uncompromising angles; a stubborn mouth, his mother had always said, and eyes that stared unnervingly back at him. "Hawk eyes," said some; with a fierce and direct gaze. Dark hair, cut as short as possible to fit beneath a helm's padding. Skin burned dark by the sun. He looked at the reflection as if he was looking at a stranger, hunting for—what? The taint of witchery?

He saw only a toughened man with eyes that looked—perhaps—a trifle haunted. Suddenly, he didn't want to look anymore—or more closely. *Introspection is for poets. Not men like me.*

He bent quickly to wash, disrupting the reflection. When he straightened to shake the water off his arms and face, he saw to his surprise that the sun was hardly more than a finger's breadth from the horizon. Shadows already filled the ravine, the evening breeze had picked up, and it was getting chilly. Last year's weeds tossed in the freshening wind as he gazed around at the long shadows cast by the scrubby trees. More time had passed than he thought, and if he didn't hurry, he was going to be late for SunDescending.

He scrambled over the slippery rocks of the ravine, cursing under his breath as his boots (meant for riding) skidded on the smooth, rounded boulders. The last thing he needed now was to be late for a holy service, especially this one. The priest here was bound to ask him for a thanks-prayer for the victory. If he was late, it would look as if he was arrogantly attributing the victory to his own abilities, and not the Hand of the Sunlord. And with an accusation like that hanging over his head, he'd be in danger not only of being deprived of his current rank, but of being demoted into the ranks, with no chance of promotion, a step up from stable-hand, but not a big one.

He fought his way over the edge, and half-ran, half-limped to the village gates, reaching them just as the sun touched the horizon. He put a little more speed into his weary, aching legs, and got to the edge of the crowd in the village square a scant breath before the priest began the First Chant.

He bowed his head with the others, and not until he raised his head at the end of it did he realize that the robes the priest wore were not black, but red. This was no mere village priest—this was a Voice!

He suppressed his start of surprise, and the shiver of fear that followed it. He didn't know what this village meant, or what had happened to require posting a Voice here, but there was little wonder now why they had submitted so tamely to the taking of their men and the confiscation of their weapons. No one sane would contradict a Voice.

The Voice held up his hand, and got instant silence; a silence so profound that the sounds of the horses stamping and whickering on the picket line came clearly over the walls. In the distance, a few lonely birds called, and the breeze rustled through the new leaves of the trees in the ravine. Alberich longed suddenly to be able to mount Silver and ride away from here, far away from the machinations of Voices and the omnipresent smell of death and blood. He yearned for somewhere clean, somewhere that he wouldn't have to guard his back from those he should be able to trust.

"Today this village was saved from certain destruction,"

the Voice said, his words ringing out, but without passion, without any inflection whatsoever. "And for that, we offer thanks-giving to Vkandis Sunlord, Most High, One God, to whom all things are known. The instrument of that salvation was Captain Alberich, who mustered his men in time to catch our attackers in the very act. It seems a miracle—"

During the speech, some of the men had been moving closer to Alberich, grouping themselves around him to bask in the admiration of the villagers.

Or so he thought. Until the Voice's tone hardened, and his next words proved their real intent.

"It seems a miracle—but it was not!" he thundered. "You were saved by the power of the One God, whose wrath destroyed the bandits, but Alberich betrayed the Sunlord by using the unholy powers of witchcraft! Seize him!"

His heart froze, but his body acted, and he whirled. The men grabbed him as he turned to run, throwing him to the ground and pinning him with superior numbers. He fought them anyway, struggling furiously, until someone brought the hilt of a knife down on the back of his head.

He didn't black out altogether, but he couldn't move or see; his eyes wouldn't focus, and a gray film obscured everything. He felt himself being dragged off by the arms—heaved into darkness—felt himself hitting a hard surface—heard the slamming of a door.

Then heard only confused murmurs as he lay in shadows, trying to regain his senses and his strength. Gradually, his sight cleared, and he could make out walls on all sides of him, close enough to touch. The last light of dusk made thin blue lines of the cracks between each board. He raised his aching head cautiously, and made out the dim outline of an ill-fitting door. The floor, clearly, was dirt. And smelled unmistakably of other fowl birds.

They must have thrown him into some kind of shed, something that had once held chickens or pigeons. It didn't *now,* for the dirt floor was clean and packed as hard as rock. He was under no illusions that this meant his prison would be easy to escape; out here, the chicken-sheds were frequently built better than the houses, for chickens were more valuable than children. Children *ate;* chickens and eggs were to *be* eaten.

Still, once darkness descended, it might be possible to get away. If he could overpower whatever guards the Voice had placed around him. If he could find a way out of the shed!

If he could get past the Voice himself. There were stories that the Voices had other powers than plucking the thoughts from a man's head—stories that they commanded the services of demons tamed by the Sunlord—and he knew those stories were true. He'd *heard* the Night-demons ranging through the dark, off in the far distance. No dog ever produced those wails, no wolf howled like *that,* and no owl conjured those bone-chilling shrieks from its throat. And once, from a distance, he'd seen the result of one of those hunts. Whatever the demons had left behind wasn't human anymore. . . .

While he lay there gathering his wits, another smell invaded the shed, overpowering even the stench of old bird-droppings. A sharp, thick smell. It took a moment for him to recognize it.

But when he did, he clawed his way up the wall he'd been thrown against, to stand wide-eyed in the darkness, nails digging into the wood behind him, heart pounding with stark terror.

Oil. They had poured earth-oil, the kind that bubbled up in black, sticky pools around here, around the foundations, splashed it up against the sides of the shed. And now he heard them out there, bringing piles of dry brush and wood to stack against the walls. The punishment for witchery was burning, and they were taking no chances; they were going to burn him now.

The noises outside stopped; the murmur of voices faded as his captors moved away—

Then the Voice called out, once—a set of three sharp, angry words—

And every crack and crevice in the building was outlined in yellow and red, as the entire shed was engulfed in flames from outside.

Alberich cried out, and staggered away from the wall he'd been leaning against. The shed was bigger than he'd thought—but not big enough to protect him. The oil they'd spread so profligately made the flames burn hotter, and the wood of the shed was old, weathered, and probably dry. Within moments, the very air scorched him; he hid his mouth in a fold of his shirt, but his lungs burned with every breath. His eyes streamed tears of pain as he turned, burning, staggering, searching for an escape that didn't exist.

One of the walls burned through, showing the flames leaping from the wood and brush piled beyond it. He couldn't hear anything but the roar of the flames. At any moment now, the roof would cave in, burying him in burning debris—

:Look out!:

How he heard the warning—or how he knew to stagger back as far as he could without being incinerated on the spot, he did not know. But a heartbeat after that warning shout in his mind, a hole opened up in the side of the shed with a crash. Then a huge, silver-white shadow lofted through the hole in the burning wall, and landed beside him. It was still wearing his saddle and hackamore—

And it turned huge, impossibly blue eyes on him as he stood there gaping at it. It? No. Him.

:On!: the stallion snapped at him. *:The roof's about to go!:*

Whatever fear he had of the beast, he was more afraid of a death by burning. With hands that screamed with pain, he grabbed the saddle-bow and threw himself onto it. He hadn't even found the stirrups when the stallion turned on his hind feet. There was a crack of collapsing wood, as fire engulfed them. Burning thatch fell before and behind them, sparks showering as the air was sucked into the blaze, hotter. . . .

But, amazingly, no fire licked at his flesh once he had mounted. . . .

Alberich sobbed with relief as the cool air surged into his lungs—the stallion's hooves hit the ground beyond the flames, and he gasped with pain as he was flung forward against the saddlebow.

Then the real pain began, the torture of half-scorched skin, and the broken bones of his capture, jarred into agony by the stallion's headlong gallop into the night. The beast thundered toward the villagers, and they screamed and parted before it; soldiers and Voice alike were caught unaware, and not one of them raised a weapon in time to stop the flight.

:Stay on,: the stallion ordered grimly into his mind as the darkness was shattered by the red lightning of his own pain. *:Stay on, stay with me; we have a long way to go before we're safe. Stay with me. . . . :*

Safe where? he wanted to ask, but there was no way to ask around the pain. All he could do was to hang on, and hope he could do what the horse wanted.

Through the darkness, under a moonless sky, through cold that froze him as his burns made him feverish. Pain became a constant; he'd have screamed, but he hadn't the strength, wept, but his eyes were too sore and dry. Yet Alberich was no stranger to pain; it could be endured, and he *would* endure it. It could be conquered; he would not allow it to conquer him.

Somewhere in the midst of the living nightmare, came the thought that if he lived through this, his own mother would never recognize him, he'd been burned so badly. He would forever wear a face seamed by scars.

An eternity later—dawn rising as red as the flames that had nearly killed him—the stallion had slowed to a walk. Dawn was on their right, which meant that the stallion was heading north, across the border, into the witch-kingdom of

Valdemar. Which only made sense, since what he'd thought was a horse had turned out to be one of the blue-eyed witch-beasts. . . .

None of it mattered. Now that the stallion had slowed to a walk, his pain had dulled, but he was exhausted and out of any energy to think or even feel with. What could the witches do to him, after all? Kill him? At the moment, that would be a kindness, and anyway, it was only what his own people wanted to do to him. . . .

The stallion stopped, and he looked up, trying to see through the film that had come over his vision. At first he thought he was seeing double; two white witch-beasts and two white-clad riders blocked the road. But then he realized that there were two of them, hastily dismounting, reaching for him.

He let himself slide down into their hands, hearing nothing he could understand, only a babble of strange syllables.

Then, in his mind—

:Can you hear me?:

:I—what?: he replied, without thinking.

:Taver says his name's Alberich,: came a second voice in his head. *:Alberich? Can you stay with us a little longer? We need to get you to a Healer. You're going into shock; fight it for us. Your Companion will help you, if you let him.:*

His what? He shook his head; not in negation, in puzzlement. Where was he? All his life he'd heard that the witches of Valdemar were evil—but—

:And all our lives we've heard that nothing comes out of Karse but brigands and bad weather,: said the first voice, full of concern, but with an edge of humor to it. He shook his head again and peered up at the person supporting him on his right. A woman, older than he, with many laugh lines etched around her generous mouth. She seemed to fit that first voice in his head, somehow . . . she was smaller than he, diminutive in fact, but she had an aura of authority that was all out of proportion to her height.

:So which are you, Alberich?: she asked, as he fought to stay awake, feeling the presence of the stallion (his Companion?) like a steady shoulder to lean against, deep inside his soul. *:Brigand, or bad weather?:*

:Neither . . . I hope. . . . ?: he replied, absently, clinging to consciousness as she'd asked.

:Good. I'd hate to think of a Companion Choosing a brigand to be a Herald,: she said, with her mouth twitching a little, as if she was holding back a grin, *:And a thunderstorm in human guise would make uncomfortable company.:*

:Choosing?: he asked. *:What—what do you mean?:*

:I mean that you're a Herald, my friend,: she told him. *:Somehow your Companion managed to insinuate himself across the Border to get you, too. That's how Heralds of Valdemar are made; Companions Choose them—:* She looked up and away from him, and relief and satisfaction spread over her face at whatever it was she saw. *:—and the rest of it can wait. Aren's brought the Healer we sent him for, when Taver told us you were coming. Go ahead and let go, we'll take over from here. If a Healer can't save you with three Heralds to support him, then he's not worth the robe he wears.:*

He took her at her word, and let the darkness take him. But her last words followed him down into the shadows, and instead of bringing the fear they should have given him, they brought him comfort, and a peace he never expected.

:It's a hell of a greeting, Herald Alberich, and a hell of a way to get here—but welcome to Valdemar, brother. Welcome. . . . :

PART ONE

Exile's Choice

HE was not dead. That much, at least, he was certain of.

At times, between the long moments when he was unaware of anything, he hurt quite enough to be in Hell, but Hell was cold and dark, and he wasn't cold. And the few times he was able to open his eyes, the room he was in was bathed in sunlight.

He couldn't be in Heaven either; if he was in Heaven, he wouldn't hurt. That was one thing that everyone agreed on; in Heaven was an end to all pain and sorrow. Pain he had in plenty, and as for sorrow—well, he'd consider sorrow when the pain ended.

Therefore, he must be alive.

The rest of what was going on around him—well. It was a mix of what he thought was hallucination, and what surely must be madness. Now, that fit with Hell, except that there weren't any demons tormenting him, only his own flesh.

Around him, voices muttered in a tongue he did not understand, but inside his head, another voice murmured, imparting to him the sense of what he heard. And that was where the madness came in. That voice, low and strong and uncompromisingly masculine, informed him that *he,* Alberich, sworn to the service of Karse and Vkandis Sunlord, the One God—

—was now a Herald of Valdemar. And the voice belonged to his Companion, one Kantor.

Impossible.

Not at all, the voice insisted. It began to wear at his stubborn refusal; he could feel his objection thinning. It clearly was *not* impossible because it had happened. He might not *like* it, but it was not impossible.

He slept, woke hurting, was murmured over and moved, fed and cleaned, the pain ebbed, and he slept again. From time to time the bandages on his face were taken off and he could open his eyes for a little. He was in was a cheerful room that seemed to be tiled, and the bed he was on was soft and comfortable—which was good, because his face and arms were in agony, his lungs stabbed with every breath he took, and if he didn't have broken collarbones, they were at least cracked. When he could see, there were generally two or three green-clad people in the room with him, and he seemed to recall that outside of Karse, there were Healers who generally wore green. So apparently—if he wasn't delirious—he was being tended to, outside of Karse, by foreign Healers. So whatever had happened, he wasn't in Heaven, or Hell, or prison—which *had* been a third option, after all. Over and over he slept to wake in pain, was given something that stopped the pain, and slept again; there was no way to tell how much time had passed, and no way to sort what he *knew* had happened from what the voice was telling him.

Except that, bit by bit, the words being spoken over his head became more intelligible, as if the language was slowly seeping into his fever-ravaged brain. This tongue—this arcane language—was like *nothing* he could have imagined. The syntax was all wrong, for one thing; these people spoke—backward, sort of. Not that he was any kind of a linguist, but for a long time he was confused as much by the *order* of the words as the words themselves. . . .

He *must* be in Valdemar. The language was as twisted about as the Demon-Riders and their Hellhorses, with the verbs coming in the middle instead of properly at the end. How could you tell what a sentence was truly about if you stuck the verb in the middle? The meaning could be entirely reversed by what came afterward!

How was he learning these things? What demonic magic was putting them inside his brain? Or was this all a fever dream, and was he lying in the embers of the chicken-shed, dying of his burns, conjuring all of this up? He *had* saved the village with his witch-power, he *had* been condemned to burn by a Voice, he *had* been imprisoned and his prison set afire. But after that?

Madness, illusion, hallucination, delirium.

Surely.

But the voice in his head told him otherwise, and as the moments of his lucidity came more and more often, it began to tell him things he could verify for himself—little things, but none of which he could have hallucinated for himself. That, for instance, the reason why he was not able to open his eyes very often was because they had been bandaged shut—at first, the skin of his face hurt so much he hadn't actually felt the bandages. And the skin of his hands was in such agony that he tried not to move them to touch anything, much less his face, which he wouldn't have wanted to touch anyway, given how much it hurt. The voice warned him when he was to be fed, and what they were going to give him—all soup, of course, and juices, and very, very often. The voice warned him when his bandages were to be changed—long before one of those Healer-people even got within hearing distance. And the voice told him about a great many other things.

:There is a large crow outside your window, Chosen,: it

would say. *:It is about to sound an alert, so do not be startled and jump, or you will hurt.:* And sure enough, a crow *would* burst out with a raucous shout, but since he'd *been* warned, he was able to keep still. Or— *:The Healers have come with a new potion for you, to soothe your burns. They think this will hurt so much that they intend to give you an especially strong dose of pain-medicine.:* And indeed, he would then hear footsteps, feel himself tilted up, and he would drink what was put to his lips quickly, because the last time they had come up with a new potion for his burns, the pain had been excruciating.

He had always been a great believer in empirical evidence, and here it was. Slowly, and with great reluctance, he began to sort through his confused memories. With even greater reluctance, he had to accept that what he thought was madness and delirium was nothing of the sort.

So during one of his moments of relative lucidity, he steeled himself, and confronted the voice.

Relative was the operative term—he felt that he *should* be angry, embittered, but there were drugs interfering with those emotions, keeping him oddly detached. Perhaps that was just as well. He needed to think clearly, unemotionally, and this was as close to doing so as he was likely to manage. He coughed, hoping to clear his throat, but the voice in his head forestalled his attempt to speak aloud.

:Don't, Chosen. You don't need to actually say *anything. Just think it.:*

Think it. Well, he talked to himself in his mind all the time; this shouldn't be any different.

:It isn't, except that when you get an answer, you needn't be concerned that madness runs in your bloodline. Not that it's likely that it was true madness that struck your father, all things considered. If it were my case to judge, I would have looked very carefully at his wife's family, and considered all the reasons they might have had for saying he was mad. . . . :

He'd have winced, if he hadn't known how much wincing would hurt. *How* had this voice—

:Kantor, Alberich. My name is Kantor.:

Kantor, then. *How* had this being known about his past?

:You've been quite generous in sharing your memories.: A hint of dry irony. *:Actually, you've been shoving them down my throat. I know that your mother was not married, that your father was a prominent man in your village and she anything but. I know that he was her only lover and that at some point when you were very young, he was sent away with your priests, supposedly mad.:* Alberich would have been flushing, had his face not been so painful. He was embarrassed—but embarrassed because he had been essentially blurting out every detail of his past life to a stranger, like the sort of drunk who would sit down next to you and begin telling you everything you *didn't* want to know. The very idea made him a little sick. *:Not that I mind, truly,:* the voice continued earnestly. *:It's only that Herald and Companion usually grow to know each other in a more leisurely manner—and as yet, you know very little of me.:*

Another suppressed wince. He didn't really want to know anything about this—Companion—did he? No. He didn't. This was a place full of witches—

—of which you might be one—

—and demons, and Vkandis only knew what other sorts of horrible creatures—wasn't it? Surely it was—

:Nonsense. You may be many things, Alberich, but a coward isn't one of them. I've asked the Healers to halve your pain-medicines, so that we can have this little discussion without the drugs interfering. There are several truths that you will have to face today, and the first of them is that virtually everything you think you know about Valdemar is wrong.:

Actually, the unsteady realization of that had been trickling down into his mind for the past—however long it had been. It had probably started when he'd fallen into the arms of those white-clad riders just over the Border. If they'd been half as evil as the Priests painted them, he'd have been roasting in chains right now, with demons nibbling at his soul.

:Excellent. That's another thing that you aren't—stupid. Those weren't just any Heralds, by the way. One was the King's Own Herald Talamir, and the other was the Lord Marshal's Herald, Joyeaus. We stumbled onto the end of a rather sensitive diplomatic mission, it seems.: There was a hint of a chuckle, and Alberich got the distinct impression that they hadn't merely "stumbled" into those particular Heralds—that Kantor had aimed himself quite deliberately in their direction. *:Well, no harm done.:*

He gathered his wits, and *thought* a question. *:I do not suppose that the rank of our rescuers has anything to do with the speed with which I was taken to further help?:*

The impression of a knowing smile. *:Not entirely. All Heralds are considered highly important. Even the newly Chosen.:*

He let that settle into his mind. *:Even Karsites?:*

:Well, since we've never had a Karsite Herald before, there's no basis for comparison.: There was a definite undertone there. Alberich decided that he was getting rapidly better at reading around what Kantor was actually telling him to what Kantor would rather just—imply. The undertone was that not everyone would have been as . . . open to the possibility of an ally out of Karse . . . as Heralds Talamir and Joyeaus.

:Excellent again. I do believe we are rather well-matched, Chosen. I would not go so far as to say that other Heralds would have run you through on sight—but we have *been fighting a rather nasty undeclared war with you for some time, and there are some hard feelings on our side of the Border as well as yours, even among Heralds.:* A sense of pondering followed that statement. *:In truth,* especially *among Heralds, since your lot enjoys killing us so very much. Now no Herald would ever slaughter someone who had been Chosen out-of-*

hand—but there are many, many of them who are not going to welcome you as a long-lost sibling.:

Just his good fortune that he'd never led troops against anything other than bandits, then. At least no one would be holding a *personal* grudge against him.

He licked lips that were dry and cracked, and stared into the darkness behind his bandages. Inexorably, it was creeping up on him, acceptance that he could never go home again.

He *was* in the enemy's land, he *was* exiled inexorably from his own. He *had* witch-powers, and they were not the curse he'd been taught that they were. And one of the Hellhorses—which were not hellish at all, apparently—had selected him to become one of the Demon-Riders.

:Please, Alberich. Heralds, *not Demon-Riders. And as for my being hellish—:* a pregnant pause, *:—well, although the people of Valdemar would say that we Companions are the sweetest, most marvelous of creatures, I suspect that the several of your men who got in my way* would *agree that I am "hellish." Assuming any of them survived the experience.:*

Oh.

On the other hand, if one of them had been that Voice—

:He was,: came the reply, with a certain grim glee. *:Though I am not certain that anyone like that Voice of yours—someone who goes about blithely burning people alive—has any right to make any judgments about who is "hellish" and who isn't.:*

Ah. . . .

:The fact that you have never personally fought against us will be useful towards having you accepted,: Kantor agreed. *:And there is at least one thing I can promise you. We will never,* ever, *under any circumstances, ask or require you to do anything against your conscience with regard to your homeland. I shan't promise we won't ask you to act against those in power there—:*

Just at the moment, he'd rather like to have the skinny or fat necks of some of those in power between his hands.

:Well put.: Kantor seemed satisfied with his answer. *:Now, the Healers will have my tail for a banner if I don't let them drug you again, so I'll ask you to mull this discussion over while you drowse, and we'll have another little talk in a bit.:*

He couldn't have objected if he'd wanted to, and he didn't want to, because the pain was getting unbearable and he heard the welcome footsteps of someone bringing him relief. After a quick, nasty-tasting draught, he was drifting again, cast loose from consciousness and what he'd always thought of as "The Truth" . . . . a state in which it was easier to contemplate a new set of truths—or at least, truisms—in place of the old.

He dreamed.

He sat in the midst of a vast expanse of flowering meadow, flooded in a haze of light that made it difficult to see for any great distance. He was warm, comfortable, without pain of any kind, and—completely alone. He rose, and started to walk, wading knee-deep through wildflowers and herbs that gave off a hundred luscious scents as he brushed them aside. No matter how far he walked, however, the scene never changed, and he never found a path. The only living things were the plants; there were not even insects or birds. He felt no hunger, no thirst, no weariness; this fit every description of Paradise that he'd ever heard—except that there was no one in this Paradise but himself.

As beautiful and peaceful as this place was—he was trapped here. And he came to realize, as he walked on in the thick golden light, that the peace came at the price of *being* unable to escape, and completely alone. Not Paradise. Not even close.

That was the end of the dream. As abruptly as it had begun, it was over, and Alberich dropped out of the meadow and into the usual fever dreams that he had fought since being brought here.

From fever dream, he moved into welcome dreamlessness, and from then into the pain that always woke him when his medicines wore off. But it was not as bad as it had been, and he knew that the drugs being given him were not as strong as they'd been at first. Someone gave him a different-tasting drink, then, and he drowsed for a bit.

Sometime later, he woke to the sound of someone—no, two people—walking into his room.

"Is he awake?" asked a voice that was strange to him.

"He should be. I gave him a draught that should—well—sober him up completely," replied one that was more familiar—one of the Healers who spent a great deal of Alberich's waking time with him. There was a touch on his chest, where there were no bandages other than the ones holding his cracked ribs in place. "Sir, I am going to take off the bandages on your eyes, and leave them off. The skin there is healed enough that you needn't have them on anymore."

"I understand," he said, stumbling over the foreign words. The Healer moved him as gently as could be, propped him up with cushions, and took off the bandages. Alberich blinked, and squinted in the sunlight, taking his first proper look at the room he'd been in for—well, he didn't know how long.

And now that he was thinking clearly, the very first thing he felt was a smoldering resentment.

A shaggy-haired man in stained and well-worn green robes was coiling up bandages at the foot of the bed, but Alberich had very little interest in him, or in the room itself at the moment. It was the other occupant of the room, the one sitting right beside him, that captured his attention.

This was a Demon-Rider.

:This is Talamir, the King's Own Herald,: Kantor corrected gently, speaking into his mind for the first time since he'd awakened.

Alberich's jaw tightened, but he tried to *look* at the man, rather than react to him. What he saw was a tall, a very tall, thin man with graying brown hair, perhaps forty or fifty years old, if Alberich's judgment was any good. His was a careworn, lean face, overlaid with gentle good humor, but with a strong chin that suggested a stubborn streak, and a determination it would not be wise to invoke if you intended to quarrel with him. And, of course, he wore that dreaded white uniform, the emblem of the enemy—a more elaborate version than Alberich thought prudent or practical for a fighting man—

:Those are Formal Whites. Talamir has just come from a Council session at the King's side. Defending your presence here in Valdemar, in Haven, in the ranks of the Heralds themselves, may I add.:

Alberich refused to be distracted from his careful scrutiny.

The uniform—*I would never don anything like this,* he told himself fiercely—a silver-laced, white-velvet tunic, with silver embroidery at the hems, over a heavy white samite shirt with wide sleeves caught in deep cuffs at the wrists, and white satin breeches. A wide, white leather belt ornamented with hammered silver supported a dagger in a matching sheath. He'd have called it foppish, except that it wasn't. But he could not imagine himself ever wearing anything so extravagant.

The fabric alone, if sold, could feed a family for a year—

:Ah. And, of course, the nobles of Karse, the wealthy merchants, the ranking Captains, and above all, the Voices of the Sunlord dress and live so very *austerely,:* came the unwelcome reminder.

"Well, you have been here some two weeks, sir," Talamir said, his hazel eyes scrutinizing Alberich just as closely as Alberich was examining him. "I'm sure you have been wondering."

"Wondering, yes," Alberich replied, giving away nothing, conceding nothing, offering nothing. Talamir sighed.

:You could be more gracious.:

"Alberich—yes, we know what your name is—you must know that *my* Taver has been talking virtually nonstop to *your* Kantor, and what Kantor knows about you, so do I." Talamir's eyes became very penetrating. "I know very well that you have a good command of our tongue now, and furthermore, your Kantor can easily explain anything you don't understand immediately. I should prefer not to spend this entire first interview fencing with you, if you please."

Well, that gave him the opening he'd been looking for. "*My* Kantor, it is?" he asked resentfully. "And when was there asking on my part, for this Choosing, this so-called *honor?*"

Talamir shrugged. "You could be dead right now," he pointed out. "Whether you consider it an honor or not, Kantor saved your life."

"For which blessing, to serve my enemy, I am bound?" There was a sour taste in his mouth, and his stomach muscles were so tight as to make his cracked ribs ache in protest. He'd not only been kidnapped, he had been reduced to simple-mindedness with drugs—but now that he was himself again, he had *no* intention of rolling over like a cowed dog and licking the hands of his captors.

"I was not aware that Valdemar had personally done you harm," said Talamir. "Nor was I aware that any citizen of Valdemar had hurt you. I was under the impression that *everything* untoward that had happened to you was the responsibility of the denizens of your own land. If you can point out to me who and what on this side of the Border has wronged you, I assure you it will be dealt with to your satisfaction."

"Even if it Kantor is?" he asked, and looked Talamir straight in the eyes.

There was silence in his mind.

"Kantor." Talamir gazed on him with astonishment. "Your Companion."

"Who under false pretenses and a disguise attached himself to me. Who carried me off, who brought me *here,* where I would not have gone had I a choice been given. Who—perhaps?—had to do somewhat with my witch-sight coming so clear, and in front of a Voice?" He saw Talamir wince and felt his own mouth tighten in grim satisfaction. "Who therefore could the cause be, that the Voice to the Fires condemned me?"

"You would be dead right now," Talamir repeated uncomfortably. "You couldn't have denied your Gift. With or without Kantor, sooner or later it would have betrayed you, and you would still have gone to the fires—"

"But my own death it was, and mine was the choice to face, or to escape it," he pointed out, anger and resentment coloring every word. "That choice, from me was taken. *Perhaps* the witch-sight I could have fought, taken from me also was the option to try. And in the first place, had not the witch-sight come upon me when and where it did, condemned I should not have been."

A village might have gone under the sword, though—

The silence that fell between them was as heavy and uncompromising as lead.

But it was not Talamir who answered him.

:I am sorry, Alberich,: said the voice in his mind humbly and full of contrition. *:You are absolutely in the right. You* had *a life and choices, and I took them from you. I shan't even bother to make all of the arguments that a Valdemaran would accept. You* aren't *a Valdemaran, and there is no reason you should accept them. For you, my actions were nothing less than arrogance and a smug certainty that I was in the right to run roughshod over you. All I can do is apologize, and try to make it right with you.:*

He closed his eyes, his own heart contracting at the hurt and pain in that voice, armoring himself against it with the anger and resentment in his. "A better way, there could have been found," he said aloud.

"In a sense," Talamir replied quietly, "this is between you and Kantor. But ultimately, all of us are responsible, so I must apologize as well. We take such pride in our freedom here—and then we turned around and robbed you of yours. With the best intentions in the world—"

"Even the Voice that to the Fires sent me, good intentions may have had," Alberich retorted, opening his eyes again. "If not to save *my* soul, then those souls about me."

Again, Talamir winced.

"Served my people, did I, and served them *well,*" he continued, bitterness overflowing at the thought that he had been forced to abandon those villagers who depended on him to stand vigilant guard over their safety. "Who now, protect them will? The Voices? Ha! Those who willed, in my place to stand?" He glared, daring Talamir to answer him.

"I do not know," Talamir admitted quietly. "But I have already offered any remedy that you could ask. What do *you* suggest? Name it, and I will do my personal best to see it done."

In the face of such a reasonable answer, Alberich's anger suddenly collapsed, like an inflated bladder with a pin put to it. "I—" he began, and rubbed his eyes, faced with uncertainty of monumental proportions. "I know not."

"Would you have us undo what we have done?" Talamir persisted.

Alberich snorted. "And how? Return, I cannot. *Notorious,* I am, doubtless. If ever a time for remedy was, it now long past is."

Talamir sighed. "We tell our youngsters that Companion's Choice is irrevocable, and for life, but that is not—altogether—true. The bond can be broken between you, if you both want it broken badly enough. It will leave you—damaged. But it can be broken."

That held him silent for a moment. There was a bond between them? And if breaking it would leave *him* damaged, what would it do to Kantor? He thought about the pain in Kantor's mental words when the Companion apologized, and winced away from the very idea. No matter what had happened to him, he could not be responsible for creating more pain. "This moots nothing," he replied, stalling. "Nowhere to go now, have I."

Talamir nodded. "Well, in light of that—*would* you consider giving us—giving life here—a trial period? Surely no choice can properly be made without *all* the information you need. Once you know us as we are, *I* believe you will choose to remain in Valdemar, to choose the Heralds."

He opened his mouth, and closed it again, because, logically and unemotionally speaking, he honestly could not think of a good reason why he *shouldn't* do as the Herald asked.

:I wish you would,: said the wistful voice in his mind.

"In the Sunlord, I *still* believe—" he began, bringing up the only remaining stumbling block that occurred to him

"That is not an issue." Talamir waved that objection aside. "It never was. But perhaps you would rather hear that from a true Priest of the Sunlord?"

He blinked. "A Voice of Vkandis? Here?"

"Not a Voice, Alberich—but I should let him speak for himself." Talamir murmured something to the Healer, who nodded and went to the door of this room. He passed out of it, and another, much older man stepped inside, accompanied by a second about Alberich's age.

Talamir rose, and offered his seat to the older man, who took it. "This is Alberich, Father Henrick," he said. "Alberich, this is Father Henrick, and Acolyte Gerichen, his assistant."

Alberich eyed them both with caution. Neither wore the red robes of a Voice, nor the black of an ordinary priest. Instead, the older man sported a similarly cut gown of fine, cream-colored wool, and the younger, a plainer robe of unbleached linen. Both had the familiar disk of the Sunlord on a chain that hung down over the breast of their robes, however.

"You serve Vkandis Sunlord?" he asked, rather doubtfully.

Father Henrick nodded gravely. "I was born in Asherbeg, Captain," he said, in unaccented Karsite. "I was taken into the service of the Sunlord when I was eight, and made a full priest at twenty. Even as you, I am a child of Karsite soil and I still serve the Sunlord. And at twenty-one—I was ordered to Cleanse three children from the Border village to which I had been assigned."

Alberich went very still. "And?" he asked.

The priest made a rude noise. "What sort of monster do you take me for, Captain?" he asked. "I couldn't of course; they were *children,* guilty of nothing more than having powers that the Voices find inconvenient! Instead of Cleansing them, I took them and escaped over the Border with them, where I met with a Herald who in turn took me to the temple here. We don't call it the Temple of Vkandis, of course; we refer to it as the Temple of the Lord of Light—but those who attend know it, and us, for what we are."

"Powers?" Alberich said, feeling very stupid all of a sudden, as his anger and resentment drained away, leaving nothing behind. "Inconvenient?"

Father Henrick looked as if he had gotten a mouthful of green mead. "Those abilities that *you* have been taught are witch-powers, and signs of the contamination of demons, are nothing more than—than inborn powers that a child has no more control over than he does over whether or not he will be a great musician, or a great cook, or a great swordsman."

"He doesn't?" Alberich asked, dumbly.

"Of *course* not," the priest snapped. "And when these powers are something that the Voices find *useful,* if the child is young enough to be trained, it is whisked into the temple rather than being burned! It is only those whose powers are of no use to the Son of the Sun, or who are too old to be molded into a pleasing shape, that are sent to the Flames!"

Alberich was glad that he was propped up by pillows, else

he would have been reeling. The priest looked as if he had plenty more to say, but his assistant placed a cautionary hand on his arm. "Father, enough," the younger man said in Valdemaran. "This poor fellow looks as if you had just stunned him with a club."

In truth, that is exactly what Alberich felt like. "I—" he faltered. "I—had no notion."

"You are not a stupid man, Captain," the old priest said roughly. "And you have a mind young enough to be flexible, if you will it. Try opening it."

He flushed at the rebuke, and felt horribly uncomfortable. This priest reminded him all too clearly of the old priest of his home, a crusty old man who had the respect of everyone in the village, and whose speech was as blunt as his common sense was good. So well was he regarded, despite a short temper and curmudgeonly demeanor, that when a Voice wished to have him replaced by a younger man, the entire village rose up in protest, and the scheme was abandoned.

"But—" he began, in an attempt to explain himself that he knew before he started would be futile.

"But, indeed. You have been given a great gift, Alberich of Karse, a gift that can serve you *and* our people, an opportunity that will lead—well, I cannot tell where it will lead." The old man glared at him from beneath bushy eyebrows. "There is a reason for all of this, I am *sure* of it, as sure as I am that it is men, and not the Sunlord, who have made Karse and Valdemar enemies. You say that you want to help our people? Our people are led by frauds and charlatans! Half, if not more, of the Voices are false, and every high-ranking priest is corrupt! And now this happens, a soldier of Karse is Chosen to be a Herald of Valdemar, and I doubt not it is by the will of the Sunlord himself. Does that not seem like the Hand of the Sunlord Himself to you?"

Alberich was covered in confusion. "I cannot tell—"

"Well, then trust that *I* can," the old man snapped. "This is a gift, an opportunity beyond price. If you piss it away, I shall be *most* angry with you. And rest assured that when the time comes and you stand before Vkandis' Throne, *He* will ask you why you threw away the gift He placed in your hands. For the God's sake, man, can't you see your sacred duty when it stares you in the face?"

Faced with that stern face of authority—of *legitimate* authority—what could he do or say? He tried to wrench his gaze away from the priest's eyes so that he could think—and found that he couldn't. "But I was given no *choice*—" he tried to protest.

The priest snorted. "Don't be daft," he retorted. "You could have stayed there to die, and you didn't. You made your choice when you sensibly took the rescue that was offered. And as for having your life interfered with, balderdash. If your Companion had never sought you out and *that* particular Voice hadn't discovered your Gift—the thing you call a witch-power—another would have. Only this time, there would have been no rescue. And what is more, your so-called guilt *could* have been used to bring others to the Fires, others who were innocent of anything except supporting you."

Talamir was standing very patiently to one side, pretending to pay no attention to what was going on. Although—Alberich had to wonder, given what he'd said about the Companions talking to one another and to him, if he wasn't managing to follow the entire conversation despite having no working knowledge of Karsite.

The priest glared a moment longer, then abruptly, his expression softened. "Lad, you're angry and resentful that your life has been turned upside down; you wouldn't be human if you weren't. You're bitter and in despair at being betrayed; you should be, but be bitter at the right people, not those who want only your welfare. If you're not frightened at being caught up in something you don't understand, I'd be very much surprised, and I'd suspect that one of those blows to your head had addled your wits. Now you think you're utterly alone. Well, you're not."

"I didn't know about you until a moment ago," Alberich began.

The old man shook his head. "That wasn't what I meant. I've been living here for better than forty years, and I've learned a thing or two about Heralds. No—I meant something else entirely. Open your heart—and I mean, really *open* it—to your Companion, and you'll see what I mean."

Alberich meant to shake his head in denial, but another stern look from the priest killed the gesture before he could make it. "Don't argue," he said. "Don't think of an excuse. Just do it. And while you're at it, open your mind as well as your heart."

The old man rose. "I'll be going now, but if you need me, they know where to find me, or where to send *you* if you'd prefer, once you're on your feet. For that matter, I'm sure your Companion would have no difficulty finding me wherever I happened to be without you having to ask anyone but him."

With that, he nodded to Talamir and shuffled out, followed by his acolyte. The door closed behind them, and Alberich stifled a sound that was midway between a sigh and a groan.

His sacred duty to join the Heralds, was it?

Hard words, thrown in the face of one who had lived his life by cleaving to duty, sacred or not.

Hard words, spoken by one who had been forced to abandon a potentially better life than anything ahead of Alberich, because he could not reconcile *orders* with *duty.* If anyone had a right to be bitter, it was the priest, but there was no bitterness behind that rough-hewn exterior manner. And no duplicity either. Nothing but unvarnished, unadorned truth, as the old man had seen it.

As he sees it—

But with forty years more experience of this place than Alberich had.

He swore under his breath.

"Pardon?" Talamir said. "I didn't quite hear what you said."

Alberich was going to growl "Nothing—" and then changed his mind.

"I said, make a trial of you, I shall," he answered—so brusquely, even rudely, that he was surprised that Talamir didn't take offense.

But the Herald didn't. "Good," he said instead, and moved to follow in the steps of the priest and his helper. But he turned when he got the door opened.

"In that case, there is one thing I should like to ask you to do," he said, with another of those measuring looks. "Before the Healer returns, I should like you to open your mind to Kantor. Completely. I think—I hope it will make a difference to you."

He left the room then, without waiting for Alberich's answer.

But then, given that the priest had virtually ordered Alberich to do the same thing, he probably didn't need to wait. He already knew that—eventually, at least—Alberich would make a trial of that, too.

Eventually. In his *own* time.

THE Healer fussed over him for a bit, then prepared to leave; on a low table, within easy reach, were a pitcher of water, a cup, and a vial of one of the pain-killing potions. "Take it when you need it and are ready to sleep," the Healer told him. "Or not at all, if that's your choice. But drink the water."

Alberich couldn't tell if the man's brusque manner was his ordinary demeanor, or due to discovering where Alberich had come from. It could be both . . . and maybe, now that he knew Alberich was from Karse, he might be having second thoughts; maybe that wasn't just an ordinary pain-killing potion.

On the other hand, the man was leaving him with the potion *and* giving him the option of drinking it, or not. Unlikely that it was poison—why waste all that time and effort in healing him just to poison him? If the situations were reversed, a "guest" of the Sunpriests would likely not be treated at all, much less given a comfortable room *and* pain-killing drugs.

"The potion will wear off about dinnertime if you choose to drink it," the Healer continued. "It's about time for you to start feeding yourself again instead of having someone ladle broth into you."

Evidently, they were ready to see the last of him. Well, the feeling was mutual. Alberich was more than ready to do without Healers altogether. Already he'd had more attention for his injuries now than he'd ever had for every other injury in his life combined.

Then the man left, closing the door behind him, leaving Alberich alone in his tiny cell of a room.

Not that his quarters in the barracks—when he'd actually been *in* them, which was rare—were any larger. But the two rooms could not have been more different.

The outer wall of this room held a large window with actual glass panes in it; the wall directly opposite held the door. The other two walls were blank, and the room was tiled in a pale gray-green. A restful color, if a trifle dull. Tiles on a wall, though; that was something odd.

For furnishings, well, there were the bed he was on, a little three-legged table, and a stool to match. Not much need for a clothes chest in a sickroom, he supposed. He was, he discovered, wearing only smallclothes beneath his blankets and sheet. And they weren't even his smallclothes. Everything about him that was Karsite was gone.

On the other hand, perhaps that was just as well. The less to mark him as the enemy, the better.

From where he was lying in bed, all he could see was a single white cloud, a mere wisp of a thing, drifting from one side to the other. Not a very inspiring view. In fact, there was nothing much in this place to occupy the mind.

Suddenly, he wanted to actually look out that window. He wanted to see more than just sky and clouds. He felt stifled; this was the longest period of time that he had spent without seeing the outside world since—well, he couldn't remember. Even when he'd been a cadet, he'd been outside, riding, exercising, training. Even when he'd been hurt before, he'd been in his own quarters, able—indeed, expected—to get about and take up light duties.

His hands were still bandaged, but lightly, and they didn't hurt so much anymore. He could use them—carefully. Well, the sooner he got out of bed, the sooner he'd finish healing. Gingerly, he slid his legs out from under the covers and put his feet on the cold tiled floor, sitting straight up on the edge of the bed. There was a painful twinge in his chest; an ungentle reminder of broken ribs.

Nothing wrong with my legs, anyway. There were some pink patches—healing burns—but at least no one had broken any foot or leg bones when they'd beaten him. A good thing, too—if his leg had been broken, he'd never have been able to get onto Kantor's back, now, would he?

He'd been hurt in the line of duty often enough to know to pause after every movement to see how badly he felt. There was no point in undoing the work of healing by passing out and falling on the floor because he tried to leap out of bed like a healthy person. So he hesitated for a moment with his feet chilling on the tiles, testing for a sign of weakness, waiting for his vision to blur or fade out. But other than those twinges, he was fine. So far, so good.

Now the true test; standing up. If *that* didn't make him pass out, nothing would. . . .

It didn't. Now to get to the window.

Moments later—moments that had felt like far longer, as half-healed bits of him protested his movement vehemently with every step—he stood at the window, sweating, shaking, but looking out.

What he saw was not what he had expected.

He supposed he would look out on an enclosed courtyard, certainly something with high walls around it. Surely they would not have put him inside anything less secure. Instead, he saw gardens, wonderful gardens, and they were extensive enough that he couldn't see the walls that must certainly be there. These were no common pleasure parks or bits of waste ground for just anyone to stroll about on.

Directly beneath his window was a graveled path, bordered on either side with a low herbaceous hedge. To either side of *that* were trees in ornamental clumps, with planted beds of foliage arranged around and among them.

The gardens themselves must have been very old, for the trees looked ancient, the grass as smooth and even as plush, the bushes and flowering plants as if they had been there since the beginning of time. There were stone benches and individual seats placed to best enjoy sun or shade, and lanterns hung from wrought-metal stands beside the benches. Nowhere were there fences to keep people away from the plantings, or even confine them to the paths, except for that little hedge, and it wasn't even knee-high. Once or twice, Alberich had seen gardens like this behind the homes of the wealthy, but never this extensive.

His room was on the second floor of this building, giving him an elevated view; it was a uniquely advantageous one for determining what his surroundings were like. There must have been a door directly below his window, for the path led up to it, and people were entering and leaving from directly below where he stood. *Young* people, he saw with a start. They wore tunics and trews, or long robes, in a paler color of green than the Healer he had seen. Some of them couldn't be older than ten!

:Those are Healer-trainees,: said Kantor tentatively. *:Where we are—it's Healer's Collegium, where young Healers are taught, as well as being a House of Healing. You're on the grounds of a complex that includes Herald's Collegium, where the Heralds are trained, Healer's Collegium, and Bardic Collegium. And the Palace. That's why all the gardens, of course; the pleasure gardens for the Palace, the herb gardens for the Healers, and kitchen gardens. They're open to everyone within the walls.:*

The Palace! They allowed *him,* a Karsite, to be within the same walls that enclosed the Palace? Granted, he was hurt, but still—*if* he were an assassin, he wouldn't let a little thing like that stop him! And most of the time he was unwatched, unguarded—how could they possibly trust him?

:You're with me,: Kantor replied simply.

The simple, bald statement took him utterly by surprise. He was "with" Kantor—and these people considered that to be enough to trust him within reach of the rulers of their land.

He recalled the attitude of the Healer and revised that. *Some* of them considered that to be enough.

Or maybe he is just like that with all of his patients.

He looked out on the gardens for a little, before answering. *:So these people train Healers in one central place?:*

:Mostly. Sometimes they apprentice with an older Healer, or are trained at one of the Temples of Healing, especially if they are uneasy about leaving their homes, but that's rare. We prefer that our Healers come here to learn so that we know that they've gotten a standard education—and any special training that their Gifts and talents might warrant.: Kantor paused. *:Would you rather that I not speak to you this way?:*

He thought about it for a moment; it seemed to him that this sharing of thoughts *should* have seemed like a violation, yet it didn't. He couldn't account for that very foreign feeling—unless, perhaps, he'd gotten used to it while he was semiconscious, so now it just didn't raise the instinctive alarm in him that it ordinarily would have. And he could not deny how useful it was to be able to silently speak and ask questions about this place and these people. *:No—I would rather you helped me. I said that I would give all of you a trial; I don't know that I can manage that without you. But—where* are *you?:*

:Right here.: He would not have believed that anything as big as a horse could have hidden itself virtually in plain sight—but there was just a little movement, and Kantor

stepped into view through a screen of bushes. He was followed by two more of the white Companions, then another two. They all stood just below his window, to one side of the path, looking up at him with eyes so vivid a blue that even from here they struck him with their intensity. *:We're all five of us waiting for our Chosen to heal in there,:* he said, with wry humor. *:Heralds have a habit of winding up in the hands of Healers.:*

These people permitted horses in their formal gardens? He could just imagine the mess that would have caused in the garden of the Son of the Sun. . . .

:We aren't exactly horses,: Kantor reminded him. *:And here, at the Collegia, people know they can trust us not to step on or eat the roses—or in this case, rosemary. Everyone here knows exactly what we are, and we can pretty much go where we wish and do what we want. Even into the Palace, if we need to.:*

Alberich looked down on them with reluctant interest. Now, with four more of these "Companions" to compare Kantor with, it was very clear that Kantor was distinct among his kind. It hadn't been obvious how powerful he was when Alberich had only been comparing him with ordinary horses—

:There was some illusion on my part as well,: Kantor admitted sheepishly. *:I hid my eye color, for one thing.:*

—but the other four were—well, like graceful acrobats or dancers. Kantor was far more muscular, his head perhaps a bit blockier, his neck arched and strong, his hindquarters and chest definitely deeper and with fantastically developed muscles.

:I am a warrior, Companion to a warrior. My friends need speed and endurance more than they need strength; I need strength and sheer power as well as stamina. No matter where your duties take you, I *will always be able to fight at your side and guard your back.:* Kantor seemed very proud of that, and for the first time, Alberich felt himself warm to the creature, just a little. They had that much in common, at least.

A warrior, Companion to a warrior. . . .

At the moment, he felt rather less than half of that. There was a growing feeling in his gut, as if he should be trembling, as if, in a moment, he *would.* He knew that feeling; it meant he was coming to the end of his reserves. In fact, it was becoming rather urgent to sit down. He was not going to be able to stand at all, soon. Maybe he shouldn't be surprised, considering all that had been done to him and how recently, but it did seem as if his reserves of strength were not what they should have been.

Then it dawned on him, why it was that he should feel weaker than expected—it had been a Healer, a *real* Healer, in the room with him. Presumably, the others who had cared for him were Healers as well. He hadn't just been physicked and doctored, he'd been Healed, as he would have been under the skilled ministrations of a Healer-Priest in a temple.

And that shocked him. They had actually gone so far as to have him Healed, not just wait for him to get better on his own, as had always happened in the past, except for one single time when he had been badly hurt in training—a pure accident, when a bolt of lightning hit the training field, killed three horses outright, and sent the rest into a blind panic, and he'd been thrown and trampled.

So no wonder he felt shaky, and weak in the knees; Healing took of your own strength and resources, speeding up what normally took days and weeks into hours and days. He probably even weighed a great deal less than he had when they'd brought him here! Small wonder the Healer wanted him to start feeding himself; there was no way that he could get enough nourishment to sustain Healing on broth.

:You should go back to bed,: Kantor admonished.

:I believe that I will. And take that pain potion the Healer left for me while I'm at it.: He knew that part of the drill well enough; it wasn't the first time he'd been hurt, though it *was* the first time it had been at the hands of his own people.

And that—

Well, just at the moment, he would rather go back to bed and to the oblivion promised by the pain potion than think about it.

Herald Talamir finished his informal report on the Karsite, and waited to see what his King would make of it.

"So. Our newest Trainee is not at all pleased about being Chosen, eh?" King Sendar asked—or rather, stated.

This was no formal audience, it wasn't even witnessed by another Herald, unless one counted the presence of Sendar's Heir, his daughter Selenay, who was halfway through her training as a Herald. They were all in Sendar's study, in the Royal Suite in the Palace—the *private* study, not the one where those who were not intimate with the Royal Family would see the King privately. This room had been the Queen's solar until Sendar appropriated it for himself; it faced south and looked out into the Queen's Garden, a courtyard that had no other entrance than the one in this room.

Roses still bloomed out there, beyond the glass, late though it was in the season, and it was home to other flowers and plants that needed tender sheltering from the worst of winter's wrath. It made a tranquil retreat for a harried monarch who wanted some peace—although there really was no way that Sendar could escape altogether from the troubles of the realm.

Talamir shook his head. "No, Sire, he's not," the King's Own replied regretfully. "I must confess, I'm at a loss as to how to proceed with him. This was hardly the response I expected."

He knew Sendar better than anyone else in Valdemar—probably better even than the late Queen had—but Sendar surprised him with his dry chuckle. "I'm not," the King said. "Truth to tell, I'm glad to hear it. I'm not certain I'd trust someone who would abandon everything he's believed in until now just because a talking horse tells him that he's been chosen to join the enemy."

"Oh," Talamir replied, blinking. "But—his own people nearly killed him in their Fires—I thought—"

"His own people had a perfectly good reason to burn him in their Fires, by their lights," Sendar pointed out, raising his eyebrow. "And sooner or later, he'll think of that for himself, assuming he hasn't already. Fine. Perhaps Kantor has managed to insinuate enough into his head while he's been Healing to make him a bit more receptive to us, but a thinking man doesn't just suddenly go over to the enemy without reasoning things through for himself. *And* it will eventually occur to him that just because Kantor is Mindspeaking to him, it doesn't necessarily follow that Kantor is telling him the truth. I would bet on that."

Talamir sensed Taver's surge of indignation at any such notion—and more remotely, sensed Sendar's Lorenil's amusement at both of them. Well, Lorenil always had possessed a strong sense of irony, not to mention a sense of humor that was positively sardonic. Rather like young Kantor in that regard.

"We're going to have to win this young fellow to us, old friend," Sendar said, as if he was completely comfortable with the notion. "We'll have to be completely honest with him, or he'll figure out we've been shading the truth for his benefit—but we'll also have to show him *why* we're trustworthy and his own people aren't. He'll have to come to the conclusion that we're telling him the truth and that he has a real and compelling reason to give us his loyalty all by himself. Anything heavy-handed, and we'll lose him."

Sendar leaned back in his chair—a modest affair of simple design and unornamented wood and leather, chosen for comfort rather than ostentation, and bestowed a penetrating look on the King's Own Herald. He and Talamir had known each other and been friends for a very, very long time.

In fact, their friendship dated from the hour that Talamir had been Chosen by Taver as King's Own Herald on the death of his predecessor—a premature death, brought on by too much stress, too much work, and a brainstorm. Talamir had been so young, uncertain in his office, and disoriented by the bond with Taver, which was *so* strong, and *so* life-altering.

Sendar, on the other hand, had been a very young King, but not at all uncertain in his office. Young, he might have been, but he'd been schooled in his duties since he could toddle. He'd been a handsome young man then, blond and tall and strong, with chiseled features worthy of a god, and an idealistic nature tempered with that finely-honed sense of irony. He was handsome still, though there was as much gray in his hair as gold, and age and care had continued to wield a cruel hand against those features, chiseling lines of worry that gave him a rather stern look. Kingly, but there was no doubt that people found him intimidating on occasion. His own sardonic sense of humor didn't help on those occasions; he rather enjoyed being intimidating now and again.

"He promised that he would give us a trial," Talamir told the King, knowing how Sendar would react. Sendar liked audaciousness; he'd loved it in his Queen, who had boldly proposed to *him* rather than the other way around, who had met every challenge, even the illness that killed her, with spirit and determination.

Sendar laughed as Talamir had expected, a dry little chuckle.

His daughter, Princess Selenay, who had been staring rather fixedly at nothing at all as she listened, made a face. "I don't see what's so funny," she objected.

Selenay might one day grow into the dry wit her father possessed, but at the moment, she was in a stage where she took everything quite seriously and earnestly. Talamir found that uniquely endearing, as did her father.

"Not funny, my dear—ironic," Sendar told her. "A Karsite,

of all things, giving *us* a chance to prove our good intentions. If you'll recall your history, you'll know why that seems ironic."

Selenay hesitated, toying with the end of her single braid, then evidently decided to be as forthright as her father. "He must be a man of honor, or Kantor wouldn't have Chosen him, so why should *that* be ironic? Can't Karsites have men of honor, too? It seems to me he has every right to require us to prove ourselves."

"Perhaps because the Karsite leaders have broken every pact they ever made—and have even made war on their own people?" Sendar suggested mildly.

She flushed as Talamir gave her an opaque look, but persisted. "Why should that mean he shouldn't demand we prove ourselves, though? The Karsites—well, how much do we know about them? Next to nothing; maybe in *their* minds they had honorable reasons to break their pacts. I mean, I should think that this man would have *more* reason to be suspicious—"

Sendar shook his head.

:Chosen, don't just dismiss her because she's young,: Taver cautioned. Clearly, this had gone from a discussion of one man to a more abstract problem.

"Well, I still don't see why, just because there are a few bad people in charge of things in Karse, we should assume that nearly everyone that comes from there is bad," she said stubbornly. "Well, look, *one* of them has just been Chosen! I don't see why there shouldn't be as many men of honor there as here."

"The problem with that assumption is that once a man of honor sees what his leaders are doing is wrong, shouldn't it be incumbent on him to do something about it?" Talamir asked the princess, who made a little grimace of impatience. "With the sorts of things that the Sunpriests have been doing, even the most devout worshiper of Vkandis is going to run out of excuses for their excesses."

"What if he can't?" she asked. "Do something about it, I mean."

"If nothing else, he should leave," Sendar pointed out. "By giving his support to a bad leader, he reinforces the position of that leader. People see that *he* is good, and since he continues to act in support of the leader, however inadvertently, they assume there is must be very compelling reasons for the leader to act as he is, and they continue to bear the intolerable."

Talamir nodded. Selenay looked uncertain, but not entirely convinced.

She'll learn, he decided. Experience, that was what she needed. "The point is that it's rather ironic, that *this* Karsite, who has already had his own leaders turn against him and try to execute him for the use of a Gift that has been the saving of their own people, should then expect us to prove ourselves to him. Not that we blame him at all, we just find it ironic."

"I can see that," the girl replied with a frown. "But I can also see *why* he has even more reason to want us to prove ourselves."

"What do you propose we do with this fellow?" Sendar asked, changing the subject. "There are bound to be objections to his presence once more people discover where he's from."

"I don't see any point in even trying to keep that a secret," Talamir replied, shaking his head. "It'll be out no matter what we do. It's a pretty problem, and one that isn't easily going to be solved. We can hardly expect people to set aside old grievances."

"It's one I wish we didn't have." Sendar looked as if he was getting a headache. "I suppose all these things happen for a reason, but I would be happy enough for this to be occurring in someone else's reign."

:Everyone always says that,; Taver observed.

Taver should know. *:I suppose they do.:*

"So, so, so. You and I have enough on our plate, I would say, without complicating our lives with this most difficult of

Trainees." Sendar pursed his lips. "Who can we delegate to bring the young fellow over to our side and make him admit to himself that his own leaders didn't deserve his loyalty?"

"Gerichen," Talamir said, instantly. "That young Sun-priest. He's—" He groped for words. "He's transparent. Eventually, I suppose he'll learn to mask what he's thinking, but for now his openness will work for us."

"All very well, but what about within the Collegium?" Sendar persisted. "We need a Herald—"

"Jadus, I think. He's taking a turn at instructor this term. And Elcarth. Both of them are so utterly different from anyone Alberich will have encountered before." He thought for a moment longer. "I'll have to keep an eye on things, though. The instructors can hardly be expected to act as nursemaids to him. I'd like to assign another Trainee to him, but there just aren't any that are adult at the moment. I *can't* have anyone younger acting as his guide. He'll resent it—"

Sendar nodded, but Selenay spoke up.

"Make him my bodyguard," she suggested.

They both turned to stare at her.

"Well," she said defensively, "If you make him my bodyguard, *I* can help him to settle in. He won't be offended, and in fact, he'll probably be flattered. After all, it isn't as if a mere Captain would ever be made the personal guard to anyone important in Karse! Making him *my* guard will show that we trust *him,* and I think that could be very important in making him trust *us.* Don't you think?"

"Actually," Sendar said slowly. "Yes. I do."

"And while he's at it, he can teach me Karsite. *Someone* ought to know how to speak it."

:Brilliant,: Taver enthused. *:Absolutely brilliant!:*

"Even if the rest of the Council will have apoplexy?" Talamir asked dubiously.

Selenay raised her chin. "Yes. And I think you ought to tell them that this was my idea. They might as well get used to the notion that I can think for myself. I'm too old to be chucked under the chin and called 'little one' and told not to bother my pretty head about things."

Which is going to come as a shock to no few of them. Talamir kept his sighs strictly mental. Evidently the gods had decided that he was going to have to make do with fewer candlemarks of rest from now on—because he certainly was *not* going to leave all of this to the sole attention of Heralds Elcarth and Jadus, worthy though they might be.

"So be it." Sendar gave his blessing and dismissal all in one, despite Talamir's misgivings. Admittedly, though, the misgivings were all concerned with other people's reactions to Alberich, and not anything having to do with Alberich's trustworthiness. Kantor was convinced; so was Taver. That was all that Talamir needed. "Talamir, I'd like you to organize Elcarth and Jadus. Let them recruit Priest Gerichen, not you."

"Oh, that shouldn't be difficult," Talamir admitted. "I suspect that Gerichen's superior already has something like that in mind, since he brought the fellow along this afternoon on his official pastoral visit."

"Then once he's on his feet and ready to be integrated into the Collegium, Selenay, I'd like you to see to the bodyguard business," Sendar continued. His daughter nodded, her eyes bright.

"Easily done," she replied confidently. She looked like a cat that had just made off with an entire jug full of cream and a brace of trout to boot. *Very* pleased with herself.

:She should be,: Taver put in.

Perhaps—but she still seemed very young to him. Too young to be so closely involved with this potentially dangerous situation. He could readily foresee Council members suspecting that Alberich was subverting the young Heir. . . .

:Yes, but that's supposed to be what she *is going to do to him,:* replied Taver. *:Really, Chosen, if you think that a healthy young* man *is going to be indifferent to an intelligent and*

attractive young lady, and isn't going to be influenced by her, you're very much mistaken.:

:You have a point. And I'm sure the thought has crossed her father's mind as well,: he admitted.

He sensed Taver's amusement. *:There you have it. If you take that line with the Council, it will be clear that Sendar believes Selenay can handle the responsibility.:*

:True. . . . : That would be all to the good.

:And if you point out it was her idea, it gives her more validity in her own right.:

:Also true.: He was glad that Sendar was seeing to it that Selenay was brought along as the Heir-in-fact as well as the Heir-in-name, but it meant a lot of work. Still, better a lot of work now than trying to bring her up to the job later, in a crisis. Because kings, even the kings of Valdemar, were mortal, and no matter what the circumstances, King Sendar's death would precipitate a crisis.

"Now, is there any sign of a repercussion down there along the Karse Border from this incident?" Sendar asked, and Talamir gladly turned the subject to the simpler one of espionage reports and troop movements. Well, relatively simpler.

"At the moment, the best guess is that the incident has been completely suppressed," Talamir replied. "There are no reports, not even rumors, from what our informants can tell us. We don't even really know which little village Kantor won him out of, they're keeping it so quiet. We *think* it's Sunsdale, because that's the only one that recently beat off bandits, but there's no word of anyone escaping the Fires from there."

"It must be an acute embarrassment to them," Sendar speculated. "Good. Let's hope it stays that way. I would rather they didn't have any more excuses to prod at us down there."

"You have a talent for understatement, Majesty," Talamir replied, rubbing his brow absently with one knuckle. "'Prod' is not precisely how I would put it. But the mission you sent me on in the first place is a complete success; Joyeaus has got a Border-watch based on the old fire-watchtowers everywhere along the Border except on Holderkin lands—and there's enough overlap that nothing larger than a bandit troop is going to slip past, even there."

"Then the damned, stiff-necked Holderkin can fight off their own bandits," Sendar growled, "And may they wallow in their pride until they choke on it!"

Her father's outburst caught Selenay by surprise, and she directed a look of shock at Talamir. Talamir just raised his eyebrows in a silent signal that promised *I'll tell you later.* She nodded very slightly.

"Joyeaus promised that she can have word to Haven of *real* troop movements within half a day at the worst," he continued. "It isn't just on our side of the Border that those old watchtowers exist. We can see theirs, and they can see ours, and there has been unofficial cooperation among the foresters for generations about alerting each other to forest fires."

Sendar snorted. "Fire doesn't stop at the Border no matter how many guards you post."

Talamir nodded. "The point is, of course, that we *can* see their watchtowers, and now ours will be manned in or out of fire season. And we've got one more safeguard in place. If one of our informants has a message too urgent to be sent by hand and he can get to one of the fire towers, he'll light a fire beacon or flash a mirror—on *their* side. Not a big one, or for long, but it will be a signal. *That* will warn the local highborn that something is coming, and from what direction, which means we'll have even earlier warning, if not the specifics."

"Remind me to find some appropriate way to thank my idiot South-Border highborn for having the sense to cooperate with each other for a change," Sendar growled, though to Talamir's ears, the "growl" sounded pleased and relieved.

"Remind me" actually meant "Talamir, go figure it out for me," of course. This time, however, it was a request that had been anticipated from the moment that Joyeaus had gotten all of the heads of the noble families to sit down at the same table and begin ironing out their differences. That young woman had the most remarkable talent for diplomatic maneuvering and soothing ruffled feathers that Talamir had ever seen. A touch of Empathy helped, of course, but mostly it was a knack for saying exactly the right thing at the right time, and being exquisitely sensitive to interpersonal nuances. She'd been utterly wasted on riding circuits. . . .

"I'll see to it, Majesty," Talamir murmured, glad that there was at least *one* small task that would be relatively easy to discharge.

Unlike the untimely arrival of that unlikeliest of Trainees. . . .

"Now, what about that tannery that Lord Wordercan wants to put in?" Sendar continued. "He's been nagging at me for the last week. I know it's something *he* wants, but I'm not sure the market can absorb that much more leather."

Talamir bent his mind to the business of the Kingdom, allowing himself to put the matter of Trainee Alberich aside for the moment—untimely, unlikely, and oh so inconvenient as he was. . . .

ALBERICH looked dubiously into the mirror at himself. The Healers had done a better job on his face than he ever would have thought possible, but nevertheless, he was scarred, and scarred badly. He looked as if someone had beaten his face with a red-hot whip several years ago. At least the scars weren't a livid, half-healed red, or he'd be frightening children and horses. His weathered tan had faded as well in the time he'd spent recovering, and he was thinner, not that he'd been carrying any extra weight before. His cheekbones seemed especially prominent, and his mouth—

Still stubborn, and they'd damned well better read it that way.

He was wearing what was, apparently, the standard uniform for a Valdemaran cadet—

:A Herald-trainee,: Kantor corrected. *:I don't believe that you will find that cadets and Trainees are at all equivalent.:*

This uniform was very new, and in fact, had been made to his measure while he was still staggering about trying to get his strength back. Some strange little fellow had invaded his sickroom one day, asked him to stand, measured him all over, took tracings of his feet, and vanished again. Today, one of these uniforms had appeared, along with a gentle-faced Herald he didn't know, and Herald Talamir.

The cut and design of this uniform was identical to the Heralds' uniforms—well, all of the ones he'd seen other than Talamir's. The difference was the color—a dark gray. Alberich approved of that color; it was a great deal less conspicuous than spotless white. It also suited his own somber disposition.

"You cut a good figure," Talamir said approvingly. "But then again, we don't often tailor a Trainee's new outfits to him; it would be a waste of time and effort, since most of them are youngsters, still growing."

"This isn't the usual color for a Trainee," the strange Herald (who had been introduced as Jadus) said apologetically. "We're apparently out of the usual materials at the moment, and I'm afraid that you're a bit larger than our run of usual newly-Chosen, so you wouldn't fit into the old ones from the common stock." The man was older than Alberich, approaching middle age, with sandy hair, and expressive features so open and honest that Alberich knew he would never hold his own in a game of chance. But the one thing that Alberich noticed most about him were his hands, graceful, flexible, strong, but not *powerful.* They were not the hands of a fighter, not even an archer.

The new Herald smiled and shrugged. "I suppose you're lucky, actually. When I say 'common stock,' it's because the uniforms are all parceled out by general sizes. Hand-me-downs, to be honest, worn until they aren't fit to wear anymore, and cycled among all of those who wear the same size. We find that it's not a bad thing, given that highborns or their families might be inclined to embellish any uniforms that were actually their property, which negates the whole point of having a uniform in the first place."

"Keeping to these, I think I will be," Alberich replied, and shrugged. "Conspicuous already, I am."

"True enough," Talamir agreed. "And perhaps by making you a trifle *more* conspicuous, we will at least make it evident that we aren't trying to hide you."

Alberich flexed his arms and legs experimentally. It might be new, but this uniform had been laundered several times to soften the fabric. Linen shirt, a fine pair of well-fitting boots, heavy canvas-twill trews and tunic. At least it was a comfortable uniform, practical and easy to move in. It could have been much worse.

He supposed that these garments would have to be made to take a considerable beating if they were to serve several sets of Trainees in their usual lifespan. Certainly Sunsguard Cadets were hard on *their* uniforms, and he doubted that Valdemaran boys would be any different.

:And girls,: Kantor reminded him.

Talamir excused himself; he had, after all, only come along to effect the introduction of Alberich to Jadus. That left the two men alone, in an awkward moment of silence. Alberich stared at the older man, wondering what *he* saw. Alberich could no more disguise what he was than Jadus could disguise what he felt.

"So," Alberich observed finally. "My keeper, you are?"

To his surprise, Jadus laughed. "Hardly that. No, actually, I'm one of your instructors, and since I have a smattering—a mere smattering, mind you—of Karsite, I was nominated to take you around to the Collegium, get you settled in, and introduce you to the rest of your instructors."

Alberich tried to keep his expression a neutral one, but he still wasn't at all happy about this whole "Collegium" business. *He* was the one giving *them* a trial, after all—so why all this business of putting him into the Collegium? Why couldn't he simply observe, quietly, so he could make an informed decision about what he would do next? Why start him on classes, when in a moon or two he might be shaking the dust of this place from his shoes? It seemed to be an exercise in futility, and one that might have a negative effect on people who would be wondering how much effort they should put into teaching him when the next day he might be gone.

Yet even as he thought that, he wondered. As he recovered, he'd had several visits from the earnest young Gerichen, who seemed convinced that none of this had been an accident, that the Sunlord Himself was behind all of this for some inscrutable purpose known only to the One God. He was trying, in his own self-deprecating fashion, to convince Alberich of this notion. Alberich was in something of a quandary over this.

On the one hand, he had difficulty imagining *why* the Sunlord would choose to put one of His Karsite people in Valdemar as a Herald, when there were better candidates who were *born* here. Surely someone who was Valdemaran was a better choice! He'd speak the language already, he'd know all about Heralds and probably be thrilled to be Chosen, and there would be no question of his being accepted by other Valdemarans.

On the other hand, Vkandis did not move to interfere in the lives of His worshipers often, but when He did—there was a reason. And who was Alberich to try and understand or second-guess the motives and actions of the One God? That would be hubris of the worst sort. If a Sunpriest thought *he* saw the Hand of the Sunlord in this, he might be right. In that case, the wisest and best thing that Alberich could do would be to humbly bow his head and accept what Vkandis intended for him.

But Gerichen was young. He might be right; he might be divinely inspired, but he might well be merely enthusiastic.

As for "settling in," that was proving far more difficult than any Valdemaran would be willing to accept. Alberich felt—well, he couldn't put a name to it. "Dislocated and adrift" was part of it; "unsettled" far too mild. "Utterly alien" came close, but didn't address the feeling of having no support beneath him. As if he were at the halfway point of a blind leap. It was far too late to go back, but he wasn't sure he'd land safely and he certainly didn't know what he'd find if he did. And that went for how he felt about the One God, too. For the first time, he'd had leisure to think about his religion and his own faith. He had questions. A great many of them. And none of them had answers.

For instance, if Vkandis wished to make peace between Karse and Valdemar, *why* not simply appear as He used to in the Great Temple? Why go to the trouble of having one single minor officer in the Sunsguard Chosen? It seemed an unreasonably convoluted path to follow to him.

But on the other hand—once again, the biggest stumbling block—who was *he* to be asking questions like that? He was only one man, one among many, who wasn't even a priest. How could *he* possibly know what was best for Karse?

But why had Vkandis Sunlord left His land to fester on its own for so long? What had happened to all the miracles, the appearances, of the ancient days? Where was the Sunlord, that he allowed his shepherds to turn wolf and prey upon their flocks?

He wrenched his mind away from the doubts and questions, and turned it squarely to face the here-and-now.

"You say, 'the rest of my instructors,'" he repeated carefully. "And it will take how long to learn to a Herald be?"

If I ever wish to do so, that is. . . . There was one clear answer to *why* this Jadus had been chosen to play guide to him. There was nothing intimidating at all about the man, and nothing of duplicity either. At least they were holding to their promise; they would let him decide for himself with no pressure on *their* part.

The Herald rubbed the side of his nose with one long finger. "For the usual Chosen, who come in here at about age thirteen or fourteen, and who are—lacking in a lot of skills you already have—it takes about five years. For you, though, I don't know," Jadus replied honestly. "Nobody *will* know until we find out just how much *you* know, plus there is a very great deal about the Heralds and this land that you absolutely must know before you can serve in the field and—" He paused and looked thoughtful for a moment, as if he had suddenly come up with a novel idea. "Actually, that may not quite be true. Something just occurred to me—and we might as well see if my option is a sound one right away." The Herald smiled warmly. "Let's trot you around, Alberich, and see what comes of it. The person I want you to see is on the way to the Collegium anyway."

"Well enough," Alberich replied with resignation. "Lead, I follow."

It was not his first excursion out into the grounds within the Palace walls, but it would be the farthest he had gone since he'd been encouraged to start leaving his bed. The Healers and his own caution kept him close to the building; he had not wanted to risk running into anyone who had the potential to be overtly hostile. He'd already had enough sour or sorrowful looks from some of the Healers and Healer-trainees he'd encountered. Once it was widely known that he was Karsite, well—no one was claiming that Valdemarans were without prejudice or incapable of holding a grudge, though in this case, he could hardly blame them.

So he had gone out, but hadn't taken the kind of long, arduous hikes he *would* have done, had he been conditioning himself at home. Not that he was weak and shaky; he'd been putting himself through a course of physical exercise since that first hour of getting himself out of bed and looking out the window. He knew, far better than the Healers did, what he was and was not capable of, and he knew very well that he was still young enough that his body would respond to being pushed to the limit by increasing where that limit stood. So at this moment he was as fit as he had ever been, if a bit thinner and paler.

As it turned out, it was a very good thing that he was.

Jadus led him through the gardens to a long, low building set off by itself. He had very little attention to spare for what were probably quite lovely gardens, once he realized just what that building *was*.

There was really no mistaking it, not when he saw the practice field laid out beside it, with archery targets, pells, and other equipment. *Then* the lack of ordinary windows, and the placement of clerestory windows instead, made sense.

This was a salle, a building devoted to the teaching and practice of arms. The kind of building that had been home to him for longer than any actual "home"—three years in the little hut he'd shared with his mother, then the rest of the time in the little inn where she worked as a serving girl and cook's helper.

Indeed, he must have spent half his life in a similar building. As a cadet, he had divided all of his waking hours among formal classes, reading and studying on his own, and weapons-work. He had never really taken any time for the recreation that the others did. As a low-born bastard, he was not the social equal of *any* of the others in his year, and he had figured out quite early that if he excelled in fighting, no one would bother him. He had already had a certain advantage in knowing all the dirty tricks he could pick up in the alleys and stables; it wasn't long before the rest of the cadets knew better than to pick on him. And while no one was particularly friendly with him, they treated him with respect. Two of the weapons instructors, seeing his diligence, actually unbent enough to act as his mentors. It wasn't exactly paternal, since they were still very strict with him, but friendly, in a distant fashion, and certainly encouraging. When it came down to it, probably he'd spent the best times of his cadet period in the salle. . . .

There was a line of solemn-faced children in gray uniforms practicing archery under the supervision of an older boy. He clearly knew what he was doing, Alberich noted with approval—correcting the stance of one, the grip of another, the aim of a third. But he hadn't been brought here to watch them; Jadus led him into the building itself without a pause. It was of a pattern with every other salle that he had ever been inside, from the sanded wooden floors to the mirrored wall to the clerestory windows above. It was superior to the salle he had been trained in, for the mirrors were silvered glass rather than polished metal. But the furnishings were exactly the same: dented and chipped wooden benches and storage boxes that doubled as seating. Practice armor, of padded leather, hung on the wall; racks of wooden blades were beside the armor. Even the smell was the same: clean sweat, leather, leather oil, a hint of sawdust.

The salle was empty except for a single Herald, an old, gray-haired man, slightly twisted and with swollen, arthritic joints. He sat on a bench with some of the padded armor over his legs, a threaded leather needle in his hand, and looked up as they entered.

"Jadus," he acknowledged. "That's the new one?"

"Weaponsmaster Dethor," Jadus nodded. "This is Herald-trainee Alberich, Chosen of Kantor."

"Kantor, hmm? Sensible lad, that one; can't see *him* making a mistake. Well, Jadus, what did you have in mind besides the usual?" The Weaponsmaster stood up, and Alberich winced inwardly. The man was in pain—hiding it, but clear enough to Alberich's eyes. He'd seen this before, in men who'd fought too many fights. The joints would only take so much damage; too much, and as the years set in and the pains of old age crept on, all the places that had been abused would suddenly become doubly painful, swelling until it hurt to move even a little.

"Since he was a Captain of the Karsite light cavalry, I did have a notion about him. Test him, and we'll both see if I'm right," was the enigmatic reply. "Isn't Kimel about? He's usually here this time of day."

Instead of answering directly, the old man barked, "Kimel! Need your arm out here!"

Alberich expected another Herald, but instead what appeared from a door at the back of the room was a man in a midnight-blue uniform, similar to the Heralds' in cut, but trimmed in silver. "I was about to go back to the barracks, Weaponsmaster," the man said. "Unless you've found someone to bout with me after all?"

The old man jerked his chin at Alberich. "Don't know. Need this one tested. Jadus seems to think— Well, just arm up, and we'll see."

The man glanced at Alberich, then did a double-take, eyes widening. Alberich braced himself for a negative reaction, but the man showed nothing. "Interesting to see which rumor is true, sir," was all the man said, and motioned to Alberich. "If you would suit up and—"

"Standard sword and shield, first," the Weaponsmaster directed, and put his mending aside, his eyes narrowed and attentive in a lean, lined, hard face. Alberich might look just like him one day. He hoped he would not have the swollen joints to match. . . .

He pushed that thought aside and selected leather practice armor and a wooden sword. There was more of the former to choose from than he'd thought; evidently, this man Kimel wasn't the only adult coming out here to practice. The wooden swords and shields were much of a muchness, nothing to choose among them except for weight, and Alberich picked ones that were the most comfortable for him.

Then he walked warily to the center of the room to face his opponent.

Alberich then went through the most exhausting weapons session he'd had since he'd graduated from cadet training. It began with sword and shield, progressing through every other practice weapon stored in the salle and their corresponding styles. Then, as he waited to see what else the old man wanted him to do, the Herald directed Jadus to lock the doors.

Alberich was sweating like a horse at this point, a bit tired, but by no means exhausted, and he gave the Weaponsmaster a startled glance.

"Live steel next," the old Herald said shortly, in answer to the unspoken question. "I don't want some idiot child wandering in here with live steel out and two real fighters having at each other."

"Ah." Alberich was perfectly satisfied with that answer; the Weaponsmaster was right. If mere untutored children had access to the salle, and he assumed they must (since having a Weaponsmaster implied that all of the young Trainees got some sort of weapons training), there was *always* the chance that one would blunder into the place at the worst possible time. Even in a bout rather than a real fight, he knew his concentration was focused, and he wouldn't necessarily notice anything but his opponent until it was too late. He followed Kimel to the cabinets on the wall and took out *real* armor and *real* weapons.

Working with live steel always gave him an extra—the pun was inevitable—edge. His awareness went up a degree, and everything seemed just that much clearer and sharper. Even his reflexes seemed to improve. He suited up, took the rapier in his hand, and faced his opponent with energy renewed.

He assumed that he was expected to pull his blows when necessary, and given the way that the bouts had gone so far, he knew it was going to be necessary. Kimel was good; very, very good in fact. Alberich was better. And Kimel was tiring faster. He wasn't going to be able to ward off everything that Alberich could throw at him.

And he didn't. Alberich had chosen the rapier for that reason; the lightest of the "real" swords, it was the easiest to "pull" when a blow actually fell instead of being countered.

The Weaponsmaster called a halt to the bouting when Kimel was clearly on his last legs. "That enough practice for you, my lad?" he asked, a certain ironic amusement in his voice.

The young man pulled off his helm, showing that his dark hair had gone black with his sweat. "Enough, Weaponsmaster," he admitted. "No matter what else you do, *please* make sure this fellow has a candlemark or so free every couple of days so I have someone to bout with from now on. I'm getting soft, and by the Havens, it shows." He actually smiled briefly at Alberich.

"I'll do that," the old man said with immense satisfaction. "It's about time I found someone to put you on your mettle." He turned to Alberich as the young man dragged himself toward the storage lockers to divest himself of his armor. "Well!" he barked. "Are *you* too tired for more work?"

Whatever was in this man's mind, Alberich was determined not to disappoint him. "No," he said shortly, then added, "sir."

"Good. Jadus, you can unlock the door. Trainee, we'll see how you are with distance weapons."

Ah. Alberich was already impressed with this Weaponsmaster; he had to assume the man had trained Kimel, and Kimel was *good.* Not quite as good as Alberich, but then his own Weaponsmasters had trained many boys that were good, but few as dedicated to their craft as Alberich. There were those that were naturals at the art of war, and Alberich was one of them—but being naturally good at something only took one *to* a certain point. It was dedication and practice that took one beyond that point. Or, as his own Weaponsmaster had said, "Genius will only take you to 'good.' *Practice* will take you to 'Master.'"

Now, this Dethor was a Master; it showed not only in that he had trained Kimel, but *how* he was testing Alberich's level of stamina, strength, and expertise. The point here was that the Weaponsmaster had waited until Alberich was tired to test him at distance weapons, when his aim might be compromised by arms that shook with weariness, and eyes blurred with exhaustion. *Clever. Very clever.*

Now, under the curious eyes of the youngsters as well as the critical eye of the old man, Alberich showed his mettle—with the longbow, with the shorter horse-bow, then finally with spear, javelin, ax, sling, and knife. He always hit the target—not always in the black, but he always hit the target. By now he had an audience of wide-eyed youngsters, ranging in age from child to young adult. It wasn't likely that they were in awe of his targeting skills; it wasn't as if he was putting missile after missile into the same spot. Presumably they were dazzled because they had never seen one man use so many different distance weapons before.

:You're enjoying yourself,: Kantor remarked with pleasure, and to his surprise, Alberich realized that the Companion was right.

:This—is what I do well,: he admitted. *:I am not ashamed of doing it well.:*

:Did I suggest you should be?: Kantor retorted. *:You are what you are: a warrior. Some* must *be warriors, that others may live in peace. You do not enjoy killing, but you are proud of your skill. I see no difficulty with this.:* A thoughtful pause. *:Better that you should be proud of your skill. When need drives, you cannot hold back.:*

Sensible. Quite sensible. He placed a final knife in the center of the target, and turned to Jadus and Dethor. Jadus was looking at Dethor with an expression of expectation.

Dethor was looking at Alberich. "Right," he said. "Karsite. What's the job of a Weaponsmaster?"

"So that those he teaches, killed or injured are not," Alberich said instantly. And bluntly. "However, whatever works, so that learn, they do, and well. Shouts, scolds, b—" He paused. "Not beating, perhaps. *Some*times, gentle. Not often.

Out in the world, there will no gentleness be. Better harshness to see here, and live, than softness, and die."

"Na, these're none of your Karsite thugs. No beatings. But all else, aye, and treat 'em gentle only when they're little, scared sparrows. Gentle pats and cosseting—that's for them as will never need to fight for life." He turned a somewhat grim smile on Jadus, and the eyes of the children—the Trainees—were getting round and apprehensive. "Right. By the Havens, I've got one now, and who'd have thought it'd be soft-handed peace-minded Jadus who'd be the one to find him, *realize* what he was good for, and bring him to me?"

Alberich was beginning to get the glimmer of an idea of what was up, and the Weaponsmaster's next words clinched it. Dethor turned to him. "Trainee Alberich, you're on notice. There'll be no riding circuit for you, and no riding internship. You'll be interning, starting now, with me, as the next Weaponsmaster. Call it—well, it's no apprenticeship, for you're nothing like an apprentice. Call it whatever you like; you're going to be a Trainee in name only."

"But—the classes—" he managed, as the children looked even more apprehensive, if that was possible.

Dethor flapped his hand, dismissing the entire curriculum of the Collegium as inconsequential. "Oh, you'll take 'em. You see to it, Jadus, but no more than three classes in a day, and I'd prefer one or two rather than three. And no housekeeping chores and no dormitory for him either—we'll have him out here, in my quarters, and he can start doing what I can't anymore. Kernos' bones, what you thought you'd be doing, putting a grown man in amongst a lot of boys, anyway—"

"It's been done before," Jadus ventured.

Dethor just snorted, and looked Alberich pointedly up and down—then at the children, who had put a careful space between himself and them.

"Ah," Jadus said, and grimaced. As Alberich had expected, the Herald was utterly transparent when it came to his feelings and what he was thinking, and right now, he realized just how wary, even frightened, all those young Trainees might be of Alberich. "I suppose he's right, Alberich; I don't think you would fit in very well with the rest of the boys."

"I think not," Alberich agreed quietly. Although he did not know this man Dethor—he knew the species. Another warrior. Someone who would think as *he* thought. As comfortable a Valdemaran to share living space with as he was likely to find.

"Then have them fetch his things over. As of now, he's an Internee with classes. I know the rules as well as you, but rules are made to be broken, now and then. Just tell Talamir what I've done, Sendar will decree it, and there'll be an end to argument."

:This is better than I had hoped for,: Kantor said, sounding pleased. *:Dethor fought on the Border, you see. We weren't altogether certain what he'd think of you.:*

:Why didn't you ask his Companion?: Alberich asked.

:Because Dethor doesn't have much consistency in the way of Mindspeech. Pahshen doesn't always know what he's thinking. The bond is there, and they do just fine, but when Dethor closes up—well, he's unreadable, and he's been completely unreadable where you *are concerned.:*

Ah. That put a different complexion on things.

"I'll see to it," Jadus said, and turned to look at the gaping children. "Shouldn't you be practicing?" he asked pointedly.

They flushed and looked guilty, especially the eldest, and gathered up their equipment and went back to the archery field. Alberich followed Dethor back into the building.

At the back wall was a door, half hidden in the paneling, the same door that Kimel, the man in the blue uniform, had come through. Alberich followed Dethor through that door as well, into a long and narrow room with seating and a wall of windows that looked out on a rather unprepossessing stretch of meadow and bushes.

"Come in here, and I'll show you how to clean up," the old

man said, waving him on. Apparently there was an entire suite of rooms here, behind the salle. Through another door, Alberich found Dethor waiting in a tiny room tiled floor-to-ceiling in white ceramic, holding a lit fireplace squib.

"Take this, reach up, and light that," the old man said, pointing to a metal container that looked very like a candle with an enormously fat wick. Pipes led up through the ceiling, and also from the bottom of the drum across to a perforated disk suspended from the middle of the ceiling. "Then turn that spigot, and you'll get a warm rain shower out of that plate. There's a box of soap there, and I'll bring you a towel; by the time you're clean, Jadus will have brought your things here and I'll have a new uniform for you. Then we can talk."

Then we can talk. Words both ominous and positive. This man had fought against Karse on the Border—but he had just brought Alberich into his personal quarters, and he was going to talk.

We are both warriors, he reminded himself. *We speak a common language that has nothing to do with Valdemaran syntax and Karsite verbs.*

Alberich stripped off his sweat-sodden uniform and turned the spigot on the wall, and just as Dethor had said, a "rain" of warm water came down from the perforated plate, draining away through a grate in the floor. This was an infinitely faster way of getting clean than a bath. Not as luxurious, but much more efficient. There was a second door into this chamber, but for now, Alberich figured he could wait to discover what lay behind it.

Dethor was as good as his word. By the time Alberich cautiously opened the door to the little room, there was a folded uniform and a towel in a pile beside it. He snuffed the contrivance that heated the water, then lost no time in toweling himself off and getting into a brand new uniform for the second time that day. It felt good to be clean, to have all his muscles aching—just a little—from the exertion. For the first time since he'd come here, he felt entirely like himself. He joined his new mentor in the sitting area, hair still damp.

"Take a seat," the old man said. Alberich gingerly chose a chair facing his new mentor.

"Now, before we start out, I want everything straight between us," said Dethor forthrightly. "I don't particularly like Karsites." He sucked in his lower lip. "Mind, it's the ones in charge I've got a bone to pick with. Your Sunpriests. Just the Karsite ones, mind; we've got a little sect of your lot on this side of the Border, and I've no quarrel with *them.*"

Alberich nodded, cautiously.

"Now, you're a soldier. Reckon that mostly what you did was take orders. Question I've got for you is—just how much did you *think* about them orders when you got 'em?" Dethor gave him a sharp look.

"Much," Alberich replied immediately, without even thinking about it very long. "Look you—my duty—to *what* it was? My God, and my people." He decided that he would leave his duty to Vkandis between himself and the God. "My people to *protect.* Not to the Fires to feed them. Not to bandits to leave them."

"And if them priests had told you to attack us, you'd have done it?" Dethor persisted.

Alberich could only shrug. "Then? You, Demon-Riders, lovers of demons, with witch-powers and witch-ways? Yes. A threat, I saw you."

"Hmph. Honest, at least. Now?" Dethor asked.

"Now—there, I am not. Here, I am." He shrugged. What was the point in asking such a question? Already he was an entirely different person from Captain Alberich of the Sunsguard. Tomorrow he might be a different person from today.

Dethor sighed, with some exaggeration. "All I'm asking is, are you going to knife me in my sleep because I killed a baker's dozen of *your* folk *and* a couple of your Priests a while back?"

Alberich gave Dethor the same answer *he* had given Alberich. "You, a soldier are. And your duty? To your King, and your people. This, I understand."

And if he asked me *about questioning orders, I would suspect he thought about* his *before he obeyed them. . . .*

"Farmers, killed you?" he persisted. "Craftsmen?" He hunted for the word. Kantor helped.

:Civilians.:

"Civilians?"

"Never," Dethor replied, with such matter-of-factness that Alberich couldn't doubt him. "Unless you count the priests."

Alberich dismissed the Sunpriests out of hand. "Then, no quarrel have I with you."

"Reckon you're ready to help me beat some skill into a pack of puppies that never saw blood?" Dethor asked, the wrinkles around his eyes relaxing, and a hint of ease creeping into his voice.

Some of whom may grow up to slay more Karsites. . . . "A question," he asked, and picked his words with care. "The answer, on your honor, swear. *Do* you of Valdemar—*do* you make war, and unleash demons, my people upon?"

"No!" Dethor said with such force that Alberich started back in his chair, his hand reaching automatically for a knife that wasn't there.

"No," the Weaponsmaster repeated, without the heat. "I swear to you, on my honor, on my gods, on my life, we do nothing of the sort. We'll defend ourselves—and there's bandits along the Border that prey on both sides of it, as I assume you know well enough—but never *once* in my time have we even pursued an invading army past the Border once we reached it. You already know that what you call 'White Demons' are nothing but our Companions. If there are demons preying on your people by night—" and a knowing glance told Alberich that this man *knew* that there were, "—then I say, look to your own priests. We don't have anything or anyone that calls up the likes of demons, and even if we did, we'd not set them on ordinary folk who just have the misfortune to live in the wrong place."

Dethor's suggestion that Alberich look to the Sunpriests for those who let demons prowl the night was not unexpected—and it was true. This was a thought that had already passed through Alberich's mind, more than once. He nodded.

And he thought of those fresh-faced youngsters at the archery field, how unless someone taught them all of the thousands of ways in which they could die and how to counter their opponents and save themselves—then they *would* die. For no more crime than serving their people, as he had. This man would not have taken him, a foreigner, to apprentice as his replacement, if he'd had any other choice. He could turn Dethor down, and have all those needless deaths on his own conscience. Or he could accept the position—

—and accept that he was going to stay.

:You are needed here,: Kantor said simply. *:Perhaps only a handful of people even among the Heralds know this—but you* are *needed here. Whatever else comes, whether your God had a hand in bringing you here, whether or not He has further plans for you here, there is that. No one else can do what you can; Dethor has looked a long, long time for his replacement, and you are his last, best choice.:*

"Then—yes," he replied, answering both Dethor and Kantor. "Yes. Learn I will, and teach."

"Then here's my hand on it." Dethor held out his sword-callused palm, and Alberich clasped it. A powerful and strong hand, that one had been; it was strong still, under the swollen joints and past the pain.

"Now, let me show you your quarters." Dethor got up out of his chair; Alberich forbore to offer him a hand. There would be a time for that later. Right now, Dethor could manage, and as long as he could manage alone, he would want to. Alberich rose, and followed in the old man's footsteps.

The quarters behind the salle turned out to be a series of interconnected rooms, with no space wasted on halls. This was a sitting room, primarily; the sun came in here on winter afternoons, which probably made it a good place for Dethor to sit and bask his bones. At the rear, it led into the "showering room" which had a cistern on the roof that fed both it and a privy on the other side of the room—which was where that second door led. On the other side of *that* was Dethor's bedroom, then a second room, which looked mostly unused, but which did have a bed and a wooden chest in it. Then storage rooms and an office, which led, in turn, back into the salle. If one followed a path around, it would be in the shape of a "u" with the two points of the letter representing the two doors into the salle.

A pile of clothing and gear lay on the bed in the second room, which Alberich assumed was going to be his. Jadus worked quickly, it seemed. The arrangement suited him, actually. And comforted him. There would be no one sleeping between him and a direct line out of here. Oh, there were windows to climb out of, but that was awkward and had the potential to be very noisy.

"This has always been laid out with the idea that the Weaponsmaster shares quarters with his Second," Dethor told him, then grinned evilly. "The Second's closer to the salle, so if there's a crisis in the middle of the night—?"

"The Second, the one who answers, is," Alberich said with mock resignation. "Master."

"Exactly. Just got one question for you. *I* have 'em bring my meals over from the Collegium—there's a fireplace in the sitting room where things can be kept hot. Wastes my time to be hauling myself over there and back, three times a day. But *you*—you might be wanting to be around people more."

It's too painful for him to be dragging himself back and forth. Alberich found it very easy to read between *those* lines. *But—he's lonely. No, I won't desert him, not even for meals.*

"If you, my master and teacher will be here—then going *there* of what use is?" he asked logically. "A waste of *my* time. Asking questions, having advice, I could be. Besides, soldiers are we. Understand each other, we do."

Was it his imagination, or did Dethor actually soften a bit? "You'll find that boy Kimel is another of our sort," he said. "Head of His Majesty's Personal Guard, that boy, and hard on himself. Always after someone to make him better and keener, but he just hasn't what's needed to be Weaponsmaster. Trained him myself, though."

"Then, on himself, he would hard be." Alberich knew that much for certain. "Like master, like man, at home we say."

"We say the same thing here," Dethor replied, and it seemed, with some content. "Not so different after all, in some things, at least."

"No," Alberich agreed.

"Right. *I* have a gaggle of youngsters coming in a moment. *You* get this room arranged to your liking, then come out and give me a hand with 'em. No time like the present to start." Once again, Dethor was all brisk business, and as he limped out, Alberich made haste to follow his orders.

He made up the bed with the linens and blankets he found in the chest, and put his things away. Not that he had a great deal to put away—those uniforms, light ones for summer, heavier materials for winter, a cloak—some toiletries, which he was pleased enough to see. He took the opportunity to give his short-cut hair a good combing, thinking as he did so that he probably ought to let it grow out now. Longer hair seemed to be the fashion in Valdemar, and there was no use in looking more conspicuous than he already did.

:You've decided to stay.: Kantor exuded satisfaction.

:Yes.: He knew he had made up his mind that the so-called "trial" was over, probably the instant that he realized Dethor wanted him to train as a replacement Weaponsmaster. Maybe

that was all it had really taken, the knowledge that they weren't going to *make* work for him, and fit him in somehow, but that there already was a place here that was crying out for someone like him. *:Yes,:* he repeated. *:It seems I'm needed.:*

Which was by no means a bad thing. Not at all.

JADUS returned about noon, as Alberich and Dethor were picking up the discarded bits of armor and practice weapons in the salle and putting things away. With Jadus was a young man in yet another sort of uniform—this time including a tabard with the Valdemar winged horse on it belted on over his clothing. A servant? It seemed so, since the fellow was carrying a set of stacked metal containers that fitted neatly into a common woven-straw cover. Jadus and Dethor led the young man through the door into the living quarters, while Alberich put the last few bits in a cupboard and followed them.

The young man opened up the straw cover and took out the metal containers one by one, and opened them in turn to disclose the components of their meal, kept hot. Clever, that; Alberich admired the arrangement. Certainly the Collegium was seeing to it that Dethor didn't suffer for taking his meals away from the rest.

By Alberich's standards of camp cookery, it was a sumptuous meal. All of it was laid out in the sitting room, with cutlery and plates that Dethor produced out of a cupboard that Alberich hadn't noticed until Dethor opened it. The servant departed, but Jadus did not; evidently he intended to share their meal. There were four different dishes, plus bread and butter; Alberich took an equal portion of each. Something like a stew, some sliced vegetable, beans, and what appeared to be baked apples. The flavors were good—when in the hands of the Healers, he'd first noticed that the food was good—but not quite familiar. The spices were all different; flavors he was used to were missing, new ones added. And these people didn't seem to use as much spice as Karsites did. It *was* good but—not exactly right. Even the bread was lighter in taste, texture and color than Karsite bread, and not as chewy. As much as the language, the *food* brought it home to him that he was on alien soil.

"Your classes won't start for another three days, Alberich," Jadus said, when the edge had been taken off Alberich's hunger. "Dethor, up at the Collegium we've decided that *you* should establish a schedule with Alberich first, and we'll work his classes in around that." The Herald sighed gustily. "At the moment, there are so *many* classes he will need to take, it won't be a problem to work a schedule of three in around whatever you set him up for."

Dethor nodded, and refilled all their cups. Alberich was mildly surprised to find that they were drinking, not beer or common wine, but some rather tasty herb tisane. Tisane—well, that just wasn't what a soldier generally drank. Not that Alberich had any *objections* to the beverage, after all, most of the beer he'd gotten over the years was indifferent at best and vile at worst, and all of the wine had been harsh and rough. Still—tisane. It conjured up images in his mind of little old ladies puttering at sewing and gossiping.

Perhaps it was meant to serve as a good example to all those children populating the place. If so—well, if he was allowed to leave this place, he suspected he would be finding a tavern fairly soon.

Perhaps, if he asked, someone would find him a little cask of some good strong ale.

"At any rate, you won't be seeing nearly as much of me, Alberich," Jadus continued, "You've got another guide coming, a fellow called Elcarth, a bit of a scholar. You see, we reckoned he'd be the best one to help you over some of the classes I'm hopeless at. I'm to bring him around to meet you in the morning."

:Which really means, what?: he asked Kantor. *:What isn't he telling me?:*

:That you aren't everyone's favorite Trainee,: Kantor replied promptly. *:Elcarth is in line to become the Dean—that's the head—of the Collegium within the next ten years or so. He doesn't look like much, but he's as sharp as a poniard, and nothing gets past him. If he approves of you, no one is going to openly contest your being here.:* Kantor paused, and Alberich "felt" him ruminating. *:Our Kings and Queens, you see, don't rule so much as* reign, *and not at all autocratically. King Sendar will probably have trouble over you with his Council for some time to come. But Elcarth—well. Elcarth comes from one of the most powerful families in the land,* and *he has a reputation for sharpness, as I told you. The Dean has a traditional place on the Council, but Elcarth is the one who's actually taking the seat for the Dean* in absentia. *That gives us a majority if we need it.:*

Alberich kept his face straight and showed no sign that Kantor had imparted this amazing information to him, but he had a very hard time doing so. The Priests of Vkandis had things so completely under their hands and wills that he couldn't imagine a ruler who *didn't* rule completely. Oh, of course, there was a King in Karse, too, but he was no more than an impotent figure who didn't rule so much as preside over a gaggle of wealthy aristocrats and would-be aristocrats with nothing better to do with their time than vie for position in a do-nothing Court that was little better than an elaborate social club. It was the Son of the Sun who held the real reins of power, and behind him, so far as Alberich knew, ranged the solid phalanx of the Sunpriests, who fulfilled the Son of the Sun's orders with nary a murmur of discontent.

Then again, what do I know of what goes on behind the closed doors of the Temple? It might be the same there. Really, the most astonishing thing might not be so much that there was contention in the King's court, but that ordinary people seemed to know about it. *That* would be unheard of in Karse.

So much had happened to him in a few short marks. This morning he had been quite willing to walk out of here forever; now he wasn't merely a Trainee, he had a real position here. It felt a bit dreamlike, as if days had passed in the course of the morning. He had gone *straight* into the life of this place without a pause for breath. That wasn't *like* him. It made no sense. There was only one way to account for it. That blasted Kantor.

:Me?: his *(his!)* Companion replied, oozing innocence. *:Don't go laying your so-called conversion at* my *doorstep. I gave you every opportunity to escape. I even had Talamir tell you the great secret—that you could have shaken our bonding loose if you really decided you couldn't bear this life. How many people have been told that in the course of our history?:*

:How should I know?: Alberich asked rhetorically.

:I was about to tell you. No more than a dozen, that's what. You're here now—:

:Because you laid a trap for me, you and your precious Heralds, and baited it with the one thing I'd find irresistible.:

"Then that leaves him free, this afternoon?" Dethor asked, gesturing with a slice of buttered bread. "Good. We'll start you in as my assistant right now, Alberich. Get the youngsters used to seeing you as my assistant first before they start hearing rumors about the evil Karsite Trainee."

Alberich nodded. Well, what else was he to do? He *knew* it was going to happen—the "evil Karsite Trainee" business. How could it not? If the situations were reversed . . .

Not that they could be. The first sight of a white uniform, and the wearer of that uniform would find himself the object of target practice. Thoughtfully, he bit off a hangnail.

"The difference, I see not," he offered. "The Weaponsmaster, if good he be, always hated is."

Dethor smiled wickedly. "Better to have 'em hating you as the tyrannical Weapons Second, the brutal taskmaster. That way there'll be no room in those rattling little skulls for the evil Karsite Trainee." He finished his bread in a way that suggested the devouring of small children.

Alberich smiled, just a little. The Weaponsmaster was absolutely right, of course. Children—and, to be fair, a great many adults—were apt to label people and stick with the first label they'd come up with. "A brutal taskmaster, I surely will be, as ever," he replied, with a touch of grim humor. "My recruits, ask."

Dethor rubbed his hands together. "I'll keep the small ones, but you—ah! You, I intend to unleash on the older ones. I've been easy on 'em—too damned easy, tell the truth. *I* can't bout 'em anymore, and there's never anyone here consistently that can give 'em proper workouts. And—oh, glory!—*you've* fought real fights. None of this court fencing, oh no! That's the trouble with the teachers the highborn have; they learn to duel, to do fancy court fighting, but not how to *fight.* Plenty of Heralds do, of course, most of 'em trained by me, but they're needed out *there,* and can't be spared." He shook his head reluctantly. "And, truth to tell, it takes more than knowing how to fight to make a Weaponsmaster."

Kantor put in a few words of his own. *:The "older ones," the best fighters among them, anyway, have been getting above themselves lately. We have a flock of them that are one, maybe two years from getting their Whites that were almost* *all out of the highborn, noble families. Before they were Chosen, they got private swordsmanship lessons, and those continued even after. They think they're masters of the sword now because they're so much better than the rest of the Trainees; Dethor can't give them the sort of workout they need to show them that they aren't.:*

Alberich knew exactly what Kantor meant, and was beginning to warm to his new task. And as for Dethor, well, it was clear that he was doing more than merely "warm" to the task. He bordered on gleeful.

Alberich caught some of his spirit. It wasn't malicious, but there was a certain edge that suggested that there were a couple of these adolescent Heralds-in-training who were due for a comeuppance. Thought themselves immortal and invincible, and it would have to get pounded into their skulls that they weren't. The usual adolescent hubris, of course. Over and over, they came into the Sunsguard, sure of their skill, and thinking only of glory and fame. Time after time, if they *didn't* learn that war against bandits was dirty, perilous, and inglorious, they got their fame by having their names inscribed on the Tablets of the Fallen in the Great Temple. At least none of *these* youngsters would be looking to make a name for himself by taking their officer out in a practice bout—or worse. Worse was an ambitious and unscrupulous recruit who was hoping to advance *himself* by removing the obstacle that Alberich represented. Or to do the same, at the behest of one of Alberich's under-officers.

"That sort, I have seen," he said shortly, and left it at that.

But he did get a bit of a shock when they finished their meal—a relatively light one, appropriate for two men who would be doing very physical work, shortly—and he followed Dethor out into the salle again. Of the six adolescents choosing practice weapons or limbering up, two were female.

Girls! True, one of the Heralds that had first found him had been a woman—he vaguely recalled that now—but it hadn't really occurred to him intellectually, even though Kantor had reminded him of that fact, that he would be teaching *girls.* Females just didn't put themselves forward. Not in Karse, anyway. Females had very clearly defined roles in Karse, which did *not* include being fighters.

:Don't hold back with them,: Kantor said instantly. *:You won't be doing them any favors.:* And when he still hesitated, Kantor added sharply, *:There are barbarians in the North, pirates and slavers in the West, and bandits in the South. And they will probably face all three before they're middle-aged, if they live that long. It will be one woman and one Companion out there, alone, and you* have *to prepare them for that.:*

:Yes, I do see that.: It made him feel a little sick, but Kantor was right; they *were* Trainees, they *would* be Heralds, and he would do them no favors at all by going easy with them.

In fact, he might well kill them. Or worse. There was always the probability of an "or worse." It was a simple fact that the probability was higher for a female.

:Or both,: Kantor added grimly. *:They can't be as strong as the boys; you'll have to give them skill to make up for that. If anything, the girls will need your skills more than the boys.:*

"Well, Trainees, I have a little surprise for you," Dethor said cheerfully. He gestured at Alberich, who lingered near the door. "This is my new Second—and from now on, *he'll* be putting you through your paces, while I watch."

Alberich had no difficulty in keeping his face expressionless. This was no different than facing a line of new recruits. Even the ages weren't *that* dissimilar; he guessed these youngsters to be between sixteen and eighteen years of age. He'd had recruits that young, although, since he'd been in the mounted troops, they'd all come from some background where they'd been riding since they could walk. And, mostly, the cavalry came from recruits rather than conscripts. He supposed Trainees probably fell under the same banner as recruits;

surely *he* was the only Trainee who had ever felt as if he'd been conscripted against his will.

:Not exactly the only one, but very nearly,; Kantor said.

In their turn, they eyed him without any shame. Mostly with curiosity, although two of the boys had challenge in their eyes. Well, they'd soon see what he was made of. They were the two oldest, he guessed. Definitely the two tallest. One very dark, muscular, and blocky, the other half a head taller, with brown hair and knowing eyes. Of the other four, the girls were a pretty creature, blue-eyed, with a smooth cap of brown hair cut no longer than her earlobes, and a smaller, lighter girl with blue eyes, a generous mouth, and blond hair done in a knot on the top of her head. The boys were both brown-haired, one of medium height and one short, both with grave faces.

But it was the first two that held Alberich's attention.

:Just as you thought, those are two of your problem children. Mind, all you need to do is disillusion them. They've got good hearts, they're just, well—:

:Arrogant in some ways, because they're ignorant and don't know it,: he supplied.

:Exactly. I can tell you that they are currently the despair of their Companions. Nothing Trevor and Mik can say shakes them out of their conviction that they are never going to find themselves in trouble that they can't come out of, covered in glory.:

At least he wouldn't have the problem with these boys that he often had with recruits—bad attitude, bad breeding, either spoiled by indulgent parents and thinking that everything should be given to them, or beaten as youngsters, figuring it was every man for himself. Too many of the Sunsguard troops were like that; hardened, with no morals to speak of.

:Why, Chosen—I believe you are beginning to like *your decision to stay with us!:* Kantor said with gentle mockery.

Alberich ignored him.

"I Alberich am," he said gravely, and waited for Dethor to

give him his direction. Dethor, after all, was the Weaponsmaster here; it was Dethor who should set the lessons, and Alberich who should carry them out.

He didn't notice any reaction to his name, which was nothing like a Valdemaran name, or at least, so he supposed.

"It is the new Weapons Second I am," he continued, meeting their eyes, each in turn. "Chosen by Master Dethor. Himself. Who now, direct us will."

Dethor quickly divided the group into pairs and set them working with each other. Interestingly, he paired the girls, not with each other, but with two of the brown-haired boys. The last two—the boys Alberich had marked as being a possible source of trouble—Dethor motioned to join Alberich.

"Sword and shield, and make them work, Alberich," he said shortly. "These lads are ahead of the rest by a bit; treat them as trained, because they are. They can go two-on-one against you."

The boys exchanged a look; the darker, more muscular one with a touch of smug glee, the other, (the one who was taller, less blocky, and brown-haired) with a look of dawning misgiving, which was replaced by anticipation when he saw the expression on his friend's face. His friend was wildly optimistic about their chances, and he had come to trust his friend's judgment.

Alberich knew that look of old. Overconfidence, poor young fools, because they were large dogs in a pack of small dogs, and had never been shown any better. They thought that they were the kings of the world, and immortal. An attitude like that would get them killed—

Unless Dethor and I can knock some better sense into their heads.

"Sir," Alberich acknowledged, and picked up a practice sword and shield from the piles at the side of the salle, while the boys did the same. They looked cocky. Alberich figured that they must have had sword training from the time they were barely old enough to hold a practice sword and shield. Five or six, maybe. From families of wealth or the nobility, he figured these were part of that "flock" of youngsters that Kantor had described; they had that particular healthy, confident, well-fed look that only *being* well-nourished from infancy imparted. Maybe only someone who as a child had never been certain whether there would be a next meal would have noticed the difference, but Alberich had learned early which were the well-fed children (and thus, dangerous, for they could bully him with impunity) and which the starvelings like himself (which he could defend himself against without fear of retribution).

"Standard or—special, sir?" he asked Dethor, when the boys had finished arming themselves. *He* had not bothered with padding, arm- or shin-guards, or even a helmet; they had prudently taken advantage of all of these. At least that showed *some* sense of self-preservation. *They* were shortly going to be very glad of every bit of that protection.

"Oh, special, Second," Dethor replied airily—and he must have known or guessed just what Alberich meant by "special." "Tammas and Jahan have had plenty of *standard* training. I believe it's time they learned what real field fighting is like."

"Sir," Alberich replied, and without a pause, whirled and laid into the nearest.

He didn't go at them as if this was a pitched battle, because he'd have taken them both out in moments. They'd been expecting the usual polite exchange of salutes, followed by a measured opening to the bout—not an attack right out of nowhere, with no warning, and that had been enough of a shock for them; he didn't need to go after them full-out.

And the way they reacted was telling; they both stood their ground, but neither close enough to defend each other, nor far enough apart to make him work harder to reach both of them. *They* might think they were trained, but they weren't, not really. So Alberich knocked the first one's shield aside with a brutal blow that nearly knocked it from his arm, without regard for "lines" and the "rules" of swordplay. He followed it up by ramming the boy with his own shield. The lad stumbled backward, and before his friend could come to the rescue, Alberich sidestepped, made a wide, low sweep with the flat of his practice blade, and knocked his legs right out from under him. It was a good thing the boy was wearing shin-guards—though he couldn't have been expecting the low blow, or he'd have guarded against it.

He turned back toward the first as the second scrambled to his feet. Once again, Alberich rushed the boy, this time herding him toward his friend with a flurry of blows. Predictably, they got tangled up with each other, and he backed off to let them sort themselves out, though the next time he did this, he wouldn't give them the respite. Then he simply chased them around the salle for a full circuit of the place, using all the dirty tactics he knew, and hitting them just hard enough that they would have bruises to show for it, even under the padding and protection. He made their ears ring a time or two as well, with unexpected blows to the helm. Neither of them, of course, got so much as a love tap on *him.* He hadn't bothered with a helm, because he wanted to be able to see them easily; he trusted to his reflexes to keep him out of trouble. Oddly enough, he would have worn the helm and padding had they been utterly untrained, for there would be no predicting what they would do. Part of their problem now was that they were rather too well-trained. If they were going to come up against lads who'd been trained by fighting and killing, instead of by self-styled Masters of the Sword or fellows with equally fancy titles, they were going to have to unlearn some of what was now ingrained. Good habits—if all you were doing was fighting other gentlemen. But very bad if you were going out to kill brigands.

By this time he was just feeling warmed up, and beginning to enjoy himself. Not a chance that they could even get a tap on him; not only because he was a far better fighter, but because they were so shocked by his tactics that they couldn't think. They *were* shocked, the patterns they knew were all disrupted, and they hadn't yet seen that what appeared to be random attacks had patterns of their own, more primitive and brutal, but the patterns were there.

Not that fighting—in the frontline, basic, dirty fighting—had much to do with thinking. It was all muscle memory at that point, because before a mark was up, you'd be so tired that it had better be your muscles that remembered what to do—your mind would be numb with fatigue and no longer working properly. But what Alberich was doing was what any good bandit fighter would do, two-against-one. He certainly wouldn't stand in one place and slug it out, nor would he move forward and back in a single, straight line.

The other Trainees stopped their practice and watched him chase his two victims around the perimeter of the salle. They watched with their mouths hanging open in amazement, and no little shock and surprise. Dethor didn't make them go back to trading blows, so Alberich concluded that *this,* and not what they'd been assigned to do, was the real lesson today.

Good. Let them think about it. Not now—they were as shocked as his two victims—but they would remember, and talk about this in their rooms together, later. If they were smart enough, they would learn from what they watched now, and the next pair he chased around the salle would be better prepared for what he was going to do to them.

He drove the boys back for a good while, which probably felt like an eternity to *them,* taking on first one, then the other; they fought as two separate individuals rather than a pair. Another mistake, for he could hack at one long enough for the other to take heart and try something, then move on the second boy before he'd rightly got his move started. And oh, they were *not* anticipating the shrewd blows to shins, the absolutely *rude* blows to the groin. . . .

The latter he pulled, and pulled *hard;* he didn't want to lay them out, he just wanted them to know what he *could* do if he wished.

And what a bandit *would* do when they came up against him.

And if he'd wanted to lay them out—helmets or no, he'd have had them measuring their length on the floor first thing. The ringing blows he landed on their helms, he hoped, would tell them that. He used the flat of his blade on the helmets, rather than the edge, but one day, when they were better prepared to counter him. he'd use the proper weapon against a heavily armored man, the mace, against them. He'd known men to die of mace blows to the helm with blood pouring from their noses and ears. . . .

Then he feigned getting tired, though he was barely warmed up—which, since they were feeling the strain themselves, they fell for. They pushed him for a few paces right into the position he wanted them, whereupon he turned the tables on them and dashed right between the two of them, catching both of them with blows in the back as he passed. Then he ran them around the salle in the opposite direction.

They had probably thought they were fit, and by most standards, they were. They were no match for a man who had spent the last seven years fighting and riding and living hard, and years before *that* in an infinitely harder "school" than this one. Never mind the past sennights he'd been flat on his back with the Healers; he'd been in top condition before that, and since he'd been allowed up, he'd been regaining what he'd lost.

Besides, these two were nothing like a challenge.

He took pity on them when he caught the telltale signs of true exhaustion—the stumbling, the uncertain aim, the trembling hands. He backed off—and they didn't follow, they just stood there, like a pair of horses that had been run off their feet and just couldn't go another step. Their weapons hung from hands that were probably numb, and their heads drooped. In a moment, if he let them, they'd collapse on the floor where they stood.

"Enough," said Dethor (with immense satisfaction in his voice), the moment before Alberich would have said the same. "Now this, my lads, is what I've been too creaky and gouty and damned old to do to you. You've just faced a *real* fighting man in his full fit trim, and what's more, before luncheon, he was giving one of the Guard a similar workout. *This* is what you'll be fighting, when it comes to it, my children," he continued, raising his voice so that it carried to the rest of the salle. "This is what you'd better be ready to face when you're given your Whites. And this is why Alberich is now my Second, and it will be his job to see to it that you can stand against him before you go out in the field. Any questions?"

Silence, broken only by the panting of the two boys that Alberich had just finished with.

"Right, then. You two—" Dethor gestured at the young men. "Off with the armor, and walk laps around the salle until you're cool. *Then* you can go back to the Collegium and clean up. Not before. You walk out of my door sore, but if you walk out stiff, it won't be my fault."

A groan issued forth from one of the helmets, but both youngsters did as they were told. Alberich almost felt sorry for them; hard luck on them to be used as examples, but they must have warranted the treatment, or Dethor wouldn't have set them up to be knocked down a peg the way he had. Alberich recalled the expressions that they had worn when the exercise began, and stopped feeling sorry for them.

"Now, Alberich—do you note, my children, that he isn't even *sweating* heavily?—take young Theela here, and show her what she's doing wrong."

Young Theela, the girl with the short hair, looked as if she would much rather have died than have Alberich show her anything at all, but her problem of telegraphing certain overhand blows was quickly sorted, and Alberich went on to the next problem, at Dethor's direction. And while Alberich was dealing out lessons to each youngster in turn, Dethor was keeping an eye on the first two recipients of Alberich's attention, making them stop and do stretches at intervals to keep from stiffening up.

As the lesson wore on, Alberich paid attention to what Dethor did and said, and when, whether or not it was addressed to Alberich himself. Dethor was brilliant, really. Despite that Alberich was doing the hands-on work of instructing the Trainees, *he* was in control of the salle and the Trainees, there was never any doubt of that. Alberich was merely an extension of his will, precisely as a good Second *should* be. But Alberich had to admire the man, for he manipulated the youngsters and the situation flawlessly, invisible. They never even guessed they were being manipulated.

By the time the Weaponsmaster was ready to let them go, it was time for *all* of them to return to the Collegium, so if the two young men had thought they were going to get off early and sneak off to some sport or other, they were sadly disappointed.

A great bell rang somewhere outside, which was, evidently, the signal for the next class. This lot was off like a flight of arrows from bows even as the first tone still shivered the air. Alberich looked sideways at Dethor, who chuckled.

"Now, why do I think that my new Second is going to be the *least* popular instructor in the Collegium?" the Weaponsmaster asked the empty air. "Barring me, of course."

"The Weaponsmaster, popularity cannot afford," Alberich said dryly, as he began picking up discarded weapons and returning them to their places.

"True, my friend. Very true. And what did you think of the two young colts who think they're stallions?" Dethor asked.

That was easy to answer. "All spirit, no sense," he replied shortly.

"Ah, but can you drive some sense *into* them? That's what I want to know." Dethor waited for his answer, head to one side, and interest in his eyes.

Alberich snorted. "Not I. *Bruises.* Pain teaches, what I cannot."

And Dethor laughed.

"But yes, learn, they will," he continued. "Stupid, they are not. Nor stubborn. Ill-taught, or *mis*-taught. But unlearn, they can."

The next class was one in archery for younger children, and Dethor took this one himself, although he commended one young lad to Alberich for some special attentions precisely because the youngster was a natural marksman. Alberich soon had him shooting from several different positions and helped him find ways of getting a full draw even when shooting from a prone, partly hidden posture. Following that class was another like the first, weaponswork in the salle, with slightly younger Trainees. This time there was a change in the uniforms, however. Among the Herald-trainee Grays was a boy in pale blue, a boy in a sort of brick-color and a girl in Healer-trainee pale green. The boy in orange was quick, but not very strong; the girl slow, but patient and deliberate. Neither were very good, but eventually their determination would enable them to hit what they aimed at though, for now, as many arrows flew over the targets or buried themselves in the grass in front of it as actually hit.

At least they were both trying to the best of their ability, which was more than could be said for the third child that was not in Trainee Gray. The boy in blue looked bored, and not at all interested in trying; he played at the archery, shooting haphazardly, not really aiming. Alberich waited for Dethor to say something or assign more "special attention" to that boy, but Dethor never did, and Alberich concluded that there must be something special about the blue uniform.

:There is,: Kantor said into his mind, startling him, for the

Companion had been silent for most of the day. *:He's not a Trainee at all. The students in light blue are the children of some of the nobles in attendance on the King; their parents don't see any reason to hire tutors when the Collegium is here and perfectly capable of educating their children. But the Blues don't have any real consequences to* not *learning if their parents don't care about their progress, so—:* The pause invited him to draw his own conclusions.

:Ah.: That certainly explained things. *:Are there consequences for beating their backsides with the flat of a practice blade?:*

:Alas, yes,: Kantor said. *:Political consequences, I fear. Now, the ones in that orange-red sort of shade are Bardic-trainees. They aren't* required *to learn weaponswork, but they are encouraged to do so. Bards are often out in the wilds and in dangerous places—and while most of them* can *talk or entertain themselves out of trouble, it's a good idea to be able to fight your way out as well. But when you work with them, be very, very careful of their hands. The last thing you want to do is injure the hands of a Bard; it would be a catastrophe for them. You could set their musical training back a fortnight or more, depending on how badly the hand was hurt.:*

He made a mental note of it. Interesting. He knew what Bards were, of course, but he had never seen one, much less heard one. Something more to look into.

He ignored the boy in blue, but once it was clear that Alberich wasn't going to single him out for attention, the boy watched *him* with a kind of speculation in his eyes. Alberich wondered if rumor had already begun to spread that the dreaded Karsite Trainee was one and the same with Dethor's new Weapons Second.

:It has,: Kantor confirmed. *:Although I don't know that he would have heard it yet; the youngsters from your first class are beginning to put two and two together. I suspect that it*

will be one of the main topics of conversation over dinner. Certainly, by nightfall the whole Collegium will know.:

Unfortunately, it wouldn't stay there. And once it got out into the Court, the nobles and the rest who hung about here, well, things were likely to get very interesting.

:Things are interesting now,: Kantor said.

If Alberich had been a stag, he'd have thrown up his head and sniffed the breeze at that, trying to find the scent of trouble. The statement boded no good, no matter what language it was spoken in.

:Just what does that mean?: he thought probingly at Kantor.

:I'll tell you later,: Kantor promised. But that was all that the Companion would say, and eventually Alberich gave up trying to extract something from him.

Easier to pound sense into a foolish Trainee. So Alberich set about doing just that.

But it was going to be a long afternoon.

THE sunset outside the sitting-room window made a fine backdrop for the meal that another servant had brought them. There were not too many different ways that one could roast a pig, nor stew apples in honey, and beans were beans no matter what you did to them, so at least this dinner had not left Alberich with that particularly odd feeling of dislocation when flavors he expected weren't there.

"A remarkable first day," Dethor said, with more than a hint of satisfaction. "Hand me those plates, would you?"

Alberich handed over the stack of soiled plates, and Dethor packed them neatly in a straw container like the one that their dinner had come in. The servant that had appeared just after darkness fell waited patiently to take it away; the clean plates it contained, evidently meant for tomorrow, (so *that* was where they came from!) were already stowed in Dethor's sitting-room cupboard.

Alberich could only shrug. "And I would know this, how?" he asked logically.

Dethor laughed, a sight which would, no doubt, have astonished his pupils. Weaponsmasters, of course, *never* laughed. They also, according to popular repute, never ate, never slept, and were possessed of the ability to know *instantly* whenever one of their pupils had done something he shouldn't, because he was always punished for it with an extra-hard lesson the next day. It obviously never occurred to boys that their guilty expressions always gave them away. . . .

"Don't get coy with me, my lad," Dethor replied. "You know very well how remarkable it was."

Alberich gave the servant a sidelong glance; the man took the hint, picked up the carrier, and took himself off. Dethor sat down beside the fireplace and motioned to Alberich to take his own seat.

"I—I feel—unsettled," Alberich said at last. "I am treated as if I belong—yet I do not. I *should* not. So how comes it, that it is as if I do? And how comes it, that it feels to me as if I should?"

"I wish I could tell you, lad," Dethor sighed, and stared out the window at the darkening trees. "If I could, well, I suspect we'd not be at odds with your land. You're not the first Karsite to come over the Border, as you know—though I suspect you didn't until you found it out here. You're not even the first Karsite to be Chosen, though all of the rest were tiny children when they escaped, and were basically Valdemaran when they became Trainees. But you *are* the first adult Karsite ever Chosen, and I have to think that it's something in you that makes you different from your fellows."

Well, that answered one question—why Vkandis, if indeed His Hand was behind all of this, hadn't arranged for one or another of the former Karsite children to be Chosen. Clearly, he had. And clearly, whatever He wanted from such an arrangement hadn't happened. Alberich stared at the fire in the fireplace. "But it is to Karse—to the Sunlord—that I belong," he said softly. He *knew* that; it was at the core of him. Nothing about that part of him had changed. If that part had changed, he would no longer be himself.

"Your god is no issue to us; we respect a man who keeps to his own gods, and it makes no difference to the Heralds who another Herald gives his soul to. But are you vowed to Karse?" Dethor asked shrewdly. "Or to your people? That's two very different things, my lad. A country—well—that can be a lot of things to different people; some would say it's the land itself. But land can change hands. Some say it's the leaders, but leaders die. Or the religion—but I'll tell you something you'll *never* have heard in Karse—and that's this: religions *change.* I've seen it happen, and I'll bet my boots that if you ask your priestly friends down in the city, they'll tell you that *yours* has changed from what it was."

That was such an astonishing statement that Alberich could only stare at him. Change? How could a religion *change?* Didn't truth come directly from God?

Dethor poked at a log sticking out on the hearth with his toe. "Don't look at me that way, ask your priests, and see if I'm not right," he said, calmly. "Ah, this is daft. I'm only giving you too much to think about. Look, Alberich, I know this isn't easy for you, and there isn't much I can do about that. You'll have to reckon out what's important to you, and stick to that. Do that, and you'll have *one* thing you can hang onto, no matter how unsettled you feel. That'll give you a bit of firm ground to hold to, as it were, and once you've got that, you can take the time to figure out more." He raised an eyebrow. "*Have* you one thing, right this minute, that's worth everything to you?"

"Honor," Alberich said promptly, without thinking. Without *having* to think. Which meant, he realized, even as the word left his lips, that the choice was *right.*

"Then you stick to that, and you'll be all right, and eventually you'll find your feet under you again," Dethor told him, and yawned. "Me, I'm off for bed. I may not have chased lads around the salle today, but it's been a long one for me anyway." He laughed again. "Good thing I don't get fighting Karsites turn up to become my Seconds every day!"

Alberich immediately got up, but Dethor waved at him to seat himself again. "Now, that doesn't mean *you* need to! Maybe you wear Grays, but you're no Trainee; you set your own hours."

"Only so, I alert and awake will be, when first arrives the class," Alberich replied dryly. Dethor chuckled under his breath, got stiffly out of his chair, and shuffled off into the shadows. Alberich sagged back into his own chair, but in the next moment, he was on his feet, staring broodingly into the fire. He wasn't tired, not even physically—that single workout with the young Guardsman had been good, but he was used to that sort of exercise all day long. When he wasn't drilling or actually fighting, he was riding, in all weathers, without the luxury of hot meals and showering baths. He was used to going perpetually short of sleep; riding before dawn and not finding his bedroll until after he'd stood first watch. When he got a bath, it was usually out of a stream or a rain barrel. When he got a meal, it was field rations augmented by whatever someone had managed to shoot or buy from a farmer.

No, he wasn't tired, not physically, and certainly not mentally. He hadn't heard anything in the back of his head from Kantor for a while, not since that class of children at archery practice. On the whole, that suited him. Kantor was very facile, very persuasive, and he didn't want any interference with his own thoughts right now. He wanted to work through them on his own.

He turned away from the fire, clasped his hands behind his back, and began to pace up and down the long sitting room. He didn't trouble to light any of the lamps; he was used to firelight, and his night vision was very good.

A suite of rooms—even a bed—I haven't slept in a bed for so long that it's going to feel strange. The last time he'd been in a bed—the one at the House of Healing didn't count—had been just over a year ago, and he hadn't had possession of it for more than a single watch before he'd been turned out by the man he was relieving. It hadn't been much of a bed, just a sack filled with straw in a box on four legs, but it had been better than sleeping in the mud that had passed for ground around there.

Beds, hot meals, willing pupils to teach. Pupils who, with rare exceptions, were singularly devoid of "attitude." Oh, this place, these people—they were so very seductive! If he could have said, "This is what is wrong with my life, and this, and I would change this, and *this* is what I want above all else—" and then have all of that come to pass in a single stroke, *this* is what he would have picked as the way to spend the rest of his life.

The only trouble was, he wasn't where he "should" have been, and he was irrevocably bonded to a White Demon.

He wasn't in Karse. These people were not his people; their gods were not his God. All right, it wasn't a White Demon, it was a Companion, but Kantor was still keeping out of his sight, because he still got a reflexive chill whenever he saw the creature unexpectedly. And yet—

And yet—

If Kantor wasn't the best friend he had never had before, he was certainly the next thing to it. Uncanny, that was—the way they fit together. It was not unnerving, but that was only because Kantor's personality seemed to fit into his without a single rough edge. Strange, yet completely familiar, and the longer that this day had gone, the less possible it seemed that he could ever properly live without the Companion's presence in the back of his mind.

He paused, staring blindly out the window. Full dark it was out there, and as a consequence, what he saw was himself, outlined by the fire, reflected in the glass. Outlined in fire—

well, *that* was appropriate. In a sense, he had gone from one fire into another. . . .

As for the life he'd been offered—well. It was all there, virtually everything he could have asked for. Even the fact that he was *not* being asked to fight anymore. At least, not for the moment, though that could change, and he was too wise in the ways of conflict not to know that.

He hated fighting. Oh, not the physical exercise, that he loved; he loved the feel of a solid hit, the surety of a stroke, the way that his body knew what to do without his head having to tell it. Perhaps it would be better to say that he hated killing, despised hurting people. Even when he was ridding the world of bastards that pillaged and raped helpless villagers left without even the means to defend themselves, he hated it. Intellectually speaking, there had to be a better way of dealing with those mad, two-legged dogs than killing them.

Practically speaking, there wasn't, of course, not really. It was kill them or face the consequences of not killing them, and know that they would go on doing what they had been at before you caught them—knowing that even if you locked them up, eventually they'd either get loose or kill themselves and probably others *trying* to escape. Then the deaths of people who absolutely did not deserve it were on *your* head. So he had long ago resigned himself to that fact, and concentrated on ridding the world of murderers as expediently, dispassionately, and humanely as possible.

But there was a part of him that had uncomfortable questions about that, questions he had tried not to think about until this moment. Brigands were not the only creatures that preyed on his people. . . .

Yes, indeed, when tax- and tithe-collectors strip folk of all but the bare essentials, leaving them sometimes not even that. And what of the Sunpriests and their Fires, hmm? Shouldn't you have thought about ridding the world of them, too?

The fire popped and crackled as he passed it, as if his

thought of the Sunpriests' Fires had somehow roused it. He shuddered, as the memory of flame licking over his own flesh interposed itself between *then* and *now.*

Before this moment, before he had crossed the Border into this strange land, he had shied away from that question; he had told himself that priestly business was none of his concern—well, except for the uneasy knowledge that they *might* one day come for him. But, in truth, he had tried not to think about that at all, tried to focus on his duty, his men, the job at hand and getting on with it.

Was that cowardice? He had to admit that it probably was, and he was ashamed of it. But what could he, one single man, have done, more than he had *been* doing, other than declare himself against the priests, be denounced, and sent to the Fires himself?

And that was even if they hadn't learned what he was, the powers he harbored. Anathema. Unclean. *If thine eye gaze upon the forbidden, put it out with thine own hand, lest ye be tempted.* That was the Writ and Rule, and he had not obeyed it. Yet how could he have eliminated something over which he'd had no control, except by denouncing himself? And if he'd done that—he'd have done the enemy's work for it, taking a competent fighter, a good officer, out of the fighting.

Had he put so much effort into being a perfect soldier in Vkandis' service so that he might, somehow, expiate the fact that he had those witch-powers?

Which aren't evil. You know *they aren't evil, and you knew it then, no matter what the priests claimed. You had no control over those dreams and visions—and what was more, the things they showed you actually helped you to protect Vkandis' people. So why would the Sunpriests* say *they were evil—unless there was something about those powers that they were afraid of? Was it that they feared one day you might see something about* them *that you shouldn't?*

It was twenty paces from one end of the sitting room to the

other, and he measured it a hundred times with his restless walking.

He had prided himself to a certain extent on being brave. He just hadn't been brave enough. . . .

Honor. Dethor asked me what I cherished above everything else, and I said, "honor." But what did I mean when I said that?

He fretted and gnawed at his own soul, tearing into it obsessively, digging deeper than he had ever done before. He had never had so much time to think. Yes, he'd done a fair amount of contemplation while in the keeping of the Healers, but most of *that* had been spent in fighting the assumption that everyone else here had taken as a given that he should be *pleased,* even thrilled, with this whole business of being Chosen. He'd been so concerned with resentment that he hadn't really put any time into thinking about his position. Kicking against the traces—

Oh, what an image that conjured up! The warhorse pulling the cart, and fighting every step of the way.

And such a cart as he was hitched to now; the entire burden of *accepting* Companion, title of "Herald," and all! But it included something he had wanted for so very long.

Yes, I hitched myself to it. I walked into the harness, willingly, because the harness was so handsome. To become a Weaponsmaster—Sunlord! If anyone had ever asked him what he would have chosen to be above all things—to emulate the men he had most admired, from the day he had stepped into the cadet corps.

Those competent, strong men who, when he was a cadet, had offered their own austere brand of distant affection to him, who had counseled him and given guidance and an example to follow—who had given him, when he was forced to bid farewell to his mother, enough to feed his hungry heart.

They must have taken the place of the father he had never known. And he wanted to be like them; had wanted it then, and wanted it now. Others had called them heartless, but he knew, and he had always known, that they were anything but heartless. They held themselves apart, not because they did not care, but because they feared to care too much. Even for him—though that resolution had not been proof against his need and theirs.

There had been two of them; two he would have done anything for, men he would have rather died than disappoint.

Berthold. Aged Berthold, white-haired but still strong and vigorous, able to hold his own with men half his age—he was the man who was Weaponsmaster to the youngest boys, the ones who barely knew which end of a blade to hold. He was patient, but unforgiving when it came to slackers. He had seen how Alberich was trying, watched him, though Alberich hadn't known it at the time, when Alberich had slipped into the unoccupied salle for extra exercise and practice. He had "chanced upon" one of those practices, and from that moment on, had made certain that Alberich never had to practice alone. A pat on the back or the head, a few well-chosen words of praise or condolence—that was all the physical demonstration of affection he ever allowed himself, but Alberich would have gone through fire for such rewards.

And when Alberich passed out of the junior class into the senior cadets, so Berthold had seen to it that *his* student, Aksel, took up Alberich's education where Berthold had left off.

Aksel, a powerful little man as flexible as he was strong, probably knew more about fighting styles and weapons than any twelve ordinary fighters in the Sunsguard. His first words to Alberich were, "Berthold thinks you have it in you. If it's there, we'll bring it out together."

Alberich had never known just what "it" was supposed to be, but Aksel offered instruction and approval in equal measure, and Alberich had drunk it in as thirsty ground drank rain. They were the finest two men that Alberich had ever known. . . .

And they *taught me what honor was.* Which might be why, when Dethor had asked what he most valued, it was "honor" he had seized on instantly.

He had learned from their example as much as from anything they actually said to him.

Honor was never taking the easy way when it was also the wrong one. Never telling a falsehood *unless* the truth was painful and unnecessary, or a lie was necessary to save others. Never manipulating the truth to serve only yourself. Protecting the weak and helpless; standing fast even when fear made you weak. Keeping your word.

Perhaps that was all part of the problem; serving the Sunpriests had turned him away from the path of honor. How was it protecting the weak and helpless, when he and his troops were turned aside from their duties on the Border to shepherd a tithe collector and his treasure boxes from village to village? How could he keep his word when those about him were making idle promises that *he* was expected to fulfill, promises that again, took him away from real duty to satisfy some idiotic whim or moment of vainglory? How could he speak the truth when the truth would simply have gotten him thrown to the Fires?

In the simpler world of the cadet corps, no such compromises had ever entered into his personal equation. They only came when he left that world.

Perhaps that was why Aksel and Berthold hadn't left it, themselves . . . perhaps they had known, in their heart of hearts, that going out into the world would only begin a long train of broken vows.

Vows like the ones he broke when he accepted his place here, his position as the partner of a Companion.

But a vow went both ways. He had pledged himself to the service of Karse and the God; only later were vows required that he pledge to obey the word of any priest, and he'd had misgivings, but it was too late to try and back out at that point. At that same ceremony, though, there had been another set of vows—the priest who administered the oaths to the new officers had pledged on behalf of *all* priests to regard the new officers as Vkandis' chosen, to stand beside them if accused, and succor them in need.

And he had quickly learned how little they honored *those* oaths.

The Sunpriests broke their vows to me long before I ever broke mine to them. Did that mean the pact between him and them was also broken? Was it wrong of him to feel that *their* betrayal released him from his oath? Or was he just trying to rationalize his own sins?

He realized, belatedly, that all this pacing was probably keeping poor Dethor awake. A glance outside showed him that the moon was well up, and there was plenty of moonlight silvering the grass outside; more than enough for him to pace all he wanted to without tripping over something in the dark.

With a silent apology, he let himself out through the salle, pacing across the wooden floor by the light entering through the clerestory windows, opening the outer door and stepping out into the waiting embrace of the night.

The chill air carried a hint of damp and a scent of grass; from the distance came the sounds of voices, too far off to be more than a murmur. But the very cadences were strange to his ear, and he felt an involuntary shiver of alarm he couldn't suppress.

Oh, these Valdemarans! Not four marks into his first real day among them—he couldn't count the time spent with the Healers—and look what had happened. They had told him the one thing he longed to hear, and had not realized that he longed to hear it—that he was *needed.* They offered for his inspection a gaggle of green children, *good* children, and told him that these young people would go out, unprepared, against the kind of animals *he* had fought against—unless he helped train them. And how—*how*—could he *not* have responded to that?

To defend the weak and helpless—how much better could he do that by training others to do the same job? How could he allow anyone to *send* the weak and helpless—well, all right, the half-trained—out to throw themselves down and be trampled on, when he knew he could remedy the situation?

There was nothing dishonorable about taking that job. There was nothing honorable in refusing it.

Yes, but these are not your *people . . . so where does your honor come into it? Or is there some reason why it doesn't further break your vows to train Valdemarans?*

But then came additional questions. When he already knew, from the evidence of his own experience, how utterly *wrong* some of the things he'd taken as truth were, why should it? When had that definition of "honor" ever demanded absolute adherence to the Sunpriests of Karse?

Just because the Sunpriests would have put any Valdemaran they found to the Fire and sword—well, he knew how wrong the Sunpriests could be. He had found a Sunpriest here, an upright man who everything in him cried out to trust, who had *told* him in no uncertain words that the Valdemarans were good and true, and that it was his duty to Vkandis Himself to ally himself with them. So where did that leave his vows and his honor?

He did not realize how fast he had walked, or how far, until an angry *snort* brought his attention back to his surroundings.

He looked up, and found he was in the middle of a meadow or clearing, ringed with trees. From where he stood, he could see some lights, a few, through the trees to his right, but otherwise he could just as well have been in the middle of a meadow in farming country.

The snort had come from a very large, white, four-legged creature just under the trees in front of him. It moved out into the moonlight, and quickly resolved itself into a familiar shape.

A Companion. It wasn't Kantor; it wasn't stocky enough, and besides, it didn't "feel" like Kantor. There was, in fact, a disturbing absence of feeling about this Companion, as if there was a wall between him and it.

A moment later, it was joined by a second—then a third, a fourth, and a fifth. They moved toward him, slowly, but deliberately, and he hadn't spent most of his life around horses not to recognize the menace in their movement. Every muscle was tense. They weren't so much walking as stalking toward him, their narrowed eyes glittering in the moonlight. There was no mistaking their hostility, and he was the object of it.

A chill ran down his back as he turned slowly, preparing to go back the way he had come—only to find his path to escape blocked by another pair of Companions. He turned back, to see that the rest had spread themselves out, and were encircling him in an all-too-familiar pincer movement. A moment later, he was surrounded.

They were huge creatures, and came armed with their own hooves. Their weight—an ordinary horse in a panic could easily kill and trample a man—a trained warhorse was as formidable an opponent as any warrior that rode him. How much more dangerous would Companions be, who had minds and intelligence of their own? His heart hammered with a surge of fear, and his throat tightened.

"Your pardon, I beg—" he said aloud, cautiously, as all the stories of White Demons rose again in his mind, no longer tales to frighten a child into obedience, but very tangible. "Intrude, I did not intend."

His words had no effect; none at all. These creatures were so full of deadly malice that he could feel it where he stood. He didn't know what they intended to do to him, but their eyes glittered anger at him, and he felt exactly as he had at the moment that the Sunpriest denounced him. . . .

Like the Sunpriest, these creatures looked at him and condemned him. Like the Sunpriest, they fully intended to wipe him from the earth.

Sunlord, shield me— Suddenly he heard the angry trumpet of a stallion and the thunder of hooves behind him, and dropped instinctively to his knees, *knowing* it would do no good, but trying to make himself less of a target anyway.

The trumpet turned to a scream, and as he winced away, a new Companion pounded out of the night, hooves throwing up clods of sod as it pounded toward him.

But the new one charged through the enclosing circle and brutally smashed his full weight into the shoulder of the nearest Companion threatening Alberich. Knocking it half off of its feet, whirling to lash at another with flailing hooves, snaking his neck around to snap at the neck of a third, the new Companion skidded to a halt beside him—

And Kantor stood with his Chosen, snorting defiantly, pawing the torn earth in challenge.

Instantly, Alberich rose to his feet, taking his stance at Kantor's shoulder.

:What did I do? What do they think I did?: he asked as the other Companions laid back their ears and tore the ground with their own hooves. *:Why are they so angry at me?:*

:It's nothing you *did,:* Kantor replied shortly, and rumbled warningly when another stepped forward a pace. His own ears were so flat to his head it looked as if they'd been cropped. *:It's what you are. Karsite. Which they, young fools that they are, will not abide.:*

Kantor whipped his head around, baring his teeth at all of the others, screaming defiance with voice and mind. *:But you are* my *Chosen, and they will not touch you! Nor will they reach you, except going through me!:*

But the others seemed just as angry—and just as determined. And there were seven of *them* to Kantor's one. They snorted and added their trumpeting to Kantor's, pawing up the sod savagely.

:Come, then!: Kantor "shouted," so that Alberich winced at the strength of the voice in his mind, following the mental shout with a challenging scream. *:Try and take me, if you dare, you impudent young puppies! Try—and see what fools you are!:*

"Kantor, *no!*" he protested, knowing that, no matter how formidable his Companion was, he was still no match for the power of so many. "Don't—"

:Stop.:

The single word rang in his head like a gong, completely driving out everything else, so *powerful* was it. For a moment, it was as if he'd been punched in the gut, unable even to breathe. He was blinded and deafened, and when he was able to think again, he found himself on his knees, as if the Word had driven him there.

He wasn't the only one so affected; Kantor stood with head hanging and eyes glazed, and the others were shaking their heads, staggering about, looking utterly dazed. *He* had recovered first, and so he was the one who saw the final Companion come pacing into the meadow, striding as a king would stride across a royal carpet spread for his pleasure.

This—this newcomer was the very essence of *Companion.* His shining coat glowed pearly and silken in the moonlight, his mane and tail fell like waterfalls of silver, and his eyes held the wisdom of ages past and the knowledge of ages to come—and Alberich knew, in that moment when he looked into the stallion's eyes, that the knowledge held as much sorrow as joy. . . .

The stallion swung his head about to stare at the others—all but Kantor, that is—with the kind of *look* that Aksel and Berthold would give pupils who had gone so far beyond merely disappointing their teachers that even the most irrepressible or arrogant of boys could not have gone unaffected.

:What is this?: the newcomer asked—no—*demanded,* in tones of disgust. *:What do I find here? Companions—threatening someone else's* Chosen? *What were you thinking? How* could *you?:*

One of Alberich's attackers raised his head and stared at the stallion; Alberich "heard" nothing, but he got the distinct impression that the other was trying to justify his actions, rather like a defiant little boy who knows very well he's in the wrong, but simply cannot bear to admit it. The others were making no such attempts; if a Companion could have flushed or paled with shame, these would have done so.

The stallion gave the defiant one short shrift. *:Enough!:* he said, but the effect on the other Companion was as if he'd been struck between the eyes with a hammer. He literally dropped to his knees, as the others winced. *:You, Jasker,:* the stallion said, more in sorrow than anger, *:What you and yours have endured is* no *excuse. What happened to these others is no excuse either. You should have learned that by now.:* The stallion swung his head around, and again Alberich felt the full force of his gaze. *:You, Alberich—Chosen of Kantor—have you, yourself, ever brought harm to a single soul of Valdemar?:*

"Not unless bandits they were, and with a band of brigands riding," Alberich said truthfully. "Claim I cannot, that my men and I did not make it so that others freed were, to come against your folk—but never a Valdemaran I touched, nor did any of those under my command."

:So I thought.: the stallion turned his attention back to the errant one, who had all but shrunk into a mere pony beneath that gaze. *:Well.:*

It was very clear that the defiant one was the target of a scathing lecture. He was not to hear what the stallion said to the other, but it made the formerly defiant one shrink even further. And if something the size and shape of a horse could have been said to "slink on its belly," then that was precisely what the Companion did—toward Alberich.

:I beg your pardon,: the young one said—whispered, rather.

:I can't hear you,: the stallion rumbled, like a storm on the horizon.

:I—most humbly beg your pardon and ask your forgiveness—: came the humiliated response. *:Chosen of Kantor, I acted vilely. I am unworthy.:*

:I should say so!: Kantor snorted, ears laid back, and teeth bared. *:Arrogant little beast, I should—:*

:Kantor!: the stallion said warningly.

But Kantor only raised his head and looked the other in the face, with no sign of the profound shame they displayed. *:I only said that I* should, *Taver. I* should *thrash this little cretin around Companion's Field twice—but I won't. I won't* ever. *Because I'm stronger and a better fighter and it would be no contest between us, so long as it was a* fair *fight, and not a case of a mob against one—:*

Somehow, the other's head drooped even lower.

:Kantor, I beg your pardon, too,: came the sad voice—if a voice in the mind could sob, Alberich sensed that this one was on the verge of just that. Alberich decided that enough was enough.

For whatever reason, this boy—and it might *look* like a horse, but it *acted* like a boy—had a grudge against all Karsites. Apparently he had decided on his own that Kantor had been deceived or subverted.

And he elected to take out his grievances on this Karsite—Alberich—who had somehow come within his reach. Why the child felt this way, Alberich had no idea—but it was apparently a driving passion, and had driven him to gather up a pack of his cronies to act when Alberich had unwittingly put himself in a position where he could be attacked with relative impunity.

But there was also no doubt in his mind that the boy—colt?—had been forcibly shown the error of his ways. And that his contrition was real, his repentance sincere, his shame overwhelming. And there was only one answer that Alberich could make to that.

He stepped forward, and put a hand under the colt's chin. The Companion started at his touch, and began to shake, his skin shivering with reaction, as Alberich forced his head up so that he could look into the colt's eyes.

"Pardon I give, freely," he said, as he felt the colt fighting to keep from bolting. "But more. Forgiveness I give also."

:Jasker?: prompted the stallion.

The youngster blinked, and Alberich was startled to see two crystal teardrops form in his eyes and slide down his pale, moon-silvered cheeks. *:I am so sorry—thank you—:*

"From you, I will have a promise in exchange," Alberich replied grimly. "Never again to act without due thought, or so terribly without *honor!*"

:I promise!: the young one replied fervently—but Alberich was not finished.

"And you—the rest!" he continued, raking them with as stern a gaze as the stallion's. "Never, ever again to let one with passion lead you to unreason!"

He "heard" murmurs of assent, so subdued that he could only hearken back to the day when Berthold had discovered that some of the cadets had slipped into his personal quarters to assuage their curiosity and had been caught rifling through his possessions. Not Alberich—but he had witnessed the tail end of that confrontation, when the miscreants had been brought up before the entire corps.

"Then your punishment to this gentleman, I leave," he said. "My forgiveness you have. *His*—you must earn, I suspect."

The stallion nodded gravely. A few more moments passed, during which there were, no doubt, a few more silent exchanges. Then the others slunk away.

The stallion turned his attention toward Alberich and

Kantor. *:Brave, Kantor. And very wise, to call me, rather than take them on yourself.:*

:I am glad you took no longer to arrive!: Kantor bowed his head. *:Taver, they are children—and we both know how Jasker. . . . Well. One of us elders should have seen to him before this. We are fortunate that nothing worse came of this.:*

:Probably.: The stallion's flanks heaved with a sigh. *:One cannot foresee everything.:*

:No. One cannot. Thank you, Taver.:

The stallion turned to Alberich, and suddenly he knew why he had that nagging sense of familiarity—

"You are of Talamir bonded, no?" he asked.

:I am. And the chief of the Companions; and as such, it was by my neglect that this child was able to menace you. So I, too, ask your forgiveness—: But Alberich interrupted him with a shaky chuckle. "Nah, who can tell, what in a boy's head will be? No need, there is. And no harm either. But, I think, good it would be to return to my place."

Taver's ears pricked forward. *:You are gracious—:*

"I am tired," Alberich corrected. "And late, it is. Good night, I bid you."

:Good night. And know that after this, you will find a warmer welcome among us. No matter who else troubles you, you will always be welcome among the Companions.: The great stallion ghosted off after the others, leaving Alberich alone with Kantor.

"Thank you," he said to his Companion. Kantor tossed up his head and looked satisfied, if still a bit ruffled.

:Jasker—underwent much horror at the hands of the Sunpriests,: Kantor explained. *:He, and all his family. All lost, and in great fear and pain—:*

Family? Companions have families? He supposed, on second thought, they had to come from somewhere. And to lose one's whole family—

:Night-demons?: he asked, with a shiver. He had seen what

Night-demons left behind, or at least, that was what he had been told had happened, and had heard the things, only once, off in the far distance. He never wished to come that close again. The Sunpriests claimed that Night-demons were sent only against the traitors and heretics and enemies of Karse—but Alberich could not imagine how those ravening horrors could determine just who was a traitor, or a heretic—

:Yes,: Kantor replied, simply.

:Then I understand.: The Night-demons did not leave very much to bury; often it was only enough to tell whether the victim had been male or female, and sometimes not even that much. *:I hope that Taver will not be too hard on him. Shall we go back to the salle?:*

:You do have the first class in the morning,: Kantor reminded him, *:I believe it would be wise.:* Then, very quietly, *:You are a man of much honor, Chosen.:*

Alberich started. Then, slowly, smiled.

"I hope I may be," he said after a moment, "I only hope I may be."

ALBERICH contemplated a substantial pile of books waiting beside his chair in the sitting room with a sigh. If he'd seen half that number of books in the past several years, he'd have been very much surprised. Lessons. *Classes!* At *his* age—

Still, only a fool wishes to stop learning. And he needed these classes if he was going to understand these Valdemarans.

He had two of these classes (not three!) for now, both of which entailed an enormous amount of reading. In the interests of preserving his authority as Dethor's Second, however, he was not having his classes, his lessons, with the rest of the Trainees. That idea had been suggested and discarded within two days of being officially appointed and functioning as the Weaponsmaster's Second—four days after actually accepting the job. Dethor had been the one insisting on some alternate form of tutoring, though; Alberich hadn't had anything to do with that particular decision. Not that he'd been particularly enamored of squeezing himself into a desk beside a lot of children. It wasn't just that it was undignified, it was that he needed to impress those same children with his authority, and he wasn't going to do *that* if he was bumbling through classes as one of their "peers." Evidently Dethor felt exactly the same, and had gotten rather testy about it.

In fact, he hadn't even *seen* the Collegium yet. All of his time had been spent in or around the salle; when he wasn't kicking youngsters into shape, he was catching up on the thousand and one little things that Dethor hadn't been able to get to for the past few years since the bone-aches got into his hands. He tried, Sunlord knew, but he had to do things slowly and the work built up faster than he could do it. And often enough, he couldn't do it at all.

There was a shed full of practice armor and real armor discarded by the Guard and Heralds that needed only a bit of mending to be useful again. Shoulder plates and elbow and knee protection just needed broken leather straps or the padding replaced, the bit of chain lying about could be repaired with a few new rings and some patient weaving. Practice armor of leather and canvas generally had to have the same treatment, or tears mended. It took a little bit of skill and strong fingers, nothing more.

Then there were practice weapons in need of mending, and archery targets to be salvaged. The things that got mended soonest tended to be in the sizes that everyone could use, which left children who were smaller, taller, or thinner than the usual struggling with poorly-fitting armor. *He* was fixing the odd-sized items first, and had the satisfaction of seeing at least two of his smallest pupils looking comfortable in practice.

In the shed he had also uncovered two or three crates of oddments. The oddments were very odd indeed and, unlike the things needing mending, had been packed carefully away. Alberich hadn't had a chance to do more than look into the crates, but it almost appeared as if the Weaponsmasters of the past had been collecting and storing anything that ever came into their hands that *might* have been a weapon, on the chance that someday, someone might be able to add it to the weaponry lessons.

Now, Alberich just might be that someone, for Weaponsmaster Aksel had learned a great many strange forms of weaponswork over the years, and had passed it all on to Alberich—at least in the form of knowing what a particular piece was *for* and how it was handled, if not in expertise. He wanted very badly to go delving into those chests . . . but the Collegium had other ideas for his so-called "free time."

Those lessons, for instance. The first of which was History; not only of Valdemar, which he had expected, but also some of the history of their neighbors. It was a good thing that the understanding of the written language had come part and parcel with the spoken word, or he *would* have been floundering. Though how something that looked like a horse could come to know how to read—or have any reason to—was beyond him. At the moment, he wasn't asking many questions of his world; he was just taking things at face value and trying not to think too hard about them. It wasn't that he didn't want the answers, it was that the answers only led to more questions, and *those* to more in their turn. He needed to budget his time carefully; he needed to concentrate his mind (and his questions) on the matters at hand.

His History tutor was yet another Herald, a little bird of a man called Elcarth, who had probably read more books in the past year than Alberich and any two other Karsite officers combined had seen in their lives. He did have a knack with history, though, being able to get at the story behind the history—and breezing right past the things that didn't have a lot of relevance to what was going on in the world at the moment. He'd concentrated on the Founding of Valdemar in regard to Baron Valdemar's issues with the Great Empire and his decision to flee with his people, then skipped over all the years between settling and the coming of the Companions with a dismissive "hardship, suffering, sacrifice, the usual sort of tales of our heroic ancestors that you'd expect to see, and you can read about it all later." Then, stopped on the tale of how Valdemar had prayed to *all* gods for help in ensuring that his Kingdom was well led after his death. The answer had taken the form of the Companions . . . which had given Alberich a double shock, for Elcarth had unearthed a dusty account of the event, too tattered and ancient to have been created just for Alberich's benefit. If it didn't date all the way back to King Valdemar, it was old enough to have been copied directly from a document of that time. And in that account was the supposed litany of all of the gods that Valdemar had prayed to. One of them had been Vkandis Sunlord. . . .

Which implied that either Valdemar had been familiar with Alberich's God, or the author of the account had been. Now, in either case, the further implication was that Vkandis would be favorably inclined to Valdemar and her King. Oh, there were a lot more implications than just that one, but that single suggestion was enough to undermine everything *he* had thought of as "history."

But Alberich wasn't allowed to dwell on that, for Elcarth had accelerated past the rest of Valdemar's reign, and that of the next few of his descendants with "there are a great many legends, songs, and tales, and you can look into them at your leisure," settling into the point where Valdemarans first encountered folk who were as strong or stronger than they were, who were self-sufficient and self-governing, and had no interest in uniting with them. Up until that point, as they expanded their borders, all they had come in contact with were small and isolated settlements that were perfectly happy to have the protection of the Kingdom of Valdemar, or "countries" (more like "counties," seeing that some of them could have been crossed in a day) that were willing to ally, and later be absorbed by, the greater nation. It was the Kingdom of Hardorn that they initially contacted, in a cautious probe back in the direction from which they had come, and that was the chapter that Alberich was dealing with now.

The other class was concerned with the government of Valdemar and how it worked; a good bit drier, this was. He'd been given the books yesterday by Elcarth, with instructions to read the first twenty pages or so. Apparently, his tutor would turn up this afternoon when Dethor would be instructing the youngest of the Trainees in their first lessons in edged weapons.

He'd read the first twenty pages as he'd been told and found it all rather . . . different. A complete contrast with Karse, which was ruled by the Son of the Sun who was in turn selected from the priesthood by the Sunlord Himself.

Supposedly. *Alberich* had never been near the Great Temple himself, never seen any of the Priests of the upper hierarchies or their ilk, nor had anyone he had ever met. Not bloody likely he ever would have either; the common folk were not supposed to trouble themselves about such things. Writ and Rule said that the Son of the Sun was selected by the Sunlord, and that was the extent of his personal knowledge. He had suspicions, of course, that the Sunlord had as much to do with the selection of His highest representative in Karse as He did in selecting Dethor's favorite hat. When had there last been a Son of the Sun selected from the village priests, for instance? They all seemed to come from among the high-ranking lot that never stirred out of Sunhame and were ever-increasingly out of touch with what was going on among the common people.

Karse actually had a king, but the position was purely symbolic, and had been for centuries. King Ortrech largely presided over a court concerned with the social functions of the old nobility and moneyed classes; the Sunpriests made all the real decisions insofar as the actual running of Karse. The King merely ratified what the priests decided, and occasionally the priests would in turn implement some small thing that the

King wanted, such as the creation of a new title or the granting of property to make a court noble into a landed one.

This, of course, was probably one of the causes of strife between the two lands—that Valdemar was ruled by a purely secular figure, and Karse by (supposedly) a divinely-guided one. Alberich wished that he was far enough along in the History classes to see what had happened when the Borders of Karse and Valdemar first met. Had *that* been the primal cause of the enmity? Or had it been something else?

The first few pages of the text on Valdemaran law and government had been perfectly straightforward. But then, toward the end of the assigned segment, he encountered a passage that left him blinking.

Of course, in the circumstance (which has only occurred three times in our recorded histories) that there have been no children of the reigning monarch that were Chosen, it falls to the nearest blood relative who is also a Herald to take up the Crown.

The text had gone on to describe how such a selection was made, based less upon the degree of consanguinity than of ability. Most of that had seemed irrelevant to Alberich—until he came to the part that said "*. . . and the vote of the Heraldic Circle as a bloc in the election of a new Monarch—provided that the candidate is at least a Trainee, if not a full Herald—comprises one third of the total, with that of the Council comprising two thirds.*"

Ordinary Heralds got a one-third vote in the selection of a King? That was tantamount to the officers of the Sunsguard having a say in the selection of the Son of the Sun!

He didn't know quite what to think about that. There was no question, however, that the Heralds had as much to do with creating the laws and government as they did in disseminating and dispensing it.

The morning classes kept him too busy to worry about all that, however, and by the time his putative tutor showed up, theoretical questions about the government of Valdemar had been pushed so far to the back of his mind that they didn't impinge on his thoughts in the least.

Then, when he saw his "tutor," the question foremost was if someone at the Collegium intended to mock him.

The "tutor" was a young woman in student Grays, slim and blonde, with a determined jaw and blue-gray eyes that considered him thoughtfully. He recognized her from the advanced weaponry class held at the very end of the day, although Dethor had never yet assigned Alberich to work directly with her.

"You might not remember me from the afternoon classes, Alberich," the girl said, in a matter-of-fact manner, as she held out her hand. "I'm Selenay."

"My tutor you are?" he replied, clasping her hand briefly. He didn't bother to hide the doubt in his voice.

She laughed, which surprised him a little. "Unlikely, I know, but the powers that be intend for you to get a practical exposure to how things are done in Valdemar, and they decided that we might as well—as the saying here goes—shoot two ducks with one arrow. You see, I'm the Heir. *Princess* Selenay. And every other afternoon, I serve in the City Courts. No one likes me being there without a bodyguard, and with *you* as my bodyguard, you can observe—as Elcarth put it—'government in action.' Anything you don't understand, I can explain, or Kantor can. Meanwhile, your presence will make the Council less nervous about my being there in the first place."

Alberich controlled his expression, and managed not to splutter. "At your side, the presence of the *Karsite* less nervous will make them?"

"But they won't know it's the Karsite who's my bodyguard," she replied, with a bare hint of irony. "Who I pick—with the senior Collegium staff's recommendations, of course—to act as my bodyguard is *entirely* the Collegium's business, not the Council's. All they will know, unless one of them decides to observe me, is that I've got someone in Grays to keep a weather-eye on my safety. They'll rightly assume that since Dethor must have had a hand in picking him, my escort will be quite competent. Oh, eventually they'll find out, you can't keep anything like that a secret, but by that time it will be so long established that objecting to my choice would make them look like idiots."

:Don't spoil her fun; she's been planning this for a fortnight,: Kantor advised.

:But—to trust me *with the safety of the Heir—:* He was utterly flabbergasted. He might have to look as if all this was just a matter of course, but at least he could drop any pretense of composure with Kantor, and he did so.

:Aren't you trustworthy?: Kantor countered. *:I know you would be the best person for the task; no one would take it as seriously as you will, because the Heralds all have a blind spot where the safety of Selenay is concerned. They believe that no one realizes that "Trainee Selenay" and the Heir are the same person, which is ridiculous—it's not exactly a secret, and even if it* was, *you couldn't keep information like that secure for very long.:*

Not very bright of them. *:And just because no one has tried to harm her, no one ever will, hmm?:* he replied. *:Perhaps it does take someone from outside to see the danger.:*

:Too true, I fear. And that isn't all, of course. You need to see how we work, so to speak, and you'll learn more from watching a common Herald's court than you ever would from books.:

:But when the great men find out who it is that is standing guard over their princess—:

:By that time you'll have proved yourself, and no one will think anything of it.: Kantor sounded very certain of himself; Alberich wasn't certain of anything except that there would be repercussions.

But who would be the ones facing the repercussions? Not I. No, that would be Dethor—Talamir—

"The King, your father—" he ventured. "Knows he of this?"

"Of course; he was the first one I suggested this to. I suppose you're ready?" Selenay asked, as calm and casual as if he'd asked what time of day it was.

"Ready?" What was he supposed to be ready for?

"You're coming down into the city with me, correct? As my bodyguard. You might as well start right now." She looked him up and down, critically. "That set of Grays should do, I suppose; they don't *look* quite like Trainee Grays, but they'll be all right. Are there any particular weapons you'd like to carry?"

"Weapons I would like to carry?" he repeated, feeling as if he'd been run over by something. "Ah—knives. A sword?"

"Well, let's get them and get on our way." Selenay waited for him to collect a set of plain knives and a common sword that he had just finished working on. He'd found them in that shed, and he had liked the balance immediately and had taken extra care with them, rewrapping the grips, cleaning, polishing, and sharpening. They were of sound make and good steel, and if old and much-abused, at least he knew they were in decent shape, with no hidden weakness in tang or blade. And he had never been the sort who got attached to a particular chunk of metal; as far as he was concerned, one blade was as good as another so long as it was balanced and sharp.

He'd never had any patience with those sagas wherein the hero found, was given, or created a famous blade with a name of its own. Ridiculous! These things were just pieces of steel, not something sentient. And when you focused too much on "my famous blade, Gazornenplatz," you were apt to forget that it was a tool, to be used and as readily left behind if need be. Aksel had felt the same, and when he'd caught cadets naming their blades and refusing to use any other, he often took the weapons in question to the forge himself and had them melted down, if they happened to have come out of the common arsenal. There wasn't a great deal he could do about heirloom blades or gifts, other than to ban them from the salle, but that's exactly what he had done. Fortunately, the question hadn't yet come up here, but if it ever did, Alberich intended to follow Aksel's example.

Alberich got sheaths and a belt and armed himself while Selenay waited with no signs of impatience.

When they left the salle, he discovered that Kantor had managed somehow to get himself saddled and bridled, and was waiting with a Companion mare in similar tack. How had he done *that?*

:Easy enough. When we show up at the stable door, the helpers know to get us tacked up. Don't forget, here *everyone realizes very well that we aren't horses, and treats us accordingly:*

Alberich shook his head a little and mounted; Selenay was already in the saddle. The two Companions wheeled and trotted away from the salle, toward the Collegium.

"I'm on a long-track internship, just as you are," Selenay explained, over the chime of bridle bells. When he looked at her without understanding, she quickly explained. "When a Trainee is considered ready to become a Herald, *normally* they're given the white uniforms and they're sent out along with an older, experienced Herald as a mentor. At first, all they do is observe and discuss what the mentor did afterward. Then, over the course of a year and a half, they gradually begin to take on every task that the older Herald does, until *they* are doing all the work and it's the mentor that's observing. But I can't do that."

"Not wise, the Heir out alone with only one other to have as guardian, and not possible, *ordinary* to be, a troop of guards trailing," Alberich observed. "Not wise as well, the Heir to be out of reach, the countryside in, but worse, the Heir to be unguarded, a strange city within. Therefore, *here* the only option is."

She nodded "Exactly. The Heralds and some of the Council assume that staying within the city is safe enough, but not even the most optimistic of them is mad enough to send me out in the field on Internship. And *because* I'm the Heir, once I put on Whites, I need to have every bit of the authority and experience of a seasoned Herald. The moment I'm a full Herald, I'll have a Council seat and a lot of responsibility. So instead of doing a regular Internship in Whites, I'm on a long-track Internship in Grays. I go sit in on Herald Mirilin's sessions of the Court of Justice, and every so often he asks me to make a judgment or take an action. Rendering justice is a lot of what a Herald does, you see, and you can study it all you like in books, but you never really understand it until you see it done and do it yourself. Justice isn't just *laws,* it's *people.*"

By this time they were approaching the graveled road that ran beside the enormous building of the Collegium. A Herald waited for them there, a nondescript man with long brown hair in a single braid down his back, and a small beard. He eyed Alberich with a stony expression.

"The new Trainee, Elspeth?" he asked.

"And my bodyguard, Herald Mirilin," she replied, with perfect composure. "This is Alberich, and actually, he's on a long Internship, just like I am."

"I should think so," Mirilin replied, giving him another stone-faced look. "I will be interested in trying a blade against you at some point, Alberich."

Alberich just bowed slightly. The Herald wasn't being actively unfriendly, so there was certainly no point in taking exception with his passive hostility, when all that Alberich was there for was to observe and watch out for young Selenay. "At your convenience, sir," he replied, making certain that his voice was absolutely neutral.

They rode down into the city in silence; Alberich didn't care that Herald Mirilin made no effort at conversation. Most of his attention was taken up with watching for trouble—for if the Council was nervous about Selenay going out in public unguarded, there must be at least *some* reason for their concern. What little of his attention was left over was involved in simple observation.

Even if he had not known very well where he was, he would have known immediately that this was not Karse.

Nearest to the Palace and the Collegium, just outside the complex walls, were the manors of the nobility and wealthy. In Karse, such buildings were the property of the priesthood, each holding the staff and acolytes of one or another of the high-ranking Sunpriests. There was a great deal of difference between these places that held secular families and those manses. For one thing—sounds. *No* sounds of prayer, chanting, that sort of thing. Dogs barking, occasional voices of children and young people, and also the sounds of domestic animals; some homes had music drifting from them, some the sounds of a party or friendly gathering coming out of the gardens.

The farther the three of them got from the Palace, following a road that wound back and forth in a manner of which Alberich strongly approved (defensively, it made sense not to have a direct path to the Palace), the less expensive and more crowded the buildings became. And soon after that, rows of shops anchored by taverns, cookshops, or inns began to displace houses, and temple facades poked in among the shops, with shrines in city squares or on corners. The noise level increased with increasing traffic and population, of course. But again, it was obvious that this wasn't Karse, because there were so many different temples and shrines, and, as he noticed on closer observation, not all of the things that had appeared to be shrines were anything of the sort. Some were public fountains, some statues that (so far as he could tell) had no religious significance whatsoever.

Some were clearly statues of Valdemaran heroes, and it was no surprise that a great many of them were Heralds (who were invariably shown with their Companions). Not all, however, which was interesting. Equally interesting were the statues that almost always surmounted the public fountains, which were not martial in any way. In fact, given that the figures were dressed in quite elaborate clothing and often held tools or implements, he had a guess—a quite astonishing guess, since nothing of the sort would have been permitted in Karse. Common artisans and merchants, no matter how wealthy or talented, should never be allowed to exalt themselves to the point of putting up public statues of themselves. Vkandis frowned on spending money putting up vainglorious statues when the same money could be given to the temple, and at any rate, exalting yourself or your ancestors in such a fashion was an indulgence in the sin of pride.

"That is who?" he asked finally, catching Selenay's eye and nodding at a statue of a round, balding little man, who clutched a plumb-bob and compass and beamed at passers-by. Alberich rather liked his statue, for not only was there the usual spigot and basin of the public fountain, but the upper basin spilled over into a trough at street level, just the right height for dogs and cats to drink from.

Selenay followed his gaze and smiled. "I don't know *who* that is, but I know what he is, and why he's there," she said. "These statues began going up in Elspeth the Peacemaker's time. Valdemar had been pretty much at peace for more than a generation, and a lot of people were getting very prosperous. So they started putting up statues of themselves, which rather annoyed my ancestor, who thought it was a silly waste of money. She made a law forbidding people to put up privately-owned statues on public streets, so they'd have the statues put up, then *give* them to the city. So she had another law made that forbade the putting up of anything on public streets unless it served a practical use and was for the public good, and being able to tie a horse to it didn't count. Oh, and you had to leave money in your will to see anything you put up was kept clean and in working order."

Alberich smiled at that. "Clever, that was," he responded. "And good for the city folk."

Selenay grinned. "Especially since the corners in the best part of the city went early, so people who wanted to do things had to take what they could get. Most people went for fountains and water pumps; the Queen said it was a pity that we were stuck with all those statues of a lot of vain old men, but at least now every street had a public water supply without taxes going to pay for it."

Mirilin overheard them, and unbent enough to smile slightly. "A wise woman, your ancestor," he said mildly. "If she had taxed them to pay for such things, they would have been calling for her head. But when they were able to make them into self-aggrandizing statuary, they were climbing all over themselves to oblige."

"Probably." Selenay shrugged. "I think she said something like that herself. At any rate, you'll find statues like that all over Haven now; when they aren't fountains and pumps, they can be almost anything useful. After a while, the artists that people hired to put up such things got to enjoy thinking up practical purposes. There's a clever basin over in the square where Pitcher and Bright cross where women can wash clothing—it was made that way on purpose. And there's dry mangers with stone canopies over them for feeding your horses or whatever at nearly every market square. There are covered benches, too, with inscriptions instead of statues, and an enormous public pigeon cote, which serves the purpose of giving poor people a place for birds for their pot, and gives the birds a place to go besides making nests in peoples' roofs." Both of them looked at him, clearly expecting some sort of comment from him; he thought about the larger towns in Karse that he had been in. Nothing this size, of course, but the only public sources of water were the wells in temple courtyards, and to use them. . . .

To be fair, there were plenty of Sunpriests who encouraged all comers to take the water freely. But—well, it seemed to him there were fewer of the generous ones from year to year, and more who at the least, if they did not exact a tithe of work, cash, or goods for the water, insisted on daily attendance at one of the services *before* you got your water. That might not sound like much, but in the day of a busy woman, there were not many marks to spare, and in order to fetch her water, she might face a choice between leaving some task undone or walking farther to fetch water from another source. "One wishes," he said slowly, "that all leaders like-minded were."

Selenay beamed; Mirilin grunted, but at least he didn't seem displeased.

The Court of Justice was held in a building over the Corn Market—literally *over* it, for it stood on four pillars above the valuable stall space. If the courtroom was filled, this covered space below—used on market days for the most valuable of merchandise, and food vendors—enabled people who were waiting their turn to wait out of the weather or sun.

Herald Mirilin was the sole arbiter here; those who brought grievances to him either had tried the regular courts and were unsatisfied, or felt that a regular court would not be as responsive to their grievances as a single Herald would. The Herald sat at a table at the back of the room, within a sort of partition that took up the back fifth or so, divided from the rest of room by a low balustrade. Those whose cases were being heard stood before him, while those still waiting, and interested parties, sat on rows of backless benches on the other side of the railing. Selenay sat beside Mirilin, industriously taking notes, while Alberich stood behind them both and attempted to look like a superfluous statue.

As far as Alberich could judge, the people here ranged in income level from well-off to impoverished. In age, they tended to be middle-aged folk, with a sprinkling of elders. The cases were astonishingly petty, which surprised him. Someone had loaned an object, or money, and the person to whom it had been lent now claimed it was a gift. A child had vandalized something, and the parents disclaimed responsibility. A dog was permitted to run loose and had bitten someone. A chicken flew into a yard and ate seeds and young plants; the angry householder caught, killed, and ate it, and the owner claimed compensation.

None of this was earth shattering, and all of it would have been settled in Karse with some form of personal confrontation among the parties concerned. In a village, it was usually the responsibility of the headman or council of elders to sort it all out—in a city, well, it generally came to blows.

Alberich wasn't quite sure why anyone "official" was involved in these cases at all. And even if the idea was to keep public fighting at a minimum, there *were* courts to handle these cases, according to Selenay. Why were Heralds concerned with these ridiculous little domestic problems at all? More importantly, at least as far as this "bodyguard" business was concerned, what was Selenay learning here that was vital enough to put her here, where she was very vulnerable?

His questions remained unanswered for the moment. But he did, gradually, begin to see the *shape* of what was called "justice" in Valdemar. When a grievance was between a rich person and a poor one, it was settled in the favor of the poor one as often as not. In the villages of Karse, rich men had influence. No one wanted to get on their bad side, for the most part. They might be cordially loathed, but no one dared to offend them. At least, no one dared except the Sunpriests—but even they tended not to upset the best source of their golden tithes. So justice tended, especially in small matters, to weigh in on the side of the fellow with the most coin. And in the cities of Karse, "justice" was for open sale, as often as not.

But here, to his bemusement, justice was simply that.

But the poor man didn't always win. Not when the poor man was in the wrong.

There was a case of a shabby, shifty-eyed fellow claiming that a merchant's horse had trampled him and broken his leg, and the merchant's coachman had agreed that, yes, that was what had happened—when the shifty fellow had thrown himself deliberately under the horse's hooves.

That was when Mirilin glanced over at the Princess. "Truth Spell, please, Selenay," he murmured.

:Watch this, Chosen,: Kantor said instantly. *:This is important.:*

Selenay nodded and closed her eyes, a tiny frown of concentration on her face. And slowly, a faint blue glow began to gather over the heads of both parties, growing stronger and stronger, until it stood out clearly even in the well-lit courtroom. Alberich kept his face expressionless, but he felt the hair standing up on the back of his neck. When anyone in Karse used magic—well, the only people who *did* were Sunpriests, and the very few times they ever did so outside of the inner sanctum of a temple, someone usually died. . . .

"Now," said Mirilin to the coachman. "Tell me again what happened, precisely."

The coachman, an earnest old gentleman who kept his gaze fastened on Mirilin the entire time, repeated his story, virtually word-for-word, while the light about him glowed steadily. He didn't even seem aware of it, although those in the courtroom who were paying attention to this case murmured with satisfaction.

"And now, sir, would you tell me what happened again?" Mirilin continued, with a courteous nod to the shabby fellow.

"Nah, lookit me *leg!*" the fellow bleated indignantly, gesturing at the limb in question, which was splinted and bound with clean rags—the only things that were clean about him. "Any'un with 'af an eye kin tell what's what!"

"Nevertheless, please tell me again," Mirilin replied, with

far more patience than Alberich would have shown. The man began his tale with ill grace, but the moment he got to "—an' I stepped inter the street, an' this bastid comes *whippin'* up 'is 'orses—"

The light went out.

Although the man clearly was unaware that anything had happened at all, the onlookers saw what Alberich had. A gasp—not of surprise, but of satisfaction—went up, and Mirilin cut the rest of the man's speech off with a wave of his hand.

"Sir, you are lying, and this man is telling the truth. He owes you nothing." Mirilin glanced meaningfully at the constables that waited just beyond the barrier. "Now, the penalties for perjury are substantial in a regular court, but since this is a Heraldic hearing, and I have discretion, I shall allow you to leave in peace—providing you *do* leave quietly. I suggest that you find a more honest means of employing yourself from here on, because you are now in the official records as a perjurer, and the next court you bring yourself before will take that into account."

The man followed Mirilin's glance and set his jaw angrily, but didn't even try to dispute the judgment. Instead, he shuffled off, quickly getting himself out of the door (or at least, as quickly as a splinted and wrapped leg would allow) while the coachman thanked Mirilin effusively.

But Mirilin waved him off with a slight sign of irritation. "Do not thank *me* for simple justice," he said. "Now, please, we have a heavy docket to see—"

The coachman took the hint and followed in the path of his accuser.

:That was the Truth Spell, Chosen,: Kantor said with satisfaction, *:And it is nearly the only sort of magic that you will ever* see *a Herald using. There's mind-magic, of course, which is things like Mindspeech, ForeSeeing and FarSeeing, but unless you are the Herald doing the mind-magic, well, you aren't*

going to actually see anything. Mirilin is better at the Truth Spell than Selenay, but he wants her to have the practice in setting it, because when she needs to use it, she'll be doing so with many more eyes on her.:

:Is that all it does?: he asked. *:Just show which person is telling the truth?:*

:There is a more powerful version that can compel the truth, but it's not likely to be used here,: Kantor replied, as an old woman with a cat came hobbling up to the table. *:That's saved for things that are a great deal more serious, and not all Heralds can invoke it. You have to have a very strong Gift, and it usually has to be one like Mindspeech.:*

:Will I—: he began, and stopped.

:You will. You'll probably be very good at it.: But Kantor was evidently sensitive to feelings as well as actual thoughts, for he quickly added, *:But given that you're going to be the Weaponsmaster, I doubt you'll be called upon to do it much. If at all.:*

The afternoon trundled on, under its own momentum of petty grievances, minor misunderstandings, rancor, greed, selfishness—and bewilderment, hurt feelings, a certain amount of genuine grief, and the genuine trust that a Herald *would* put things right. As the afternoon went on, there were several inheritance cases that came up, and in one, Mirilin worked something like a miracle, not only getting compromise, but in getting all of the aggrieved parties to apologize to each other and reconcile.

Sometimes both parties were equally right and wrong, and it was then that Mirilin truly showed his worth. Somehow he always managed to get both sides to see the rights as well as the wrongs of the case, and for the most part, managed to get *them* to work out a solution without having to have him decree one for them. That was sheer genius, and Alberich did not see how he managed it. Astonishing.

No wonder he's assigned to this! Alberich thought more

than once, as Mirilin played near-invisible midwife to yet another compromise.

:In many ways, Selenay will have to do exactly this when she is Queen,: Kantor pointed out. *:A court is a little like a village or a neighborhood; everyone knows everyone else, everyone has his own particular agenda to pursue, there is an entire pecking order within the group that outsiders would never be aware of, and above all, you can never forget that someone has to be aware of all of the undercurrents and keep conflicts from breaking out into actual feuding. The actual complaints here will be different from those within the Court, but the dynamics of personality are fundamentally the same.:*

So *that* was what Selenay was learning here. Perhaps these people weren't as daft as he thought.

The court was closed around dinnertime, with a backlog of people still waiting. But no one complained overmuch, perhaps because Mirilin had kept things moving fairly briskly.

On the way back, Selenay and her mentor discussed the intricacies of case and personality with great animation; Alberich achieved his goal of becoming unnoticeable, as he rode behind them. This was good; he actually learned far more than he had expected as Mirilin offered the fruits of his hard-earned experience to Selenay.

And when Selenay took her leave of Alberich, he found that he was looking forward to the next session down in Haven. If Mirilin hadn't exactly warmed to Alberich, at least he hadn't rejected Alberich out of hand.

He returned to the salle and headed for his shared living quarters with the feeling, on the whole, that he was rather pleased than otherwise with the way that the day had gone. But Dethor's first words, spoken as he walked into the midst of a conversation that had certainly been going on for at least a mark before *he* arrived, put a chill on his good humor.

"There you are," Dethor said, as the other two Heralds in the room looked up at his entrance. "What do you know about a group that calls themselves the 'Tedrel Mercenaries'?"

"WHAT of the Tedrels do I know? Huh. Nothing good," Alberich replied, but only after standing there for a moment, blinking stupidly; such a completely unexpected question left him feeling slightly stunned. *The Tedrels?* What on earth could *that* sinister group have to do with Valdemar? And why ask *him* about them?

"Why?" he asked, as the others sat there looking at him, waiting for him to say something more.

"Because there's word Karse is hiring them." Dethor's eyes could have pierced a hole in steel, but evidently Alberich's reaction of further shock pleased him, for his expression softened immediately.

The Tedrels? Why would Karse hire *them?* Who could have learned of them to hire them in the first place? Most people in *Karse* had never heard of them, let alone anyone this far north. The only reason *he* knew anything about them was because of Aksel.

And the only reason that Aksel knew anything about them

was because *he* still had contacts within the Mercenary Guild, friendly contacts, which was not within the norm for anyone in the Sunsguard. One evening Aksel had told him that the Mercenary Guild was issuing warnings about the Tedrel Companies; since that was just before Alberich was commissioned out of the cadets, Aksel had seen fit to warn his protégé in case he came up against any Tedrels in the course of his duties. He'd shown Alberich the broadside carrying the message, in fact.

Don't trust them, said those warnings. *Don't fight with them, and don't take a fight against them.* And the reasons for these flat edicts had been chilling. . . .

Now Karse was not in good odor with the Mercenary Guild. The Sunpriests expected men to fight for the glory of the Sunlord, and not for such venial considerations as money and booty. They had, on two separate occasions, hired Guild Companies and then reneged on the contract. They had *paid* for those mistakes; with full Guild backing, enough caravans led by Karsite merchants crossing the southern Border of Karse had been confiscated to pay for the arrears—and since it had been high-ranking Sunpriests who had backed those caravans with their personal fortunes, the bird of ill luck had come home to roost in the right nest. But the Guild Companies now refused any and all overtures from the Sunpriests, and of all of the military leaders in Karse, only Aksel—who was not a "leader" as such—still had friends in the Guild.

That had all fallen out while Alberich was still sweeping out the stables to earn extra coppers for his mother. By the time he was in the cadet academy, Karse was learning that not even non-Guild mercenaries would take their coin. Being cut off from the Guild left Karse without a reliable source for extra troops; being refused by nearly everyone left them forced to supply their needs from within.

And therein lay the rub. The regular troops were few. Standing armies were expensive beasts to maintain. Men had to be recruited or conscripted—and if you took too many men off the land, who would till and plant and harvest the fields or tend the herds? Once you had the men, you had to train them, and house and feed them *while* you were training them. Then, when they weren't actually fighting (which was most of the time) you *still* had to feed and house them. The Sunpriests might be able to induce religious fervor enough to get their men to fight without pay (or at least, with minimal pay), but they still couldn't get by without food and shelter, no matter how fanatic or pious or even desirous of paradise they were.

And besides that, there was a limit to how many troops you could recruit in the first place. Many places in Karse had poor soil; poor soil meant that a great deal of work had to be put into a farm to make it prosper. The boys might get dreams of glory in the Sunsguard, but their fathers would see to it that they didn't run off when they were needed at home. No matter how hungry for the land and riches of other realms the Sunpriests were, they were not mad enough to deplete their own land of the very people needed to keep the farms going. By the time Alberich was about to get his first commission, they had conscripted so many of the poor in the cities that there was an actual labor shortage, and women were taking jobs that once only men had filled. That had been the reasoning behind permitting bandits to use Karse as a base to raid into Valdemar; bandits didn't require the support of the state, and they kept up the ongoing feud with Valdemar without—in theory, at least—costing Karse anything. Except that, of course, bandits didn't keep their bargains, which had required the Sunpriests use all of their Sunsguard to quell them, leaving no fighters for any other little projects they might have in mind.

Which left hiring troops as the only viable option, if troops were needed for a campaign against anyone. That meant either Mercenary Guild companies, which were trustworthy, would not loot or otherwise molest your people, and in general were welcome in the lands of those who hired them—or non-Guild troops, which were unpredictable at best, and a hazard to those who hired them at worst. By betraying the Mercenary Guild, the Sunpriests had shaved those options to a narrow little rind, because not even the non-Guild Companies operating anywhere near Karse would touch a contract.

Of course, the only reason why you would need more troops was if you were going to start a war. The *last* time when the rulers Karse had reneged on a Guild contract—the war had been internal. Some madman out of the hills had decided that Vkandis spoke through *him* without any evidence or real miracles to back up his assertions. But his cause was convenient for some of the nobles, moneyed merchants, and even a few priests, so they backed him and began a civil war. Both sides of the conflict had been decimated, which was, in part, how a bastard-born peasant like Alberich had managed to get into cadet training. And if it came to more than Border skirmishing, frankly, in Alberich's opinion Karse couldn't possibly raise the troops needed from among its own people.

If Karse was planning a real war again, non-Guild mercenaries were the only way in which an army could be raised in a hurry. But—the Tedrels? Could they possibly be mad enough to use the Tedrels?

A war? With whom? Rethwellan, perhaps. In the last conflict, Rethwellan had seized the opportunity to increase its borders, and the Sunpriests badly wanted the province of Menmellith. Not Valdemar, surely not—surely the lessons learned in the past were enough by now! No matter *how* fanatically the Sunpriests hated Valdemar and the Demon-Riders, surely they knew better than to engage in open warfare. Now Rethwellan—that made more sense, and there was some justification for warfare with that land. Menmellith had once been Karsite. Very, very long ago, of course, but the Sunpriests had long memories.

But—to use the Tedrels! The very idea made him feel a little sick.

Honor. . . .

It was hardly *honorable* to hire creatures like the Tedrels for anything. *They* followed none of the laws of combat; they were more apt to turn to massacre civilians than they were to fight the battles for which they'd been hired.

"But little, I know," Alberich said slowly. "And that, hearsay for the most part is."

"Figure we know less," Dethor said, settling back in his chair, and motioning for Alberich to take the one remaining seat left.

Alberich did so, but not with any feeling of ease. He sat on the very edge, back straight, muscles tense. "It is said," he began, "and long ago this was—three, perhaps four generations—that a war there was, in a land south and far, far east of Karse. Brother fought brother, in a cause none now recall. But those who the Tedrels became, lost that war, and instead of surrender, into exile went. Determined they were to gain back what lost had been—a land their own to call, where called they no man 'lord.' But nothing they had—except their skill at arms. And so, mercenaries they became. All of them. Company after company, after company. Which, even in defeat, enough men was, to fill up a country."

Now it was his turn to watch as Dethor's eyes bulged just a little with shock. "An *entire nation* of mercenaries?" the Weaponsmaster asked, aghast.

Alberich nodded; interesting that Dethor had not known that, which was the thing most notable about the Tedrel Companies. "Now, that was long and long ago, and wanderers they became as well. No wives would they take except those who would wander and consent to being the property of who could hold them, and no women in their ranks as fighters at all. Camp followers only, have they decreed that women may be. And—" He found this next part difficult to articulate, but he tried. "They—altered. It is said."

"In what way?" one of the others asked, abruptly cutting into his narrative.

It was the King's Own, Talamir, not in one of his more elaborate uniforms, but in a set of Whites like everyone else's. No wonder Alberich hadn't noticed him until he spoke. *Talamir here, and waiting to hear what I know . . . it may be rumor, but they are taking the rumor seriously.*

"Once, they had honor and purpose, and things they would not do. Now," He shrugged. "Nothing there is, they will not do, should the reward be high. *Anything* for loot. War they bring against the unarmed, as well as fighting true battles. I have heard—dreadful things." He had to pause, shaking his head. "With no wives, only women held by the strongest, no families, their ranks then grew but slowly, and difficult, it was, to replace those who fell. So now anyone they take into their ranks, who presents himself—thief, murderer, it matters not, has he a strong arm. And thus, cruelty upon cruelty piles."

Dethor and Talamir exchanged a worried look.

But Alberich wasn't quite finished. "The greatest change is this. No more seeking *the* home, they look only for *a* home. Should any offer a new land in reward, it is said—it is said that there is *nothing* they would not do." He gnawed his lower lip, thinking about the cold-blooded killers that Aksel had described, and what they would willingly do for anyone who was so foolish as to offer them a new homeland. His blood ran cold at the very idea. "But this, hearsay only is," he amended. "None I know has seen them, spoken to them, fought against them nor with them. Should any in Valdemar seek them to hire, warned they should be. It is said, moreover, that no sworn word do they truly hold by but their own, *to* their own, and they can and have turned against those who hired them."

"Someone had better find a way to get that message across to your own people," Dethor replied grimly. "Because word has reached us that they're thinking about hiring the Tedrel Companies. And not just one of 'em. *All* of 'em."

Now Alberich went icy cold all over with sudden dread, and was glad he was sitting down. Hiring one or two of the Tedrel Companies, he could just barely see. Aksel was not high enough in the ranks for his warnings to be heeded overmuch on that score. But all of them? There was only one reward that would tempt *all* of them together. "Madness," he said flatly. "Surely not—" *Surely not even the maddest and most fanatical of priests would hazard all to cast their lot with the Tedrels!* That would be insane. As Aksel had described them, having the Tedrels in one's midst was like playing host to a large pack of wild dogs. So long as they were full-bellied and content, the worst that would happen was that there would be a little damage to small towns here and there, if the scum that now filled out the ranks of the Tedrels grew bored. Perhaps rape, a bit of looting, possibly a few houses burned.

The "worst" that would happen if they are satisfied . . . rape. Looting. Oh, my poor people. . . . His stomach turned over. He thought about his border villages, and his throat and chest tightened, his gut roiling.

No worse, perhaps, than the bandits were already doing on the Borders.

But to face it from bandits, and then receive worse from those beasts—who in turn were hired *by the Priests supposed to protect them!*

That would be bad enough, But if the paychests were not as full as promised, or stopped altogether—the pack would turn. . . .

And fire and the sword would reign, at least until the paychests came again.

His chest felt too tight; his heart ached at the mere thought.

If this were true, the only way to hire the whole nation *was* to promise a homeland. Would Karse offer Menmellith?

Possibly. Menmellith was no great prize, but would Karse then want the Tedrels as neighbors?

So it would be Valdemar. The priests hate Valdemar enough to allow anything so long as Valdemar is left gutted, Kingless, and without the Heralds. . . .

Karse as a new homeland probably would not tempt them; it was too hard a land. They wanted something like that dream that their land had become for them, a place fat and rich, soft and sweet. But they would take out their spleen on Karse if it promised them such a homeland and failed to deliver it into their hands.

"That's what we've heard," Dethor said, shrugging. "Anything more you can tell us?"

Alberich shook his head; what more *could* he say? Dread was a sickening lump in his belly. "This rumor—I hope it false proves."

"Our sources are good," was all that Talamir would say. The third man, who was *not* in Whites and did not identify himself, only grunted. *He* looked about as friendly as Mirilin—which was to say, not at all. There was no doubt in Alberich's mind that the third man did not trust him.

And why should he, if even some (if not most) of the Heralds were ambivalent about Alberich?

:But we aren't,: Kantor said with some force.

The warmth that followed that pronouncement made the cold nausea lift a little, and eased some of the churning of his gut. It certainly made him feel less as if he was standing alone, facing a suspicious mob.

:I know. Thank you.: Knowing that the Companions now accepted him helped a little, but—

He knew what he wanted to say—that he had given up everything, *everything,* when he was brought here. That he had thrown his lot in with Valdemar, given his *word,* and that word was not given lightly. Couldn't they see that? This unknown man, who watched him from under furrowed brows, didn't he realize that?

And he wanted to say that—if his own people had sunk so low as to hire the Tedrels to do their dirty work, then surely even the Sunlord would abandon them. . . .

But he said none of this, for it would not matter if he did. Instead, he sat stone-faced and silent, and waited for the others to say something.

Even if it was only to "suggest" that he leave.

Finally Dethor hissed a little between his teeth. "I don't s'ppose," he said carefully, "that you'd know anybody likely to—well—be *helpful?* Inside Karse, that is? We'd like to know more about these rumors from someone with good, hard facts."

That . . . was a little better. Even if it sniffed around the edges of that promise they'd made him, the promise never to ask him to work against his own people.

But if those who are supposed to lead my people have already betrayed them? How can knowing if that betrayal is true or false be acting against the people?

"Depend it does," Alberich replied, just as carefully, "on what it is, by *helpful,* you mean."

"Information," Talamir said. "Nothing more. And nothing that would hurt Karse. Only what will protect *us* without hurting your people."

Alberich turned Talamir's words over and over in his mind, as the other three watched him. Because he *did* know someone who might—just might—be willing to be "helpful." Of all the people that Alberich knew, Aksel Tarselein was the most likely to be enraged and offended if this tale of hiring the Tedrels was true, and was, because of his own contacts, the most likely to know if it was truth or rumor spread to discomfit the enemies of Karse.

For Aksel Tarselein, trainer of cadets, had already been a deeply troubled man when Alberich knew him. Someone—

another young, highborn officer—had once described him, with a sneer, as "one of the old school," as if being a man of honor and integrity, whose word was seldom given and always kept, was somehow unfashionable and old-fashioned. And the shifts to which the Son of the Sun had fallen by the time Alberich had been commissioned had left Aksel profoundly disturbed. He was glad, he had confessed to the younger Alberich when the two of them had shared a farewell flask on the night of Alberich's commission, that he was no longer in a position where he found himself forced to obey orders which went against his conscience. "And it is a harder world today," he had said sadly, staring at the last few drops in the bottom of his flagon. "You may discover that you have to stop thinking—or stop obeying. I hope that the Sunlord will guide you, young one."

He had said no more on the subject, but Alberich *knew* which path he had taken, though not without qualms, and not without remorse.

I stopped thinking, at least until Kantor came to me. . . .

Just as he knew that Aksel had *not* stopped thinking. That was not Aksel's way. But as long as Aksel remained a Weaponsmaster to cadets, he would never be given an order that forced him to disobey either. Aksel held fast to his own honor only by making sure he was in a place where he would not have to sacrifice it.

Which of them had been given the easier path? Was it better to obey and not think, or think and try to ignore and be glad you, personally, *didn't* have to disobey?

"Possible, it is," he said, very slowly, "that there is a man. But possible it is *not,* directly to approach him. Friends he keeps, in the Mercenary Guild. There it is you must go. Speak with you he may, deny you he may." Alberich shrugged. "I cannot say; his own decision, he must make."

"Fair enough. And we've got enough friendly contacts with

the Guild to ferret out whoever knows him," Dethor said, nodding agreement. "His name?"

"Aksel Tarselein. Weaponsmaster to the Sunsguard Cadets." Once again, Dethor and Talamir exchanged a look, this time a startled one.

Should he add something from himself, so that Aksel knew who had revealed him?

:Do you think your name would make Aksel change his mind?: Kantor asked.

:It might. . . . : The now-familiar sickness rose in him again.

:And would you want it to?: Kantor continued, *:Or would you rather—:*

:I would rather there was no pressure on my old teacher but that of his own thoughts,: Alberich said firmly. Kantor let the matter drop. And to his immense relief, Dethor made no request for some token from Alberich. Nor did the third man—who felt, perhaps, that a message from one already branded as a traitor would do *his* cause with Aksel no good.

"Aksel Tarselein." Dethor and the third man exchanged a look, and the third man grunted. "That's one name more than we had before. Especially if he decides to talk."

"Yes." Alberich didn't elaborate; Dethor didn't pressure him to. The third man got up to leave.

Dethor poured a tankard full of beer and pushed it across the table to Alberich, as the third man turned at the door, gave Talamir and Dethor a little nod, and walked out. Alberich picked up the tankard and drained half of it in one gulp.

He felt a great need of it, at that moment, and it did a little, a very little, to settle his unsettled stomach and nerves.

:It is only a rumor,: Kantor said suddenly. *:That is all. No matter that this spy of Sendar's has convinced everyone that it is more than that. He has no proof. He has only heard stories and a name, for no one* he *has spoken to has seen the Tedrels*

or their Captains, or even an agent that may be said to come from them.:

Relief made Alberich's hands a little steadier as he put down the tankard. *:If anyone will know the truth of the rumor, it will be Aksel,:* he replied. *:And if it* is *true, I believe that Aksel will speak.:*

:And in any case, it is out of your hands.:

"Well, no matter what, Talamir, it's out of *our* hands," Dethor sighed, echoing Kantor's words. "This is a thing for those with talents you and I don't have. Nor Alberich either."

Alberich regarded him broodingly. "I *could.* But a pledge you made to me—"

"And we'll keep it," Talamir said with finality. "Though I will admit to you freely, that this is one reason why the Lord Marshal's man was here. He wanted us to pressure you into crossing the Border again, to spy for Valdemar."

Wordlessly, Alberich shook his head.

Dethor snorted. "Aye, we told him as much, then asked him to his face if he'd really *trust* you if you agreed. And he had to admit that he wouldn't, so what's the point? *We* know you're sound as a good apple, but to the likes of him, a man that turns may well turn again. Gods help us, though, I sometimes wonder what we're to do with you."

Alberich eased his dry mouth with another swallow. "What you have done. There is, what else to do, to bring trust where there is none?"

"Not much. Doubters can't accuse you of much, here with my eye on you, and keeping you apart from the rest means that nobody's going to try and make trouble for you. What d'ye think of young Selenay?" An abrupt change of subject, but Alberich answered it quickly enough.

"Steady, thoughtful, careful, and untried." He saw the questions in Dethor and Talamir's eyes, and tried to answer them. "No opposition, has she met. No loss, no pain. No great joys either, no love. With the single eye, she sees now—clearly, in black and white, as young things do. Until she has more wisdom, well, who knows how she will see then? When great events come upon her—*then* will you see, of what she is made. Not until. But the makings of a king, she has. And she thinks, which, with more than most young things, is not the case."

"Told you so," Dethor said in an aside to Talamir. The King's Own just shrugged. Dethor turned back to Alberich. "She came up with this bodyguard notion on her own, but I think it's no bad idea, having you instead of one of the Guard, especially when she's with Mirilin. Lad in a Guard uniform puts people on edge; fellow in Whites makes 'em wonder if the Heralds have some reason to haul in more than one for a simple Herald's Court. But a fellow in Grays? Nah, that makes 'em relax. We want someone with her to keep *her* back covered, without making people nervous that he's there. People don't necessarily *expect* a fellow in Grays to be much of a fighter, and they don't think of him as a fancier sort of constable. They take you, I'll be bound, for another Trainee on Internship, maybe another highborn."

Alberich smiled slowly, seeing what Dethor was getting at. Talamir only looked strained. "But once the Council finds out, there will be difficulties," the King's Own said reluctantly, then shook his head. "Yes, and I admit, it *is* my responsibility to smooth them out. Well, the easiest way will be by simply not saying anything for now, I suppose. I'll have a word with Mirilin—"

:We already have, via Estan, and he won't be mentioning Alberich's presence as the Heir's bodyguard to anyone, not even to other Heralds,: Kantor said promptly, and by the sudden, startled look on Talamir's face, Taver must have said the same thing at the same moment. Dethor laughed aloud; the word must have reached him, as well.

Talamir coughed. "Well. Apparently you have *far* more friends here than I had thought, Alberich. So unless someone from the Council actually sees you at Selenay's back, and realizes who you are, apparently we'll keep that much from their attention for a while." His face grew distant again for a moment, and he added, "Long enough that perhaps by the time the Council realizes just who Selenay's bodyguard is, there will be far fewer doubts about you."

"Occurred to you, had it, that we being managed are?" Alberich asked him, in a moment of stark frankness. "By *them?*"

They knew who he meant—the Companions. He half expected Kantor to be annoyed by the statement, but he sensed instead a dry amusement.

He got a look of startlement, then one of understanding, from both the Heralds. "Oh, always, at least to an extent," Talamir replied, with the same utter honesty. "And in some cases, that's all to the good." His voice took on a different coloring then, a hint of wry tartness. "But let me tell you a bit of home truth, Alberich of Karse—something that I do *not* tell the children, because they *are* children and need managing—it is your right and privilege to tell your beloved Companion just where he can shove anything he tells you or asks of you if it goes completely against your better judgment." He raised an eyebrow. "As even my Taver has found, to his occasional shock and dismay."

Dethor whooped with laughter, and applauded. "By the gods, Talamir, good for you! And well said!"

Now Alberich expected Kantor to be completely offended, but instead, he "heard" an ironic chuckle in his mind. *:Tell the King's Own that it is our right and privilege to do the same with our Chosen, you know.:*

Alberich started to repeat the remark, but Talamir held up his hand. "Never mind. Taver has said the same as your Kantor, I expect. My point is that we are adults, and although the Companions have certain abilities and information that we, their Heralds, may not—well, the reverse is true as well. You've got a mind of your own, and experience that your Companion doesn't have, and, I presume, sound judgment. Don't be afraid to use them, and if you feel strongly about something, be prepared to insist you be heard. The Companions don't know everything. As Taver pointed out to a few of them the other night, they aren't infallible. They can make mistakes, and advice can go both ways. Herald and Companion are meant to be *partners,* not superior and servant."

"In the beginning for most Trainees, exactly 'cause they *are* younglings, that isn't always the case," Dethor put in. "Sometimes Chosen and Companion are the same age and learn together, but sometimes one's full grown while the other's still a child, or just a little older. But in your case, you're both adults, and you start out with a partnership from the beginning."

Talamir nodded emphatically. "We each give, and we each take, and what we do should be the result of cooperation, not dictation. Don't forget that."

"I shall not," Alberich replied, "But for the moment, Kantor it is, who knows this land and people. Not I."

"True enough." Talamir hefted his tankard and looked at Dethor, who poured him (and, without his asking, Alberich as well) another round. The beer foamed up, leaving a pleasantly bitter aroma in the air.

Dethor and Talamir exchanged another pregnant glance. Alberich's neck prickled. Something was still in the air. Talamir was not here *only* because of the rumors coming out of Karse.

"Alberich, I'm here for more than one reason. I think that you already have some inkling of this, so I am going to put it in plain language," Talamir continued, rubbing his thumb along the side of the tankard. "As a fighting commander, I suspect that you have, more than once, had to do what was expedient, rather than what was—"

"Ideal?" Alberich suggested. "An idealist, I never was."

:Liar,: Kantor objected mildly. *:Who was it, agonizing over*

the fate of the border villages just now? Who is it that values honor above everything else?:

:Hush: He flexed his shoulder muscles; they felt tense. Something was coming; he was just beginning to make out the shape of it, and he wasn't certain he was going to like it. "You have a thought."

"More than one. Actually, I have—we have—a job that needs doing. It's something *I* used to do, before I got too crippled up," Dethor said, with just a hint of . . . regret? Bitterness, that he was no longer what he had been? "I don't know that you'd have the stomach for it—but I've got to tell you, Alberich, for all your skill you're the *last* person I'd have looked to for this, except for one thing. Taver trusts you. He thinks you can do this, so Talamir says."

"Taver said to ask you," Talamir added, and sighed, his brow furrowed with concern and uncertainty.

:Taver might have made a suggestion, but Talamir is not completely certain how good an idea it is,: Kantor put it.

Well, that was clear enough.

Talamir cleared his throat awkwardly. "You saw the Lord Marshal's man—you know that there are such things as—agents. Well, we Heralds have them as well—and we need another."

He nodded warily, but might have prevaricated, except that in that unguarded instant, Kantor simply edged into his mind and *showed* him what it was that Dethor and Talamir wanted him to do.

"Agent" was too small a word to encompass the task.

In fact, Alberich was more uniquely suited to the job than even Dethor had been, *because* of his foreign origin. There were places where Dethor would always stand out—because Dethor was nobly-born for all that he pretended he was common. What you'd been born and bred to was difficult to hide, especially when you were under stress. But Alberich was as common as clay, and used to moving in the lowest of circles.

Under stress, he slipped into that world as easily as a bottom-fish slipping into the muddy river bottom.

Mostly, Dethor had collected information—in the Court and out of it, from the servants' common room in the Palace, to the vilest alleys near Exile's Gate, to the scented rooms where courtiers fenced with words.

Mostly— But a time or two, Dethor had done more than collect intelligence and pass it on to Talamir. A so-called "agent" who was also a Herald had an extraordinary degree of freedom to act as he saw fit, and once, Dethor had used his knowledge of traps to cause a single fatal "accident."

And he had agonized over that murder, for murder it was, and never mind that the man had been the hidden heart of a vile trade and no one had been or would be able to bring him to justice. Dethor had murdered and knew it, and *still* agonized over it.

:As you would. As you would act, if there was no other way, and you would be decisive about it.:

Yes, he would, on both counts. But although he would regret murder, for he hated killing, he would not allow such a thing to ride him with guilt afterward. He felt his pulse throbbing in the hollow of his throat, and his collar felt too tight. Yes, he would. Some things had to be done—and was it better to stain innocent hands with blood, or add one more stain to the sleeve of one already steeped in it?

The King *could* have "agents" like the Lord Marshal had, men who would take their orders and carry them out, and leave the question of whether the orders were morally justified to someone else. The King did not want that. He wanted a Herald; he wanted someone who did not simply take orders. He *wanted* someone who would think—weigh—and act. And agonize over it afterwards perhaps . . . because there would be that necessary question when it was all over.

But it had to be a particular kind of Herald, and such folk did not emerge from among the children—children with their shining certainty of right and wrong—that came with their Companions to fill the rooms of the Collegium every year. He would not besmirch those pure hearts, would not twist them into something that they were not.

It took a Herald like Dethor, like Alberich, who was Chosen as an adult, full-grown, who knew about moral ambiguities and difficult choices. Like Dethor—who had himself been one of the Lord Marshal's agents, before he was Chosen. Like *Dethor's* master, the Weaponsmaster before him, who had grown up a child of poverty, seen the evils of the world very young, wiser than his years, though his parents had sheltered him from what they could.

No such man (or woman, though perhaps it would have been harder for a woman) had come to Dethor and Talamir until now, and they were not altogether certain that Alberich was the right material for this task. But he was what they had . . . and they were in terrible need of *some* man for the job. Talamir was altogether too recognizable and too desperately needed to have the time for such covert walkings, and as for Dethor, who could barely hobble to the Collegium for a Council meeting or a meal now and again—well.

All this poured into his mind as the other two sat quietly, waiting for him to assimilate it all. Did they know what Kantor was showing him?

:Of course they know. It is our way. I can show you in moments, what would take them days to explain.:

Ah. Expedience . . . so the Companions knew it, too. Somehow that made him feel more akin to Kantor, not less.

He took a deep breath, and regarded both of them with somber eyes.

"It is much of me, that you ask," he said slowly. "It is surprised, I am. When I have here been—how long?"

"Conscious or unconscious?" Dethor retorted and shrugged. "You've been a real part of things for maybe a fortnight. And I would never in a hundred thousand years *think* to trust you with this—except for Taver."

:Why Taver?: he asked Kantor silently. *:Why, if Companions are as fallible as any other?:*

:Because Taver can make mistakes, but never that *kind of mistake. Never, ever, a mistake in judging a person's character, his heart, and soul,:* came the reply—and then he got the sensation that Kantor was conferring with someone else.

Talamir and Dethor watched him closely, weighing his least expression, just as Kantor added, *:Come outside, if you trust* me. *There is something more you need to have that Taver wishes to share with you. And not just for making* this *decision.:*

There were so many overtones to that deceptively simple statement that it was Alberich's turn to start with surprise. There was more than a hint that this was something as important as *anything* that anyone had ever told him in all of his life—something life-shatteringly important. And a subtle shading that this was something Taver had never shared with any other Herald.

Not even Talamir. *Not even Talamir.*

Suddenly, he had to know what this thing was. "Rude, I do not wish to be," he said abruptly. "But think on this—with no eyes on me—I must, for a little." He stood up even as he said this, and the other two Heralds watched him measuringly, but with a leavening of understanding.

"You don't have to give us an answer right away," Talamir said, as if making up his own mind about it. "But if you would consider it—"

"Tedrels—and now this—" Alberich shook his head. "I must think alone. But consider it, with all seriousness, I will. And—I will answer you soon." He did not define "soon."

The other two remained in their seats as he stalked off, head swirling dizzily with a dozen contradictory thoughts.

He wanted to go back to Karse. The very notion of the Tedrels being *near* there made his skin crawl. He wanted to hide here, and never hear of Karse again. He *didn't* want this new job that Talamir and Dethor had suggested, and yet, if he didn't take it, the tasks *would* be done, but by men who left their thinking and their morality in the hands of others, and merely followed orders . . . and never cared what the repercussions would be, never wondered if they had done the right thing, never thought at all. The bare idea was repugnant.

And he wanted to see just what this secret that the Companion Taver held could be. And how could it possibly, *possibly,* have any relevance to him?

Taver was waiting outside, just out of sight of the windows of Dethor's sitting room, with Kantor beside him. The sun was setting, and the air lay thick and sweet and still among the trees around the salle—but there was a hint of the bitterness of dying leaves in the sweetness, and the poignant suggestion of autumn coming soon, soon.

:Thank you for coming,: Taver said gravely, directly into Alberich's mind, startling him. Taver's mind-voice was distinctive; rich and deep, with a little breath of echo to it. There was a certainty and a stillness to it, as if Taver was a great tree, with his head in the clouds and his roots reaching down to the bedrock. And powerful, without ever making Alberich *feel* the power as anything other than potential.

"You are welcome," Alberich replied awkwardly, pulse hammering in his throat, feeling as if *he* was the one being granted the favor. This was strange. This was *very* strange. Perhaps the strangest thing that had happened to him since he had arrived here. That odd *thing* that they called his Gift fluttered in the back of his soul with something that was not—quite—warning.

:I think—I hope—that what I have to show you will make many things clearer for you,: Taver said, with infinite gentleness. *:Please, come and place one hand upon my neck and look into my eyes.:*

Puzzled, Alberich did as he was told. He touched the electric softness of Taver's neck—looked into living blue—

And paradise engulfed him, as the heavens opened up and spilled out glory.

And when he came to himself again, he was lying on the grass, staring at the hooves of the two Companions—*silver hooves, why didn't I notice that before?*—with a mind so full it felt as if it couldn't possibly fit in the narrow confines of his head.

Mortal men should not look into heaven. If they do, they should not be surprised when all they can remember is that they were there, for one brief, radiant moment. *He* certainly was not.

But that moment had given him something he had needed, and had not known he needed, until the need was not there anymore.

He sat up slowly and felt the back of his skull gingerly. But the lump he expected to encounter, and the headache he anticipated, were not there.

:I took your body, and caused you to lie down, rather than fall down, Alberich,: Taver said, as Kantor whuffed at his ear. *:I knew what would happen, and it was no thought of mine that you take hurt from it.:*

Alberich stared at the Companion—who was more, so *much* more than he appeared that it made him dizzy even to nibble at the edges of the thought. "You've *never* done this to Talamir?"

:Talamir never required it. He is of Valdemar, blood and bone. You—were floundering, drowning, without a foundation. I think you were not even aware of it, except that you sought for it desperately, without knowing what you sought for. Have I given you what you needed?:

He *had* been looking, and yes, desperately—Taver was

right. He *thought* that he'd been thinking, but he'd really been cluttering up his head with the minutiae of his new life here so that he didn't have to think about anything deeper. But if it came to that, he'd been looking for that foundation all his life. He'd tried to make his honor into a place to stand, but honor needed something to be based in.

:Ah.: There was contentment in that thought. *:Good.:*

Good? Oh, this was so much more than *good.* He had been drowning, with no land in sight. Yet, suddenly, Taver had put firm ground beneath his feet. Uncertainty that had been with him for so long it had become an uneasy part of him had been dispelled, popped like a bubble, exploded like the inflated bladder that it was. The monster in the closet was gone. And something so much better had taken its place. . . .

Taver nodded his graceful head. *:Alberich, will you trust me again?:*

Alberich blinked at such nonsense. Trust him? *Trust* him? Trust to so pure a spirit—a being so near to the divine that he could scarcely believe there was no glow of holiness about him? Trust a being that he should, by all rights, be worshiping?

Taver shook his head and mane, and whickered a laugh. *:Oh, come now, Alberich, I am not so much as all that—a servant only, nothing more.:*

A servant! "As much a servant as—as the Firecat of legend!" he whispered, hardly daring to speak. "As the Guardian of the Gates of Paradise!"

:Exactly so. No more than that.: Taver bent to touch a soft—and very, very material nose—to Alberich's ear. *:Come, stand—put your hand to Kantor's neck, and look into his eyes as you did mine. And this time, open your heart to him, as you have not yet done. Give up your walls, Alberich of Karse. Take them down, and let him inside.:*

He could fight the command of one of Vkandis' Priests—he could no more stand against the same command as given by

Taver than he could have fought a whirlwind. He did as he was told.

He looked deeply into those sapphire eyes, and opened his heart. And Kantor stepped gracefully into it, and filled it, and until that moment, he had no notion how empty it had been, nor how lonely he had been.

And as all of the knowledge and understanding and revelations that had come to him in the past few moments settled into place like doves coming to rest on their proper perches for the night, he knew, truly and completely, that there *was* Something above them all, call it Vkandis Sunlord or any other name. He could no more understand that Something than a flea could understand a man—but it *was* there. He would continue to have other doubts, other fears, but that one was gone.

And there was something else, much nearer and homelier, that would also be with him as a *certainty* as rock-solid as the earth beneath him and undoubted as the sky above. No matter what happened, in the next moment, or moon, or year, or lifetime—he and Kantor would never be alone or lonely again.

"Chosen—" he whispered, and buried his face in Kantor's mane.

:Chosen,: Kantor replied, with all the love that great heart could hold.

And it was—oh, yes—it was more, so much more, than enough.

PART TWO

The Tedrel Wars

ALBERICH heard a sound that once would have prompted curiosity, and now only brought a dull, aching despair. Wagons were coming up the road to the Palace Gates, enough of them that the rumbling noise was audible even from the practice ground outside the salle. He knew what that meant. These days, there were no more fetes and celebrations at the Court that needed fancy foods, wines, and decorations. The burdens these wagons bore were grimmer by far. More grievously wounded folk, soldiers and civilians alike, coming from the battlefields to the south, where the forces of Karse grappled with those of Valdemar. People too badly hurt for their own Healers to tend, who had been sent here, in hopes that the masters at Healer's Collegium could make them whole—or, at least, mend as much as could be mended.

All the fault of the Tedrels . . . the Tedrels, who had been set against Valdemar after all. It had been no rumor that Karse was hiring them, and once the lands lost to the Menmellith Province of Rethwellan were retaken, to be used as the Tedrel base, it had been Valdemar's turn to face them, face Karsite troops and Karsite Sunpriests backing the most ruthless mercenaries this world had ever seen.

All of Valdemar—except himself—was of a single heart and mind in this situation. Everything must be done to defeat Karse. And had the enemy been anyone other than Karse, no doubt he would be feeling the same.

But it *was* Karse, and he was torn, heart and soul, ripped in half between honor and desire. He *wanted* to go to the front lines himself, to put his considerable skill and knowledge to serve Valdemar. But there was a chance if he did, he would be fighting and killing his own people, and he wouldn't know it until it was too late. The Tedrels had no livery except among their own blood; it could be anyone in the front lines. He would not have cared, if only it had been the Sunpriests and the generals that served them that he slaughtered, but it wouldn't be, would it? *They* would be safe in the rear, or far, far away, and he could not depend on anything except that it would not be only Tedrels he helped to kill. No, mixed in among the Tedrels, and certainly serving them in their camps, would be ordinary people, simple people, who had no quarrel with Valdemar and would have been happy if they had been left in peace. His people, the ones he had pledged himelf to serve.

And besides, even if he found a way to help without facing his own folk across the edge of a sword, he wouldn't be allowed to go. If he set foot outside of Haven, there were powerful people who would be certain that he was doing so to betray Valdemar. And having deserted Karse, how could he blame them for that assumption? When a man turned his coat once, it took no great stretch of the imagination to think he might do so again.

Whenever his mind wasn't otherwise occupied, it was thoughts like these that came flooding in, and with them, a tide of guilt and depression. People who had become his friends, his brothers and sisters, were going south into danger—and here he was, safe in the sunshine of high summer in Haven.

He was glad that at least he had a task, something he could do honorably. Now he knew, only too well, some of the pain that Aksel must have felt when he remained training the cadets, while his trained cadets went off to do the fighting. And he knew the agony of being torn between desiring the best for his land, and knowing he could not support what the leaders of his land had joined hands with. Aksel himself must be feeling that same agony, for Aksel had given Valdemar's spies some of the information that warned them that the rumors of the Tedrels' hiring was true. It must have been by Vkandis' will, surely, for the information had come well before the first attack on the border of Valdemar, with enough time to prepare for that attack and those that followed.

These were not battles, these were wars—where the Tedrels moved into land opposite the Border, fortified it, then launched campaign after scorched-earth campaign from spring through autumn and then vanished, only to pick and fortify a new spot during the winter from which to pillage a new territory. Each time they did this, they effectively halted all farming, all commerce in that area, decimating it and leaving it barren and trying to recover. It was a diabolical plan, and there was nothing that Valdemar could do to thwart it without crossing the Border into Karse themselves, which Sendar (wisely) would not allow.

And damn-all use my ForeSight is against them. The magic that the Heralds called Gifts and that Karse called "witch-powers," Alberich found less useful than the exaggerated tales had led him to expect. Oh, he had Mindspeech, and very powerful, but it was of use only with other Heralds with Mindspeech and with Companions—and in setting the Truth Spell, which he seldom used. He probably could reach across the length or breadth of the country with it, but he never left the city of Haven; he was never allowed to leave. And he had Fore-Sight, that ability to glimpse what was to come—but it didn't stretch ahead more than a mark or two. It was a Gift that might be invaluable on a battlefield, except that he wasn't allowed near the battlefields. Of course, it was also an erratic Gift, which manifested irregularly and unpredictably, certainly not one he controlled . . . certainly nothing he could use from *here* to help in the Tedrel Wars. It seemed to work only in cases where something *he* could do, immediately, would change what was to come.

The Tedrel Wars; everyone called these seasonal blights by that name now. Little wars, leeching wars, stretching now into the fourth year. Every spring, a new little war, more deaths, more fresh-faced youngsters going out to face the foe, and Alberich wondering—as surely Dethor wondered—*had* he trained them well enough, prepared them well enough? Could he? Could anyone? It wasn't only Heralds he trained, it was young Guard officers, those Healers that would accept training in the use of weapons, and even some of the highborn youths who volunteered, out of a sense of duty and with dreams of glory in their hearts. He trained them, and he sent them out, and he never knew if *any* of them would return.

Valdemar bled from a wound that was not allowed to heal, that weakened her steadily. Alberich *knew* this, knew that when the Tedrel commanders judged the land weakened sufficiently, they would turn a little war into an all-out campaign. And there was nothing he could do about it. If it hadn't been for Kantor, he would never be able to sleep at night—but Kantor had his own ideas about what was good for his Chosen, and when Alberich was prepared to spend another sleepless night staring at the ceiling, his gut in a knot and his head throbbing, he would sense Kantor moving into his mind like a storm front, and then—

Well, then the next time he saw the ceiling, it would be morning. Last night had been one of those nights, leaving him singularly irritable, and not at all inclined to be charitable toward any of his pupils. Charity could—would—get them killed. *Especially* the one before him now.

Alberich surveyed his latest pupil, and reflected that Trainee Myste was at least providing one thing for him: a distraction from grief. Although she was providing a little grief of her own, of a different sort.

The middle-aged woman looked right back at him, her hazel eyes unnaturally large behind the thick glass lenses she wore, held to her face by a frame of wood, with leather straps that buckled behind her head, flattening already straight brown hair. She had a set that she normally wore that had lighter frames with sidepieces of wire that hooked over her ears, but those kept flying off during any sort of exertion; this had been the best they could do for weapons' practice, and it wasn't very good. Her peripheral vision was poor enough, and the frames of the lenses made it worse. And they were a handicap in another way; the *first* thing that an attacker would do would be to try to smash them. But she was virtually blind without them, so what could he do? Her short-sightedness was just the first in a string of handicaps that made her woefully unsuited to be a Herald.

He thought she looked particularly aggrieved this afternoon, but it was difficult to tell what her expression was on the other side of that wood-and-glass mask.

Physically, she was utterly unprepossessing, and looked like what she had been before she'd been Chosen; a sedentary scribe and clerk. He had no idea why she of all people had been Chosen, at a time when fighting Heralds were what was needed, not clerks, and how he was going to *turn* her into a fighter he had no clue. He despaired; she—well, he didn't know for certain how she felt. Frustrated, surely, at the least.

She was the single *clumsiest* Trainee he had ever attempted to teach, bar none. He didn't think this was on purpose, though, for even though she clearly didn't want to be here, she did try until she was black and blue. Even if she'd come here as a child, she'd have been clumsy, he suspected, but this business of learning weaponcraft late in life, a task to which she was utterly unsuited, must seem utter madness to her. He didn't blame her for being irritated and unhappy.

What was the point of putting her in this position anyway? She couldn't *see* without those lenses; she would lose them in a fight, and then she would be blind, and how was he supposed to train her to overcome that? Though there were tales of blind warriors with preternatural abilities in both Karse and Valdemar, those had all been about men and women who had been trained since early childhood in their craft, who brought skilled bodies and the finely honed senses of hearing and smell and touch to bear on the problem of being unable to see.

Not a middle-aged clerk who had been bent over a desk all of her life. She would arrive at the front lines only to return in days in one of those wagons. If she returned at all. Which he doubted.

She sighed and shifted her weight from one foot to the other, recapturing his wandering attention. "Weaponsmaster, all due respect, but we both know I'm hopeless at this. It's a complete waste of your time to try and train me to use *this.*"

She gestured at the sword she carried—and she spoke in Karsite.

In point of fact, if it were not for the fact that she couldn't fight, couldn't shoot, and couldn't defend herself, she'd be in Whites at this very moment. Self-defense was the only skill she lacked to enter her Internship, for she'd known most of what a Trainee learned long before she was ever Chosen. There was nothing about the history of Valdemar and the Heralds that she didn't know before she came here. She mastered the fine points of the law with the indifferent ease of someone who had spent years copying legal briefs. In fact, anything having to do with the written word, including no less than four languages, was of no difficulty to her. And she was the only person besides Alberich himself who was a fluent and natural speaker of his own tongue, learned directly from old Father Henrick before Alberich had set foot on the soil of Valdemar.

"There's a saying in Hardorn," she continued. "'You shouldn't attempt to teach a goat to sing. It will waste your time, hurt your ears, and annoy the goat.' I can say without fear of contradiction that the goat is getting annoyed."

He had to smile at that; she blinked behind those thick lenses, and emboldened, continued. "I keep asking this question, and no one will answer me. Can you give me one single, *good* reason why I have to learn weaponswork? And 'because all Trainees have to' is *not* a good reason. After all—" she set her chin mulishly, "—you don't make all *Healers* learn weaponswork, so why should every single Herald have to?"

Since he had just been about to say *because all Trainees have to,* he found himself stymied. He opened his mouth, closed it again, and regarded her thoughtfully. "Just what would you do if you were ambushed in the field?" he asked.

"Run," she replied promptly. "I'd cut loose my saddlebags, if I was mounted, throw away my belt pouch if I was afoot, and run. Chances are, whoever attacked me would be after my things and any money I had, not *me.* I'd let them have what they wanted. Things can be replaced, and while they'd be scrambling after loot, I'd be getting farther away."

:That was a good answer,: Kantor observed.

"And if you had to help villagers with a bandit attack?" he persisted.

She laughed. "Give my advice and go for help!" she replied. "Not that anyone would be likely to take the military advice of a dumpy, bookish female who's half blind, no matter what uniform she was wearing. But riding Aleirian, I'm as fast as any Herald, faster than any other messenger, *and* once I'm within Mindspeech range of any other Herald, I can relay my information."

:Another good answer. She's full of them, isn't she?:

:She's full of . . . something.: He sighed. She wasn't intimidated by him, not in the least, difficult creature that she was. She didn't *care* that he was Alberich of Karse, only half trusted even by the Heralds. "I know all about you from Henrick. And from Geri as well, of course," she'd said on meeting him, meaning Gerichen, once-Acolyte, now Priest; Geri, who'd become as much of a confidant as Alberich ever made of anyone. Simple sentences, but the *way* she'd said them had left him wondering just what it was that they'd told her. And later, he wondered what, and how much, she had written down, for she seemed to be always writing everything down in little notebooks. She always had one with her. When she wasn't writing things, she stared in a way that made him feel she was memorizing everything, so that she could write it down later.

:So how are you going to answer her?: Kantor prompted. *:She has a good point; you're never going to make her into any kind of a fighter. You were just thinking that the first thing that anyone seeing her would go for is those lenses, and then what?:*

Then she'd *be* blind, of course, and utterly helpless. No, she was right, very right, the best thing she could *ever* do if attacked would be to run away.

Could running be the answer, then?

:It should never be said that Herald Alberich refused to find a better way when one existed,: Kantor said. *:Besides, if she* can't *fight, they won't send her to the front lines; they'll use her to replace a Herald who* can *fight and send him instead.:*

"Put that away," he said abruptly. "You are right. I would be no kind of Weaponsmaster if I could not match the weapon to the student, not the student to the weapon. And *escape* might be the answer, however unlikely that weapon might be. Come into the salle, into the sitting room, and we will discuss this."

He didn't miss her smile of triumph, not that it mattered. She wasn't going to get off as easily as she thought; there might not be fighting practice, but she *was* going to find herself training until she was in far better physical shape than she'd ever been in her life. There would be extra riding classes for one thing; if her Companion was going to be running, *she* had better be in shape to stick with him, no matter what he had to do to get away. And if *she* was going to count on being able to run away, Alberich was going to make her into a competitive foot racer, whether she liked it or not.

Some of that clumsiness, at least, can be trained away.

She followed him into his living quarters; Dethor wasn't there at the moment. One of the Healers was trying a new treatment for his swollen joints, a course of bee venom, for beekeepers swore that the stings of their charges kept the ailment away from them. By now, Dethor's bones were painful enough that he was more than willing to tolerate even the stings of angry bees in hopes of getting some relief.

As a reward for his cooperation, he'd get a massage with hot stones and a treatment for his hands of hot sand afterward, something that *did* give him consistent relief, even if it was only temporary.

Myste took one of the chairs in front of the window; Alberich sat opposite her. "We need to think," he told her. "We need to find a way to make the things you *can* do into weapons. Running, for instance." He pondered that for a while. "I'll trade you saying for saying—in the hills in Karse there's a proverb, 'The hound that chases two hares catches neither.' If you are going to run—we need to contrive a way that you can create more than one thing for your pursuers to go after."

"Dropping my packs—" she began.

"But what if there is something in your packs that you've been entrusted with?" he countered. "What if it's in the winter, with no Waystations near? If you drop your packs, you won't have what you need to survive. It won't do you much good to escape from bandits only to freeze to death in a blizzard." He brooded over the idea for a moment, then the answer came to him. "I think we should add a bit of extra equipment specifically for you—packs and belt pouches that you're *meant* to throw away."

"What?" she asked, "Stuffed with straw or the like?"

He shook his head. "No, *not* that, actually. If you drop worthless decoys, it won't be long before bandits and brigands all *know* that the packs you drop are worthless, and they'll ignore them and go for you again. No, that hare won't run—there will be *just* enough in the decoys to satisfy an ambusher without making it look as if you're an especially juicy target, and to make certain that attackers chase the packs, and not you. And the same for belt pouches; from now on, you'll be carrying at least two small extras, both full of coppers, and if someone attacks you, you'll throw them in opposite directions, one to either side of your line of flight."

She was happy enough about the planning, but visibly unhappy when he brought her back outside and put her in front of the obstacle course. "Run the course, then run it again," he told her mercilessly. "And keep running it until I tell you to stop. Running away isn't going to do you any good if you can't actually run any better than Dethor on a bad day."

And he left her to it, with a faint feeling of having—for once—gotten the better of her. Irritating woman. Not that he didn't *like* her; she not only had the advantage of being one of the few people he could converse easily with in his own tongue, she was an interesting and lively conversationalist. And besides not being afraid of him or intimidated by him, he got the feeling that she respected him in a way that was quite flattering, when she wasn't trying to get the better of him. Why was it that she entered every conversation with the goal of somehow trying to *win?*

Well, she could just work some of that out over the hurdles. Meanwhile, he had a class of young archers to put through their paces.

When he told Dethor of his solution to the problem of Myste over dinner, the Weaponsmaster chuckled. "Good solution," Dethor replied. "A very good solution. But I hope it isn't one we need to use. I'd much rather that the Heraldic Circle can find a position for her that makes the best use of her talents here in the city. Whatever those talents are."

"At the moment," Alberich replied, with just a tinge of sourness, having had to find reasons why every single obstacle in the course was one she needed to learn to negotiate, "Arguing and writing. Little enough of anything else, have I seen."

"Heh. I've seen those little notebooks of hers—" Dethor blinked. "Now, why didn't I think of this before? Herald-Chronicler, of course! Elcarth's doing it now, but we want him for Dean of the Collegium, and we need to start training him in that—" His voice faded off as he got that faraway look in his eyes that meant he was thinking, and probably Mindspeaking with his Companion. Alberich now knew that look very, very well.

And Dethor was right, of course; with all of his own reading of the Chronicles, he could see how being the Herald-Chronicler would easily be a full-time job. It wasn't just the doings of the Heralds that the Chronicler covered, it was *everything;* anything that had any impact on any part of the Kingdom larger than a small village.

:What do you think?: he asked Kantor.

:That it's probably the reason she was Chosen,: Kantor replied. *:She gets onto a story like a rat-terrier and won't let go of it until she's shaken it free of all the facts.:*

Annoying little dogs, rat-terriers. All yap and idiotic courage—or was that "stubbornness?" Still. Come to think of it, that described Myste rather well. . . . Or, perhaps, she was more like a cat, one of those mouthy ones that wouldn't stop caterwauling, came when you didn't want them, and wouldn't come when you did.

:We're in nasty times. Someone has to be willing to put down nasty facts without editing them,: Kantor continued. *:And you* like *cats. You like rat-terriers, too.:*

He ignored that last. *:Hmm. Nasty facts like my little exercise tonight?:* he replied.

:It ought to be written down somewhere,: Kantor countered. *:Maybe not for common consumption, but if someone doesn't record* everything, *no matter how unflattering to the Heralds it is, the next generation is going to get the idea that we're all plaster saints. Then when someone has to do something underhanded for a good reason, nobody will be willing to do it. . . . :*

He sighed. There was that. And plenty of Chroniclers in the past had created "auxiliary Chronicles" that not everyone was allowed to read, Chronicles that recorded mistakes, blunders, errors in judgment, and jobs undertaken that were somewhat less than the letter of the law, all in unflinching detail. Not the sort of thing one gave the children, of course, but these Chronicles, and not just the standard texts, were what Alberich was studying as history. Just now he was in the middle of the very brief Chronicle of Lavan Firestorm; some of the soul-baring on the part of Herald Pol and King Theran was enough to make the heart ache. He could relate all too easily to the litany of "should haves" and "could haves."

Well, if Trainee Myste—who was certainly being allowed to read and study the unexpurgated versions of the Chronicles—was able to combine the qualities of detachment and tough-mindedness that the job required, especially *now,* well done to her. Elcarth probably wasn't; he was too tenderhearted to be unflattering to people he liked, even when it wasn't possible to get to the truth without being unflattering.

Mind, only a handful of people would know *that* for certain within Myste's or Elcarth's lifetime, because the Chronicles weren't written for the present generations, they were written for the future, and very few Heralds other than the King and the King's Own were allowed to see what their current Chronicler wrote. And then it was in terms of editing by similarly tough-minded Heralds, and only to ensure accuracy.

As he knew very well, the Chronicles could be extremely caustic at times, and no one really wanted to see himself, his presumed or even actual motivations, and his failures, stripped bare and put down in uncompromising writing.

In his opinion, a young person didn't have the perspective nor the experience to write what needed to be written. So there, again, Myste was fully qualified. Appointing her as Chronicler Second would solve the problem of what to do with her very neatly indeed.

Dethor abruptly came back to himself. "I believe that will work," he said, as if Alberich had been privy to whatever thoughts were going on in his mind. "You're going out in the city tonight?"

"No other choice, have I," Alberich replied with a shrug. "Much result, I do not expect, but sow silver I must, a harvest of villainy to reap."

In this, at least, he was able to aid Valdemar with a clear conscience. In disguise, one of half a dozen personae he had concocted and established, he prowled the less-savory quarters of Haven, looking for trouble. "Trouble" came in various guises, but money usually lured it out of hiding. The money wasn't bribes—Alberich was more subtle than that. Sometimes he posed as someone looking for a particular sort of creature to hire, sometimes as a bully-boy looking for work himself. Sometimes he bought information, and sometimes sold it. In all cases, there was nothing to connect the less-than-honest characters he portrayed in the seedy drinking houses and alleyways with Herald Alberich, the Weaponsmaster's Second. There was some benefit in having a scarred and scowling countenance that looked the very acme of villainy. If there wasn't a woman born who'd give him a second look, no one looked askance at him in a low-class bar either.

And fortunately, there were enough foreigners in Haven that his accent caused only a little comment, and no one recognized it as Karsite. Most accepted his story that he came from Ruvan, Brendan, or Jkatha. All three were so far away he might just as well have told the inquisitive that he was from the moon. Virtually anything he claimed would be believed. The only people who *might* know better would be true Guild Mercenaries, and so far he'd never seen one of those in Haven. They weren't needed here; Valdemar fielded its own standing army of full-time soldiers, called the Guard, and always had. Even Guild Mercenaries didn't bother to go where there was no need of them.

"Well, you be careful out there tonight," Dethor said, putting down his empty tankard. Alberich automatically refilled it for him from the pitcher on the table between them and raised an eyebrow. Dethor wasn't known for having the Gift of Fore-Sight, but one never knew. "A reason for the warning, you have?" he asked carefully.

But Dethor only shook his head. "Not really. It's just that it's been quiet, and it's usually quiet just before there's a lot of trouble."

"And trouble then comes in threes," Alberich agreed gloomily. "*And* a full moon there is tonight. I shall walk carefully."

"Full moon." Dethor groaned. "You're going to get into a brawl tonight, aren't you?"

Alberich felt his muscles tighten with automatic anticipation. He suppressed his reaction as much as he could. Dethor was very good at reading body language.

"Probably." Alberich shrugged with an indifference he didn't entirely feel. A bar fight would at least give him something on which to take out his frustration. He always slept better after being able to pound some villain's face into the floor. The wretches that tried to pick on *him* were at least as bad as he pretended to be. The only reason they were at the tavern instead of jail was that they hadn't been caught at anything lately, and they well deserved whatever punishment Vkandis decreed they meet at the hands of His transplanted worshiper.

:Oh, very nice reasoning,: Kantor said, with more than a touch of sarcasm.

"Try not to give the Healers any more work, will you?" Dethor requested with resignation. "They had a few words for me the last time you needed patching up, and since I couldn't tell them *why* you'd gotten cut up, they assumed I'd been working you and Kimel with live steel and you'd gotten the worst of it. So, of course, it was *my* fault."

"That, I can promise," Alberich replied, gathering up all the supper dishes and placing them in the empty basket. "For that the wretches whose bones I break, seeking a Healer would not be, ever. Too fearful would they be, that in seeking Healing, it would be justice they found." With a salute to Dethor, he left the rest unsaid, and headed for the door. He couldn't help it; there were frustrations in him that were crying out for release. He wouldn't *look* for a fight, but if one came to him—

He sensed Kantor's sigh.

He left the basket just outside the door to their quarters for a servant to collect, and went out into the flooding light of the full moon to saddle Kantor. His Companion was waiting for him at the special stable only the Companions used.

Just inside the door was the tack room, but Kantor's gear was all stowed on racks near his stall, just as it was for every Companion who resided primarily at the Collegium. On a warm summer night like this one, all the half-doors on the stalls were open to the night air, and with all of the moonlight pouring in, the lanterns weren't needed at all.

They were quite alone in the stable, which suited Alberich's mood perfectly. *:You've told Taver and Talamir we're going out tonight?:* he asked Kantor, throwing only the plainest and most basic of saddle pads and blankets over Kantor's back.

:Of course.: Kantor looked back over his shoulder as

Alberich tightened the girth. *:We're going out the private entrance?:*

:Of course.: Alberich swung up into the saddle, and they made their way across the Field. Kantor's hooves made no sound at all on the soft grass; they moved across the silver expanse like a pair of spirits gliding over the surface of a silent sea.

There was a little gate at the far end of the wall around Companion's Field that would have been a dreadful security hole had it not been closed by three doors—the final one of iron cunningly cast to look exactly like the rusty-brown stone that the wall itself was made of. Only Talamir, Sendar, and Dethor had held the keys to those doors, and Dethor had given his to Alberich. Furthermore, the iron one was so heavy that it required a Companion's strength to haul it open from the outside, and it wasn't likely that anyone with a horse or a mule was going to be able to get along the outer wall of the Palace without a challenge. And *then* a would-be intruder would have to get his mount to push instead of pull. Not too likely, that. It was an amazingly clever door, that actually could swing in an entire one-hundred-eighty-degree arc—but there was a spring-loaded stop on it that worked as a fairly high doorsill to keep it from swinging outward; a stop that could only be dropped down level to the ground from the inside. So Kantor could push it to swing *out* when they were on the inside, but no one could *pull* it out from the outside. Locking the door released it again, and as Alberich turned his key in that final lock, he heard it *smack* up into place on its spring.

There was no one on the road, but several times he looked up to see one of the Guards keeping watch on the wall, so well hidden in the shadows that only he, who knew *every* hiding place along it, could have spotted them. He nodded to them, and got a little hand signal in recognition. The Palace Guard, at least, now knew and trusted him.

Of course, he'd trained a good many of them, and bouted

regularly with all of them. You learned a lot about a man, sparring with him. Once Kimel had accepted him, the rest had started coming around.

He wasn't in Whites tonight—and that would have made him instantly recognizable to the Guards no matter what. He could have Whites if he wanted them . . . but he didn't want them. He'd become accustomed to those dark gray leathers; they suited him, suited his nature, suited his wish to be something less conspicuous.

:As if you could be anything other than conspicuous,: Kantor scoffed.

:When I'm with you, perhaps not,: he acknowledged. *:You are rather conspicuous all by yourself.:*

By alleys and shortcuts that only he knew, he and Kantor slipped quietly among the mansions of the highborn, through the townhouses of the wealthy, and suddenly came out on a side street in a neighborhood of inns and taverns. They were only paces away from the Companion's Bell, a respectable inn that was their intermediate goal.

Alberich felt that tightening of his muscles again, and a quickening of his pulse. It was time to go to work, work that he understood, work that he, and only he, *could* do.

The Bell had several distinct advantages for what he was about to do. Firstly, it was a place often frequented by Heralds, so the sight of a Companion in a loose-box would not go remarked, nor would the sight of Alberich entering the stableyard. Second, the Heralds had a private taproom available to them—Heralds could and *did* mingle with the regular customers, but no one would think twice about Alberich not appearing among them, for plenty of Heralds who came here kept to the private room.

Ah, but then there was the third reason. . . .

He dismounted, and Kantor followed him into the stable. There were two other Companions there already, who whickered a welcome to both of them. *:Excellent,:* Kantor said. *:I shall have reinforcements—if you need them.:*

Alberich snorted, and left Kantor to make himself at home in a third loose-box as he approached the far wall, and the third reason for his being here.

The third reason for his being here and no other place, was that the Bell had a locked room at the back of the stable that contained a trunk, and had a second locked door that let out onto an alley. A very dark alley, and one that, somehow, never had patrols of constables or City Guard at night.

He unlocked the door. He paused just long enough to light a spill at the lantern beside the door, then locked himself inside. There was a second lantern there, which he lit.

In that trunk had been Dethor's disguises; now it held Alberich's.

Someone else—Alberich thought it was probably the innkeeper himself—had a key to that room, for any clothing he left atop the trunk was taken away and laundered and placed back inside it. Some disguises, of course, *shouldn't* be cleaned—the stains and yes, the odor lent verisimilitude to his persona. Those he put back in the trunk himself, wrapped in a waxed canvas bag to keep from stinking up the rest of his gear.

Tonight, however, it was about time for Aarak Benshane, a common enough thug with a reputation for not asking too many questions of prospective employers, to put in an appearance at the Blue Boar. Aarak was not too noisome a fellow; Alberich could get away with cleanliness tonight.

Alberich opened the trunk and selected his disguise with care; leather trews, battered boots and hat, scarred black leather jerkin strong enough to turn most blades, and a shirt of no particular color that was a bit frayed about the cuffs and collar. Over these, he slung a belt holding two knives, but no sword. Aarak did most of his work with his fists.

:That should suit you, considering the mood you're in.: Kantor was not being ironic nor sarcastic this time.

:As a matter of fact,: Alberich replied, *:it does.:*

By day, the tavern that was his goal, the Boar, was a quiet enough tavern, serving manual laborers at the nearby warehouses. At night, however, it took on a rougher clientele. Some of the laborers returned to drink away their earnings, and they were joined by others, for whom the warehouses were of less-than-legitimate interest. Aarak fit right in there; he *might* hire himself out as a day laborer, if he was inclined to do manual labor, or forced into it, but he would far rather serve as the lookout for thugs who planned a little late-night looting.

Alberich let himself out into the alley. It was dark back there, shadowed on both sides by tall buildings, but he knew his way around Haven even in pitchy black. He kept to the alleys for the most part, only crossing streets when he had to, and at length, found himself in the warehouse area where the Boar stood.

There was a lot of coming and going around a warehouse, and no one asked what was being stored there very often. And, of course, warehouses were full of things that were already packed for transportation; what could be more attractive and easier for a bold gang of thieves?

Alberich had been recruited by such gangs, once or twice, though never out of the Blue Boar, and never as Aarak. He had hopes, though, and he nursed his thin, sour beer at a table here several times a moon, waiting to see if his patient fishing would catch him another gang of thieves.

He opened the door quietly. It wasn't a good idea to make any kind of an entrance into the *Boar.* There were always people there who would take that sort of hubris amiss.

Flash of blue—a tangle of thrashing bodies on the floor—

He paused, just inside the door, and caught himself.

Damn. Come on. Don't show anything, or you're dead. He shoved on inside the door on strength of will, until his vision cleared and he could pretend that he hadn't just had a flash of ForeSight.

The regular servers knew him by now, or at least, they knew Aarak's distinctive hat. He caught the eye of one, nodded at a vacant table off to one side of the room, and took his seat there. Within a reasonable length of time, the server appeared with a jack of beer.

Despite Kantor's needling, he'd had a few hopes that someone *might* try to recruit him tonight—a full moon now meant moon-dark in a fortnight, and moon-dark meant the possibility of work.

But the truth was, from the moment he'd crossed the threshold, he knew that Dethor had been right about a tavern brawl in the offing. Even if he hadn't gotten that brief—very brief—glimpse of a tumble of fighting bodies on the floor of the place from his ForeSight, he'd have known it. There was something in the air tonight, something wild and edgy, something that made Kantor, back in his stall, prick up his ears and ask wordlessly, and in all seriousness this time, if Alberich thought he'd need any help.

Alberich never actually got a chance to reply. He was just starting on the first swallow of his beer, when the fight erupted over a card cheat, three tables down.

The cheater had friends, and the friends waded in, and Alberich saw—

Flash of blue—

The fight was only a pretext to rob the only person here with any real cash. That was the owner of the Blue Boar himself.

Three people swarming the bar, as combat seemed to thrust them toward it by accident.

He came to himself long enough to dodge out of the way of a tumbling body, and shoved his hand into a special belt pouch he always wore as Aarak. It held weighted knuckle guards, his preferred weapon for brawling. He didn't like using blades in a brawl—he was there to immobilize people, not kill them. No point in killing them, when, if they were what he *really* wanted, he wanted them alive, to question.

Another flash of blue, freezing him for a moment.

The three thieves—he assumed that was what they were—waited for the fight to reach the bar and then threw themselves over it, the surprised tavern owner trying to get out of the way as they all three landed atop him. There were short, heavy clubs in their hands.

They clubbed the tavernkeeper senseless.

Alberich shook his head to free it of the vision, as shouts and cries of pain marked the center of the brawl. A drunk, stinking of beer, blundered into him and made a wild swing at him.

And that was just enough. Alberich sprang into motion, like a mastiff held leashed and suddenly released. A savage grin with nothing of joy in it split his face. He ducked under the other's swing and gut-punched the drunk with his laden fist, stepping out of the way and shoving him to one side to topple him before he spewed the contents of his stomach all over everything in front of him.

Flash of blue, and he saw the three thieves vault over the bar and make off with the cash box while a larger fight still engaged the bouncers and everyone else they could draw in.

That was it; that was all his ForeSight showed him. But it was enough. When his eyes cleared for the third time, he saw the three men beginning to make their way towards the bar.

Ha. Another drunk approached, got one look at his face, and flinched away. Alberich shoved him aside, straight-armed another, shouldered into a third.

And when the three would-be robbers reached their goal, he was already there, waiting.

They only saw one more temporary obstacle in their path, and moved to clear it.

They weren't very good with their lead-weighted clubs, which was probably why the clubs were weighted in the first place. And they hadn't practiced fighting as a team either. He managed to get the first two to tangle each other up for a moment, by grabbing the first and shoving him bodily into the arms of the second. They weren't expecting anyone to reach *for* them—

While the first two were shouting and tripping over each other, he stepped in toward the third, came in low, and laid out his target with a brass-laden right to the point of the chin.

His fist connected solidly, with a satisfying impact that snapped the fellow's head back and sent him sailing across the floor to land over a table. It didn't break, of course. The tavernkeeper didn't want the expense of replacing furniture every moon. The Boar's tables and chairs would stand up to a charging bull and the bull would come away second best.

Now he felt it, that heady pleasure—which would be a guilty one, later, when he came to think about it—that rush of energy and unholy glee that only came during a fight. Fighting-drunk; that was what Dethor called it, for it wasn't the berserk rage that wiped out thought and sense. On the contrary, it made him sharper, and he enjoyed it when he was fighting in a way that would make him feel a bit ashamed of himself later. But now, it widened his manic grin and filled his veins with lightning.

When the first two got clear of each other, he grabbed them both and shoved their heads together with a *crack* that echoed even over the noise of the brawl. One went down; the other didn't.

He was stunned, though—stunned just long enough.

Alberich grabbed his shoulder and spun him around to face forward; pulled back his fist, and delivered a gut-punch that made the fool's eyes bug out as he toppled to the floor.

He looked around for the trio's friends, the ones he'd seen in his vision, but they, seeing that the cash snatchers were down and out and there was no reason to continue the fight any further, began breaking free of their little knots of combat and scuttling away.

He thought about pursuing. His blood was up now, and he was ready to chase down half a dozen of the young thugs.

:Chosen. Enough. You've ended the problem; that will do for now.:

Kantor's demand cut across the fire in his veins, and chilled it.

He shook his head and backed up out of the way, against the wall. With the instigators gone, the bouncers were managing to quell the remaining belligerents without any help from him. He slipped his knuckle guards off his hand and back into his pouch.

Part of him regretted that the fight was over. Most of him sighed with relief. When the last of those still trying to fight had been tossed into the street, he gave the bouncers a hand with sending the unconscious after them. The three *he'd* done for were among them, but he saw no point in saying anything about what might have happened. After all, there was no proof.

He accepted a somewhat better tankard of beer as his reward for helping out, and stayed only long enough to drink it before returning to Kantor. His glee was gone; his guilt had started, and besides, nothing more was going to happen tonight. If anyone was thinking of hiring Aarak, they wouldn't do it tonight. The men he'd downed might have friends watching, who would take it amiss if someone "rewarded" Aarak with a job.

The moon was down by the time Alberich got to his hiding place, and he had to feel carefully for the keyhole to let himself inside. He discovered bruises he hadn't felt when he changed back into his gray leathers.

:Maybe you didn't, but I did,: Kantor sniffed as he mounted.

:They'll heal,: he replied, sending Kantor back up the street toward the Palace. He felt as he always did after a fight; weary

and with emotions dulled except for a fierce and bitter satisfaction. The weariness was welcome; he'd sleep well tonight for a change.

:There was someone watching you from the corner,: Kantor went on, giving him a flash of something that the Companion had noted through Alberich's eyes. *:I think you'll be offered a job next time you go there.:*

The bitterness eased a little; Alberich recognized that vague glimpse. It was someone he'd been watching for some time now, a legitimate businessman who somehow seemed to have more goods in his warehouse than he'd actually *purchased.* . . . Now—now he might find out just where those goods came from.

"Good," he said aloud. *:That is why we come there, isn't it?:*

:Not entirely,: Kantor retorted. *:At least,* you *don't.:*

Alberich started to reply, and thought better of it. Kantor was infinitely better at warring with words than he was. He let his silence speak for him, letting Kantor come to his own conclusions.

Eventually, the ears flattened, and out of the silence came—

:I apologize.:

:And you are also right,: Alberich acknowledged. *:I* do *seek out fighting more often than necessary. I* could *go about the same business without getting involved in altercations at all. But it is what I need, right here, right now.:*

Kantor sighed, but his head nodded. *:So be it. If you need it, then we will continue to seek it, and I will say no more about it, except to ask you to take care.:*

Alberich closed his eyes for a moment. *:Perhaps, someday, we will no longer need to go hunting trouble for trouble's own sake.:*

It was all he could offer. But Kantor seemed to find it enough.

DETHOR had invited Talamir to his quarters tonight, in a way that had been less "invitation" and more "demand." Talamir was fairly certain that he wanted to discuss the current situation with his Second. Alberich, the probable subject of those discussions (now officially a full Herald, though he kept stubbornly to those peculiar gray leathers of his) was gone when Talamir arrived.

Dethor interpreted his curious look correctly; not a surprise, considering how well he and Talamir knew each other.

There was a small fire in the fireplace, although the weather was not yet so cool in the evenings that a fire was necessary. But the Weaponsmaster seemed to crave both the extra warmth and the emotional comfort of a fire more and more often of late.

Come to that, they all craved extra comfort. The Wars seemed both too far away, and too near. A feeling of dreadful tension underlaid everything, no matter how trivial, a frantic feeling as if whatever was being done *had* to be done, or enjoyed, or dealt with *now,* for there was no telling what the next day, or even the next candlemark, might bring. Small comforts took on enormous importance, yet one indulged in them in a spirit of guilt, quite as if throwing on another log was somehow going to deprive the Guard on the Border of heat and light.

Dethor had lit only two lanterns, one behind each of the two hearthside chairs; the fire provided the rest of the light in the room tonight.

The Weaponsmaster's Second was nowhere to be seen. "He's out. In town," Dethor said, as Talamir looked inquiringly at the third seat that Alberich usually used. "He won't be back for a while. I believe he's got something on the boil tonight."

"He's doing good work down there," Talamir observed as dispassionately as he could, and settled himself into the padded chair opposite Dethor's. It was difficult to be dispassionate about Dethor's bland statement. Every time Alberich had "something on the boil," there was usually a great deal of violence involved before it was over. Alberich was directly involved in that violence at least half of the time; if Talamir hadn't been aware of just how much he despised unnecessary force, he'd have suspected that the man was seeking out opportunities to thrash someone.

But—perhaps he is, and he's simply making sure that the opportunity calls for necessary violence. That wouldn't be too difficult in the neighborhoods Alberich had to prowl.

"I wondered how much you'd kept track of," Dethor said. "What with everything else you've got going on."

"All of it, I think," Talamir admitted. "And he's as good as you ever were in the covert work, and better, far better, than I. We are, perhaps, too much the gentlemen. He fits in down there better than we ever could, no matter how much we deluded ourselves about our acting abilities."

The words hung heavily in the air, and Talamir glanced

out the window of the sitting room. It was moon-dark, and a Companion ghosted into and out of sight among the trees out there, a glimmer of white in the darkness.

"There's too many bloody bastards taking advantage of the situation to make trouble. Or money. Or both," Dethor muttered. "You cut one down, and two more spring up to replace him. It wasn't like that when I was doing the dirty work. It was never that vile down by Exile's Gate."

Talamir shrugged; they both knew that was true enough. Haven had been stripped of all but a skeleton staff of the Guard; constables and even private bodyguards had gone to join the army. The opportunities for the criminal and unscrupulous were legion. Alberich and a trusted handful of constables and the Palace and City Guard were accomplishing more than even the Council guessed. None of it had anything to do with being a Herald, of course—other than an occasional use of the Truth Spell and his communication with Kantor, Alberich never did anything that could not have been done by an ordinary constable.

Providing, of course, that an ordinary constable had his knack for subterfuge and covert work. Which, of course, none of them did. There was only one Alberich.

He couldn't rid the place of crime forever, but every time he removed a criminal from the streets, it look a while for someone else to fill the void left behind, a breathing space for the constables still at work on the street.

Alberich had a real flare for working clandestinely, something he'd probably never explored back in Karse. Talamir wondered how Alberich felt about this new skill; it didn't seem to match the persona of a simple military man.

As if Alberich would ever be a simple *anything.*

"It was never that vile because there were never that many opportunities," Talamir pointed out. "And what are we to do? Demand some sort of certification of virtue from everyone who passes the gates? Haul them away and question them under

Truth Spell as to their motives? I think not. The best we can do is what Alberich's doing, and thank the gods we have him."

The fire flared, revealing Dethor's troubled expression.

"You know the man's in a real mental state," Dethor said, leveling a long and accusatory look at his old friend. Talamir shifted uncomfortably, but his conscience forced him to meet Dethor's eyes. "I have the feeling that he's overworking, just so he can sleep at night. I have the feeling that he's *looking* for trouble just so he can work out his frustration on a legitimate object. The problem is, when you start looking for trouble, it starts looking for *you.*"

Talamir sighed, deliberately looking down at the plate of fruit on the table between their chairs. Slowly and methodically, he picked up an apple and began to peel it. "I know," he admitted. "I wish there was something that I could do about it. But even if we hadn't promised we would never ask him to do anything against Karse—"

"—the Council won't allow him out of Haven." Dethor snorted, and Talamir looked up from his apple with reluctance. The creases and wrinkles of Dethor's face turned his frown into something demonic, and the firelight only amplified the effect. "Dammit, Talamir. Can't you do anything about this? I *know* he wants to do something about the Wars, and I see his face every time he watches another batch of youngsters going south. It's tearing him up!"

"What? Vouch for him? I have, a hundred times and more," Talamir replied, nettled that Dethor would even *think* he'd been doing less than he could for Alberich. "Then there's the little matter of what he calls his honor."

"Which he's damned touchy about," Dethor growled.

"Exactly so," Talamir agreed. "So what are we going to do? Truth here—I'd give both legs for a dozen Alberichs, all willing to go spying back there among his own people. Damned insular Karsites! Strangers stand out among 'em like a chirra in a herd of sheep. Accents, mannerisms, what they know without even *knowing* that they know it—" He threw up his hands in frustration. "—you just can't *teach* those sorts of things!"

"Tell me something I don't know," Dethor said, throwing an apple core into the fire in a gesture of exasperation. "Just how many agents have we lost?"

"Too many." Talamir was just glad that none of them had been Heralds. *He* had argued—successfully—that the Heralds were too few to risk inside the borders of Karse. But the fact was, from the beginning he had doubted the ability of any of them to pass as Karsite, and when the Sunpriests got their hands on Heralds, the results were traumatic for *every* Herald. It wasn't just the Death Bell tolling that sent everyone into a spate of mourning, it was that everyone *knew* what happened to Heralds that got caught in Karse. There was a sick fear behind the mourning, and the same kind of frustration and anger that sent Alberich out looking for a fight.

The Lord Marshal had been perfectly willing to send in his own people, however, and when he did, exactly what Talamir feared, happened. Karse devoured agents as a child devours sweets. They seemed to last about a moon before they were discovered; certainly not much longer. What happened to them after that, Talamir was all too aware; he preferred not to dwell on it, for at least all the men had been volunteers and knew precisely what awaited them if captured. Certainly, no more than a handful had returned.

Horrible. And there didn't seem to be a great deal they could do to change that. No matter *how* much information they gathered on Karse, no matter who they spoke to or how many old books they read, they were *not* able to fool real Karsites for long.

If at all.

"What we need," Dethor said glumly, "is what we can't get. Real Karsites. Someone who's got all the little nuances, habits, all the things you just can't study. Someone who *fits.* Someone who can't give himself away, because what's second-nature to him is all based on real Karsite memories. But the few folk who've come over are all too frightened to go back, and I can't say as I blame 'em." The scent of burning apple, sweet and bitter at the same time, added a strange nuance to his words.

Alberich wouldn't be too frightened to go, if he could; Alberich had everything they needed in an agent. If only they could use him—

And—the other stumbling block—if only his sense of honor would allow him to be so used.

It was so intensely frustrating. Sometimes Talamir just wanted to howl with the frustration.

If it was bad for him, it must be worse for Alberich. He was facing enormous pressure from those who didn't know about the covert work and saw only that he spent little time in the company of the other Heralds and less *doing* anything that might help the war effort. There was even more social pressure from those who had no idea that the Council had effectively shackled Alberich to Haven. There was a feeling from some that he had somehow betrayed the land that had taken him in, the brotherhood into which he had been admitted.

But what could they do to change that? Nothing. Everything he was doing, other than his position as Dethor's Second, was covert, and had to remain so.

Especially the work with the Lord Marshal's agents—though for all the candlemarks he spent with them, there was little enough to show in the way of success.

But then, the agents were only men—clever men, facile men, but just ordinary men. They couldn't *be* him for a day, or a week, or somehow pluck the deep memories that made him *Karsite* out of his head and plant them so solidly in their own minds that they *became* Karsite themselves.

Which brought him back to the problem all over again. If only they could make all those agents into little Alberichs . . . if only they could link those agents into Alberich's head, so that every time they did something wrong, he would catch them and correct them.

And a blinding revelation hit him.

"Good gods—" Talamir exclaimed, staring unseeingly at his reflection in the window. "I do believe I have the solution."

"To which problem?" Dethor asked skeptically.

"To the problem of how we can get effective agents into Karse," Talamir replied, holding his half-peeled apple tightly. "And to the problem of Alberich contributing to the war. You know how MindHealers are able to get into someone's head and do things with their memories? Extract ones we need from someone who's unconscious, and all that?"

Once again, he found it unnecessary to explain to his friend where he was going. "MindHealer. You think they'd be willing to get into our Karsite's head and get *his* memories out, then plant them in someone else's head?" Dethor looked interested, but skeptical. "They're damn near as touchy about what's moral and what's not as *he* is about his honor."

"If he agrees, I can ask," Talamir replied. "I lose nothing by asking, and if I already have his consent, what can they object to?"

"And will those memories be *real?*" Dethor continued. "I mean, you *know* how faulty even trained memory can be. Memory isn't reliable—especially not childhood memory."

"Which doesn't matter!" Talamir responded triumphantly. "Not in this case. What *matters* are the little things that make him Karsite, not the particulars. In fact, I wouldn't be at all averse to some inaccuracy, even a little childish fantasy; if we can make agents who aren't Alberich but *are* common Karsite folk, all the better."

Dethor brooded over the idea for a while. "I'm not sure that could be done with the Lord Marshal's men," he began, sounding very dubious indeed.

But Talamir shook his head. "I'm not talking about the Lord Marshal's men," he replied. "If this works, we can risk

Heralds. And we'll have to; I suspect it will only work with those who've got Mindspeech."

"Ah, hellfires." Dethor was clearly dismayed. After a moment, however, he scratched his head and shrugged. "I suppose you're right. And I have to think we'll get volunteers."

"I'd be shocked if we didn't." It was a depressing thought, actually—his yearmates, students, teachers, people he knew, rushing eagerly into the worst danger. It was bad enough for the Lord Marshal to send spies, but if the Karsites found *Heralds* on their soil—

Yet if those Heralds could pass as common Karsites and be able to discover and pass on what the Tedrels were going to do well in advance—

The alternative, though, was not to be contemplated. Alberich was not the only one who thought that the Tedrels were engaged in a campaign to drain Valdemar until it was so weak that one tremendous push would collapse everything.

They don't know us very well if they think we'll just collapse, Talamir thought, grimly.

:They know us not at all,: Taver said, although Talamir had not deliberately used Mindspeech, sounding just as grim as Talamir felt. *:But the cost of holding against them, never knowing when the push is coming—:*

It didn't bear thinking about. *:So we must know what they are about to do before they do it, so that we can appear to weaken without actually doing so. Then we can lure them into making their final push while we are still strong.:*

That, really, was the only possible option. Sendar and the Council had weighed all the others, not that there were many. By emptying the treasury and conscripting every able-bodied man and woman in the Kingdom, they *might* be able to mount a counter-campaign. There wasn't enough money in the entire Kingdom to hire a force equivalent to the Tedrels. . . .

:There is not enough money in all of Karse twice over to hire the Tedrels,: Taver reminded him. *:They are fighting for*

themselves, not Karse. Karse has not hired them, per se—or at least, they offered them something more than just gold. Karse has merely provided them with a platform from which to launch a campaign to conquer a new homeland and the resources to support them while they do so.:

"Why do the Karsites hate us so much?" Talamir asked aloud, in something like despair. "Why?"

Dethor shrugged. "Religion's at the heart of it, I'd guess," he opined. "But don't ask me, ask Alberich."

Religion. What about Valdemar could *possibly* seem so threatening to a religion?

:There is no one true way,: Taver said. *:That is what threatens the Sunpriests; that is what terrifies them. If you offer* that *to people, you offer them freedom, and you challenge those who claim ultimate authority. If you offer that, you give people options. The Sunpriests rely on being the ultimate, unchallengeable authority; their lives depend on the very opposite of options. Their rule depends on their followers having* no *options, and relies on blind belief and even blind obedience.:*

:Perhaps, but how do they expect to keep their people in the dark?: Short of building a wall around the country and guarding every exit point, there was no way of keeping people from finding out what was going on outside their borders.

:Ah, but a war builds *that wall, doesn't it?:* Taver responded. *:You don't need stones when you've got an enemy.:*

"Interrupting, I hope I am not," Alberich said from the doorway. He sounded exhausted; when he came into the light, Talamir took a good long look at him, and decided that he was at least as exhausted as he sounded.

"Hmm. Another fight?" he asked. The Weaponsmaster's Second was somewhat the worse for wear. He had a bandage across his forehead and another binding his forearm (suggesting that he'd already been to the Healers), bruised knuckles, and other signs that he'd been getting into trouble down in Haven. Small wonder he sounded tired.

"Fruitful," was all Alberich said. "But to drink, something wholesome, if you please?" He made a face. "The taste of sour beer, to remove from my mouth."

"I very much please, lad, and get off your feet," Dethor said quickly, and Alberich limped into the room. Dethor tilted the kettle at the hearth and poured out a mug of mulled wine, handing it to Alberich who sat down and accepted it, draining half of it in a single go. "So, what'd you net us this time?"

"Smugglers," Alberich replied. "Of vile things in—of information out." He raised a weary eyebrow. "One leak less, there is, and the jail, full." He still looked troubled, though, and Talamir knew why; it wasn't that he hadn't done well, it was just that he was concerned that there were informants who were eluding him. Anyone that Alberich caught down in the slums of Haven would not likely be sending the most sensitive information. Not that there was any sign that there *was* such a leak, but they always had to assume that one could exist.

Finding *those* leaks was Talamir's job; Alberich could not function in Court circles, while Talamir could, cultivating a mild-mannered and quiet demeanor, saying little and all of that agreeable and sympathetic. He came across as unworldly and just a bit absent-minded. People confided in him a great deal, and generally had no idea how *much* they had told him.

Nevertheless, there was no doubt in Talamir's mind that if saboteurs and couriers were to materialize in Haven, they would be living and operating in the area that Alberich was responsible for. Elsewhere, people were curious about their neighbors. In effect, each little quarter outside of the *most* impoverished areas was a kind of village, where everyone knew everyone else and wanted to know what they were up to. Not so around Exile's Gate. The inhabitants were utterly indifferent to the doings around them, and with good reason. Those who were too curious often ended up on—at best—the wrong end of a beating.

"Plenty of damage can come out of Exile's Gate," Talamir

assured him. "Anything you do to stop it from traveling to our enemies is another arrow in our quiver."

Alberich sighed. "It seems like not enough." But he leaned back and accepted a refill and an apple, which he peeled with a frown of concentration, getting the entire peel off in one piece. The knife made a crisp sound as it passed through the flesh.

"If you were a maid, you'd be tossing that over your shoulder, and looking for the letters of your husband's name in it," Dethor observed, as Alberich carefully set the long curl of peel aside.

Alberich regarded him somberly. "Is that so? In Karse, such are for the children fried and dipped in honey. I have told you, divination a thing of witchcraft is. No Karsite maiden would dare such a thing, for the fear of the Fires."

Once again, Talamir was struck by how very different the Karsites were. A Valdemaran wouldn't think twice about tossing an apple peel, reading the tea leaves, wishing in a fountain. And that was the essence of the problem that faced the agents sent into Karse.

"Have you eaten?" Talamir asked, instead of commenting. "More than just that apple, I mean."

Alberich shrugged; Talamir took that as a negative, and made up an impromptu meal for him from the remains of supper's meat and salad and some bread. Since Alberich took it with polite thanks, then absently ate it in less time than it had taken Talamir to make it, the King's Own was certain that he must have been famished.

"Glad enough, I am, to be rid of such filth as were locked away," Alberich continued, swallowing the last bite whole and absently licking his fingers. "Only, I wish it were more that I was doing. In the South . . ."

That was as good an opening as Talamir was likely to get, and he took it, explaining what he had in mind. He knew Alberich very well now; he didn't waste his breath in trying to convince the man of anything, just stated his case. He watched as Alberich's eyes took on that curiously unfocused appearance that meant he was discussing the idea with *his* Companion.

This gave Talamir plenty of time to study Alberich, and he didn't like what he saw.

Besides the bandaged forehead and forearm—*not* his sword arm, which was telling—there was a bulge beneath the sleeve covering the biceps of that same arm that suggested another bandage, perhaps of a previous wound. The scars left from the burns on his face were crisscrossed by others now. That, as Talamir recalled, was a favorite tactic of low-and-dirty street fighting—to go for the face, figuring that the pain and blood that any facial cut produced would be such a distraction that it would be easier to go in for a kill.

Not that facial scars were going to make him stand out in the neighborhoods and the company where Alberich was going at night. The opposite was true, actually; the more scars, the more he would fit in. Beneath the scars, the face was good, if carved on harsh lines—a long oblong with a stubborn chin, high cheekbones, wide brow, heavy eyebrows set in a permanent scowl, aquiline nose, and the eyes of a goshawk, fierce and wild, with the barest hint of something that was not quite sane. Or at least, it was a peculiar sort of sanity, that saw deeper into dark places and could stare into the abyss without flinching. Perhaps it was the curious quality that Alberich's eyes had of never being the same color twice in a row, varying from the gray of a threatening storm through a muddy green-brown, to (as they were tonight) something close to black.

For the rest, well, there was no doubt that even in the company of Heralds, who were a fit and athletic group, Alberich stood out. It was not that he had a perfect body—at least, not in the sculptural sense—it was something else. The practiced eye picked out the quality of muscle, the way every movement was *just* enough and no more, the absolute stillness at rest, and the immediate response when one was called for. Every movement was exact. It was difficult to describe, but easy to see when one knew what to look for. There was a fine economy in Alberich's actions, not a bit of energy wasted, and nothing held back when it was needed.

All of which, of course, came across as predatory and threatening, and probably all to the good down there in the slums.

"So," Alberich said at last. "I will think further on this."

It was a disappointing reply, but Talamir tried not to show his disappointment. There was nothing more he could add to his argument, and anything else would be nothing more than pressure that Alberich would probably respond poorly to.

"Seeking my bed, I should be," Alberich continued, rising, and looking down at them solemnly. "Dethor's Second, I still am, and there Trainees always are."

They bade him good night, and once he was out of the room, Dethor shrugged. "Well, there it is," he said philosophically. "It's up to him now."

"And hope he can find a straight path through all our tangles," Talamir added—wondering if he ought to begin praying to the Sunlord, just for a little help. And whether, if he did, the Sunlord would take it amiss and tangle things up even further.

Alberich lay in his bed, hands tucked behind his head, staring up at the ceiling. There was no fire in his room, but a dim light from the lanterns and torches lighting the gardens came through the curtains at his window and created soft shadows, contrasting with the deeper pools of darkness among the beams. He was acutely conscious of little things, all of them so alien, so very different to the things he found ordinary. . . . The crisp herbal scent of the sheets, *not* Karsite sairel, but Valdemaran lavender. The shape of the room, long and narrow rather than square. The flavors lingering on his tongue. The cadence of conversation in the next room. All these things speaking eloquently of another place than the one he called *home.*

And his mind buzzed with activity, though his body was still. This was a pretty little quagmire that had been set at his feet. . . .

Granted, he *had* been helping the Lord Marshal's men, but he'd done so knowing full well—and having *warned* them all, as well—that no one not born in Karse, or at least raised there from early childhood, could ever pass as Karsite. Now he was punished for that, for that had been sophistry, a way of appeasing both sides of his conscience without having to compromise either, and he had known it. Now he was caught, and there could be no evasion. Either he could aid Valdemar against Karse, or by withholding his aid, help Karse instead, knowing he was handicapping Valdemar.

Such a choice, and at the moment he could see no way of acting, or not acting, that would not cause harm. Violate his pledged word, or effectively cripple the abilities of those who had succored and adopted him to defend themselves. Betray his home, or those who had saved him.

:Talk to me, Chosen,: Kantor demanded. *:You've closed yourself off to me. Trust me as I trust you; let me hear your thoughts.:*

:You won't like them,: he replied mordantly.

:Perhaps not,: Kantor countered. *:But at least you will be talking to me about it. Perhaps we can find answers if we both look for them.:*

He took a moment to frame his thoughts. *:If I do what Talamir asks of me, I go against my oaths. And it is of no use at all to claim that the spies will work only against the Tedrels when my people are working hand-in-glove with them. Act against the Tedrels, and Karsites will bleed.:*

:Little doubt,: Kantor agreed, as he stared at the shadowy ceiling, listening to the indistinct murmur of voices in the next

room. *:But how are you being true to your oaths if you withhold help that could shorten this fight? You know that your Sunpriests will not hesitate to add Karsite troops to the Tedrels in order to defeat Valdemar, and the longer the wars go on, the more Karsites will die.:*

:I have no control over what the priests do or do not do,: he said stubbornly. *:And I do* not *know, not for certain, that they will order my people into this affray. What they do is in their own hands, and the will of Vkandis. I can only control my own actions, and I am the one who is responsible for what comes of them.:*

He felt Kantor ruminating over that one; well, he'd spent enough time agonizing over the problem himself, and it was the only answer he could come to. No matter what *other* people did, if he was to remain true, he could only do what *he* felt was right.

:Pah,: Kantor said in disgust. *:Why must the right answers be so unsatisfactory? But, Chosen, this might be right by your oaths, but must you remain bound by oaths to those who violated* their *responsibilities, not only to you, but to the people they lead?:*

:If I break those vows,: he replied slowly, painfully, *:I become no better than they. Who will trust me, if I break my vows? How can I trust myself?:*

Silence again, as Kantor considered this as well. This time, his reply was only a frustrated sigh.

:I have no argument for you that would not also be sophistry,: Kantor admitted, after the silence had gone on for what seemed to be a candlemark at least.

Strangely enough, that reply brought him a modicum of relief. Kantor was with him. Kantor was at least as uncomfortable with the situation as Alberich was, but the Companion was *with* him. Kantor, his best and truest friend in the world, was not going to use that friendship to try and persuade him of something against his conscience. Now all he had to do was argue with himself.

He sensed Kantor thinking furiously and waited to see what the Companion would come up with. *:I don't suppose,:* Kantor offered diffidently, *:that you could get some sort of dispensation from the Priests of Vkandis absolving you of those oaths?:*

:Geri won't *give that. He can't offer it on his own authority, and I wouldn't accept it from him even if he did.:* No matter what the Sunpriests down in Karse did, Geri knew that, short of an apparition of the Sunlord Himself, there was *no* way that he could absolve Alberich of previously made vows.

And as for asking for some sort of message from Vkandis Himself— He flinched away from the very notion.

For whatever reason, the Sunlord had elected to permit the Sunpriests to act as they were. Only He knew what was in His mind. Alberich could speculate, but—

Here was the truth of it all: who was he that Vkandis should appear to him to absolve him of his oaths? Only one man in exile, one man who could only prove his faith by remaining faithful. . . .

:Chosen—: Kantor said suddenly, interrupting his thought. *:Let me ask you this. Suppose, just suppose, that you were not bound by those oaths. What would you do in that case, if you were completely free to do what you wished to do?:*

What would he do? *:I haven't thought about it, haven't even considered it. There was no reason to,:* he replied honestly. And, then answered just as honestly, *:If I were free, I would aid all those agents without a moment of hesitation. I'd go myself, if the Council could be persuaded to trust me. In fact, I'd demand to go—:*

:Why?: Kantor interjected. *:Why would you* demand *to go?:*

That was an easy question to answer, for it was the sum of all of his turmoil. *:Because no one born and raised in Valdemar could* ever *be so careful of the lives of the children of Karse as*

I. No one but I would care enough to take the extra effort to be sure *no harm came to them.:*

Alberich was no Empath, but the sudden flood of triumph that welled up from Kantor was a thing so tangible that it felt like the beams of the rising sun, reaching upward into the heavens at dawn. It so surprised him that he felt stunned, too shocked for words.

But Kantor had words enough for him.

*:Then, Chosen, Alberich, Herald of Valdemar and Captain of Karse—*make *more of you! Make them out of the Heralds that Talamir brings to you! Give them not only the things that Talamir wants, but the memories, good and ill, that have made you what* you *are! Do that—and they will be as tender of Karsite lives as you, and you could ask for no better stewards in your absence.:*

He lay blinking for a long moment as the sense of that penetrated. Then he closed his eyes and considered the advice from every possible angle.

And he could find no flaw in it. What better thing *could* he do for his people than this? How could it violate his oath to create *more* protectors of his people? Kantor was right. Kantor was *right!*

Relief flooded into him with such force that he felt dizzy with it, and he clutched the sides of the narrow bed as it seemed to move beneath him. And when the feeling of release ebbed a little, he felt his face wet with unexpected tears—

Oh, my people—oh, my beloved people—I can send you protectors to take my place at last, at long last!

He rubbed the tears away with his sleeve, swiftly controlled himself, and realized that the murmur of voices in the other room had not stilled. Dethor and Talamir, Sunlord bless them, were still deep in their plans, searching for answers—

:—trying to find a way to persuade you without pressuring you—: Kantor pointed out.

Yes. They would be. They had been as careful of his honor

as he was. More, perhaps, because they did not understand the reasons behind what he did, they only honored his conviction that he needed to do them.

He got out of bed; it wouldn't be the first time he'd rejoined a discussion while in a nightshirt and sleeping trews. He made his way to the doorway of the sitting room, and stood there a moment, silent, seeing again the strain, the care, the burden of duty weighing both of them down.

At least this time he'd be able to lift some of that, not add to it.

He cleared his throat, and they looked up, startled.

"I believe, my brothers," he said, with a nod to both of them that acknowledged their kinship without unnecessary words, "I believe, help you I can. And must. So speak you with your Healers, and tell them, Alberich of Karse wishes this, most devoutly."

He waited just long enough to enjoy the look of stunned shock and amazement on both their faces. Then he turned and made his way back to his bed—there to enjoy the first untroubled night of sleep he'd had since the Tedrel Wars began.

THE MindHealers, with one adventurous exception, were not happy about the plan, which was not really a surprise. Alberich did not give a toss whether they were *happy* about what he was doing. All he cared about was that they had agreed to the project.

The Heralds he had recruited for his agents were a diverse lot; four of them, which was *all* he would risk on this venture. He didn't know any of them well, which was another good reason for having chosen them. Three of them were too old for him to have trained, and the fourth had been so average that he was entirely unmemorable. One sun-weathered, dark-haired man who *was* a tinker, and thus had all the skills to pass successfully as a Karsite tinker. One, in his late middle-age years, was from a family of herdsman, and thus able to pass as another goatherd who had been displaced from his home in the hills by the war. In fact, he could probably make a fine case for having had his herds confiscated by the Tedrels, leaving him with nothing but the meager possessions he could carry on his own back. The third was a youngster, a lad who had *just* gotten his Whites—but he had three advantages. First, he was from a forester family just on the Border near Burning Pines. Second, he had been an orphan, forced to take responsibility for himself from an early age. As a consequence, he acted more like a young man in his late twenties than one just barely eighteen. And thirdly—thirdly, he was *smart.* He had a strongly developed sense for self-preservation; he thought before he said or did anything. He, of all of them, was the likeliest to be recruited by the Tedrels themselves and the most likely of anyone who had volunteered to be able to keep his head and stay plausible when within their ranks. There was something to be said for being the type that has been knocking about in the world before becoming a Herald, in this case.

The fourth was a woman as old as the old man; she would try to get taken on as a laundress or cook. Alberich didn't hold out much hope for that, but if she could, well, an old woman would hear a lot from the Tedrel camp followers. Even if the Tedrels themselves didn't speak to women, the recruits were of the type that wouldn't be able to keep their mouths shut.

None of them would have their Companions with them; all of them were confident that their Companions could stay out of sight, but within call, so if things began to look the least bit dangerous, they could get out of the camp and escape before suspicion mounted to certainty.

Alberich was quite certain of one thing, at least. When they were done with these sessions, they would *be* Karsite, or he would call a halt to the whole scheme. That was how he had sold his plan to the MindHealers; he had to wonder how much they really understood what he meant, but he had to take a chance somewhere.

No one knew how this was going to work, but the MindHealer who had agreed to mediate the experiment had some ideas of his own that he wasn't inclined to share with anyone, not even Alberich. He had only promised this much: if what he planned worked, the Heralds were not going to get Alberich's memories, *per se,* and Alberich was not going to be reliving his own memories. "I won't say anything more," he'd repeated stubbornly, no matter who asked him or how many times he was asked. "I don't want anyone going into this with any preconceptions to muddle things up. If this works, it will work very well indeed."

Though how they were supposed to enter into the situation "without any preconceptions" was beyond him.

When the time came, Alberich appeared at Healers' Collegium at the appointed hour, with three of the four Heralds he had recruited trailing in after him, one by one. It probably would have been amusing if they all hadn't looked so serious, even apprehensive; he could have been a tutor or nanny trailed by his three of his four charges. They were sent to a quiet chamber that held two narrow beds and a chair between them, and stood, as Alberich thought to himself, "like a gaggle of useless idlers," none of them particularly wishing to take a seat either on the couches or the chair. The young man still hadn't arrived there when Healer Crathach, long and lean and sardonic, appeared in the room to which they had been sent.

"Ah, good. I only need one of you volunteers at a time," he said, looking entirely too gleeful for Alberich's comfort. "Hmm—you, I think, Orven. Take a couch. Alberich, you take the other. Try to relax, and close your eyes."

The former herdsman made a bit of a face, and did as he was told, taking the farther of the two couches. In silence, Alberich did the same, taking the nearest. He closed his eyes, and heard a creak as the Healer sat down in the chair, felt a hand laid atop his forehead and suppressed the urge to knock it away, and—

And suddenly, he was in Karse.

But this was not exactly a memory. He had never lived in this cob-built hut—too small to be called a cottage—though he had seen plenty like it over the years. This was a typical mountain hut of the poorest sort, yet there was a poorer state than that in Karse, and that was to be the lowest of the kitchen or stable staff, who had not even a scrap of floor to call their own. Scullery maids, cook's boys—they slept on the kitchen floor and ate what they could scrape out of pots, never washed except what parts of them got immersed in water when they scrubbed things, never changed their clothing until it dropped from their body.

He and his mother had, thank Vkandis, never been *that* lowly.

However, in this incarnation, it appeared that the protagonists of this "memory" *were.*

A little boy, who was him, and was not him, about three years old, was watching a woman who was his mother, and was not his mother, scrubbing the floor of this hut—a floor, made, as was usual in these huts, of the scrap ends of boards gathered and pieced together. She did not own this place; whereas his mother *had* owned, or had at least rented, their little dwelling. This woman was a servant here, the only one; sleeping on the hearth, doing the heaviest of the work, taken on by the mean old woman who owned the place only because, in her outcaste state, she asked nothing but food and shelter for herself and the boy that was him, and not him. He looked through that boy's eyes, yet he did it from an adult perspective.

Now, he recognized the memory from the framework. *If* this had been his real memory, he would have been watching his mother scrubbing the floor of the inn where they lived. But this wasn't his village, it was another, in herding country, where he had served in his first year with the Sunsguard. It wasn't an inn, for this particular village had been too small to have one; this was just one of the many little houses, with a bush above the door to show that it sold ale and food. He didn't recognize the woman; she was something like his mother, but mostly not. And although he somehow knew that Orven was actually experiencing this episode as if *he* were the toddler, *Alberich* was watching it as a sort of dispassionate passenger in Orven's head.

This was fascinating; living fiction. Except that Orven was living it. Had *he* come from a background that was *that* impoverished? It could be; the MindHealer could be taking both sets of experiences and melding them together in a Karsite setting.

The bones of the experience were the same as his own; a group of fellows who considered themselves to be young toughs strolled past, and decided to abuse the woman because of *his* presence, calling her "whore" and worse. True, she was not married, and now had no prospect of ever wedding. True, she had not named his father to anyone but the Sunpriest. But his mother—and, in this manufactured memory, this woman—were hardly whores. They sold themselves to no man, and had been so tight-lipped about the identity of Alberich's father that *nothing* had ever made them reveal it except to their priest.

The boy knew none of this, nor did Orven who was actually living through this instead of observing it—nor had Alberich at the time. Orven, from his childish perspective, only knew that the men were large and loud, and were making his mother unhappy. They frightened him, and he began to cry.

Now all of this came with an incredible load of detail that Alberich had not even known was *in* his memory—the scent of the harsh tallow soap the mother was using and of the wet wood of the floor, the beer smell from the cask just inside the door, the aroma of the pease porridge over the hearth, and woodsmoke, the sharp not-quite-spring scent of the air itself, the sour-sweat smell overlaid with goat and sheep of the men. And that was just scent. There was the quality of the sunlight, thin and clear, giving a great deal of light, but not much warmth. He somehow *knew* the look of the cobbles and the dirt path outside the door, the shape of the hut, with its rough cob walls, whitewashed some time last spring, the whitewash shabby from all the winter storms—the shape of the other houses of the village, of the village itself, a straggle of houses along the road. He even knew the road, cobbled only where it passed through the village itself. Alberich knew where it had all come from; he'd seen dozens of villages like this one over the years. The story came from his life, and the setting, but both were tolerably confused together, creating a new "life" entirely.

It wasn't him. Orven, taken back in his mind to the level of a toddler, was the one feeling all of this; it would be Orven's reactions that counted here.

The flood of external detail was giving Orven plenty to take in; internal, of course, was something a good deal more primal, the uncertainty and all the turmoil of a small and terrified child.

Then *he* came striding up the path, as if the crying had summoned him; tall, bearded, straight-backed, dressed in a long black robe with something bright and shining and immediately attractive to the wailing child on the breast of it. He wasted no time, verbally laying into the men in a voice like thunder, somehow making it clear that it was their good fortune he wasn't going to lay into them physically as well. There was a great deal of what Alberich—from his dispassionate distance—recognized as Holy Writ being quoted, mostly about the poor, the fatherless, and the repentant. There was also a great deal of Writ quoted about the ultimate destination of those who abused the poor, the fatherless, and the repentant.

And a curious thing happened. The more the man spoke, the larger he seemed to become, and the smaller the woman's harassers became. As they shrank into themselves, unable to look either at the woman or the Sunpriest—that was clearly what he was, although it was Alberich, and not Orven, who knew this—the woman took on more confidence. Since none of the thunder was being directed at him or his mother, the child calmed and crept near to her, and she hugged him close.

"Now, go!" the man finished at last, in tones dripping with disgust. "And if you don't wish another taste of my tongue, find yourselves something godly to do for a change!"

They slunk off, exactly like whipped curs. Now the man came to stand over the boy and his mother. "How long has this been going on, woman?" he asked curtly, but not unkindly.

She shrugged. "Since he was born, Holy Father," she replied, in a resigned voice.

Now the Priest looked down at the boy. "Then it is time I took a hand," he pronounced, in a way that said quite clearly that it would be useless to protest. "I will have the boy with me for two marks in the morning, every morning. It is time he learned the ways of the Sunlord, blessed be His Name, and when the village sees that *my* eye is on you, there will be no more of scenes like this."

Then he turned and stalked away again, and the memory—or, more accurately, manufactured memory—was over.

Alberich "woke," suddenly released from the experience, and opened his eyes. *He* was as calm as he had been when he took his place on the couch, but from the tear streaks on Orven's face, it was clear that he had experienced, and quite directly, everything appropriate to that young child in that situation.

The Healer was grinning with great satisfaction, so Alberich had to suppose that what he had planned had worked. But he put one finger to his lips, and motioned to Alberich that he should leave the room for the moment.

Alberich felt a little unsteady, but did as he was "told." The other three were waiting outside, sitting on a long bench, and looked up at him expectantly when he emerged.

"The Healer, pleased is," he said laconically, and left it at that. It was not very much later that Orven left, looking quite composed for a man who'd been dissolved in tears only a short time ago, and the Healer called in Alberich and the young man, Herald Wethes.

The next three sessions were similar, with Alberich serving more as observer than participant, but each setting being appropriate to the persona being created for the people involved, and rich with vivid detail. Wethes had another mountain village, but *his* mother was from a forester clan, for instance, and for the old woman, the village was down in the plain.

Even the identity of the Sunpriest changed, and Alberich had the notion that here, too, the image was coming from the other Heralds, each of them contributing the face and figure of some authority in *their* childhood, trusted and wise.

He was thoroughly exhausted before the sessions were over, but to his surprise, very little actual time had been spent in the enterprise, no more than a mark or two. But if he was tired, the others were completely drained by what was, for them, a highly emotionally-charged experience.

And it was just beginning; he wondered if they were already starting to regret volunteering for this.

But although it was as physically wearing as a good, long practice session, this first set was not as emotionally difficult as Alberich had feared. Well, truth be told, although he had known that the only way to make these fellow Heralds into what he wanted to be was to give them bits of his own life, that was entirely what he had feared as well. He hadn't wanted to expose himself and his life to others so nakedly.

But it appeared that, somehow, he wasn't going to. The others had no idea how much of what they were going through was really part of his life, and the emotions they were feeling were theirs, not his.

Perhaps that was what had bothered him the most of all about this whole project; he had not wanted his feelings to be so exposed. If this was the Healer's doing, then he owed the man thanks. More than thanks.

He lingered while the last of his four volunteers collected

herself and tottered off, looking dazed. Healer Crathach gave him a knowing look when he didn't leave, and leaned back in his chair, arms crossed.

"I'll save you trying to wade backward through our language, and tell you straight up the answer to what you're going to ask me," the MindHealer said with a grin that had just a touch of smugness about it. "Yes, I planned this whole business of only *using* what you know to build seminal Karsite experiences for our four victims, rather than taking your memories entire. It's all been very deliberate. I've got a lot of reasons for doing it that way, as much for their sake as yours. You wanted them made Karsite, not made into duplicate versions of you. And *I* didn't want them subsumed into your rather formidable personality, Herald Alberich. But most of all, I did not want *you* to have to expose yourself in a way that would have been difficult for you to come to terms with."

Alberich let out the breath he'd been holding in. "You knew—" he said, with just a touch of hesitation.

"That you didn't *want* everybody and his Companion knowing every sordid detail about your past?" Crathach looked sardonic as well as smug, an odd combination. "I'd be a pretty poor MindHealer if I hadn't been able to pick *that* up, now, wouldn't I?"

Alberich just shrugged; it was only the truth.

"At any rate, things will diverge more from here, in the little life stories we're concocting," the MindHealer continued, and scratched his head with a slight frown. "How to put this? The powerful *incident* that formed you into what you are now will remain the same, and all of your background, but the way our agents will react to it, and the details of the incident will be driven by their own personalities. Am I making sense to you?"

"I—" Alberich hesitated.

"Well, never mind, you'll see it as we go along. The point is, the more we do, the *less* it will be anything like your own experience." The MindHealer shrugged, stretched, and got to his feet, then he paused, giving Alberich a long, measuring gaze. "Go, *do* something," he said. "Something purely physical. There's such a thing as thinking too much, especially for you."

Since thinking was all that Alberich had been doing for the past several marks, the advice seemed good to him, and he nodded. "My thanks," he replied, and went off to follow his Healer's orders.

Sendar coughed unexpectedly. Selenay pressed down too hard on the goose quill, and it leaked, leaving a trail of ink spatters on the parchment. She cursed and tried to blot the damage but only made it worse. She dropped the quill and made a grab for the edge of the parchment in irritation.

Her secretary snatched it away before she could crumple or tear it to pieces, as she had two others. "Let Crance take care of it," her father said, without looking up from his own work. "He has your notes, he has what you've written so far, and he should have been doing this in the first place. You don't need to be here, and you're getting hunched shoulders from sitting at a desk. Go do something purely physical."

When she didn't respond, he looked up at her. "*You* do not need to write every word of your judgments yourself. Crance doesn't have enough work from you as it is. For Haven's sake, you don't need to replace the entire Circle, clerks and all! You've already freed up two Heralds from the city courts so that they can go South, and that is *enough,* Selenay."

He sounded exasperated, and he probably was. She was trying so hard—and in her head she knew he was right, but in her heart, she kept feeling that she should be trying harder still.

She rubbed one of her tired eyes, and let poor Crance take

the offending paper away to his own desk. "It doesn't seem like enough," she said; she felt forlorn, but she was afraid she sounded sullen. "I feel like anyone who isn't feebleminded or sick, or afflicted somehow, ought to be *there,* not here."

Her secretary, a young man who was nearly as short-sighted as Herald Myste and afflicted with wheezes when he ventured near anything in bloom, looked at her mournfully. She immediately felt even more guilty for making *him* feel guilty for not being in the fighting.

"My dear—" Her father sighed. "Selenay, you sit in Council with me, you're serving in the city courts, and half the time you don't let Crance do his job. You are doing more than you need to, and probably far more than you should. Get out of here into the sunlight before you forget what it looks like and you turn into a troglodyte."

She stared at him, blinking. He rose, took her hand, pulled her out of her chair, and shoved her forcibly out the door of the Royal Suite as the two guards at the door tried not to stare.

The door closed behind her, and to her astonishment she heard him slide the lock slide home. "And don't come back until your nose is sunburned!" she heard Sendar say, his voice muffled by the closed door.

For a single moment, she thought about pounding on the closed door, demanding to be let in. . . .

The right-hand guard made a choking noise, and Selenay swiveled just in time to catch him screwing up his face in an attempt to keep from laughing aloud. She knew him very, very well, indeed; he'd played Companion to her Herald too many times to be counted when she was little. In that, he had been more fortunate than most patient fellows who allowed toddlers to bounce on their backs; Companions were expected to have minds of their own, and didn't wear bitted bridles. And they didn't suffer being drummed upon by little heels when they didn't move fast enough. He'd bounced her off a time or two when she exceeded the bounds of the allowable.

She made a face, but didn't comment, because there was great relief in being *ordered* to do what she wanted, but had been too guilty to pursue.

"Beggin' your pardon, your Highness," the Guard said, composing himself. "But I believe that sounded like an order. I'd obey the King, if I was you."

He stared straight ahead, but his eyes were twinkling.

She gave a theatrical sigh. "Orders are orders," she agreed, and with a wink, turned and headed for the nearest exit.

:Caryo, I'm on my way!: she Mindcalled, feeling just a bit giddy, as if she'd been released from classes for an unexpected half-holiday. *:I'll need—:*

:Done. Your Alberich's been ordered off to gallop out his megrims by the MindHealers,: Caryo replied cheerfully. *:Perhaps your father knew that already when he ordered you out. It wouldn't surprise me. You can* both *do with an outing.:*

It could well be; there wasn't much that Sendar didn't know. It saved her hunting up her bodyguard and trying to determine whether he could be pried away from duties of his own, of which he seemed to have rather too many. If she'd been ordered away, she wanted to leave Haven altogether. She hadn't been outside the walls in—well, ages. Certainly not since the Wars began. They wouldn't go *far,* not far enough that anyone could rebuke him for leaving the city. Not that he had a choice if he was guarding her, and she would point that out if anyone dared to say anything.

By the time she reached the stables, Alberich was waiting, with both Companions saddled and bridled. As usual, it was impossible to read him, and she had long ago given up trying.

"A destination, you have?" he asked, though it was more statement than question.

"Outside Haven. The Home Farms," she replied. The so-called "Home Farms" actually belonged to the three Collegia, and supplied the needs of hearth and table. There was a separate farm, the Royal Farm, that took care of the Palace; it wasn't much larger, but it had twice the staff, for the Palace tables required something more sophisticated than the vast quantities of plainer fare devoured by the Trainees. Selenay was in the mood for *simple,* and besides, the Home Farms had the river flowing along beside them, and she had a notion to go fishing. After all, Sendar had told her not to come back until her nose was sunburned, and there was no better way of doing that than "drowning a worm," as the old gardener who'd taught her used to say.

Alberich just nodded; evidently both Caryo and Kantor were more than ready for an excursion, because off they set at the trot. They took a shortcut across the velvety lawn, briskly heading for the Palace, curving around the New Palace and getting onto the paved drive in front of the Old Palace. This was the side of the Palace that the working Heralds rarely saw, and the Trainees, almost never. The facade of the building was interesting, showing as it did the old "fortress" face of the building, with its doors meant to hold against a battering ram. But it had been softened by a planting of formal cypress trees in enormous tubs, and was fronted by a paved courtyard centered by an octagonal pool and a geometric granite fountain, and Selenay had *no* idea what the material paving the courtyard and drive were. The paving dated from just after King Valdemar's time, when the need for defense had begun to take a secondary place to other Palace functions. It wasn't cobbles or bricks, for there wasn't a sign of seams or joins. It was a solid pale gray, very nearly identical to the color the Trainees wore, from edge to edge, and the feel of it was slightly springy. The entire pavement was surrounded by a wrought-iron fence, tall and formidable, like a row of linked pikes twice the height of a man, with the wide drive of the same substance as the courtyard leading up to it and through a pair of gates that were usually left ajar. Nevertheless, there were Guards stationed here, on either side of it, with little boxes to keep the weather off them when it was truly awful.

Alberich led her past them, his back absolutely straight, his seat so easy that there was no doubt in anyone who knew cavalry that it was in the cavalry where he'd learned to ride. For their part, the Guards did not seem to pay any attention to them, staring straight ahead. She knew better, though. They weren't there as ornaments.

The drive went toward the tall proper-walls, that surrounded the entire complex, velvety grass on either side of it, but no plantings other than a row of cypresses right up against the wall itself, the same sort of cypresses that were inside the fence. And there were yet more of them, planted in boxes arranged with mathematical precision on either side of the drive. The cypresses softened the look of the stone wall, and probably helped give the guards up there a little protection from the wind in winter, and shade in summer.

There were more Guards on the wall and on either side of the passage that led through it, both inside and out. This was still defensive; there were portcullises on both ends, and a rather nasty murder-hole in the middle, through which all sorts of unpleasant liquids could be poured down upon a would-be invader. Not so incidentally, the murder-hole had made a good place for a young Princess to drop petals and peas down on unsuspecting visitors, with extra points awarded for the pea that landed squarely in the middle of a fashionable hat without the wearer noticing.

There was no one up there to drop peas upon them now, and they trotted through the cool shadow and out into the sunlight and down into the city.

Nearest to the Palace, predictably enough, were the enormous mansions of the highborn, each a smaller palace in itself. The farther one got from the Palace, the less expensive (and more crowded) the buildings, until by the time they passed out of the final set of gates and walls—for the city had outgrown its walls several times, and a new set had been built around the new construction that had spilled over on the other side—the final set on *this* road were a mix of shops with apartments above, stables for hire-horses, and inns and taverns. The road was not, however, a straight line to the final city gate; there were no straight lines to the complex within Haven. Everything had been laid out like a maze, so that if the city ever did come under attack, the defense could be fought street-by-street.

Before the Wars, that very notion had seemed laughable. Not anymore. Though it would probably take having the Tedrels appear at the gates before the citizens of Haven believed that.

Out yet another set of gates with yet another set of Guards they went, following the river which ran under the walls at this point. Here, the transition went abruptly from the urban to the rural, for this was where all market gardens that supplied the city with fresh eggs and vegetables were located. While the urban had edged out past the final walls outside other gates, here it had not, for the profit to be derived from such well-watered and fertile property was not to be trifled with. And here, in the midst of market gardens, suddenly loomed a true *farm,* the Home Farms, so named in the plural because they *had* been several smaller farms at one time. All of the buildings from each of these separate farms had been thriftily disassembled and reassembled in a central location; all of the cottages joined into one big building where the farm workers lived, all of the barns ranged around a single yard and each allocated to *one* form of livestock. Even the henhouses had been moved, and were lined up in a neat little row, free-ranging chickens efficiently pecking up every bit of stray grain in nearly every weather, and cleaning up insects in summer.

Here the river curved away from the main road, and the lane leading to the Home Farm's buildings ran alongside it. Behind the Home Farms, also watered directly by the river and situated on this lane, was the Royal Farm—but that wasn't Selenay's destination. The Royal Farm was a showplace of its kind, the chickens segregated by meat-birds and layers, kept separate to keep their breeds pure. Everything on the Royal Farm was a purebred, from the chickens to the plowhorses; every building was spotless and immaculate. The hothouses were there, for forcing flowers, fruit, and vegetables out of season. Pens of gamebirds were there and exotic food plants too difficult to grow in quantity. Ponds of delicately-nurtured fish for the Royal table, even.

Too formal for Selenay today.

The lane was clear, with not so much as a turtle on it, and both Companions broke into a canter that took them all the way to the farmhouse. Selenay found herself grinning as they pulled up with a flourish in the yard in front of the building, and even Alberich looked a little less mordant. The farm manager, an ancient fellow indeed, hobbled out to determine what they wanted, and when Selenay explained her wish to fish for the benefit of the Collegium tables, was happy to direct them to a shed where the fishing tackle lay.

"Eels," Selenay muttered to herself, selecting the appropriate tackle, knowing very well that the Collegium cooks made a fine eel pie. She looked askance at Alberich, who was examining the poles dubiously.

"You *do* know how to fish, don't you?" she asked.

He turned solemn eyes on her. "No."

:Doesn't mince words, does he?: Caryo chuckled.

"Then it's time you learned," Selenay told him ruthlessly, and with a touch of glee. "It's a standard skill all Heralds are supposed to know. You might have to find your own food in the wilderness, after all."

"And I, in wilderness will be allowed? Not likely, that." He sighed with resignation. Or disgust. Or both, perhaps. She didn't care. He might as well learn to fish; it wouldn't do him harm, and it might do him good.

She spent the next candlemark or so in a position every Trainee ever schooled by the Weaponsmaster's Second would probably have given his last hope of the Havens for. Schooling the infamous Alberich, playing stern and implacable tutor to the Great Stone Heart himself! And it was highly entertaining as well.

She presented Alberich with his pole, and had to show him how to bait the hook—and the formidable Alberich proved to be very reluctant to touch the bait!

"Now don't be so squeamish," she ordered, pulling a worm out of the earth of the bait pail and handing it to him. "I've shown you what to do, it's not that difficult."

He took the worm in his thumb and forefinger, and held it stiffly in front of him. "Must I?" he asked in a strangled voice.

She suppressed her mirth, and instead fixed him with the same sort of gimlet-eyed stare *he* gave reluctant Trainees. She didn't even need to say anything.

He barely skinned the worm onto the hook, and she *knew* it wouldn't stay. Sure enough, the third time he pulled the hook up out of the water to check on it, the worm was gone.

He glanced aside at her; *she* was pulling in eels at an astonishing rate and already had a bucketful. She just gave him that look again, and nodded toward the bait bucket, without saying a word.

With a long-suffering expression on his face, he probed the loam with a reluctant finger for another worm.

By the end of the afternoon, she was highly satisfied with her half of the expedition. She had a fine mess of eels, *far* more than a mere bucketful, certainly sufficient to provide Heraldic Collegium with an eel-pie supper. She had a properly sunburned nose (but not so much that it was going to hurt later) and Alberich was—

Well, it was comic. The incredibly competent Alberich *did* have something that he couldn't do. He had caught exactly two fish, both of them little sun-perch, and neither big enough to keep. He had lost most of a pail of worms, and it was a good thing that he *hadn't* hooked anything large, or Selenay suspected he'd have lost the rod as well. He, who couldn't miss a target, couldn't cast a line to save his life. He, who was so dexterous with any weapon of any sort, tangled his line with appalling frequency.

Mind, he *had* managed to relax, if only by cursing under his breath at his pole, his line, the wretched fish that stole his bait. Practicing with his students out of doors as much as he did, *he* hadn't had a clerical pallor, but there weren't quite as many frown furrows cutting across his scars.

She put up her gear with a sigh of regret; he put his up with a sigh of relief. The old man came to take charge of the tub of eels, which was as well, since she couldn't exactly take them back to the Collegium in her saddlebag. Together they rode—at a walk, this time—back down the lane to the road.

"How did you manage never to learn how to fish?" she asked him, after they rejoined the traffic on the road heading into Haven.

"I should learn, where?" he asked. "When very young, helping in the inn, I was. Then it was in the Academy, and fishing, a sport for gentleman is, or a subsistence for the poor. No part has it in training for a cavalry officer."

He must have been *very* young when he first began to work, then. . . .

:And very poor,: Caryo told her, knowing that she needn't say more. Although fishing was traditionally a way for the poor to add another source of all-season food to the larder, the poor *also* had to have the time to fish. Which, clearly, Alberich had not. The very poor also might not have enough to spare for hook, line, and bait.

"Besides," he added meditatively, "where lived I and served I, no great rivers there are. Swift streams only. Trout, have I heard of, which great skill takes. Wealthy man's sport."

"Well, you've got the knack now," she replied cheerfully, and was rewarded with his sour look.

"Then best it is that to Haven I am confined," he said. "And should fish be required of me, purchased at market they can be. Else, it would be starvation."

She couldn't help it; she tried to hold back her snickers, but they escaped. He looked—pained.

"Oh, really, Alberich, it's so nice to find *something* you can't do!" she exclaimed.

"Glad I am, that such amusement given you I have," he told her crossly. "Perhaps a new title, I should have? Herald-Jester?"

She couldn't help it; he looked so irritated now that the giggles just burst out all over again. And finally, one corner of his mouth began to twitch, then both corners, then, although he didn't actually *laugh,* he unbent enough to admit that the joke, although on him, actually was rather funny.

And it wasn't until he had delivered her back to her father, sunburned nose and all, that she realized that she hadn't thought about the Wars once all afternoon. But what was truly satisfying, she also understood in a flash that in wrestling with worms and hooks and poles that would not do what he wanted them to, neither had Alberich. And that Sendar had sent her off to "do something" at the same time that someone in authority over Alberich had evidently decided that *he* needed some distraction.

So perhaps her father was even cleverer than she'd thought. *No, there's no perhaps about it,* she decided, making her way back toward the Royal Suite. *He's much cleverer than I'd thought.*

However, of all the thoughts that had occurred to her today, that was, perhaps, the very *least* surprising.

OUTSIDE the tavern, a storm raged, effectively ensuring that no one would be leaving or coming in any time soon. Water poured off the eaves of the tavern in sheets, like a waterfall, as the gutters overflowed. The rain spouts added to the mess, spouting like geysers, sending a torrent of water over the cobbles. It was *cold* out there, the temperature had plummeted, and the rain felt like icewater.

Inside the tavern, those who were stuck here nursed the last dregs of their drinks and contemplated another. Or perhaps, a nice pigeon pie or a good slice of mutton. . . . The innkeeper, anticipating the needs of his customers, had started a kettle of mulled cider, even though it wasn't the season for any such thing, and the spicy scent began to drift through the inn, turning heads and sharpening appetites. It was unexpectedly cozy in here, with a small fire going, just enough to take the chill off the air. And the ambiance was a million leagues away from the atmosphere in the last tavern Alberich had been in.

Alberich had come out of the secret room at the back of the stables here at the Companion's Bell, only to find that the storm which had been threatening all day had finally broken. Since he was effectively trapped here *and* starving, he decided to make a virtue of necessity and avail himself of the little private room reserved for Heralds and their guests.

Of course he was starving; he'd left before suppertime, and you just didn't eat what was offered in, say, the Broken Arms. Not unless you wanted to have an intimate and detailed knowledge of the inside of the privy, sooner or later, when your stomach objected to what you'd put there. Granted, the indoor water closets at the Collegium were fine things, but not as a place for an extended stay.

He'd already had his fill of watching people tonight; on the whole, he'd rather just sit back on a comfortable settle alone, and watch the storm. Here, once he was *out* of that secret room where he changed his identity from that of a Herald to any one of half a dozen personae he wore in this city and back again to a Herald, he felt almost as secure as at the Collegium itself.

It wasn't only the wretched neighborhoods he prowled, as a cheap thug-for-hire, as a ne'er-do-well of dubious reputation, as a sell-sword. No, he had some respectable personae as well; he was a small merchant in imported knives, he was a votary of some obscure god whose cult was so tiny that no one had ever heard of it (for good reason, since it didn't exist), he was an honest caravan guard. . . .

But most of his time was, admittedly, spent in places most Heralds never saw but the city constables and Guard were all too familiar with. And most of it was spent accomplishing very little but waiting for one or another of his patiently-laid traps to catch something. Far too much of it was spent in places that could be called "taverns" only because they sold alcoholic drinks. And he thought he'd been served some wretched brews as a Karsite officer! At least those had been *drinkable;* rough, strong enough to lift the hair on your arms, but drinkable.

Tonight had been one of those nights when nothing whatsoever happened, or was going to happen, except, perhaps, a common brawl or two. The threatening storm had made people think twice about leaving whatever cramped little corner they called "home"—people with only a single change of clothing had to shiver in it until it dried on their backs if they got soaked through. The taverns had been half empty, and none of his informants had poked their noses out of their holes. When the sky above the rooftops to the west began flickering with far-off lightning, he had given up. He'd hoped to get back to the Collegium before the rain began, but luck wasn't with him, it seemed.

Then, again, perhaps it was.

Heralds were common enough visitors here in the Bell that no one remarked on their presence. When Alberich arrived here, he didn't wear his trademark gray leathers anymore, he wore Whites, which made him blend in with the other Heralds who frequented the place. Sometimes a Herald just wanted to get away from the Collegium, have a tankard or a glass of wine, flirt harmlessly with a serving girl. And why not? Heralds, as Talamir took pains to remind him, were only human.

Sometimes a number of friends wanted to get together when they all came in at once; there really wasn't a big enough room in the Palace where five or more could put their feet up and talk as long and as loudly as they wanted. You could get food anytime you wanted it, but it tended to be the sort of thing that could be fed to a great many people at once—and a bespoke meal, of *exactly* what one had a craving for, was something even Heralds sometimes fancied.

The innkeeper took him to the Heralds' parlor and showed him to a seat by a window, from which he could see, in the frequent flashes of lightning, rain pouring down as if it would never stop. A moment later, a serving girl brought him hot pigeon pie of his own, and a tankard of the innkeeper's own bitter ale. It wasn't Karsite, but it was close, and unlike the harsh brews of the mountains, it was *good.*

The high back of the settle screened him from most of the room, which, in any event, was empty and likely to remain so if the weather continued to be this bad. There was no closing door to this room, and a low hum, like a hive of drowsy bees, came from the common room, in between peals of thunder. The contrast between inside and outside was so striking; storms like this commonly occurred in the mountains of Karse, but this was the first time he'd ever spent one sitting in a comfortable, warm seat with a hot dinner in front of him and the spicy scent of mulled cider in the air.

He could remember dozens of these storms when he was a tiny child, when he'd huddled beside the smoking, struggling fire on the hearth in the middle of the room, while the roof leaked in a dozen places and more rain dripped down through the smoke hole in the middle of the roof. The shutters would rattle with the force of the wind, and his mother would hold him close as she carefully fed the fire with the driest bits of wood, to keep it alive. He didn't remember the ones when he was in the temple, though; that sturdy wooden structure never left him with the fear that at any moment the roof would blow away. But the ones when he was older, helping out at the inn—yes. He'd be in the stable, helping to calm the horses, struggling to get doors closed, running all over with buckets to catch leaks. Or he'd be out *in* it, tying things down, bringing them in, and never mind the lightning striking near—too near!—and the cold rain soaking him through. The Academy was down in the valley, in a place that didn't get storms like *that,* but once he was out with the cavalry—oh, he lived through plenty more of them. Most of the time, out in the open. You *hoped* for a chance to get your tents up first, and you'd wrap every blanket you had around your shoulders and watch the rain stream down off the edges of the canvas and know it would be a cold supper again. Being caught without shelter, though, was worse. The best you could do was get down in a valley, try and find the scrubbiest, lowest stand of trees, and get under them. You'd get off your horse, because with the lighting and thunder, even a trained cavalry horse could bolt. You'd use the canvas of your tent as a raincape, and hope it kept the worst of it off you, standing with your head down, one hand holding your horse's bridle up near his nose, the other holding the canvas just under your chin, shivering, both you and the horse.

Oh, this was better, much better, like so much of his life since he'd come to Valdemar. And yet, it was not enough, and he was not certain if the problem was within himself or Valdemar.

He was glad enough that there was no one here. It allowed him to be left alone with his thoughts. He was rarely truly alone for very long.

"I understand you've lost your first fight," said someone at his elbow.

The voice was female—familiar, but he couldn't put a name to it immediately, for the words startled him so much.

"Eh?" was all he could manage, as he swiveled to see who it was that had interrupted his solitude.

"With a fish," Herald—no longer Trainee—Myste amended, her glass lenses glittering with reflected lightning. She sat down across from him without waiting to be invited. "A rather small fish," she added in Karsite, with a chuckle.

The serving-girl, laden with Myste's dinner, set her dishes down opposite Alberich's, then she whisked back through the door to the common room, leaving them together.

"Ah." He found trying to see past those lenses rather disconcerting. "You have been speaking with Selenay."

He found it a relief to speak Karsite; Valdemaran was still a trial to him, and he had the sinking feeling that it was going to take years, even tens of years, before he was comfortable in it. He managed with his low-class personae mainly by being taciturn, knowing that the people around him wouldn't recognize a Karsite accent anyway.

"It's more-or-less my job," she replied. "It's thanks to you I've got the job, I'm told—training with Elcarth, and Interning in the city courts with Selenay as the senior judge. I'm Elcarth's Second, and Elcarth believes I should be ready to step into the Herald-Chronicler position within a year or two."

"Good," he said, and meant it. "And what has my ignorance of fishing got to do with the Chronicles?"

"Not a thing," she admitted. "It just came up in our discussions. I just let people rattle on, you know; it's the most effective way to learn things." She paused, and tilted her head to the side. "I don't suppose *you* would be willing to rattle on at me?"

He opened his mouth to say no, then closed it again. It was an interesting thought. "And this would go into the restricted Chronicles?" he asked instead.

"Possibly. Some things should be common knowledge, and by the time anyone *reads* my Chronicles, all of those covert identities you've got now are going to be outdated."

So *she* knew about what he was doing! Well, he shouldn't have been surprised if she was Elcarth's Second; she'd be reading the restricted Chronicles that *he* was writing. He wondered, knowing that *she* must know about the secret room here, if she'd come down on purpose to waylay him.

She ate two or three bites, reminding him that his own dinner was getting cold. He started in on it; delicious, as always from the Bell's kitchens. Pigeon pie was a delicacy in Karse; the only pigeons there were the larger wood pigeons and calling doves, hard to catch and reserved for those with falcons to take them. Here in the city, though, there were pigeon lofts everywhere, and the common rock doves bred like rabbits. It was rabbit pie that was the ordinary man's fare in Karse, in fact. Rabbit pie, rabbit stew, rabbit half-raw and half-burned on a stick over the fire. . . .

"I grew up on this—" Myste said, gesturing with her fork to her plate. "We had a loft in the back yard. I find I miss the taste at the Collegium."

"Hmm. It *is* good," he agreed. "Not common fare where I come from."

"Well, here—in the city especially—you make up your pies with whatever you have to eat for supper in the morning, and drop them off at your neighborhood bake shop as you go off to work and pick them up when you return, along with your bread. Most people with small apartments or single rooms don't have a bake oven; in fact, especially in the city, most people only have the hearth fire to stew over and not a proper kitchen at all." Myste didn't seem to want a response; she went back to her dinner, and he followed her example.

"It is much the same in Karse," he offered, "Save that there is no bake shop, or rather, the baking place is often the inn. And we steam food as often as stew it." He well remembered the smell of the baking rabbit pies in the kitchen of the inn where his mother worked. They'd come out, and woe betide anyone who touched them, each with a particular mark for the family that had left them, and a star cut into the crust of the inn pies. He'd never gotten a quarter pie like this, hot from the oven. He and his mother had been on the bottom of the hierarchy of servants, and were treated accordingly. First were the customers, of course, then the innkeeper, his wife, and children. Then came the cook and the chief stableman, who got whatever intact portions the innkeeper's family left. Then the cook's helpers, the serving girls, the potboys who served the drink. Then the grooms in the stables and the chambermaids. *Then,* at last, Alberich, his mother, and the wretched little scullery maid and turnspit boy. Which meant that what *he* got was broken crust, gravy, bits of vegetable. Or anything that was burned, overbaked, or somehow ill-made—too much salt, he recalled *that* pie only too well. But they got *enough* to eat, that was the point; once his mother got that job at the inn, scrubbing the floors, they never went hungry. There was always day-old bread and dripping, the fat and juices that came off the roasts and were collected in a drippings pan underneath. There was always oat porridge, plain though that might be, and pease porridge, the latter being such a staple of the common fare and so often called for that there was always a pot of it in the corner of the hearth. Pease porridge was the cheapest foodstuff available at his inn, and they sold a lot of it; when the pot was about half empty, the cook would start a new lot, so that when the first pot was gone the second was ready to serve. All of the inn's servants could help themselves to a bowl of it at any time, even the scullery maid and the boy that sat in the chimney corner and turned the spit in all weathers. The innkeeper was thrifty, but generous with the food, not like some Alberich encountered over the years, who starved their help as well as working them to exhaustion.

"Ah." Myste stacked her emptied plates to the side with a sigh of satisfaction; Alberich pushed his beside them. "I don't mean you to begin nattering at me at this moment, Alberich. I just meant that when you feel like it, I'd be glad of your addition to the Chronicles. And I don't mind being a listener if all you want to do is talk. Think out loud, maybe. Or just talk to hear Karsite."

He smiled slightly. "Knowing your unending curiosity, I thank you for your patience."

"My curiosity has as much as it needs on a regular basis right now," Myste replied. "You know, before Elcarth took me on, I was never satisfied. I wanted to know, not so much what was going on, but *why*. That was the thing that drove me mad, sometimes. *Why* had this or that law been made, *why* were your people such persistent enemies, *why*— Well, there are always more questions than answers. Now I'm able to find out my *whys,* more often than not, and more to the point, I'm entitled and encouraged to do so." She smiled, and her lenses glittered. "Maybe that's why I was Chosen; I can't think of any other reason."

He laughed. "Is that why you were always such a thorn in my side, as a Trainee? That you could not be told to do a thing without wanting the reason for it?"

She shrugged. "I don't take orders well unless I know why the order is being given. And I'll be the first to admit to you that I'm very lucky and have been unusually favored in that way. Most people can't afford to indulge that particular luxury; they either follow their orders without question, or—well, there are unpleasant consequences for wanting answers." She rubbed her thumb absently against the little "clerk's callus" on the side of the second finger of her right hand, a callus created by hours of pressure from a pen.

He nodded, wondering suspiciously if she was hinting at *his* past.

"The more I'm in the courts, the more I realize that," she continued. "As a clerk, well, I *knew* why I was doing what I was doing. It was obvious. Pointless, perhaps, but obvious." She glanced up at him, sideways. "You know, you have to be a clerk, I think, before you realize just what a pother people make over nothing. And the sheer amount of ill-will that people seem to think *must* go down on paper, or die. Dear gods!"

"What, letters?" he asked.

"No. People mostly write their own vitriol in letters. We're a literate people, Alberich; that's mandated by the Crown. Just as Karsite children are required to go to the temple for religious instruction, ours are required to get instruction in reading, writing, and figuring. No, I meant legal documents, that's mostly what a clerk handles. At least, my sort of clerk. There are others who do things about money, but I've never had that kind of head for figures. I saw a lot of wills." She sighed. "A *lot* of wills. And depositions. And the documents involved in lawsuits. Well, since you've been acting as bodyguard to young Selenay, *you've* seen what happens when something gets as far as the courts!"

He nodded again. "But it is important to them."

"Some people have too much leisure, if that's what's important to them," she said sourly. "Wrangling over dead granny's best bedcover, as if the fate of the Kingdom depended on it, when all the while down there in the South—"

She couldn't finish; she just sat there, shaking her head.

He thought back about all of the things he had observed while Selenay sat, either in judgment as the principal judge or as an assistant when she was still a Trainee. "I do not understand it either," he said, then added, with a touch of humor, "but then, I never had so many possessions that *things* took on a great importance to me."

She burst out laughing at that. "Whereas I have too many, thieving magpie that I am! So I suppose I *should* understand them! Then again, most of my possessions are books, so I still don't understand why people would get into such a state over a few pence or a set of silver." She looked ever-so-slightly superior.

"And if it was dead granny's library that was in dispute?" he asked shrewdly, to puncture that superiority.

She saw it—and bravely took the blow. "There you have me. Dead in the black." She laughed. "Oh, look. The rain's starting to slacken up!"

He glanced out the window. She was right; the downpour had turned into something lighter, and the lightning had moved off into the far distance. "It could be just a lull," he warned, as she made as if to get up.

"Could be, but I'll take my chances. I need to get back up the hill; I'm tutoring a couple of Trainees." She did get up then, and he found himself wishing she would stay.

He stifled an impulse to catch hold of her hand to prevent her leaving, but she seemed to sense *something,* and turned back toward him.

"I meant that, about nattering at me, Alberich," she said. "You know, I don't put personal things in the Chronicles. Not unless they're reasons for something happening, and it would have to be a pretty important something. And Alberich?"

"Yes?" Something had passed—was passing—between them. Something he didn't recognize and didn't understand. She stared at him; he sensed her eyes behind those lenses, oddly intent.

"You might try talking to Geri as well. After all, that's what he's there for, isn't it?" She had an oddly wry smile on her face. "Well, all things considered, that's part of his job, I'd think—to be talked at."

And with that remarkable statement, she was gone.

He sat there for some time, in the half-dark, wondering why this conversation seemed to have—well—a feeling of *importance* about it.

:Perhaps because it's another Herald?: Kantor asked.

He hadn't ever gotten such an odd feeling from anyone else, not even Talamir. *:No, it's not just that. She's not an Empath, is she?:*

:Not so far as I know,; his Companion replied thoughtfully. *:But she does have one rather odd little Gift. She doesn't have to cast the Truth Spell to know if someone is telling the truth, so long as she's in close proximity to them. It's why she's in the city courts, in fact.:*

Interesting. Perhaps that was why she seemed to be able to get the people to *tell* her so much. Perhaps that was why she was so focused on needing to know the why of things. If you always knew that something was true or false, maybe your focus shifted from finding out the truth, to finding out the reasons behind it.

If you knew that something was true, maybe that impelled you to talk to others, as well as listen to them.

:Am I needed up the hill?: he asked. Kantor would know;

the Companions always seemed to be more-or-less in contact with one another.

Kantor's reply was immediate. *:No. And I've no objection to staying here in this nice, dry stable if you have something you need to do. Shall I tell them you're going to be down here a while?:*

:Please do.: Myste might not be the right person to talk to about some of the things that were troubling him, but she was right about one thing. Gerichen *was,* and if he couldn't take counsel with one of Vkandis' own, who could he speak with? *:Tell them—:*

He hesitated. *:If anyone wants to know, tell them I'm going to visit a friend.:*

The Temple of the Lord of Light in Haven was a small one, situated between a saddlery and a chandler. Alberich thought the chandler a particularly appropriate neighbor, all things considered. Candles—next to the Temple of the Light? He wondered if the chandler knew.

He'd gone back to the secret room and donned the garb of one of his more-respectable personae, in no small part because that persona was possessed of a raincape, an article of clothing that Herald Alberich had forgotten to bring with him this evening. Besides, it wouldn't hurt for Lysander Fleet to be seen here. It was one more layer in the persona.

The duties of a Sunpriest began at sunrise and ended at sunset, but Geri would be accessible for another couple of marks—

Candlemarks, he reminded himself. He *had* to start thinking in Valdemaran terms, or he would *never* get the hang of this confounded illogical tongue. . . .

The Temple itself, though modest in size, did not skimp on illumination. In fact, it showed itself to be a most hospitable neighbor; at the gates of the forecourt, directly under the two large oil torches, were benches that were, in nearly every kind of weather but rain or snow, occupied by one or more of the neighbors taking advantage of the "free" lighting to read by. The forecourt was illuminated by six more torches, and there were benches beneath them as well, although normally only a member of the temple congregation was likely to venture in there to read. Or socialize; Henrick encouraged people to feel as if the temple was an extension of their household, and there were plenty who lived tightly packed into a couple of rooms with their entire family who were happy to use the space in good weather. The forecourt was a good place for meeting friends, taking very small children to play, or just to get away from the rest of one's family.

They weren't uncomfortable benches either; of wood rather than stone (though wooden benches would have been more in keeping with Karsite custom anyway) and constructed with a subtle curve that welcomed a sitter. They glistened wetly in the rain, like great, sleek river beasts looming under the torches that had been extinguished by the first of the downpour. With the torches out, the only illumination came from two lamps on either side of the door of the temple itself. That wasn't a lot, and Alberich cursed the invisible bumps and cobbles that made for unsteady and slightly slippery footing.

He pulled open the wooden door and slipped quietly inside, trying not to disturb anyone who might be there. But the place was empty, holding nothing more but the Presence Flame on the altar, and the sharp scent of the oils used to polish the wooden interior. The aroma sent a shiver and a pang of homesickness over him. All Temples of Vkandis had this scent, since (except for the Great Temple in Throne City), all Temples of Vkandis were made of wood. Polishing some of that wood had been one of his tasks as a child. . . .

Not that his old priest had any notion of taking him in as a novice. It was only too clear from the very beginning that Alberich had no vocation, and at any rate, *he* would not have lasted five marks in the cutthroat game of politics that most Sunpriests played.

But the scent brought back memories of his childhood, pleasant ones, in fact, which would have surprised people had they known it.

Well—not his four agents. Thanks to his memories, they now knew what a Sunpriest *should* be like. A little stern, perhaps, but *not* unforgiving; a truly upright person.

Geri came in after Alberich let the door fall closed again, and it did so with a hollow *thud.* The priest—for Gerichen was a full Sunpriest now, just as Alberich was a full Herald—peered toward the shadows enshrouding the door, and made out at least the basic form enshrouded by a rain-cape. "What can I do for you, my s—" Geri began, as Alberich threw back the hood of his cape and stepped forward so that Geri could see *who* it was.

"Don't call me your son, Geri," he admonished in Karsite, "You're nowhere near old enough to be my father."

"Keep coming at me out of the dark like that, and my hair will soon be white enough to pass for your father," Geri replied. "Of all people, you were the last I would have expected to see tonight."

"A mutual friend suggested that I don't come visit nearly enough." Alberich felt himself relaxing in the familiar surroundings that said *safe haven* to his younger self, no matter what had happened to him later at the hands of Sunpriests.

"Ah?" Geri raised an eyebrow, and then a hand. "Well, in that case, since this is a social call, shall we take this to my quarters?"

"Lead on." Alberich came up the aisle toward the altar. The sanctuary, the entire temple in fact, was a harmonious construction of carved and shaped wood, from the vaulted roof to the parquetry floor. The bench pews were finished with finials carved in the shape of a torch flame, and the Sun-In-Glory was inlaid in very subtle parquetry behind the altar. The several woods used to create it were of shades so near in color that you had to *look* for the pattern, and know what you were looking for, in order to see it. More patterns, geometric this time, were inlaid in the backs of the bench pews, in the floor, in the altar itself—and these were anything but subtle. Every color of wood possible had been used here, and Alberich reckoned that the artisan in question was either now a very wealthy man, or else was a devoted member of the congregation doing it for the glory of the One God, for it was quality work, and wouldn't have come cheaply.

Geri led him in past the altar and the door behind the altar itself. This was a kind of robing room, with vestments hung up all over the walls. A door in the opposite wall led to the priests' quarters.

"Here," Geri said, motioning him into a tiny kitchen. "It's warmer in here than anyplace else. Have a seat; Henrick's asleep, but don't worry about waking him. He could sleep through a war and a tempest combined. Do you want anything to drink? Beer? Tea?"

"Tea, please," Alberich replied, and watched with interest as Geri moved efficiently about the tiny kitchen, heating water in the pot over the hearth and getting mugs for both of them. "I don't know why I haven't come here before, instead of making you come up the hill."

He said that, because the kitchen *smelled* right. Those were Karsite spices he could taste faintly in the air, and a uniquely Karsite black tea that was steeping in that kettle. There were sausages hanging up in the corner of the hearth—both for further smoking and because the smoke kept insects away—sausages Alberich would bet tasted like the ones from the inn where he'd grown up.

"So what is on your mind?" Geri asked.

"A great many things," Alberich replied, now fully relaxed,

with Geri's good tea on his tongue. "Tell something, though. What do you think about Myste?"

"I like her, but she's deceptive. I don't mean that she lies, I mean that her appearance is deceiving. She looks and sounds harmless, but she's a hunter," Geri said instantly. "She won't let anything stand in her way once she's on a scent. Though I'm not sure what quarry she's stalking. Probably a lot of things, one of them being answers."

"Ah, but to what questions?" Alberich replied.

"She's stalking those, too. Why do you ask?" Geri responded curiously.

"I'm not sure. Now that I'm not having to browbeat her into training properly, and she's a full Herald *and* Elcarth's Second, we're peers, so we're no longer in conflict with one another; she intrigues me, I suppose. It must be that instinct, one hunter recognizing another. She's the one who sent me here tonight, in fact." He took a sip of tea and savored the flavor. It was the *right* flavor, the one from his childhood although the flavor from his childhood was a diluted version of this. "I'm hunting answers myself."

Geri regarded him with a somber gaze. "You, of all people, ought to know that you aren't going to find many of those *here.* Questions, certainly, but precious few answers. Ours is a *faith,* Alberich, not a map or a guide, and certainly not a set of certitudes. At least, that is the way it should be—"

"Not what it has become." He said that sadly, and once again, he was back in childhood, with that kind, yet stern priest, who tried to show him in ways a child would understand, just what the Sunlord was and was not. "We are the mirror of Valdemar—"

"More like the twin. Or we were, before things disintegrated." Geri sighed. "I've had this discussion with Henrick, actually. *He* is of the opinion that the long slide began with a will to power. I think it's more complicated than that. I think that the priesthood was corrupted by the congregation."

Alberich blinked. "How, exactly?"

"The laity wanted absolutes, answers, and the priesthood finally elected to *give* them answers, the simpler the better," Geri replied. "The Writ took second place to the Rule, and a poor second at that. The answers took away all uncertainty, and what is more, took away the need to think."

Alberich frowned; not for nothing had he spent so much of his childhood under the tutelage of a priest who knew—and lived—the old ways. "Above all, the Writ demands that a man—or a woman, for that matter—learn how to think."

Geri nodded. "You see? The *old* ways require that each person come to the Sunlord having thought through everything for himself. The current Rule requires that men become sheep, herded in one direction, following one path, pastured in one field, ever and always, so will it be."

"Sheep." It occurred to Alberich that it was probably no coincidence that the Sunpriests of Karse had taken to calling their congregations by the name of "flock."

"Sheep don't *have* to think for themselves, do they?" Geri made a face. "The Sunlord was reshaped from the Unknowable into the remote but predictable Patriarch, from the Whirlwind to the windmill that grinds—exceedingly small. Do this—you are gathered unto His bosom. Do that—you are cast into the outermost hells." Geri shook his head. "Answers are terribly seductive. The simpler they are, the more seductive they become."

Alberich turned that over in his mind, and found it certainly matched some of his own experience. "But that isn't the whole of it," he objected.

"Of course not. I just suggest that *this* was where the corruption started," Geri replied. "*Then* came the power, power that came from giving people what they wanted instead of what they *needed,* and power is just as seductive and even more addictive than any drug. Now—I don't know, Alberich. I don't know how it can be fixed. Or even if it can. It would take the Sunlord Himself in manifestation, perhaps. And someone as the Son of the Sun who is willing to hold to the hard course and be disliked, even hated."

"And loved."

"And loved," Geri agreed. "At one and the same time, and probably by the same people. Because when you demand that each situation be considered separately, and not responded to with the predigested Answer, you are always going to anger *someone* since you're always going to disagree with someone. Probably even someone who agreed with you the last time, and now takes this new response as a betrayal."

Alberich smiled sourly. "It would take the Sunlord Himself to protect someone like that."

"I fear so, and I am very, very, glad it isn't me." Geri drained his cup and poured himself another, then smiled. "So, since I am *not* going to give you any answers, what can I do for you?"

"Give me an opinion." He outlined, as best he could, what he was doing with his four putative agents. "They have seen the very best that Karse is, in the form of Father Kentroch, my protector and teacher, and if I'm reading them correctly, they have warmed to him just as I did, and more importantly, responded to his ideas of responsibility and honor. We're just about up to the point where I first learned I had a witch-power; I suppose each of them will have a similar experience, but the witch-power will be his or her own Gift in real life."

"If you're wondering if you have somehow betrayed your vow to protect the people of Karse, let me tell you now that both Henrick and I are *positive* you are doing nothing of the sort," Geri said firmly. "If anything, you are going to put four more protectors in place, just as you had hoped. Did you know that all four of them have been coming down here for practice in the language? Or so they say."

Alberich shook his head, surprised.

"Well, they have—and what Henrick and I figured out after

the first two visits was that they didn't want lessons in Karsite—their accents are impeccable, by the way—but an understanding of how *our* version of the Sunlord differs from what they're going to encounter in Karse."

Something about the way he said that made Alberich stare at him. "Oh, no—" he said, feeling his heart sink. "Please do not tell me that they want to convert."

"We wouldn't accept them as they are now if they did," Geri said with a laugh. "No, actually, I think they're integrating their two personae; *then* once they know how things are now, they'll react as a Karsite who was brought up in the old ways would."

Alberich felt a profound relief. The last, the *very* last thing he had wanted to do was to change anyone's religion. "That's sensible. Geri—" he hesitated.

Only now did Kantor interject something. *:Geri is your priest. This is surely a question for your priest.:*

"I'm torn," he said at last. "It feels as if there must be something more I can do, for Valdemar. Valdemar has given me so much—what should I be doing in return?"

Geri considered that question carefully. "Alberich, my friend, it is also my duty to tell you things that are true. You *are* doing as much as any other Herald; someone has to be helping to keep the peace here in Haven, and you are doing that. You still serve as Selenay's bodyguard, and thus free someone else to go South. And in case you were wondering if you should offer your military expertise—no.

"No?" That surprised him. "But—my training—"

"One of the things that is true is that you are *not* a great general. Not yet, anyway. Valdemar has great generals, and it doesn't need you in that capacity." Geri gave him a look shaded with pity and understanding.

"Ah." He felt deflated. But—well—

:We have the Lord Marshal, with decades more experience than you. Perhaps you have the advantage of training at the

Academy, but we have the Collegium, which is, dare I say, just as good. It isn't only Heralds who are taught here. Occasionally, among the Blues, there is a young military genius from the Guard, and the Lord Marshal was one of those.: Ah. Geri was right, then. He stared down at his cup. "So—"

"So other than doing what you are doing—you should be getting *yourself* prepared for the day when the King and the Heir and everyone else that can hold a blade goes down to the battlefields of the South to hold off that last big push that you know is coming." Something about the tone of Geri's voice made him look up—because it was odd. Very odd. It didn't exactly sound like Geri.

Geri stared off into space, his face blank, his eyes looking—elsewhere. And Alberich felt an unaccountable chill on the back of his neck. There was something going on here, something he didn't recognize. "You are Selenay's bodyguard, Alberich, and when the day of that final battle dawns, she is going to need you more than she ever has before—because the last, the very *last* thing she will think about is her own safety, so it is the first, indeed, the only thing that *you* must be concerned about. *That* is what you must be readying yourself for. Nothing else, nothing less. If need be, you must save her from herself on that day, so that you save her for her Kingdom."

Alberich had never believed those stories about how "the hair on the back of someone's neck stood up" when something very, very uncanny happened. Now he did—because he could feel that exact sensation. Geri continued to stare off into space, with that peculiarly blank expression on his face, but something glinting in his eyes. And Alberich had the distinct impression that whatever was speaking, it *wasn't* Geri. Which left—what? Here in Vkandis' own temple, it couldn't be anything inimical . . . but it sounded almost as if this was a prophecy.

He wanted to speak and ask something for himself; wanted

to ask a question, a dozen—but they were all questions he really didn't *want* to know the answers to, honestly—

If I did, I'd be trying to tame that Gift of mine and make it serve me predictably.

The Writ said that the future was mutable and unknowable, until one passed through it and it became the past. That was why the Writ spoke against the witch-powers of those who tried to predict the future—not because the attempt to know the future was wrong in itself, but because being told *a* future closed some peoples' minds to the possibility of any other and they focused all their attention, their hopes, and their fears, on *that* future to the exclusion of other possibilities . . . which defeated the entire Prime Principle of Free Will upon which all of the Sunlord's Writ was based.

All this flashed through Alberich's mind in the time it took for the cup to slip out of Geri's fingers and drop to the table with a clatter.

"Botheration!" Geri was back, startled, seizing a cloth and blotting at the spill before it escaped to make an even bigger mess. "Look at me—woolgathering! I'm sorry, Alberich."

"No matter." The hairs on the back of Alberich's neck had settled, but not the uneasy feeling that *something* had wanted him to know more than he should about the future. *A* future.

Except that we know there is going to be a final battle. We're planning for that already. And if I had taken thought about it, I would immediately have known that Selenay would never consider her own safety under battlefield conditions. I haven't been told anything I couldn't have figured out for myself. Have I?

"I should be going. My day starts early, and yours, even earlier," he said, trying not to show any of his unease.

"True enough; good thing for me that I'm a real lark-of-the-morning," Geri said cheerfully as he walked Alberich to the door. "Come by here more often, won't you?"

Alberich almost, *almost,* prevaricated. Then he hesitated.

Because the Writ also said that when Vkandis *wished* the future to be revealed—or steered—He would find a way to do so.

"I will," he promised, and went back out into the cold, dark, and the rain—ordinary things.

Ordinary things.

He didn't think he was going to sleep well tonight. Probably not for many more nights to come.

PART THREE

The Last Battle

HE had been expecting it for months, with a feeling of heavy dread and sick anticipation that put him off his food and kept him staring at the ceiling at night. All winter he'd worried and wondered. Were the Tedrels going to break with their pattern and attack in the winter? After that strange evening when Geri briefly spoke for—Something Else—how could he not have felt that the storm was about to break?

He'd wished for an inkling that he was doing the right thing—and he'd gotten it. Nothing inimical could have used Geri as a mouthpiece, *not* a Sunpriest, and *not* inside the sacred confines of the temple. Everything in the temple was sacred, no matter how homely it seemed. Vkandis was the Lord of All, from the Sun-fire to the hearth-fire, and he did not scorn the small and commonplace. So even if what had spoken through Geri was not Vkandis Himself, it was *certainly* some spirit that was doing so on behalf of the Sunlord.

Be careful what you ask for. Well, now he had it, and now he knew, well in advance of everyone else, that Sendar and

Selenay would go into combat, no matter who tried to stop them. Now he knew . . . and didn't dare tell anyone.

Now he knew but didn't know when. He only knew it would be soon. But how soon? Every night he went to sleep on edge, and every morning he woke with the feeling that a storm was coming. And certainly this was what everyone including the now-successful agents had been working toward, all this time—to lure the Tedrels into thinking that the Valdemaran defenses were a hollow shell, and a single concerted drive would crack through. And thanks to the four that *he* had planted, when that time came, Valdemar would know as soon as the Karsite troops themselves did. They would know days, weeks earlier than they would have before his four demi-Karsites got planted successfully on the other side of the Border.

Yes, he was expecting it. But when the word came, it still hit him like a blow to the gut.

It was Talamir who delivered the blow; that didn't make it *better,* but at least it was from the hand of a friend and delivered as calmly as that worthy could manage.

It was early spring—or tail end of winter, take your choice. Raw weather, in any event, the trees still leafless, though there were a few, *far* too optimistic for his way of thinking, that were swelling into bud. The snow was gone, but a bite in the air and the snarl of the wind suggested that it wouldn't be too wise to tempt fate by rejoicing aloud that it was gone. Half the days were clear and cold, half raining, that miserable, dripping rain that would come up without warning and then stay a week, and by the time it crawled away, half the Collegium would be down with head colds. It never stayed clear long enough for things to dry up, in any event, and it was a good thing that the Trainees' uniforms were gray, because you couldn't help ending up with mud from the eyebrows down by midday, no matter what you did. Tail end of winter, *he* would call it, for all that the days were longer, and you could, if you searched diligently, find a few foolhardy crocus and snowdrops coming up in the gardens.

Spring, and he hated to see it, because it meant at least another season of war. And Spring came sooner, the farther South you went. True, in the mountains at the Border, it actually came *later,* but once out of the mountains, or when you stuck to the valleys, Spring was well on the way.

Spring was no longer a season of hope and renewal, and had not been for some time. But would this be the *last* season of war, or only the latest? That was the question that hung suspended over his head like a sword.

For the past fortnight, he'd been running a cross-class with the Horsemanship teacher, an accelerated course in fighting while mounted, and each day it had taken most of a candlemark to clean Kantor up afterward; all the Companions had been mired to mid-flank and spattered above that line. He was cold as a frog, tired, and every time he licked his split lip, he tasted mud and blood. There was no other way of learning how to fight in this kind of muck except to *do* it, though, no matter how much everyone hated it. *He* was looking forward to a hot bath with utter longing, and he trudged into the quarters behind the salle, expecting only to see Dethor and perhaps get a little commiseration before he went back to see about that long soak in hot water.

It took him aback to see Talamir there—Talamir, sitting in one of the hearthside chairs, and the sun still in the sky, for Talamir *never* was free enough to come back here before sundown. Talamir's expression told him the worst even before the King's Own opened his mouth; he froze, feeling as if something had just petrified him in place. He knew; he *knew.* And it didn't take a Gift to tell him.

For a moment, he couldn't breathe. For a moment, he was stunned. The blow had fallen.

The Tedrels were moving.

"This is the season," Talamir said, and that was *all* he

needed to say. So the bait had been taken, the misinformation believed, This season, as soon as the rains stopped, the rivers subsided, and the ground was firm instead of mired, the Tedrels would make their all-or-nothing push.

He'd wanted it and dreaded it in equal parts, and now it had come.

He nodded, for there wasn't much that he *could* say at this point. Other than: "Know where, do we? When?"

"When—well, they're going to take a little longer than usual. They're going to try and browbeat the Karsites into adding troops, and if they can't get troops, they plan to demand money so they can hire whatever non-Guild scum they can hold together under a banner." Talamir sounded quite certain of *that* information, which meant that *someone* had overheard something he (or she) technically shouldn't have. "They want shock troops to take the brunt of battle, so their own can move in behind, undamaged. And they'll want a bigger base to move from than before, one that will hold *all* of their people and possessions in it, ready to move into Valdemar as soon as they take it."

"But *where?*" he persisted. That was critical. When they knew *where* the Tedrels were going to come across, they could set up their own defensive lines on ground of *their* choosing.

"Not yet," Talamir admitted. "Other than that we *don't* think it'll be Holderkin lands. The last taste of them that the Tedrels got didn't seem to agree with them."

Alberich's lip curled a little. He didn't much care for the Holderkin, but they had surely proved to be too tough for the Tedrels to digest. And it wasn't that they'd actually formed any kind of a defensive army either. By law and custom, they kept enough food in storage at each of their Holdings to keep everyone minimally fed for two years—and in that way, no single bad year could bring them to their knees. So when the Tedrels descended last summer, instead of fighting them, the Holderkin had locked every man, woman, child, and beast into their fortresslike compounds and sat the Tedrels out. After looting what little hadn't been locked up, and burning the crops, there wasn't much the mercenaries could do, except circle the walls, trying to get in. That wasn't a very successful strategy, and they wound up getting shot full of arrows for their pains any time they got within range. The places were too small to justify the amount of effort it would have taken to breach those walls, and there was no real loot of any kind if you did. The Tedrel recruits being what they were, they fought for the loot as well as the promise of a land of their own. Yet you couldn't leave the hundreds of Holds intact if you intended to occupy the land; that wasn't merely asking for trouble, it was inviting trouble in and offering it a cup of tea, so to speak. So last season when the Tedrels had tried to take Holderkin territory, the season had been singularly profitless and unsatisfying for them. Perhaps that had added to the impetus that impelled them to put in their final push now. They could not afford two lootless seasons in a row; too many of their recruits were *not* fighting for a new homeland, and would break ranks and desert if they saw no profit coming for a second year. You couldn't even tempt them with the Holderkin women; if the walls were breached, as had happened in one or two instances, the ones that didn't kill themselves were slain by their menfolk.

Given that the Holderkin would only follow precisely the same strategy a second time, it was vanishingly unlikely that the Tedrels would attempt the conquest of the entire country of Valdemar from there. It was far more likely that their plan was to conquer all of Valdemar and then cut off the Holderkin, dealing with them one Holding at a time at their leisure.

"I haven't much else to tell you," Talamir admitted. "Only that they've fallen for our ruse, that they believe we have been beaten down and depleted, and that they are gathering every resource they can for that final campaign."

"ForeSeers?" Alberich asked. He hoped the ForeSeers were

getting something, although his own rogue and unpredictable Gift hadn't even warned him of this news.

Then again—hadn't it? How much of the dread he'd felt these past several moons had been due to his Gift? It didn't always give him visions; sometimes it only gave him warnings.

"The ForeSeers just confirm that the agents are right. But since the decision was evidently made in their council a few days ago, and only just announced to the general troops, I expect that will change." Talamir sounded confident, and he had every right to be.

Mutable and unknowable Future. . . .

Well, perhaps. What the Writ had to say on *that* subject was a matter of philosophy rather than reality—meant more to keep people from closing themselves off to all of the possibilities that free will gave them. And this was particularly true when Karsite Writ met Valdemaran reality, and the Gift of ForeSight—which, often as not, showed *many* futures, not just one.

And if Vkandis really abhorred the knowledge of the future, would he have given me *that particular Gift?* For Alberich, like the Heralds, had used it to change the future he saw for a better one. . . .

He began making calculations in his mind, trying to reckon how long it would take the Tedrels to coax or coerce the Sunpriests into adding Karsite troops to their numbers—or, more likely, come up with more gold and silver—how long it would take to get all the supplies together for such a campaign—establish a base four times larger than any they'd had before—

Then he realized that there were better heads than his who were already working on that very problem, and that their agents-in-place would be able to give Valdemar infinitely better information about what was actually happening than *he* could with what was only speculation. But there was one thing he could and *would* do.

"Two targets, and two only, they will have, should the King and Heir the field take," he told Talamir and Dethor. "Sendar to slay, and Selenay to take or slay. Take Selenay, they would prefer, and sword-wed to—whatever leader survives. It is the *land* they want. Behead the leadership, they must, to take the land. Better still, to behead the leadership, and make all right by wedding the Heir. Live with their neighbors, they must—" *Now* he could deliver his warning, the warning that Geri had delivered to him.

Dethor made a sound like a groan, and Talamir nodded. "Just what I thought, and I told Sendar as much," the King's Own replied bitterly. "But trying to keep *either* of them out of the fight at this point is impossible. Stopping the Tedrels now is going to take everything we have, and Sendar believes that if he and Selenay stay safe in Haven, we will lose the fight before it even begins. If they take the field, there isn't a man or a woman who won't fight better for their presence. And much as I hate to say this, I have to concur."

With a sense of sick agreement, Alberich nodded. The warning had been delivered and heeded, but it clearly would make no difference to the King and Heir. So—

The warning was given to me. Therefore, it is I who must act on it.

"Then this, I can do," Alberich said firmly. "Heralds there will be, and Guards, to shield them in a battle guard. So, to *me*, bring them for training. To make the shield-wall for a King, a special skill is, and each man, his place must know, and know that the right- and left-hand comrade will firmly stand."

"And he has to know how to fill in when the man to his side falls," Dethor seconded grimly. "Alberich's right, Talamir. We haven't had a King go into combat in—glory!—over a century. More, I think; I never was much good at history. We haven't had a battle guard in all that time. *I* don't know the strategy except from books."

"But trained the Sunsguard is, for such a thing," Alberich told them. "Sunpriests, Red Robes, and Archpriests and Hierophants we must guard, if not the Son of the Sun—for into the vanguard they *will* go. When know you Sendar's battle guard, to *me* send them. Selenay's battle guard, *I* will choose. And Selenay's battle guard and bodyguard, *I* will lead. Remain here, I will *not.*" He was slightly appalled to feel his spirits rising a little at the prospect of a fight at last, and something he *could* do. Action, rather than sitting.

But that was just it, really; it was a fight at last. No one could deny him his right to be in the thick of it now. He *would* be the leader of Selenay's battle guard; no one could stop him now.

"So far as the Palace Guard members are concerned, I would just as soon that you chose for both Sendar and Selenay," Talamir said thoughtfully. "You are the best judge of them, since you work with them all the time."

"Then, not solely Palace Guard it will be, but City, too." He honestly didn't think that there would be enough men in the Palace Guard who were young and fit enough to supply what he wanted for two sets of bodyguards. And that wasn't being snide either—so many of the Palace Guard had resigned their posts to serve down South that men who had retired had come out of retirement to fill their places. Those old men were perfectly fit to stand indoor guard duty at a door; if their reflexes were a little slower than in their youth, they had a world of experience to take the place of fast reflexes. They might even be good enough to fight with the army as a whole. But they couldn't march like younger men, couldn't *run* like younger men, and hadn't the stamina that was needed for this job.

"Whatever, whomever you want," Talamir told him. "I'll see to it that you get it. Or him."

"Or her. She-Heralds and she-Guards for Selenay, can I get them, half and half with men," said Alberich, and grinned fiercely to see the surprise on both their faces. "Tcha! *Think,* you! No thanks from the Princess, would there be, for clumsy men in her tent trampling. And with her, they must be sleeping! *And* follow her other elsewheres, that a man should not go!"

"You mean to guard her that closely?" Talamir asked, his face reflecting an interesting mix of shock and approval.

"One man, with a knife, all our efforts can overset," he pointed out to them. "Sendar your charge is, Talamir. Selenay is *mine.* And, say I, guarded she will be in every moment of every night and day. Battle guard there will be, but also bodyguards, will she, nil she, waking and sleeping."

He did not say that he expected Sendar would rebel over being so closely watched and would disregard anything Talamir had to say on the subject. But Selenay would listen and obey his orders once he'd explained them, thanks be to the One God. She wouldn't *like* them, but she'd obey them.

Unlike her father, she could not disregard orders. He could and would have her tied up and locked into a secure tower if he had to. He hoped it wouldn't come to that, but at the moment, he thought he could count on her good sense. Especially when she saw her father being less than sensible.

Tcha. All it takes for a youngling of that *age is to see the parent doing one thing, and it is certain they will try and do the opposite.* How refreshing to have youthful rebellion working for him instead of against him! And perhaps, when *Sendar* saw his daughter being sensible, he would be shamed into sense as well. Not likely, but he could hope.

"You'll want Heralds Keren and Ylsa," Talamir said thoughtfully. "Neither of them will be in the least impressed with rank and birthright; they saw Selenay as a first-year Trainee and helped me whip her into shape."

"Women there are in the City Guard as well—" And he couldn't help the wry smile. "Locasti Perken, Berda Lunge, and Haydee Dellas." His spirit rose a little at the thought of recruiting those three to his bodyguard. Selenay would have to be a deal older and craftier before she could outwit or overawe *them.*

Dethor raised an eyebrow. Talamir chuckled. "Oh, I believe I know those names," the King's Own said, matching

Alberich's smile. "They have night patrol around the Compass Rose and Virgin and Stars, don't they?"

"And just last week frog-marched young Lord Realard back to his father, *then* delivered a lecture to the old man that fair pinned his ears back," Dethor said, with a nod. "Or so I heard."

"Correctly, you heard. Impressed with rank, *they* are not, either." Two Heralds, three City Guards, that made five, and with the addition of a Palace Guardswoman who came to his practices who was called Lotte—if she had a surname, he'd never heard it—that would give him two women at Selenay's side at all times. That would do for close bodyguards; for her battle guards, and Sendar's, he'd want another ten or a dozen. Twenty or twenty-four good fighters; he'd have to think long and hard about *who*. . . .

"These, I need—" he said, rattling off the names; Talamir nodded. "—those six at once. Special training, will they need. The rest, from Palace and City Guard, I will make a list."

"Have it to me in a candlemark," Talamir said, getting to his feet. "Send it by page. I'll have Sendar sign on it. That will cut through any objections. I'll have your six women report in the morning, and the rest to you within the week."

He would have liked it to be sooner, but that was probably the best that could be done. Replacements would have to be found, schedules juggled, and all of that took time.

Time—which was now working against them.

"Selenay, I want as well," he added. "Best it is, that she learn her guards to work with."

"Right," Dethor agreed. "And if we can get Sendar down here to work with his—" He stopped at the grimace that Talamir gave.

"Ask for the moon, and you're more like to get it," the King's Own said grimly. "If he sees his bed for more than four candlemarks in a night *now,* I'll be surprised, so don't expect him to come down here for what's 'only' a little arms practice."

"Then his Companion, we shall have!" Alberich said, in a

burst of inspiration. "One at least of the pair shall we train with!"

:Done, Chosen,: Kantor said instantly.

"And you'll have Taver to stand in for me, because I *must* be with Sendar," said Talamir in the same moment. "That way at least one half of the pairs will get some practice in this."

:The sensible ones,: Kantor said.

Alberich was not disposed to argue with that assessment.

Six women—two in Herald's Whites, three in City Guard blue, and one in the darker, near-midnight blue that marked the Palace Guard—stood at attention before Alberich. Three of the six were older than he by three or four years, and were probably at least as tough. But there was not a jot less than honest deference in their expression, and though all six of them looked sober, they did not look anxious. That was good; it meant that they trusted him, his competence, and his orders.

"You six have I selected, as Selenay's bodyguards," he told them. "Two each for each of three watches, day and night. Her side, you will not leave, while on watch, ever."

He saw the two Heralds exchange a glance; noticed a slight frown of concentration on Lotte's face.

"Now will I ask, how paired you wish to be, and which watch you wish to take," he continued. "Sensible you are, and know you that no less honor there is, for the night watch than the day."

"If it's all the same to you, I *think* Ylsa and I ought to be on day watch," Herald Keren spoke up. "Selenay will have to be in on all of the battle plans and councils and the like, and—well, not to be rude, but Heralds will just blend in with the background."

Meaning, no one will object to Heralds being there, when some of the highborn might complain to see City Guard, particularly women that they might have seen hauling their erring sons home drunk.

"Objections?" Alberich asked, looking at the other four, who shook their heads.

"That splits the night with us," said Berda. "I'll tell you what, if it's all the same to you two, I'm used to the late hours after the taverns close, and I know that Haydee and 'Casti are on—*were* on—first night watch. Lotte, think you could handle the dawn watch with me?"

The Palace Guardswoman shrugged. "It'll take me a bit to get adjusted, but I'll manage."

Well, that sorted itself out painlessly. "Make it so," he told them. "And once satisfied I am that your business you know, those watches you will take at Selenay's side."

"Whether or not we're still in Haven?" Herald Ylsa asked, looking surprised.

"Whether or not. Used to your presence, I wish her to be. Invisible, I wish *you* to be."

Nods, no objections. "What do you want us to do that we haven't done before?" asked Lotte.

He proceeded to show them.

They were used to fighting back-to-back, but *not* when in charge of someone incapacitated, or someone who needed to be kept in cover. They needed to learn how to find safe exit routes, at least two, the moment they entered a room or a situation. They had to practice defensive, rather than offensive, fighting. And later, he would teach them quick rescue techniques, how to dash in and grab the Heir if someone had snatched her, while she was still within reach. Even if that someone had a knife to her throat. The time to get her away was *not* after she was in enemy territory. He hoped that at least one of each pair was a good shot; one of the best ways to rescue someone who was kidnapped was to shoot her in the leg. Someone who had to be carried became doubly hard to take.

But he thought he would save *that* lesson for a time when Selenay wasn't with them.

By midmorning, Selenay had joined them. She was not at all happy about having bodyguards *all* the time, but she was reasonable about it. The same could not be said for her father, according to the terse report he got from Kantor.

But *Alberich* didn't have to deal with her father. That was Talamir's problem, not his.

He was just pleased that his six women were quick studies, a little quicker than he'd hoped, actually. The three from the City Guard were especially adept in defensive strategies, perhaps because of their riot training. Students, crowds of layabouts and troublemakers, and drunks in fair season sometimes turned into mobs, and the City Guards and constables were trained to deal with a mob in every manifestation, whether cheerful and manic or surly and destructive.

The two Heralds had their own set of valuable skills, especially suited to their day watch, in no small part because they were used to letting their eyes skim over a crowd, looking for someone or something that was subtly *wrong.* The two Heralds would have their Companions to help, of course—and the Companions made another good reason to have them on day watch. No one assassin, not even a group of three to six, could get past two Heralds and *three* Companions. And the possibility of getting a group of strangers past sentries and guards and other sharp-eyed sorts by day was vanishingly small.

By night—well, it was possible, but it would have to be very well coordinated, and the number of approaches to get at Selenay would be limited. So once Selenay joined them, Alberich concentrated on escapes—how to get *her* to where her Companion could reach her, for once she was mounted, she was probably safe. Safer, anyway. Her Companion could get her out of reach of *anything* that anyone could use at night, for distance weapons would be severely limited by limited visibility. Night watch did have a different problem, for Selenay would be asleep part of the time. The three City Guards solved that problem for him, though, because they were perfectly used to manhandling semiconscious bodies. Even if Selenay was somehow drugged and couldn't be awakened, with a little luck, they'd be able to get her out of harm's way.

"We won't eat or drink anything we haven't brought with us," they told him, before he even asked. "And we won't eat *or* drink at the same time. That way even if someone's somehow managed to get to our grub, *one* of us will be able to see that something's wrong."

He was quite satisfied with their progress when he dismissed them at the end of the first day. The bones were there of a good set of three pairs of bodyguards and a first-class set of battle guards. Even Selenay was impressed, and had worked as hard as they did, in a role that did *not* come naturally to her—that of hiding behind others and allowing someone else to take care of her.

Lotte was the last to leave, and she helped him to clean up the salle before she did. As the door closed behind her, he sat down on a bench in the salle, suddenly feeling exhausted. It had been a long, long day.

The salle was silent, except for the sounds he made himself. The last blue light of dusk came in through the clerestory windows up above and reflected off the mirrors behind him. He unbuckled the straps of his armor with fingers that ached from holding tightly to sword and dagger, and winced at the occasional bruise.

Training the battlefield guards—ah, that would be another question. He'd thought long and hard about it, and had decided to go with a mix of half Heralds, and half Guardsmen, and had given the list to Talamir last night.

He would head up the group around Selenay, and Talamir would be the commander of Sendar's group. The *most* experienced fighters he chose for Sendar's guards, because on the battlefield, the Tedrels that came after Sendar would be going in for the kill. The ones after Selenay would be handicapped as they would be trying to capture, not kill, so they would hold back somewhat. His people would have no such compunction against *them.*

And he rather expected that Selenay, once she saw fighting, would be eager to stay *out* of it. Not that he doubted her courage. . . .

But she was a young and sensitive person, and battlefields were horrors. *He* was sickened by them, and he was hardened to the death and carnage. Once she got her first taste of real fighting, she should be perfectly willing to stay at the rear of the battle lines with the commanders.

Alberich was not as sanguine about keeping Sendar out of the thick of the fighting.

But then, again, that was *not* his job. It was Talamir's, and if the King's Own couldn't manage it, no one could. Certainly not Alberich, the foreigner, for to some, perhaps unconsciously even to the King, that was an issue. No matter how people felt about him consciously, somewhere down deep inside, the moment he opened his mouth—

:Perhaps if you worked on your grammar,: Kantor suggested.

:Indeed. In my infinite leisure time,: he retorted as he pulled off the armor he'd worn to protect himself. He had been the "assassin" for all of this practice, and as such, had worked harder than all of them combined. He was in good condition, as good as he'd ever been, but—ah, it had been a hard day, as well as a long one.

At least he'd been too busy to think, too busy to worry.

Today he had neglected all of the Trainees, leaving poor Dethor and a couple of the older Trainees to conduct lessons themselves. Tomorrow he would have to do the same.

And the day after, and the day after that—

He sagged down on the bench, suddenly, with an overpowering sense of guilt. He was *supposed* to be Dethor's Second, to take the burden of all of this off of the old man. *:Ah, Kantor, what am I going to do?:* he asked plaintively. *:I can't be in two places at once—:*

:And if you were not here, who would be teaching the Trainees? And who would have seen to it that Selenay had bodyguards? And who would be drilling the King and Heir's battlefield escorts?: Kantor replied. Someone else, of course. Dethor, and someone else. Someone who wouldn't have Alberich's experience.

Someone else—if he could figure out *who* that someone else might have been, maybe he could recruit him (her?) to train the Trainees.

:This last lot of Trainees won't see fighting,: he said, after a moment. *:We've put everyone who is even remotely ready into Whites by now, but there're still the ones that are a year away from becoming full Heralds. There must be a dozen of them, and I've personally taught* all *of them from the time they came in as Trainees; I can put* them *to teaching the younglings, while Dethor supervises.:*

:Good answer,: Kantor approved.

:And I can see to it that Dethor stays here, no matter how much he wants to go South with the full army,: he decided, clenching his jaw. *:He'll fight me on it, but if the King orders him to stay, then no matter what happens to me, there will still be a Weaponsmaster at the Collegium.:*

:He won't like that, but it's a sensible course of action.: Kantor sighed. *:Mind, all he has to do is try* one *night in a tent to know that he'd only be a handicap and a liability. One night spent in something other than a warm bed would leave him a cripple.:*

By that, Alberich knew that Kantor and the other Companions were already plotting ways to get Dethor to make the experiment. Quietly, of course. Without anyone else knowing, of course. There was no point in embarrassing the old man.

:Or hurting his feelings.:

:Good answer,: Alberich replied, and levered his own stiff, sore body up off the bench. A hot soak, something to eat, and then— *:Do you think I'd be allowed to sit in on any strategy sessions?:* he asked. Perhaps he wasn't a great general, but there was only one way to get that expertise, and that was to watch an expert in the craft of war.

:Just slip in and stay in the background, and we'll see to it that no one notices you,: Kantor replied.

Well! That was interesting.

And he'd better take advantage of it.

He limped toward the door to his shared quarters. It was going to be a long night.

The first of many, he suspected.

:The first of many,: Kantor agreed. *:But it won't be alone, Chosen. Never alone.:*

Talamir clenched his jaw and told himself that it wasn't wise to contemplate strangling his King.

He sat, rather stiffly, in the armchair that Sendar had nodded him toward. He knew that chair of old. It was seductively comfortable, and it was supposed to make him relax. He wasn't going to allow it to.

And he wasn't going to strangle his King. "Sendar," he said instead, "I am fully aware that you are an accomplished King and leader, *and* under most circumstances you are perfectly able to defend yourself, but may I be bold and point out to you that you can neither remain awake from now until this war is over, nor can you do everything that you refuse to delegate, even though there are plenty of your humble servants who are perishing for something constructive to do. *Therefore* you can resign yourself to the fact that you *will* have to sleep, now and again and *will* require bodyguards while you do so, and you *will* have to learn how to delegate." He took a deep breath and waited for the inevitable reaction.

The King growled under his breath; something inaudible, but it sounded unflattering.

"Furthermore," Talamir persisted, "if you intend to persuade your daughter to put up with *her* bodyguards, you are going to have to set her a good example."

"That," Sendar said, clearly and distinctly, "is blackmail."

"The blackest," Talamir agreed. "It's also the truth."

He neglected to tell the King that he had pointed out the converse to his Heir. If each of them thought that the good example she (or he) was setting was the reason for the *other* behaving in a sensible fashion, it would make everyone's job much easier.

Although Sendar looked sullenly at him (recalling to Talamir's mind the rebellious adolescent that he'd been as a Trainee), he nodded. "All right. I'll accept the bodyguards. But I want to train with them," he said stubbornly.

"I don't think you're going to have a choice in the matter. I believe Alberich was going to insist on it." Talamir had the satisfaction of seeing surprise on the King's face. "He's a very thorough fellow, is Alberich. He realized immediately that having a bodyguard doesn't do you a great deal of good if someone attacks you, and you don't know what to do but they *do.* The wrong move could put you in as much danger as if you didn't have them at all."

"Selenay—" Sendar began, and was interrupted by his daughter walking into the room.

"Selenay *has* been training with her bodyguards," she said, flinging herself down into a chair with a groan and a wince. Talamir noticed that her hair was wet. She must have just come from the bathing room. "Six of them! And the so-gentle Alberich promises that it's going to get harder from here. I have, in the course of the afternoon, been thrown to the ground, thrown *onto* Caryo's back, hauled about like a sack of wheat, and taught how to dive for all manner of cover. Not to mention done just a trifle of fighting practice myself. I'm quite looking forward to facing the Tedrels; they can't be worse than this."

Talamir decided not to disabuse her of that notion. He just caught Sendar's eye and nodded. Sendar grimaced.

"Well, I'll be doing the same tomorrow," the King said, to Talamir's pleasure. "Though how I'm to squeeze more hours into the day, I do not know."

"I've already told you, and done so repeatedly. By putting the Council meetings and any other business that is not directly concerned with the war into the hands of your Seneschal," Talamir told him, with a little heat, because he had been advising this very move for months now. "That is what he is there for. You can't be two places at once, and if we don't win this thing, there won't *be* a Valdemar for you to reign over! Your Seneschal is competent, unflappable, and far better at obfuscation than you are. If it's something he *can't* do, he is supremely good at stalling things until you have the leisure to deal with it, and what is more, he knows to a nicety what he can and cannot do. Delegate, Sendar! How many times do I have to repeat that?"

Sendar shook his head. "I don't—" he began, then shrugged. "I will. But—"

"And don't tell me that you don't like it," Talamir snapped, deciding to show his King and friend the edge of his anger. After all, Sendar wasn't the only person in the Kingdom who was doing things he didn't "like."

"I won't," Sendar replied, in a way that told Talamir that this was exactly what he *had* been going to say. "What else do you want me to put on my plate?"

"A speech. You're going to have to tell the people—of Haven, at least—what's coming. And I've never been the speechmaker that you are." That was *certainly* something that needed doing that only Sendar could handle. "I can't write it, and I certainly can't deliver it."

"A speech." Sendar sighed. "Yes, that will have to be me.

Selenay, I advise you that when you take the throne, find someone else to write the speeches for you."

"I think not," she replied, so somberly that both Talamir and her father shot a look at her. "Speeches aren't just something that we deliver, as if we were mere actors. They have to come from our hearts, father, and there has to be truth in them. If they don't resonate from inside us, and they don't have truth behind them, how can we ever expect people to believe in us and what we say?"

They both focused on her at once. It wasn't so much with astonishment as—unanticipated pleasure. She sounded like an adult. She *was* an adult. And she sounded like someone who had learned all the right lessons from her father.

She returned their looks gravely. "Platitudes might satisfy for a short time, father—but soon or late, the people will realize they are being fed form without substance. What I tell them must be the truth, and I must believe it, and I must hold to it. That is what you have taught me. I have learned far more from you than that, but that is one of the important things you have taught me by your example."

He nodded, and so did Talamir. *:She knows. We've done our job, haven't we?:* he asked Taver.

:We have. She may not yet have all the skills, but she has the spirit and the heart. Skill will come with time.:

Now—if they could just be certain of *having* the time. . . .

ALBERICH stood behind Selenay's chair in an attitude that was a hair less than rigid attention. That slight degree of relaxation, he had noticed, tended to make peoples' eyes slide right over him. He had taught Selenay's Six (as they were calling themselves) that same trick; it was very useful to be ignored, especially for a bodyguard. The fact that he was in Whites rather than his own distinctive gray leathers was helpful there; people didn't *notice* that it was the infamous Alberich there because they didn't expect to see *him* in Whites.

Talamir *would* have been standing the same guard behind Sendar's seat, except that he had his own seat on the Council; in this case, his place had been taken by Herald Jadus. Jadus managed to look as if he was no more than an interested bystander, and his guileless expression reinforced that impression. If one didn't know better—and only a few people *did*—one might well assume that was the case.

Jadus was something of a surprise to Alberich. He would have expected the Bard-turned-Herald to be one of the lot remaining behind at the Collegium, not skilled enough in warfare to be of any use in the coming fight. He would never have guessed that Jadus was as grimly determined to strike his own blow against the enemies of Valdemar as any Guardsman, nor suspected that Jadus was a deadly swordsman. His skill with a blade was not something that had come to light until recently, as he had been out on circuit all this time. Dethor had remembered it since he had trained Jadus himself; he was the one who had recommended Jadus as one of Sendar's bodyguards.

There was an interesting twist to his talent with a blade; Jadus fought with a light rapier rather than the commoner broadsword, but such a weapon was much more useful in a situation of close combat. Useful, too, within four walls, or any other crowded situation. Dethor had called Jadus in to work with Alberich, and both of them had immediately suggested that Talamir assign Jadus as one of the King's six personal guards. The more Heralds they had in *those* positions, the better. Sendar was more likely to listen to a Herald than a Guardsman. Not that the King was "likely" to listen to anyone if their advice went against something he felt strongly about, but a Herald was more likely than anyone else to get him to stop and think before he acted.

But Jadus was not the only surprise; another of Sendar's bodyguards was a Healer. In fact, it was the same MindHealer, Crathach, who had mediated the transfer of all of those memories from Alberich to the four spies.

Crathach was also a wicked bladesman, although he favored a two-handed style with knives instead of longer weapons, and his skill was such that he had been able to teach Alberich a trick or two. *He* came to Alberich himself to demonstrate his skills, and volunteer his services at something besides Healing. "You don't want a Healer angry at you," he'd said, when Alberich questioned him on whether he could bring himself to kill with those knives. "A Healer knows how you're put together, and what will hurt the most. I've been working with the severely wounded ever since all this started—" his eyes had glinted, "—and this Healer is very, very angry at the Tedrels."

Alberich often wondered just what had made Crathach, a Healer, into someone who could say that and look Alberich straight in the eyes while doing so. But he of all people understood a wish to keep one's past private, and unless Crathach volunteered the information, *he* was not going to ask. He probably hadn't expected to be made one of the King's personal bodyguards, but he adapted immediately. And Alberich was not at all unhappy about having someone who was *also* a Healer serving as a bodyguard. Especially a MindHealer, who had ways of dealing with a King who was reluctant to rest when he needed to.

It was a convenient assignment, to have the Healer taking the latest of the two night watches, along with one of Sendar's former squires, knighted just after Alberich had come to the Collegium. The lad had then been sent by his father on some mission or other, and hadn't come back to Haven until a few moons ago. Alberich had anticipated a certain amount of trouble from that one, but all he'd gotten was respect. Evidently the young buck had gotten some of the arrogance knocked out of him. . . .

Just as well; any arrogance the young bucks of Valdemar still had was about to get knocked out of all of them, and for some of them, the experience would be fatal. The less arrogance, the better the chance at surviving until all this was over.

What Sendar and Talamir and the Lord Marshal were doing at this meeting was to give the rest of the Council a thorough briefing on absolutely everything that they had all learned—from spies, FarSeers, ForeSeers, and anyone else whose word they thought was trustworthy.

The Tedrels were in the process of establishing their final

base for attack just across the Border in Karse, and the size of it made Alberich grow cold all over. So far they had done nothing *but* prepare; it was not yet a campaign, much less a war, and that did not bode well either. This was to be an invasion, and as such, the preparations were being taken with all of the care that decades of detailed planning could insure.

They had been working toward this moment for—well, years, decades, at least. Alberich had known better than to hope that their focus had diminished over the years. Their shock troops might be a combination of the dregs of the mercenary trade, criminals who sought sanctuary in their ranks, and whatever young men they could recruit with promises of adventure, excitement, and easy money, but the core was the Tedrel nation, whose longing for a new homeland had only strengthened, the longer that they went without a home.

If anything, the increase had been exponential with the land of Valdemar in their sight. The bitterness of those thrown out of their homeland by their enemies had been distilled by the years. Now it was as much of a weapon as the swords, spears, and arrows in the hands of the army.

And they had done something very clever this final season; Karse was used to their strategy of making a base from which they could strike into Valdemar, and didn't think twice about it when, once again, the Tedrel commanders had set about establishing yet another. But this time, with the Karsites lulled into complacency, they had built up their own troops and established a base that could be used equally well to strike at Valdemar *or* Karse, then made it clear to their erstwhile allies that they did not particularly care if further aid was delivered voluntarily or wrested from the Sunpriests by force. The Sunpriests must have been shocked to discover the monster they themselves had created, sitting on their doorstep, not to be budged, reasoned with, or countered, demanding that it be fed, and fed royally.

That much, Alberich and the others knew from the spies.

And although he could not know this for certain, he was fairly sure that the Karsite treasury had been emptied, literally and completely, into the Tedrel coffers until even the rapacious maw of their army was sated. Shocked and dismayed, utterly undone and perhaps in a panic when they realized the position they had put themselves in, their first thought would be of self-defense. The coffers could be refilled, but if the Tedrels came in force to take what they wanted, they probably wouldn't stop with taking the gold and silver in the treasury—they would go on to help themselves to the personal treasures of the high-ranking priests . . . at the very least.

Supplies, the lifeblood of an army, were pouring in. And the means to transport those supplies, just as important, were not lacking either. If there was a cart or a beast in all of Karse that was not in the hands of the Tedrels, it was not for lack of money or effort. Trade had slowed to a crawl as carters, draymen, and teamsters flocked to make a small army of their own in the ranks of the Tedrels. Merchants couldn't find anyone to carry their goods; farmers were having to transport their own foodstuffs to market. The silver lure held out to recruit these notoriously independent souls was augmented by the guarantee that they would be sacrosanct, that no one could or would force them into the ranks of the soldiery. *They* would not fight; *they* would be guarded by fighters. The supply lines would roll, fat and heavy with everything the Tedrels needed. *This* time they would not plunder the countryside because they had to; they would not need to worry about living off the land.

Although Sunsguard soldiers did *not* go into the ranks of the Tedrel forces, there had been movement toward the Border, and now they had formed a line of defense on either side of the Tedrel base, ensuring that the Tedrels could not be flanked, at least on the Karsite side of the Border.

Brilliant. It was all brilliant. He couldn't fault their strategy.

Or their patience. They had waited all this time for their

golden opportunity, and they were clearly not going to ruin that opportunity by forgetting that patience now. The Tedrels would move when the Tedrels were ready; not before, and not a candlemark later.

Talamir and the Lord Marshal were revealing all of this to the Council now. It was new to most of them, but only because they hadn't been paying attention. It wasn't as if they hadn't been *warned,* over and over again, that the Tedrels were going to keep coming at Valdemar until it fell, or they were destroyed and dispersed.

Alberich couldn't fathom it. It was as if the moment that the Tedrels retreated in the fall, the members of the Council forgot they existed and would be back in the spring. True, there were plenty of pressing concerns, but none, to his way of thinking, as the inevitability of the Tedrels making that final push. Perhaps, in the back of their minds, they hoped that eventually the Tedrels would give up and go away. After all, they had never yet won so much as a thumbnail's worth of Valdemaran land. But if that were so, then all of the things that all of the spies and ForeSeeing Heralds and historians had been telling them had just gone right past them without being believed.

If they'd been paying as much attention as they should have been to all of the reports that Talamir had given them over the last few moons, they would know most of this. On the other hand, the fact that it was all coming as a horrible surprise was going to work in Sendar's favor. The Council could—and would, as Talamir and Sendar worked together like a pair of clever shepherd dogs—be stampeded into granting Sendar whatever he wanted.

One of those things was Alberich—no longer kept back in the shadows, ostensibly no more than a closely watched underling. Sendar wanted Alberich in the thick of things, at his or Selenay's side, seeing and hearing everything that was most important, most secret. This greater danger would make the members of the Council forget where Alberich came from and remember only the uniform, the quiet work on the seamy underside of Haven, the invaluable help in placing agents in Karse. And presumably, there would be no further objection to Alberich's presence wherever Sendar wanted him.

Granting him authority—well, that was another question altogether. Alberich didn't really need or want overt authority; he had all he could handle covertly.

But he *would* get, by virtue of being Selenay's most visible bodyguard, complete access to every strategy session. No one would think twice about it. If he really saw something important, and knew there was something that needed to be said, it would be said through Selenay, or Talamir, or even Sendar himself.

Ah, the advantage of being a Mindspeaking Herald. . . .

:I think that the position of being behind the Powers that Be suits you better, anyway,: Kantor observed.

:Why? So that no one has to look at my face?: he asked sardonically.

Kantor pretended to be shocked. *:Why, Chosen—was that a* joke *I just heard?:*

:As you know, I have no sense of humor,: Alberich responded. *:Now, hush, I want to see just how hysterical the Council members get when Sendar talks about the leaks of what should have been Council information. And how much of it is feigned.:*

Because he had some suspicions that there were a few—a very few, no more than two or three—members of the Council who were not as tight-lipped as they should have been. He didn't suspect any of them of sending information to the enemy *themselves,* but rather, that they gossiped about Council doings to others. They probably thought that their friends and cronies were trustworthy enough—if they actually thought at all, which was doubtful. These highborn Valdemarans seemed to take it as read that *none* of their friends, or their friends' friends, could *possibly* be untrustworthy, and never mind heaps of evidence to the contrary. . . .

And never mind all of the political infighting that went on between factions.

That was probably where leaks were happening, and not an overt traitor. Of course, all of this chattering made them feel very important and in the know, and their friends would be feeding them information *back* so that in their turn, they could impress the rest of the Council members with their knowledge and insight. *They* thought it was harmless, and in any other situation than the one they all found themselves in now, it would have been. But now, such loose-lipped behavior was nothing like harmless. Even without the Tedrels on the Border, there were other hazards, outside and inside of Valdemar, that could (and probably did) use this information to the detriment of poor, ordinary folk.

So Alberich was paying very close attention to the reactions of the Councilors, and he wasn't at all happy with what he saw.

Lord Gartheser. He was oh! so very concerned, shocked, dismayed, and he was acting, Alberich was certain of it. Gartheser headed up a faction that had been particularly nasty about Alberich's presence among the Heralds, but Alberich wouldn't have held a grudge if they hadn't been so underhanded about their opposition. Still, he'd have given Gartheser the benefit of the doubt—

Not with that bit of overacting. Gartheser was up to something. Gartheser knew more than he should. And where had he gotten that information?

:Hmm. Unfortunately, Sendar's old playfellow Orthallen is in Gartheser's coterie. . . . : That was Kantor, who actually knew far more about these people than Alberich did, which was saying a great deal. The Companions had their own information tree, which was as flourishing as any gossip vine in the Court, and was far more accurate.

Alberich suppressed a grimace. That wasn't good. Lord Orthallen, a few years older than Sendar, had been kind to Sendar when the King was a lonely child in the Court, before he'd been Chosen. Now, Alberich was fairly well certain that the *only* reason the adolescent Orthallen had been kind to and protective of the grubby little child Sendar had once been was because he'd had an eye to the main chance, even then. But you couldn't persuade Sendar of that, and as a consequence, as a child, he had made Orthallen into his hero, and as an adult, his close friend and compatriot. Orthallen had extraordinary access to the Royals for someone who wasn't a Herald. In fact, it was virtually a certain thing that Orthallen was going to get the Council seat soon to be vacated by Lord Tholinar.

Alberich liked Orthallen even less than Gartheser. Lord Gartheser was just pigheaded and prejudiced and interfering. He wanted things *his* way, he didn't trust anyone who wasn't highborn, and he wasn't entirely certain even of those jumped-up commoner Heralds. But although he despised Alberich, he didn't mean any harm. And though he probably had friends who were not at all trustworthy, there was no way yet to prove that to him. To give him the benefit of the doubt, Alberich was fairly certain that if anyone could bring Gartheser proof of his friends' iniquity, there was no doubt that he would drop them without hesitation.

Orthallen, on the other hand. . . .

Well, Alberich had no real evidence against the man, other than the evidence of his feelings. Or perhaps, his Gift. Either way, there was *something* about Orthallen that put his back up, like a cat scenting a snake. He had no evidence against the man, and nothing other than his instincts to go on, but—

:But I agree with you. There is something altogether ruthless about my Lord Orthallen. As if he doesn't care who or what is ruined so long as he comes out with what he wants.:

Now that was an interesting observation, coming from a

Companion. Was this purely Kantor's feeling, or did he have some other source of information? *:What if you hooved fellows conspire to keep Orthallen safely occupied with something else? Do you think you could organize that?:*

:I can try, but I'm not a miracle worker. The most difficult part is that no one seems to see anything wrong with Orthallen but me and thee.: Kantor sounded discouraged, as well he should. *:My fellow Companions don't* like *him either, but that could be only because he doesn't really like our Chosen.:*

:Then thee and me will have to do what we can.: Among a thousand other things. . . .

He pulled his attention back to the Council meeting, and was pleasantly surprised to see that the Council members, after their initial shock, were actually pulling things together. Surprised? No—astonished. He truly hadn't thought they would bury their differences and get straight down to working together, burying feuds and sparring and jockeying for power so quickly—

But they were! The horseshoe-shaped table buzzed with half a dozen overlapping conversations, as the Councilors dropped their political differences and settled down to the task at hand. Sendar somehow kept track of it all; Selenay just kept track of who was in need of a page, of writing materials, or just another pitcher of drink. As the time candles burned down, Selenay sent more pages for food and drink, while the Council organized and coordinated the resources of their territories, Guilds, crafts, and associations. They were tallying up what could be brought down South immediately, what could be collected in a fortnight or a moon, what could be spared, and how much could be done and still leave just enough left to keep everyone from starving to death over winter, and no more. Because now, finally, they *all* realized that even if the entire kingdom was left impoverished, that ruthless stripping of resources still had to be done in the face of the enormous threat that the Tedrels posed. Finally, *finally,* they understood. And at least now that they understood, they were prepared to act, and act swiftly, with no argument. The shock over, they were showing their mettle. Even Lord Gartheser.

"Better hungry and cold than dead and cold," said Lady Donrevy grimly. That seemed to sum up everyone's feelings.

Not before time, but at least it was *in* time. Alberich settled his face into a mask of indifference. It was time for him to observe, and nothing more. As the candlemarks passed, the daylight faded, and pages brought and took away laden and empty platters and pitchers, he watched and listened.

His time to act would come later.

"No, and no, and *no!*"

Selenay was in a temper; losing patience with her maidservant entirely, she pulled the useless gowns out of the traveling chest, wadded them up, and threw them on the floor. She did *not* want the creature to try and foist the blasted things off on her again.

"I will *not* take those gowns, or *these* gowns, or any gowns *at all!*" she snapped, as the maid snatched the dresses up with an expression of shock and offense, and smoothed them hastily. Selenay felt a pang of guilt over the crumpled and wrinkled state of the delicate white silks and satins, raimes and linens—but not enough to show that she felt any guilt. "How many times must I tell you? I'm going to a *battlefield,* not a fete, a ball, a state visit, or a festival!"

"But, Highness, you will be surrounded by highborn young men!" the maid protested indignantly. "Your Highness cannot possibly wish to appear the hoyden—"

Great good gods! What part of "battlefield" doesn't she understand? Selenay suppressed a groan, and wondered what demon had possessed her to accept this foolish woman as her personal servant.

Because Uncle Lord Orthallen sent her to me, of course. And now I can't dismiss her because he'd feel as if he'd let me down. And I did need a proper lady's maid, one that knows about hairdressing and all that sort of thing. . . .

Unfortunately, the creature did *not* know about Heralds, nor did she care. She cared only about the trappings of rank, the care of gowns, the importance of self-importance, and she could not seem to fathom that there was another set of duties of the Princess and Heir that went far beyond looking handsome, attracting a husband of suitable rank, and following the appropriate court etiquette. Yes, she was sheer genius when it came to dressing well and looking exquisite. But that was all she was good for. On the whole, the woman was far more hindrance than help, especially now, and finally Selenay sent her on a fool's errand into the attics just to get rid of her, knowing that *she* would be packed and gone long before the woman got back.

Then she did something she would normally *never* have done. She pulled out everything the maid had packed, and *tossed* it out, all over the furniture, the floor, wherever it happened to fall when she dumped the packs. The maid could do something useful for a change when she returned; she could pick it all up, see that the gowns were pressed and brushed, sort out all the hairdressing nonsense and cosmetics, and put it all away. Selenay could braid her hair by herself very well, and the only "cosmetic" she was likely to use "out there" was soap.

With the maid out of the way, it took just over a quarter of a candlemark for Selenay to pack. It wasn't difficult, she'd learned how to pack for the field long ago, and had watched her friends as they packed up to go out countless times. Wistfully, she had watched them then; she had known it wasn't possible for *her* to go, but she had wanted to, so badly.

Well, now she was going; and she didn't want to. Alberich probably thought that she would be excited about being in the front lines, and anticipate being in the thick of fighting, right up until she got her first real look at it, and only *then* would she lose her taste for war. He was wrong. She had already lost her taste for war, and she knew far more about it than she thought he realized. She had been making it her business to visit the wounded in the House of Healing ever since all this began, to thank them. They seemed to appreciate her attention, though why, she couldn't imagine. Maybe it was just that for most of them, it was their first (and probably last) close-up look at one of the royals.

Well, she knew first-hand what war *really* meant, and she was absolutely terrified. And was not, under any circumstances, going to show it.

She rang for a servant to help her with her trunks, but carried two of her packs herself. And she outdistanced the poor servants in her haste to get down to the stables. Probably she should have waited for an escort of Guardsmen, but she didn't have time. And if she wasn't safe at this moment, with the Palace and grounds alive with Guards, Heralds, and the last of the regiments to leave Haven, she would never be safe anywhere.

She popped out of the nearest door onto the courtyard in front of the Palace, a place that was normally quiet and empty at this time of the morning. Not this morning. . . .

The sun was just above the horizon, a sliver of red in a dusky sky; the air was a little damp, with dew slicking the cobbles rimming the pavement and birds filling the air with their morning calls. It seemed too beautiful a morning to be riding out to war.

The courtyard was awash in white: white Companions, Heralds in their white field uniforms. Selenay fit right in; her uniform was not a whit different from theirs. That was a conscious decision. There was nothing about their clothing to distinguish her or her father from the other Heralds. Of course, the moment she crossed the threshold she was joined by her two shadows, the Heralds Keren and Ylsa, who fell in behind her casually, as if they were just a couple of her best friends who'd been waiting for her to come out. She greeted them with a tense smile, and then spotted Caryo, already saddled and bridled with field tack, waiting with Keren and Ylsa's Companions, who were completely ready, saddle packs and all.

Her father was already in the saddle, but she saw with a touch of relief that she was by no means the last to arrive. It didn't take long for her to sling her basic field packs across Caryo's rump and fasten them in place; less time to get into the saddle herself. Her remaining packs and trunks would go on the wagons carrying the rest of the supplies, with her tent and her father's.

Caryo (with Selenay's two shadows in close, but unobtrusive attendance) moved to Sendar's side without prompting. The King nodded an acknowledgment to his daughter but didn't stop reading the dispatch he'd just been handed. He held out his hand and a page on horseback slapped a graphite stick into it; he scrawled a reply on the same paper and held out his hand again. The page slapped a pre-inked seal stamp into it, which he impressed across his signature. He blew on the ink to dry it and rolled it up; this time he handed it to the dark-haired, somber-faced Herald who'd brought it to him, who in turn slipped it into a message tube.

Then the Herald held the tube up at eye-level, frowning at it. One moment he held the tube, the next, his hands were empty. *He* looked a bit pale for a moment, but recovered quickly; Sendar slapped him on the shoulder.

"Well done," was all the King said, but the young man smiled, blushed, and backed his Companion off to rejoin his fellows.

The young fellow was a Herald with the Fetching Gift, of course; either he, or a Mindspeaking Herald, had told Talamir that there was a message, probably from the front, that needed a written answer. The Fetching Herald had brought it in a heartbeat, and sent it back again in the same amount of time.

Now, with this all-or-nothing war to be fought, the Heralds truly showed how invaluable they were; in fact, without them, Valdemar would have no advantage over the Tedrels at all. Heralds who were Mindspeakers rode with scouts and served to relay news, messages, and battle plans. Heralds who were FarSeers spied on the enemy without him even being aware he *was* being spied upon. Heralds with the Gift of ForeSight tried to predict what would come next; the two lone Weather Witches tried to predict when rain would fall on the enemy and when on their own troops. And those with the rare Gift of Fetching sent things to and from their commanders in the distant South.

There were other, even rarer Gifts, which might or might not come into play, depending on circumstances. At the moment, for instance, the only Firestarters in the Heraldic ranks were not very strong, which was—well, some would think it was a pity. Certainly, if they'd had a Firestarter with the strength of the legendary Lavan Firestorm, they would hardly need an army. On the other hand—the finale of the Battle of Burning Pines had very nearly incinerated both the Karsite and Valdemaran armies together. Selenay was just as glad their Firestarter couldn't do much more than ensure campfires from thoroughly soaked, green wood.

The mood was subdued, as the sun rose a little higher, and the dew began to dry. The Companions, unlike horses, were not restive; they stood rock-steady in their appointed places, with little more than the occasional head shake or switching of a tail. The Heralds themselves spoke very little, and only in a murmur. Perhaps most of them were occupied in Mindspeech—certainly Sendar was, for the King had that faraway look that Selenay knew meant he was deep in conversation with someone.

:More likely a series of someones,: Caryo said quietly. *:He's been talking to the others since he woke.:*

Selenay bit her lip; on the one hand, she wished very strongly that her own Gift was powerful enough for her to hear what was going on. On the other hand, she wasn't sure she wanted to know. She was already afraid; if she knew what her father knew—well, she wasn't at all sure that she could keep up the brave face that she *had* to show.

The last of the Heralds to accompany Sendar to the war ran into the courtyard, packs over their shoulders, to finish kitting their Companions and take their places among the rest. When the very last was mounted, Sendar held up his hand, and what little talk there had been ceased entirely.

"You all heard my speech for the people of Haven," he said, his voice sounding rough and tired to Selenay, but strong nevertheless. He squinted into the morning sunlight; there were dark rings under his eyes, and she wondered how much he had slept—if at all. "I won't bore you with repeating it, and besides, none of you need to be told why we are doing this. Before winter comes, some of us will die; many of us will be injured. No less than myself, your King, *you* are primary targets for our adversaries. Our enemy knows very well how important the Heralds are to our strategy, and as you have been aware, he has made it his business in his past campaigns to eliminate as many of you as he could. Only the fact that I have made it *my* business to withhold as many of you from the front lines as I could has kept our losses to a minimum."

Selenay blinked; she hadn't realized that, but of course it was true. It must be. There hadn't been more than four or five Heralds killed in the Wars for each year that there had been fighting! Now she knew why—and knew that Sendar had not been lulled into thinking that the Tedrels would eventually go away. He had believed Alberich, believed the spies, and planned for this from the beginning.

"This is the fight that I have been holding you for," Sendar continued. "Now, in my turn, I am going to ask you for something very, very difficult. You would not be Heralds if you were not perfectly prepared to pay the ultimate price for Valdemar, so I need not ask you for courage. Instead, I ask you for caution."

Caution? Selenay thought, surprised, even a little shocked. She was not the only one; she saw eyes widen, lips purse, and brows furrow among those closest to her.

"You are a finite resource," Sendar continued, turning in his saddle so that he could meet the eyes of everyone near him. "It will take four long years, at a minimum, to replace each one of you, and that assumes that enough younglings will be Chosen to do so. And each and every one of you is desperately needed for our strategies to work. You cannot be spared. So I ask you for caution, care, and to remember that although your duty to Valdemar may mean that you face death—your duty also requires you to live and serve, no matter what the cost to you." His voice took on a hard and implacable tone. "You must and *will* face the fact that there is worse than death on the field of combat, and be just as prepared to live with such a fate as you are willing to die. Valdemar can make use of a blind Herald—or an armless or legless one, and all you need to do is to recall the story of Lavan Firestorm's mentor, Herald Pol, to know that this is true. Valdemar can make use of even a Herald who is confined to a litter with a broken neck. What Valdemar can make *no* use of is a dead Herald."

Selenay swallowed, and wondered what was going through the minds of those around her. She hadn't thought about that. Had any of the others?

She glanced to her left, and found herself looking into the grave and grim visage of Herald Alberich. He gave a slight, tight little nod.

If no one else had, *he'd* thought of that. And probably reminded Sendar of it.

The silence within the courtyard was so profound that the twittering of sparrows in the trees and bushes in the neat boxes around the courtyard seemed loud and intrusive.

"This is no war like any we have ever fought," Sendar continued. "The Tedrels have nothing to lose and everything to gain. If they are defeated by us here, they will have lost their last, best chance at the homeland that is their only goal. They have nowhere to retreat to. After the way they have treated their allies in Karse, the Sunsguard will fall on them and destroy them if they lose. *That,* so Alberich tells me, is the message implied in the two flanking forces along the Border. The Sunsguard will not only prevent us from engaging the Tedrels in a pincer movement across the Karsite Border, it will prevent *them* from coming back into Karse. And never believe that they do not know this. They are probably counting on it to keep their own mercenary shock troops in line and under control."

Oh. Selenay repressed a shiver. *Never corner an enemy who has nothing to lose.* How many times had Alberich drummed *that* into her head? And now the enemy had been *put* into a corner. A bad situation had just gotten infinitely worse.

Sendar paused to let all that sink in. No one moved. No one spoke.

"But *we* have everything to gain by defeating them, and not just for ourselves. When this war is over, and we have defeated the enemy, no one will ever face a single Tedrel Company again, much less the entire nation," Sendar said, into the waiting silence. "They will be *finished,* for all time. And we *will* defeat them!" His voice took on a strength and a surety that suddenly made even Selenay's spirits rise. "We *will* defeat them for although they call themselves, and think of themselves as a nation, they are *not.* They have a body, with no heart. They think that the land is the nation. *We* know better. We know that Valdemar is not the land—and it is not just the people. Valdemar is a spirit, a community of spirit that binds a hundred disparate peoples with a hundred different religions and ways of life into a company and a greater whole. It is not a unity, for that would be denying our diversity, and in our diversity and our tolerance is our strength. Even if this enemy succeeded in driving us from this land—which he will *not*—Valdemar would live on. If he slew all of us—which he will not—Valdemar would live on. That spirit is what you fight for, and will live for, Heralds of Valdemar, for you are at the heart of that spirit—a spirit of tolerance, compassion, understanding and care—all things that our enemy cannot and will never understand. And in the name of that spirit—we *ride!*"

The cheer that rose was as spontaneous as it was heartfelt; Even Selenay felt a cheer bursting out of her throat, and she was so used to the effect that the King's speeches had on people that she had thought herself immune by now. Even grim-faced Alberich was cheering, and his expression had as much of hope in it as she had ever seen. Keren and Ylsa cheered with tears running down their faces, and they weren't the only ones.

Sendar and his Companion surged forward, down the drive that led out the Palace gates, buoyed on the wave of sound, and the rest of the Heralds followed.

And Selenay with them, for once nothing more than another Herald, another weapon, to serve Valdemar to the last of her strength, and even beyond.

THE King and his company of Heralds and bodyguards swiftly outdistanced the baggage train, those Council members who elected to go to the front lines, and the Royal regiment. They would have outdistanced *anything,* as Alberich soon discovered, because they were all mounted on Companions—even the bodyguards, who were being carried as a matter of courtesy by unpartnered Companions. Carried, just like sets of cooperative baggage—because these Companions would not tolerate even the excuse for a bridle that the partnered ones wore. Alberich had known, as a matter of theory, just how swiftly the Companions could cover ground. Now he discovered it as a matter of practice.

They could have been performing a sort of precision drill, for they *all* used a pace that was as fast as a canter, and as smooth as a running walk. So smooth, in fact, that it was perfectly possible to strap oneself into the saddle and doze, if one were tired enough. Their hooves didn't pound, as Alberich had noted before this; they chimed. Not as loud as bells, and not precisely *like* bells, but the effect of so many of them hitting the ground together was a bit unsettling. Like being in the same room as a thousand wind chimes. . . .

Alberich was astonished; it was his first experience of this ability, unique to Companions—

—or to be honest, it was his first *conscious* experience of this ability. Kantor must have used this pace to get him across the Border into Valdemar from Karse.

Now he knew why Dethor had packed his sleeping roll in his saddlepacks and not with his tent. He wouldn't see his tent—or anything else in the baggage train—for days or weeks. Neither would anyone else in this group; they would have to depend on the army for shelter for a while when they got to the front lines. And he supposed that they would have to hope that the weather stayed good on the way. . . .

It didn't matter; Dethor had overseen his packing, and everything he truly needed was with him. He hoped that someone with similar experience had packed for Selenay and the King.

:Selenay and the King already knew how to pack for this sort of trip,: Kantor said, and left it at that.

Once out of the capital, they moved down the road with a purposefulness that was positively frightening. There was no way to properly convey the effect—they weren't *menacing,* but they seemed to exude a sense of needing to go somewhere in a hurry, a sense that somehow made everyone move out of their way without noticing that it was happening. It was uncanny. The first time he saw it working, he felt the hair go up on the back of his neck, and Kantor's wordless reassurance.

This could have looked like some sort of parade, all of the Companions and their uniformed Heralds, with the single spots of Healer Green and Guard Blue among them. It didn't; Alberich could tell by the faces of those who gathered to watch them pass through their towns and villages that they gave no such impression. The expressions that the common folk wore were uniformly grim. Perhaps the people of Haven had not yet grasped the seriousness of the situation, but the people of the towns and villages knew it. There was no cheering, and the hope he saw in their faces was tinged with desperation.

:They know, don't they?: he asked Kantor.

:Better than those in the cities. Everyone knows everyone in a village; when their youngsters go off into the Guard, everyone knows every word in every letter that comes home. And—everyone knows when someone isn't going to come home again.:

Ah. He shifted in the saddle, careful to do so with Kantor's stride so as not to throw him off. Well, that was something he wouldn't know about—letters from the front lines, and a village's interest in them. His mother couldn't have read a letter even if he'd been allowed to send her one from the Academy.

And he remembered, for the first time in a long, long while, the first line of the oath he had sworn when he joined the Academy. *The temple is your mother and your father is Vkandis Sunlord. . . .*

It was still true. Just not in the way that those who had listened to him swear that oath intended.

They stopped for the night around dusk, outside a village—which one, he didn't know; they went past it too quickly for him to read the faded sign in the uncertain light. The Herald in the lead broke off down a side lane and the entire group followed, slowing as they did so. The lane was overgrown, entirely grass-covered, eventually bringing them to a tiny cabin set off in a clearing, with no sign of any inhabitant about it.

:That's because there isn't *an inhabitant. This is one of the Waystations,:* Kantor told him. *:We're two days' journey from Haven at my usual pace; three or four by horse.:*

Feeling stiff, though not as stiff and sore as he had expected, he slowly dismounted. He had read about the Waystations, though he had never seen one. This one, a little stone hut with a thatched roof, looked solid enough, though it wasn't very big. But sheltering no more than two Heralds at a time, and then not for very long, it didn't need to be, he supposed. The walls were thick, and so was the door; there weren't any windows, but inside he saw that the floor was slate, and there was a stone fireplace. It was a better structure than the one he and his mother had shared before she got her job at the inn.

The building itself was given over to Sendar and Selenay as their shelter. Six of the other Heralds returned to the village for provisions, while the rest, Alberich included, made camp and saw to the comfort of their Companions. Even the Guards and Healer Crathach put in the time to groom and feed and water the Companions they rode.

They completely exhausted the stores of food for the Companions in the Waystation bins, but at least there *was* plenty of grazing. It was fully dark by the time the six Heralds who had gone after provisions returned, and by then there were a couple of small fires going, sleeping rolls had been arranged according to friendships or prearrangements—Alberich's would be across the door of the cabin, and the other bodyguards would be in close proximity—and the steady munching of Companions through grass was as loud as the insects and night birds.

Alberich had expected that they would be cooking some sort of communal meal, but what was brought back from the village was both unexpected and touching. The villagers had given up parts of their *own* evening meals to send them to the Heralds on their way to the front lines. Ham, cold chicken, and bread, cheese and fruit, cold boiled eggs, sausage rolls, and sweet cakes, jars of pickles and packets of tea—

Parcel after paper-wrapped parcel came out of the saddlebags and net bags that the six had taken into the village, to be divided equally among the lot of them, Sendar and Selenay taking no precedence in what they got. There was a bit of trading as people swapped items they didn't care as much for, then things quieted down rather quickly.

"Draw straws over who washes up tonight, and who does in the morning," Sendar suggested, as conversation ceased while jaws were otherwise employed. Most everyone was probably as starved as Alberich; they'd all eaten while on the move, taking out provisions that had apparently been packed by Palace servants, since Alberich didn't recall packing the contents of the little bag on the front of his saddle—a paper-wrapped pair of sausage rolls and a skin of cold tea. But it had been candlemarks ago, and it had been a very long day.

Someone collected enough black-and-white beans from the Waystation to equal the number of riders, and put them into a bag. Alberich was not unhappy to find his was a black bean, and when he was done with his ham and pickled beans, joined the queue of those who were cleaning up now. Water straight from the well felt refreshing after the hard and sweaty day of riding; it was going to feel cursed cold in the morning. Sendar and Selenay got black beans as well, and Alberich insisted they go ahead of him. There was method in this; *they* were in the Waystation and probably asleep by the time he finished, and he was able to stretch himself out across the door without worrying that he'd be inconveniencing them. But he wondered, just before he fell asleep, if there was even the faintest likelihood that a village of Karsites would sacrifice portions of their own meals to a troop of Sunpriests and Sunsguard under similar circumstances.

On the whole, he thought not.

The next day followed the pattern of the first, except that they had to stop at midday in a large town and several Heralds went to each tavern and inn in turn to collect meat pies for all of them. Alberich had an idea that he would be heartily tired of meat pies and sausage rolls before the end of their journey . . . but of course, that was the least of his worries, and it was better fare than he'd ever gotten with the Sunsguard.

The contrast between their grim purpose and the placid, lush countryside they rode through could not have been greater. Alberich tried not to look too closely at the folk who came out to see them pass, but he couldn't ignore them altogether, and it wrung his heart to see them—middle-aged men and older, women either *with* children or as old as the old men. There were a great many children and not very many young adults. He knew what that meant. Those that could be spared, were unattached, had no families to support—they were gone. In the army, facing the Tedrels. And who knew if they'd ever return? He saw that in the faces of those that they rode so swiftly past, in the fear they tried not to show.

But if the Tedrels broke through, these same people would be taking up whatever arms they had to defend their lives—or fleeing back up that road to Haven. . . . And try as he might, he could not but help look at those peaceful villages and imagine flames rising above the roofs, and bodies sprawled in the streets.

It was better when they were riding through the countryside. And maybe the others were cursed with the same sort of imagination as Alberich, for their pace seemed to increase, just a trifle, when they were going through a center of population.

So it went, sunrise to sundown, league after league of it, and no end in sight. It almost seemed to him as if he was caught in a peculiar nightmare, riding inexorably toward a dark and dreadful fate.

Selenay had longed for a day when she might ride out like any other Herald, taking to the road with her packs behind her, leaving the Palace and all of the stuffiness of the Court behind. Now that day had come, and she thought—often—that it might have been a good idea if she had never made that particular wish. She would rather have to suffer being laced into a tight gown and listen to dull speeches every day for the rest of her life than face the Tedrels. And it didn't matter that there would be an army between them and her. She was as much afraid for the people she knew, her friends, the people she'd been with as a Trainee, who would *be* in that army, as she was for herself.

What was more, the *reason* why Alberich had assigned bodyguards to her for day and night was real now. She understood that her life was in genuine, serious danger—and worse than just her life. She had learned in several sleepless nights following a long and somber talk with Alberich that there *was* a fate worse than death. The Tedrels had every reason to want to take her alive, and many more reasons to want to make sure that she was alive, and *outwardly* well, but not in possession of her wits anymore. And there were a great many ways to ensure that she wasn't sane once they got hold of her . . . the most obvious being to murder Caryo. She was used to a Valdemar where the King could walk unguarded among his people—but her father wasn't going anywhere without his six shadows either, and that shook her to the core. He no longer trusted his own people—or at least, no longer trusted the ones he didn't personally know. It would have made her weep, if she hadn't been too frightened to cry.

The heavy, leaden feeling of fear increased day by day. It hung over all of them, making conversation stilted and unnatural, punctuating the silences, and making it impossible to *enjoy* the fragrant, picturesque countryside through which they rode. The enforced, close presence of her father, quiet and grave with worry, or absent altogether as he Mindspoke with the Heralds relaying a moment-by-moment summary of what was going on with the enemy and with their own forces, was a greater burden than she allowed him to guess. She couldn't lean on him for comfort, for Alberich and Talamir were right; he was already taking on more than he should. She could only thank all the gods that ever were for Caryo; at least she had someone to turn to, even if that someone couldn't actually do any more than she could. It helped, immeasurably, when in the dark of some Waystation, unable to sleep, she could unburden her heart to another who would understand; and in moments when she could steal away a little, with Keren or Ylsa pointedly *not* looking at her, that she could pretend to groom Caryo and cry into her soft shoulder.

There were times when Selenay wondered if they would *ever* reach the army, but more times when she hoped they never would. So long as they rode, she could put off the day when everything would change. So long as they rode, she was safe, safe as only a Herald in the company of Heralds could be.

So long as they rode, the army had not yet met the enemy, and she could pretend that they never would.

Nevertheless, the Companions, even her beloved friend, carried them inexorably to that confrontation, and it was almost a relief when that day did come. Almost. The waiting might be over, but now she was *here.*

She heard the army long before she saw it; the hum of a city many times the size of Haven transported to the rolling hills of the southland. And long before she heard it, there were other signs of it; provisioning wagons going toward it full and away from it empty, messengers pounding up or down the road.

There were other signs; more ominous signs. The countryside was empty. It was empty, because insofar as it was possible to get the people to leave, it had been evacuated. There wasn't a sheep on the hillsides, or a farmer in the fields. The fields that no longer held sheep *did* hold something else, grazing on the rich, emerald grass, grass that the Tedrels desired for their own herds. The horses, the oxen, the mules of the army grazed there—not the horses of the cavalry, which were kept within the camp, but the horses that drew the carts that supplied the army, the horses that carried messengers when the message was not urgent enough for a Herald. Common horses, but for the most part better by far than any that these hills had seen before.

But when they finally reached the outskirts of the encampment, it was something of an anticlimax, for it looked like nothing more than an ordinary army camp. They topped a hill, and saw the edge of the camp below them, across the slow river that split the valley in half, on the other side of a stone bridge. Sentries guarded the road there, the visible token of the ones Selenay could not see. Beyond the sentries, rows of pale canvas tents, rows of tents that were as even as furrows in the soil, that marched up the other slope and crowned the top of the hill, a strange and martial crop of spears and pikes planted in stands beside them. And yet, it was no larger an encampment than ones she had seen before, on the edge of the city.

She knew abstractly that it wasn't possible to *see* all of it from any one point, not in these hills. She knew that in her mind, but the emotional impact of so great a force as they had gathered together *should* leave her breathless, or so she felt. So as the sentries barring the road demanded and received passwords, she felt oddly disappointed.

But then they followed the sentry's directions down the road, with properly arranged ranks of whitewashed canvas tents on either side, each section with a central campfire, each four sections serviced by a larger cook tent. And as they continued to ride forward, the ranks of tents went on, and on, and on until she began to lose count. Over the next hill and down the other side, the tents ranged on before them, interrupted only by trees and hedgerows, the racks of pikes and spears piercing the sky beside them. Then the tents were interrupted by a drill ground, full of Guardsmen at practice, followed by another hill, another little valley, and yet more tents and another drill ground. Then a farmhouse, taken over by officers, full of comings and goings, with the yard crowded with horses, snorting and switching their tails at flies. And when they didn't stop there, at what she had thought was the command post, *that* was when it hit her; just how big their army was. . . .

Selenay tried to imagine it, and failed. She had seen several hundred people at once many times, even several thousand, crowded into one of the huge public squares in Haven for some speech of her father's, but never more than a fraction of the number that must be assembled here now. And that number didn't include Healers and Heralds either—and there were probably a lot of Bards here, too, for you couldn't keep a Bard away from something like this. Then there were all of the support people, cooks and carters, laundresses and tailors, the servants of anyone highborn—

No wonder her father had put off assembling this huge a force until now. Where would he have housed them? How long could he have kept them fed? The logistics were mind-boggling. She couldn't imagine the amount of coordination it took just to feed this army for a single day, let alone care for it for the past several fortnights. How could it have been organized in the first place? Who was doing the training? Who was keeping the place *clean,* for the Havens' sake?

No wonder Talamir kept telling her father to delegate more.

Now she knew why Alberich couldn't be jollied into a better humor. He knew this was coming, of course. Well, so had she, but unlike her, Alberich had known very well how large a force the Tedrels had when they decided to commit all of it. For their army was just equal to the one that the Tedrels were fielding, and only just.

Her heart went cold, and she was suddenly, desperately, urgently wanting to run away, to turn Caryo and go so far north that not even the Tedrels would find her. There were places up there—the Forest of Sorrows for one—where you could lose an entire regiment of cavalry and not find them for years. One girl on a single Companion could stay hidden until the rivers ceased to flow.

The truth of it was, she could *do* that. And no one would blame her if she did. Some people would even applaud her wisdom in giving the Tedrels one less available target. But if she did that, some people would lose heart, and she had no way of knowing how many. It might be enough to make a difference, and she could not take that chance. She could not do much here but this; by her very presence, one slim girl facing down the enemy, daring him to try and take her, she might give heart to those who were actually doing the fighting. And she could take some of the burden—not much, but some—from her father.

So she couldn't run away. And she dared not show how afraid she was.

But she was very glad that she had reins to hold. They kept her hands from shaking.

She had thought that they would stop at that farmhouse—but no, they went on, past more tents, more drill grounds, until she wondered if they would *ever* make an end.

The practice grounds were all in use—no slacking going on in this army, and well-drilled these fellows were, too. Alberich's practiced eye ran over the troops, and he was pleased with what he saw.

:Better than anything in Karse, eh Chosen?: Kantor asked smugly, as the men lunged and recovered in time to their leader's chants. Spears, this lot had, with cross-braces like on a boar spear that kept the enemy from coming at you once you'd stuck him. It made them a little awkward to handle in a group, but that was what practice was for.

:Not better trained, but better-motivated,: he admitted. *:That's as important a factor as food and weapons.:*

The trouble was, of course, that the core troops of the Tedrels were just as highly motivated. But *not* the shock troops

. . . and that just might make the difference. The shock troops, the ones meant to take the brunt of the attacking, were the flotsam that the Tedrels had lured to their ranks with promises of loot and blood. Once it was *their* blood that got shed, the question was how well they'd stick. Valdemar had that working in their favor.

In numbers, if all of their ForeSeers and spies were right, Valdemar and the Tedrels were evenly matched. But not, perhaps, in motivation.

:Greed might be motivation enough,: Kantor said, soberingly. *:Don't count on them to turn once the fighting gets bloody. Most of them have seen plenty of fighting; it's not as if they were a lot of sheepherders dragged in by fast-talking drummers.:*

His eye lingered on a group of spearmen and pikemen training—spears in the first two ranks, pikes in the next two. Pikemen were traditionally the positions of the least trained. Although there was some skill involved in handling a pike, it was not much different from handling a boar spear, and involved more following orders than thinking.

There was some clumsiness, but not enough to make him think that they were entirely fresh. There was a great deal of determination. Their clothing, beneath their Valdemaran tabards, told him that they were farmers.

Other men might deride farmers-turned-soldiers. Not he. Farmers knew what they were fighting for; farmers were used to death and killing, for they did it every autumn when they killed the cattle and swine that would feed them through the winter. The average citydweller might never see meat that was not already rendered into its component parts; the farmer had raised that "meat" from a baby, and had resisted his children's efforts to name it and make a pet of it.

Killing a cow was easier than killing a man? Not when the farmer had delivered the cow as a calf, had agonized over its illnesses, had called it to its food every day for all of its life, brought it all unaware into the killing shed, and stared into its eyes before killing it. Whereas the man he faced was a stranger, was hidden in his helm, and wanted to kill *him.* Then wanted to take his land, his goods, and his women. A farmer would have no difficulty in making the decision to kill a man.

No, he was happy to see farmers here. It was the city-dwellers, the craftsmen, that he was concerned about. It was one thing to train and look proficient—it was quite another thing to hold yourself together in combat.

He glanced at his charge; Selenay was looking white about the lips. He wondered why.

:She understands now what we're facing,: Kantor replied. *:It's hit her, in her gut, in her heart, just how* big *our army is, and by extension, how big theirs is, and all that this implies.:*

Ah. Well, he felt sorry for her, but better now than later. Better now, when she would have time to gather the courage he knew she had and compose herself before the eyes of those who would fight for her sake.

:For the sake of Valdemar,: Kantor corrected.

:It is the same,: he countered, as he spotted the convocation of larger, fancier tents that marked the center of the army, and the seat of its leadership. What with bodyguards, sentries, servants and all, it had been too big a convocation to house in any farmhouse.

:A philosophical difference, perhaps,: Kantor replied, *:to you. A real one to us.:*

They reached the periphery of the tents, a boundary marked by another set of sentries stationed every few paces around the edge. The edge was defined by what appeared to be ornamental swags of rope hung between stakes. It *wasn't* ornamental, and it was a device suggested by Alberich. Hidden amid the fringe and bullion were bells, very loud bells, and anyone who so much as brushed against those ropes would raise a very audible alarm. One couldn't climb over it or crawl under it. A small thing, but one more barrier between his charges and harm.

The Lord Marshal was taking no chances. It was the Lord Marshal who had suggested the second innovation, a layer of black felt lining the inside of the tents, so no one would be silhouetted against the canvas by lights within. Another small thing, but it would make the King, his Heir, and the officers less of a set of targets once night fell. Unless a spy was able to watch them closely, one wouldn't even know when they were *in* their tents.

The Lord Marshal himself was there to greet them, and Alberich moved closer to Selenay as they all dismounted. This would be another good time to strike at her, in the moment when everyone was a trifle relaxed at the end of the journey.

But Kantor had made a statement that needed to be answered. *:She is not Valdemar? Then let her* become *Valdemar,:* he said fiercely. *:Men fight better when the symbol of what they fight for is before them. Why do you think we carry a shrine of Vkandis before us when we wage war?:*

He actually took Kantor aback for a moment. *:An interesting observation,:* the Companion replied, and left it at that.

It was as well that he did, for Alberich's attention was elsewhere now—scanning every face and every body around them, even—no, especially—among the servants of the highborn. *That* was the place for a traitor to slip in, among the servants. He watched without seeming to watch, a good trick he had acquired in the taverns of the worst part of Haven. There were a great many tricks he had acquired there, or learned from Dethor, and he had taught most of them to Selenay's Six, and Sendar's too, or at least as many as he could impart to them in the short time he had to school them.

He was pleased to see that they were using those lessons; pleased to see that the ones guarding Sendar were doing likewise. They were more obvious in their watchfulness, but there was no harm there; they drew attention to themselves, and if there was anyone watching *them,* he would spot the watchers. . . .

Layers upon layers of care and misdirection, of planning and deception, and upon them Selenay and Sendar's lives might depend.

The moment passed; the King and Heir moved into the circle of guards and canvas. Thin protection, or so it seemed, but stronger than one might guess, for they were out of the milling crowd, where a knife could be employed suddenly and without warning, and into a more controlled place where more watchers watched the watchers.

He joined them, in the background, always in the background. Now, more than ever, he needed to be unnoticed.

How ironic, that he, who had trained for most of his life to be a leader, should now require of himself to be insignificant.

How ironic that he should find, as he dropped back to be a shadow-Herald in his dark gray leathers, that he preferred the place in the shadows to the one in the light. He watched young Selenay as, white-lipped, but with her head held high, she took her place beside her father at the planning table.

And then he turned his attention to those around his King and his charge. He knew what the strategy for the initial stages of battle would be, at least for now; it had been discussed and discussed until it was tattered. He knew, and he feared that the enemy knew.

But it had been too late to prevent them from knowing when the strategy was decided—and as he himself had told Dethor, "No strategy survives the first engagement." You could plan and plot all you liked, but when your plans depended on the enemy doing what you *thought* he would do, it wasn't likely that he'd cooperate with you.

Now all they could do was see what he did, and trust that they could move to counter it, whatever "it" turned out to be. Chances were, it wouldn't be anything they had planned for. The Tedrel Warlords had not survived this long by being stupid. If anything, they were entirely *too* clever; that very cleverness had caused any ruler who might consider hiring them to take a good long look and realize that they were in many ways as much a danger to the one who had hired them as they were to the enemy they were sent against. So no one, in all the time they had been roaming, had ever before hired the *entire* nation. Broken up into Companies, they were safe to have inside your borders. Only the Sunpriests, in an act of monumental hubris, had gathered all the Companies together in one place.

Now the Sunpriests were well aware of their folly, too late to do them or Valdemar any good.

We cannot simply turn them back, he thought with anguish. *If we do, they will only turn on* my *people—*

And of all of those here in this camp, he was the only one who would care if they did.

But what else could he have done, except to act as he had? He hauled his divided attention back to where it belonged, and kept it on Selenay and those around her. The tents were dark, thanks to the felt lining them; the only light came from the entrance and the unlined canvas tops. The bases had been rolled up to ankle-height to allow air to circulate. The interior of the one they were in was sparsely appointed—that would change when the baggage train caught up with them—and for now, the only seating was on folding stools. Sendar was offered one of these and refused it; Selenay did not.

Talamir called for food and drink, and when it came, made sure that both the King and Heir availed themselves of it. Sendar was, of course, completely immersed in all the reports of the commanders, even though there was nothing new in them. Selenay was looking wan, but Alberich did not suggest that she retire to her own tent. She had to harden herself; they *all* had to harden themselves, to go beyond what they thought they could do until there was no more strength left, then find more strength, somewhere, somehow.

As if she had heard his thought, she turned her head

toward him and met his eyes. Then she rose and took her place at her father's side, paying every bit as much attention to the reports as he was. Although the King did not even glance at her, Alberich watched as he placed his hand on her shoulder, tacitly welcoming her presence, and showing any who doubted that she belonged there.

Good. Now no one would suggest that she get some rest, dismissing her as irrelevant to their discussions.

A movement—an *odd* movement—caught his eye. Without turning his head, he identified the movement as someone pulling slightly away, rather than leaning *toward* the group. His peripheral vision was excellent, better perhaps than anyone guessed, for he had no trouble telling who it was without betraying his interest by looking at the man.

It was Orthallen, who was serving as the commander for the militia of his sector. His brows were furrowed, his posture tense.

And he was frowning at Selenay.

ORTHALLEN—

There were some singular holes in Alberich's intelligence regarding Orthallen. At that moment, Alberich wished that he'd spent a little more time trying to fill them.

But in the very next instant, Orthallen's frown vanished, to be replaced by his usual, affable expression, apparently leavened by worry. And if Alberich hadn't *seen* the transformation, he would have thought that the expression was genuine. Now, however, he was aware that it was a mask, one that Orthallen could don in the blink of an eye, and very seldom dropped.

A mask over what, one wonders. . . .

Alberich forced himself to be charitable. *All* he saw was a frown, which might have been occasioned by anything. That Orthallen didn't approve of anyone as young as Selenay being privy to every bit of war planning going on. That Orthallen didn't like the prospect of a Queen instead of a King. That Orthallen didn't approve of a female being involved in war planning. That Orthallen had indigestion.

Perhaps not that last, although being on the doorstep of the final campaign of a nasty war was enough to give anyone worse than indigestion.

The likeliest was that Orthallen had suddenly been confronted with the fact that he would one day be serving a Queen instead of a King. And given the urgency of the current situation, "one day" might be a great deal closer than he thought. And he didn't like the prospect.

It had been some time since Valdemar had had a Queen; there wasn't anyone now alive who remembered the last one—it had been a good long time, after all, and *she* had been a co-Consort, ruling with her King, Sendar's grandfather.

Sendar's Queen, who'd had no interest in being co-Consort, had died when Selenay was a mere infant, and Orthallen had a good reason to be wary of the problems associated with a female ruler. Women *did* die in childbirth, and even if Selenay wedded someone Chosen, who could be a co-Consort, there could be trouble if she died; the Kingdom had been left to the Council to rule while Sendar had gotten over his beloved wife's death. If that had happened when there was a crisis like *this* one looming, the result could have been a disaster.

Could have been, but *would not* have been. Perhaps Orthallen couldn't understand that; he wasn't a Herald, he didn't know what deep wells of comfort the Companions were, and he might not understand just how totally Heralds were driven by duty. If Sendar had had to deal with a crisis, even in the moment of his beloved's death, he would have. That he gave himself over to mourning was only because he knew he had the luxury of doing so.

Nevertheless, Alberich did not like that frown on Orthallen's face; there was something about Orthallen's expression that he couldn't pin down, and his instincts said it was more than just one older man concerned about the possibilities that a young woman Heir represented.

It must have come as a distinct shock to him, seeing her

here, seeing her being briefed instead of being sent to a tent to rest. It's one thing to see "the child" sitting at a Council table, it's quite a different thing to see her sitting here. After all, just because Selenay had a Council seat, it didn't follow that she was truly a part of the Council's deliberations. The seat *could* have been nothing more than show, for certainly Selenay's vote went with her father's every time. Given Orthallen's patronizing attitude toward the Heir, the shock of realizing that she *was* a power to be reckoned with and had a mind of her own must have been unpleasant. But was it unpleasant enough to cause that particular *kind* of frown? It hadn't been the look of a man surprised and a little offended; it had been the expression, calculating and angry, of one who had not realized that there was a roadblock to his plans. Or so Alberich *thought,* but everything he thought he'd observed was all in retrospect, for the expression hadn't been there more than a moment. It was distinctly frustrating not to be able to quantify his feelings, but since he'd been working in the slums of Haven, his instincts had sharpened, and he'd come to depend on what they told him.

Therefore, he would keep an eye on Lord Orthallen.

So he delegated a portion of his mind to doing just that, and turned the rest of his attention back to the briefing that Sendar was getting. The Lord Marshal and his Herald Joyeaus were getting to the end of things Alberich already knew, and they looked as if there was more to say. A great deal more. And that it was bad news.

"The ForeSeers are reporting difficulty, Majesty, as are the FarSeers," Herald Joyeaus said. Her thin face was set in an expression of solemn thoughtfulness, for this development was something new—though not unexpected, at least, not to Alberich. The fact was, he was surprised that it had taken so long for the Tedrels to block attempts to FarSee what they were doing. Possibly they had not realized that the Heralds could do such a thing with the amount of accuracy they had.

Possibly they had been blocking attempts to scry magically, and had not until now reckoned on the Gifts. Possibly they had been saving their mages for this moment.

Or possibly it had taken them this long to buy or coerce magical expertise. . . .

It seemed to take the rest by surprise, though, all but the Lord Marshal, who looked grim. "Exactly what do you mean by 'difficulty,' Joyeaus?" Sendar asked.

Joyeaus' mask didn't slip, but Alberich didn't have to be an Empath to know that she was very worried. "As you know, Majesty, my own strongest Gift is FarSeeing, and although when I Look elsewhere I have no difficulties, when I Look across the Border, I might as well be Looking into fog. In concert with two others, I made further attempts, but we managed no more than glimpses, which were confusing at best. The ForeSeers tell me that they are unable to See *anything* when they attempt to scry into the future—"

"But as we all know, ForeSeeing is chancy at best," Sendar finished for her. "The most probable answer to that is that there are so many possibilities branching from this moment that they are unable to see even one clearly. I am more concerned by the report from the FarSeers. Can FarSeeing be blocked?"

Officers and Councilors began murmuring nervously among themselves and shifting their weight. Alberich pulled at his collar, feeling stifled suddenly and wondering if he was the only one who found the rising tension in the tent to be edging close to panic.

"I—" Joyeaus hesitated. Alberich was astonished that she did so. How could she not *know* that it could be blocked? How could she not have *expected* that enemy mages would do so? And yet, from the way she looked, and the way Sendar acted, it seemed that the possibility had never even occurred to them.

Alberich didn't want to step out of the shadows and draw attention to himself, but he didn't seem to have a choice. No one else saw the blindingly obvious. He cleared his throat; the sound was shocking in the silence that had followed Sendar's question. Every head in the tent swiveled in his direction.

"Herald Alberich?" Sendar prompted.

"Senior, high-rank Sunpriests, such powers have," he said carefully. "And unscrupulous others with magic for hire are, in the Southern Kingdoms. Among the Tedrels, there may be magicians, though specifically I have not of such heard."

They looked at him as if he had spoken in Karsite, not Valdemaran. Maybe in a way he had. He cursed his lack of fluency, and the need to speak without composing what he was going to say.

He tried again, this time coming directly to the point. "Assume you must, that others than Heralds Gifted are. Surely Sunpriests are, for this I know! Surely Tedrels are, for they are a nation, and *some* must Gifted be! *Yes.* Blocked your Gifts *can* be!"

Joyeaus blinked, and looked as if she was coming out of a daze. "He's right, Majesty," she said. "We have been remiss in assuming that *only* Heralds are Gifted—and that just because we don't know ways of blocking Gifts, it doesn't follow that someone else hasn't found a way."

"So the Gifts are useless?" asked one Councilor, his voice sounding strained.

"No, no—only FarSight and ForeSight!" Joyeaus hastened to say. "Mindspeech works perfectly well, and Fetching as well, at least as far as we can tell. We've never *depended* on ForeSight, it's too rare a Gift and too erratic anyway."

I can vouch for that, Alberich thought grimly.

"And we've never depended *entirely* on FarSight either," Selenay put in, her high, young voice carrying over the muttering (and, yes, there was rising panic in those voices) of those around her. "We'd be fools to depend on *any* single source of intelligence, gentlemen! You may depend upon it, there are other ways of finding things out at a distance. Including—" she added, with a touch of irony, "—common spies."

"Animal Mindspeech," replied someone. Alberich couldn't tell who, precisely, for the background chatter distorted the sound. The voice was female, though, and very confident. "The Chronicles say that the Hawkbrothers of the Pelagiris Forest use Animal Mindspeech with their birds as spies. Surely we can do the same? Or listen through the ears of a horse or hound?"

The muttering subsided, and what there was of it sounded less panicky. Sendar turned to Joyeaus. "Deal with it, Joyeaus. Find the Heralds with Animal Mindspeech; see what you can do. Ask Myste what's in the Chronicles. Perhaps the Heralds of our generation have not needed to worry about their Gifts being blocked, but there's no reason to think it hasn't happened in the past somewhere, and if anyone will know where, when, and what was done about it, it will be Myste."

"Sire." Joyeaus bowed and edged her way out of the crowd.

No wonder the voice had sounded familiar, and he felt that familiar apprehension whenever he thought of the half-blind Herald-Chronicler-in-training. Well, at least he'd given her enough skill to get herself out of trouble if she had to, and he could count on her strong instinct for self-preservation to keep her out of the fighting itself.

Unless, of course, there was no other choice. But if *that* happened, everyone in a white uniform with a mount that was even vaguely pale in color was going to be in danger. The Tedrels knew better than to let a single Herald escape alive.

It has to be Sunpriests that are helping them, though. No mage worth the name would serve Karse or *the Tedrels. No mage worth the name will serve where the Mercenary Guild won't.* Even one of the blood-path mages wouldn't serve the Tedrels, in part because the Tedrels themselves would know better than to trust one of *that* sort. You didn't want a blood-path mage around; when sacrifices ran short, they tended to grab whoever was closest. . . .

That didn't make things any better, however. The Sunpriests had *power.* Everyone knew about the invisible creatures they commanded that stalked the night, able to see into a man's very soul and discern if he was a heretic and a traitor, and thus, their lawful prey. He himself had *heard* them, howling in the distance.

:Then why didn't they take you?: Kantor asked, with none of the ironic humor he might have put into such a question.

:Because I am no heretic,: he replied, with none of the sharpness *he* might have put into a reply, because Kantor was not teasing him, and deserved candor. *:I follow the Writ as well as I may; and though I often fail, failure does not make a heretic,* blasphemy *does. They hunt those who would deny Vkandis, not the sinner. If they hunted sinners, there would be no man or woman safe in Karse, and precious few children. And as for their other prey, I am no traitor to Karse or my people.:* There was heat in his last sentence, though; he couldn't help himself, and Kantor reacted to it.

:Peace, I only asked to see what it was that these creatures that haunt your darkness might seek,: he said soothingly. *:I suspect in part it is a feeling of guilt, and in part, the fear that such guilt would cause. Especially in those who think that such creatures can read their souls, and know that the Sunpriests would not approve of what is there.:*

Well, that was a novel suggestion. And it was one he would think about in depth—and perhaps discuss with Myste, since she was here—but later. For now, since the mere mention of the fact that other peoples had as much or more magic at their disposal as the Heralds did, seemed to cause Sendar and the others to act as if they were momentarily stunned, he had other things to worry about. *:Take it as read, you and the other Companions, that the Sunpriests are going to try to block whatever Gifts we use,:* he advised. *:I don't know how well*

Sendar and Joyeaus understood what I was trying to tell them—:

—and even now he truly didn't understand how the possibility hadn't even occurred to them.

:We probably can't do anything about FarSight and ForeSight, but I defy them to block Mindspeech with the Companions boosting it,: Kantor said with determination. *:And we* might *even be able to boost the other Gifts on an irregular basis.:*

Good enough. Now for the rest; he waited until there was a gap in Sendar's orders, and interrupted.

"Majesty," he said clearly, with a touch of sharpness. "If blocking FarSight the enemy suddenly is, when until *now* he has not, then is it not that he does not *want* to be seen? And steps is taking, of that to make certain? And that would be—why?"

Sendar stared at him a moment, his brow furrowed, and again Alberich cursed his lack of expertise in Valdemaran. But it would have taken him a quarter-candlemark to work out how to say it clearly, and they didn't have the time—

The others just stared at him, probably trying to untangle his mangled syntax as well. Selenay, who was far more used to the way he spoke, uttered an oath that would have made one of the muleteers blush.

"They're moving!" she said—no, shouted—before her father could rebuke her for her language. "Father, the Tedrels, they *knew* we'd be watching them, they didn't care until this moment since all we'd see is their troops building, but now they don't want us to see them because they're *moving!*"

Sendar swore, in language even stronger than Selenay's (and there was no doubt in Alberich's mind where she'd learned to curse so fluently). But he put up his hand to quell the raised voices around him, stilling an incipient panic with a single gesture.

Alberich hoped that Selenay was taking note. This was the

sort of thing a Monarch needed to be able to do by sheer force of personality.

"Even if they could fly—which they cannot—they could not be at our Border before three days have elapsed," Sendar pointed out. "Since they must move on their feet and those of their horses, it will be longer than that. We have a dual task—to find another way to gain the intelligence that Far-Sight would have given us, and to prepare the army to meet them. The former is in the hands of Joyeaus and Myste, and if any two Heralds can find what is needed in the past, *they* can. So, my friends, let us bend our minds to the latter, for it is time to finish our strategies. That is what *we* can do."

Alberich withdrew a little, for at the moment he was best as an observer. *No battle plan survives the first encounter with the enemy,* he reminded himself. He'd reminded Myste of that truism often enough as well; with luck, she'd remember it and she and Joyeaus would add several more layers to their plotting.

And if he paid a little more attention to Orthallen than the rest, well, that also was part of his responsibility. It was not only an enemy that could do damage. Sometimes the danger came from within, and the one who brought it could even have all of the best intentions in the world.

It was a very small tent—more like a pavilion, actually, showing old and much-faded colors on its canvas—pitched among the slightly untidy cluster of those belonging to Heralds assigned to the King and his officers. No two of these tents were alike, taken as they were from whatever was available after the Guard, the officers, the King and his servants were done picking over the available canvas, but this one stood out for both its inconvenient size and its shabby state. As the sun dropped toward the horizon, Alberich looked at it askance. Surely not.

"My home away from home," Myste said, gesturing at the canvas square with its peaked top. She held the flap open to let him in.

"This must be the oddest campaign tent I have ever seen," Alberich remarked, as he squeezed himself into the tent that Myste had taken, ducking his head to avoid the low cross-beams. "It's certainly the smallest—"

Myste shrugged. "That's probably why no one else was particularly eager to take it. I think it must have been cut down after the canvas around the bottom started to rot and stitched together with replacements, because the floor is newer than the sides and top."

He *had* expected something entirely different, a tent that was more a semiportable library. Well, there were books, but nowhere near as many as he'd expected. His glance at the neat packing case that served as a bookcase as soon as the cover was unstrapped made her smile. "I brought copies of War Chronicles, and some odd bits, and nothing more than would fit in that case," she said. "Only copies. If the army retreats and I have to flee with nothing more than the uniform on my back, may the Tedrels have joy of them."

He didn't tell her what he thought the Tedrels would use the paper for, he just folded his legs under him and sat on the canvas floor. "And this is interesting—"

He pointed at the arrangement where anyone else would have had a cot or a bedroll. He *thought* there might be a cot under there, but one third was propped up to serve as a chair back and the opposite end dropped down, and the rest had a strange tray raised over it on some sort of folding legs, with everything needed for writing arranged atop it; a brazier no bigger than the palm of his hand, stacks of very cheap wood-pulp paper, graphite sticks, and pen and ink, and a lantern she could hang on the tent pole overhead. Which she did at that very moment, raising the chimney after it was hung to light it with a coal from the tiny brazier. And a moment later, she sprinkled the coal with a powder that sent up a haze of insect-repelling incense.

She grinned as she saw what he was looking so closely at. "That's my invention. Bed, chair, and table in one, and it all comes apart and fits together. It even makes part of its own case. My clothes and bits are packed in the back half under the cot, and the desk is the top. And since we've got messengers going to Haven twice a day anyway, they take what I've written with them whenever they go. No matter what happens, we won't lose more than half a day's rough notes from meetings and anything else I know about, and if everything goes pear-shaped, Elcarth will at least have a record of what led up to it." She swung the "desk" away on a pivoting arm, and sat down.

He hoped that losing a half-day's rough draft would remain her only concern.

For all that the bed thing was amazingly compact, there wasn't much room left in her tent. He'd seen her rooms at the Collegium. She was a woman addicted to clutter and a collector of *things.* This sparse minimalism was totally unlike the Myste he knew. She gave him a side glance as if she guessed what he was thinking, and a half smile, which swiftly sobered. "Joy and I have had our little conference and we have some plans, and you were right, there *have* been times when Gifts have been blocked, and—oh, do hold back your surprised look—by Karsites. But there are things we can do, and they have never managed to block Mindspeech on our side of the Border. Or battle line, whichever came first. Another point of interest, if you will, is that since Lavan Firestorm's time, apparently they have been unable to coax those night-stalking things you were talking about anywhere *near* the Border because they haven't appeared *at all* over here. Now, can I count on that continuing, do you think?"

Alberich chewed on his lower lip and considered what he knew. He had only heard the things in the distance, and had never asked any Sunpriest about them. But then, one didn't ask *them.* Interest in what they sent out might cause them to suspect guilt, or worse, heresy. But it did occur to him that although he had never heard them *too* near the Border, the reason for that was probably less than arcane. The Sunpriests would not risk *themselves* anywhere near the Border, and they probably had to be within a certain proximity to their charges to control them.

And if the Tedrels were providing a screen of bodies, they wouldn't hesitate to follow.

However, the situation at the moment suggested that the Sunpriests had a great deal more to concern themselves over than their ancient enemies.

"I think—I think perhaps that even if the Sunpriests *could* send their servants across the Border, at this point they *wouldn't.* I believe that they hold them back in reserve to make certain the Tedrels, after conquering Valdemar, do not turn on them as well." He raised an eyebrow. "Consider, if you will, the troops we know are flanking the Tedrels, the ones my spies said are *not* to cross the Border. No, I think the Night-demons will stay within Karse."

"That is a distinct relief." She made a note amid the rest on the desk at her side. Then closed her eyes for a moment. She looked tired, and he wondered how long she had been here, for he hadn't noticed her among the Heralds around the King.

"It is one small blessing," he replied. "Another is that *our* troops have limited choice of ground, given where we think they must come. And a greater blessing is that our troops will be fresh."

"All they have to do is stop overnight, their troops will be just as fresh as ours," she pointed out. "They know *we* won't cross the Border. But frankly, all I know about battles and war is what I've read, and everything I've read just makes me want it all to go away."

"Unless he is a madman," Alberich said soberly, "I believe you will find that even the great generals feel the same.'

She looked down at her hands. "May I ask you a horrible favor?"

He was going to say, "It depends on the favor," but something about the way she had asked that question made him answer, unequivocally, "Yes" instead.

She fixed him with that glittering gaze of eyes shielded behind thick, glass lenses. "Shielded" was a good thought—she probably used those lenses as shields to hide what *she* was thinking.

"May I stop pretending that I'm brave and cheerful around you? I feel as if I can trust you, more even than the rest of the Heralds, I mean; you've seen me at my worst, I suppose, and you seem to know, somehow, why I *have* to be here." She shrugged, helplessly. "And I do. It's important that a Chronicler be here, and it can't be Elcarth, since he can't make himself detached enough—but it's also important that someone be here who knows history, because things that have been done in the past are likely to solve a problem now. I daren't pretend I'm anything other than insanely optimistic around anyone else; Joy is not entirely certain I should even *be* here—or at least she wasn't until this afternoon—and if they have any idea how terrified I am, they'll be certain I'll freeze up at the worst moment and try to send me back."

He felt his expression softening, and for once, he let it. How odd to see her looking vulnerable! It wasn't that she ever attempted to look warrior-tough, but she wore this facade of cool indifference, even when he'd been training her—when she wasn't wearing an aura of annoyed irritation. He didn't think he had *ever* seen her look so helpless, much less on the verge of tears. He held up his hand to stop her. "Of course you can," he said, with sympathy that surprised even him. "And although I did not expect to see you here, I understand what you can do that no one else can; the amount of information you must carry about in your mind is astonishing."

"Not so much that, as I know where to look for things. I can ask Elcarth to find what I need, and he can Fetch handwritten notes down here." She shook her head. "I *can't* do that from up there in Haven. It depends on being *in* a meeting and seeing a problem and knowing where to look for an answer. And telling people that there *is* an answer, right then, before they get hysterical. You have to *be* there to know what priority to put on the problem; reports don't tell you that. But nobody wants me here; they look at me and see a half-blind, clumsy liability who's likely to be in the way, or worse, need rescuing. So I have to put up a facade so they don't find another reason to send me back."

He hesitated. "As the Weaponsmaster, I am concerned that you are the person least able to defend herself here."

"Which is why I'm *petrified,*" she replied, in a very small voice. "And I want to go *home.* But I can't, and I won't, and I won't ask anyone else to look out for me."

"I never thought for a moment that you would." The tent was *so* small, he could easily reach over and pat her shoulder, which he did, awkwardly. Her face crumpled, but she didn't cry. Just as well. Women in tears unnerved him. She did put her own hand up to hold his on her shoulder, though, and he didn't mind—

:Bollocks. You like it.:

:You stay out of my head,: he said sharply. *:Or at least be quiet about being there.:*

Kantor wisely did not reply.

"Don't think I want *you* to take care of me either," she continued, even though she was shaking. "I don't! I *can* take care of myself, even if I'm not a good fighter, I won't freeze up, and *will* be sensible and be the first to run away, if the time comes to retreat!"

"I didn't think you would ask, not for a moment. As your

Weaponsmaster, although I am concerned, I am certain that I have trained you well, and I trust you to be intelligent enough to do what you must." He tightened his hand on her shoulder. "But as your Weaponsmaster, you need not be brave with me. In fact, if you have concerns and feel you cannot voice them to others, do tell me. The night stalkers, for instance; that was a reasonable thing to consider."

She sighed, and some of her shaking eased. "I'm not a brave person," she said reluctantly. "Actually, I'm rather a coward. I'm afraid of so much, it's easier to say what I'm *not* afraid of. I think about what can go wrong all the time, it keeps me awake at night, and it makes me want to dig a hole and hide in it. And even if things don't go wrong, it's still going to be horrible—people dying and blood and pain—and it's one thing to read about battles, but it's something else to have one happening around you."

There were so many things he could have said—that she was right to be afraid, that she would be less afraid if she stopped thinking so constantly about all the dire possibilities—

He said none of them, for none of them seemed quite right. And after a moment, she let go of his hand and he took it back. With a touch of reluctance . . . which felt a bit odd.

:Because you don't know how to act around a woman who might be more than a friend, but isn't either out of bounds or a whore,: Kantor said bluntly.

Well—that was true enough. But this was no time to try and learn how. Later, perhaps, if there was a later. *And now who is dwelling on the dire possibilities?*

She took a deep breath, squared her shoulders, and turned those glittery lenses in his direction with a wan smile. "Thank you for being my friend as well as my Weaponsmaster and fellow Herald, Alberich. It helps to have someone human I can be at ease with."

He nodded. "As you help me. Think of the relief I feel, not

only to drop my mask, but to have someone with whom I can speak my native tongue." He managed a wry smile. "Perhaps you can help me with my Valdemaran, so we don't have a repetition of that scene in Sendar's tent. Only Selenay understood me!"

Myste shook her head. "At least it made *her* look very competent, and gave her credit a strong boost. Poor little Selenay! I hope she can find someone to take her mask off with."

"If no one else, it will be me," he promised, reading the request for exactly what it was. Then he deemed it time for a change of subject. "Now what else have you found in those Chronicles?"

"All the routes that your people have *ever* used to come at us." She reached under her cot, and pulled out a roll which proved to be a map. "I traced them all on this."

"*Very* useful." The hilly, sometimes mountainous terrain along the Border only permitted so many practical routes for an invading force, and here they all were, or at least, as much about them as the Valdemarans knew, since most of Karse was unknown land to them. But *he* knew the Border, if not as well as he'd like, certainly better than anyone here, and perhaps with the help of some of the FarSeeing Heralds or the ones with Animal Mindspeech who could see through the eyes of a high-soaring hawk, he would be able to fill in the terrain on the other side a bit, and they'd know which paths and passes to watch.

"Myste, I shall be sure and let it be known that you are *monumentally* useful," he said. And was rewarded with a genuine smile. "Now I shall go and present this to Sendar so that I can do that."

"And I shall write up the next lot of notes to dispatch." She tucked her legs under the tray and pulled it toward her, and that was how he left her, head down, lamplight shining down on it, an island of peace in the midst of frantic preparations for war.

But his night was not yet over. He went to Selenay's tent, and found her toying with the remains of her dinner—a dinner which, for the most part, looked uneaten. Her two guardians were right with her, and her tent was ringed with regular Guardsmen.

He nodded with satisfaction as they challenged him, then sent one of their number to fetch someone from Selenay's bodyguards who could verify his identity. That was quite right; they should never assume that someone was who he said he was if *they* didn't know him on sight. One of the two bodyguards recognized him the moment she put her head out of the tent, of course. Only then was he allowed inside the perimeter they had established.

Selenay gladly put aside the plate at his entrance. There were several lamps suspended overhead here, which didn't matter, since the felt lining the walls made it impossible for anyone to see silhouettes on the canvas. He noted the arrangement of the cot in the middle of the tent—now folded—with approval. "Is there any news?" she asked, her expression somber and a little pinched.

He shook his head. "That I have heard, nothing. But for you, a task I have."

She actually brightened at that. "Good. I feel as if there is something I should do, but I can't think of anything." She reached up and tucked a strand of hair self-consciously behind her ear. "I don't think there are many people besides you and father who think I should even be here."

He regarded her gravely. "Come. Among the troops, we must walk. Speak to them, you shall, this night and every night. Of their homes and families, must you ask; speak you must as your heart tells you, to put heart in them, to put a face—*your* face—on Valdemar."

"You mean, make myself some kind of mascot?" she asked,

as he gestured to her guardians to take up their weapons and follow. "Create a symbol?"

"Of a sort. Speak of Valdemar, you must; not just of the evil that comes to tear her, not of fear alone, but of hope." Hope. *He* hoped she was up to this; Sendar would likely be making his own forays among the troops, but there was a limit to his time. Selenay had more of that available to her, and Selenay was a handsome young girl, golden-blond and fresh-faced, and not unlike the pretty girls the men and women wearing the uniform tabards of the Valdemaran army would see at home. He wanted to put *that* face on the abstract notion of "my land, Valdemar." He wanted them to see that their leaders served *them,* as much as they served their leaders. When they saw their leaders, remote and at a distance, he wanted them to remember the night *this* one walked and talked with them.

"But what should I say?" she asked, sounding a little desperate, as they left her tent. He motioned to the sentries to stay in place. Mounted on Companions, they were as safe as they would be in a knot of guards. Kantor waited for them; Caryo came out of her lean-to, and Alberich helped Selenay throw her saddle on her.

"Ask, first. Ask of home and family. Ask of their welfare. Then, think, and as your father would, speak." She had spent all of her life listening to her father's speeches; it was time she learned to make some of her own. In fact, there was very little she could say that would be *wrong.* Her mere presence out here with the troops, asking after their well-being and their background, would be enough. She would be showing the concern of their monarch, putting a face and a voice under the crown. And word of that would spread.

They rode down the torchlit paths between the tents at a walk, so that the two bodyguards could keep pace afoot, until they came to the first campfire of common footsoldiers. As fighters did, the world around, they had gathered around their common fire, and there was talk, some rough joking, a small cask of beer to be shared. It all stopped, when two Companions loomed up out of the darkness. It ceased altogether, when they dismounted, their officer (good man! thought Alberich) recognized Selenay, and scrambled to his feet, then tried to drop to one knee. "Highness!" he stammered, as Selenay prevented him from going down by taking his elbow and keeping him erect.

"Just Selenay—ah—lieutenant?" she replied, her cheeks going pink.

"Lieutenant Chorran, Ma'am," he said, his cheeks pinker than hers, his eyes anxious under an unruly thatch of dark hair.

"Well, then, Lieutenant Chorran, would you make me known to your men?" she replied with admirable composure. If Alberich hadn't known this was her first foray out into an army camp, he would never have guessed it.

She stood, hands clasped gravely behind her back, as Lieutenant Chorran introduced her to every one of the round-eyed men encircling the fire. When he was done, she picked one at random. "So, Nort Halfden—what part of the world are *you* from?" she asked, as if his answer was something she burned to hear.

"Boarsden, Ma'am, east of Haven," he replied, looking as if he was having to concentrate to keep from tugging his strawberry-blond forelock at her.

"I know it; good grain country." She smiled at him, and he looked about to faint, yet couldn't help beaming with pride. "And perfectly *lovely* morel mushrooms in the forest in the spring."

"Aye, Ma'am!" he enthused, losing a little of his shyness. "That there be!" She gave him a nod of encouragement, and he warmed to his subject. "Why, there's a copse just by our duck pond that—"

That was all it took; he was off about his father's farm, and that led her to single out others who looked as if they were losing their awe of *her* to want to boast about their own lands. A leading question or two was all it needed; she just gave them a cue, and let them run on. This lot was all farm folk, though from differing parts of Valdemar; companies were made up of men (and women, though it would have to be a sturdy wench who was in the pikes) who came into the force at about the same time, so that they all worked through training together and got to know one another well. Alberich approved of the arrangement; it created cohesiveness.

When Selenay showed interest in their lives, their homes, and their families, they swiftly warmed to her. When she showed them that she was not that different from them, they took her to their hearts. The firelight shone on their young faces, and Alberich tried not to think about how *very* young they were, how it was certain that some of them would not be going back to those homes and families. It wrung his heart; he reminded himself that they would only be worse off if war had come to their little farms, and they had to face it all untrained.

"But what about now?" she asked finally, looking around. "Your lieutenant is obviously a fine officer—"

"The best, Ma'am!" said one stoutly, and young Chorran blushed.

She nodded with earnest satisfaction. "If there is there anything you need, then, I'm sure he'll see to it. But are you getting enough to eat—"

"Well, no one and nothin' is gonna fill up Koan, there—" said one fellow slyly, and the rest laughed; this was evidently a joke of long standing among them. "But barrin' that, it ain't home, here, but we're all right, Ma'am."

She looked at each earnest, friendly face in turn, and Alberich watched them watching her, intent on her. It was clear that she had it, that subtle charisma that marked her sire. She had more than their attention; she had won their loyalty.

"My father and I want you all to get home again," she said

softly, as the firelight made a golden halo of her hair, giving her, had she but known it, a slightly ethereal look. "We want that more than anything. And we want you to go right on gathering mushrooms every spring, chestnuts and potan roots every fall, telling tales beside the fire every winter. But that isn't going to happen if *they* win."

Nods all around, each of them looking as if they were hearing this for the first time, even though it was hardly news to any of them.

"But we have what *they'll* never have," she continued, holding her young head high, her pride in *them* showing in every word. "*They* don't have a home and they don't want to trouble to build one for themselves; they want to steal ours. *They* don't have families, even, so Alberich says," she gestured at Alberich, who contented himself with looking somber. "And I'd feel sorry for them, I'd even invite them to come settle if they'd just *asked* us! That's what we're all about, is Valdemar—we *don't* keep people out if all they want is peace! That's the way we've always been, haven't we?"

Murmurs of assent, with a growl under it.

Good.

"But since these Tedrels don't *want* peace, don't *want* to build, and only want to steal our land and homes from us—there's only one way we can meet them," she continued, with a look of fierce pride that would have been incongruous on such a young face, but for the circumstances. "We didn't begin this war, but by all that is holy, I swear we will *end* it!"

It wasn't the best speech he'd ever heard, but it did exactly what Alberich wanted it to; it galvanized them. Partly it was Selenay's personality, partly it was that they *wanted* to find a figurehead for their cause. They cheered for her, and that was what counted; she thanked them in a way that made them cheer for her again, and when she mounted Caryo, she was glowing with enthusiasm and flushed with pleasure.

Then it was off in another direction, to another campfire,

wandering in a random fashion, skipping some groups that seemed to be intent on some business or entertainment of their own, going on to others who might need her speech more. Selenay was beginning to run out of energy and wilting a little when Alberich called a halt to the visits for the night, and led her and her guardians back to her tent.

"Did I—" she asked quietly, as the encampments quieted and the fighters around them let their fires die down and sought their bedrolls.

"Well, you did," he assured her. "Very well. And tomorrow, again you will do so, and the next night, and the next. Each time, a different direction, a different set of fires. And know, all will, that their Princess cares for them, and thinks of them, and their King cares for them and his daughter sends to see they are well. So for you they will fight—"

"Not for me!" she exclaimed. "For Valdemar!"

"But Valdemar, *you* are," he countered. "A face they need, upon the idea. That face, you are."

She might have continued to voice her objections, but they had reached her tent, and he bundled her inside without standing on ceremony as soon as she had unsaddled Caryo and rubbed her down. "Sleep now," he told her. "Think and argue on the morrow."

And there he left her, too tired, really, to do more than he had told her to do. She let the tent flap fall shut behind her, Caryo ambled into the lean-to that served as her stable, and he mounted Kantor again.

:She has the spirit in her,: he told his Companion with intense satisfaction as they reached his tent, and he dismounted to free Kantor of his burden of gear. *:And she found words enough that were right to do the job.:*

:Caryo helped. But you're right. And this is something that's needed.: Kantor flicked an ear back in his direction. *:She's putting heart in them.:*

He heaved the saddle onto its stand, and hung the bridle

up beside it, taking up a wisp of straw to give the Companion a quick rubdown. *:And they in her.:* That was the beauty of the thing; even as she gave them something tangible to fight for, they gave *her* confidence, and helped her to find her courage. The more courageous *she* felt, the more heart she'd put in *them. :There. That should hold you until morning.:*

The Companion gave himself a brisk shake, and walked into his own lean-to. *:You're wasted as Weaponsmaster,:* Kantor said thoughtfully, from out of the shadows under the canvas. *:You should have been a Councilor.:*

:Vkandis forbid!: he exclaimed indignantly. *:I would rather muck out stalls!:*

:There—it's a similar occupation,: countered Kantor, and his mental chuckle followed Alberich all the way to his bed.

FOR days, there had been nothing but drill and drill for the men, plan and replan in the commanders' tent. Every day Selenay sat at her father's side and listened, putting in a word or two that was always apt, always to the point. Every night she and Alberich and her bodyguards went out to another set of campfires, talking to another set of fighters. He tried to see to it that she had words with every sort—from the young Knights of the heavy cavalry to the archers and pikemen, from the half-wild hill folk serving as scouts to the massive brutes of the heavy foot. He had his own ears to the ground, and he was satisfied with what he heard—as he'd hoped, the men and women she spoke with *talked,* and soon it spread like wildfire across the entire army that the King and his pretty daughter were "right folk" worth fighting for, who knew their people and *cared* for their people and would be right in there slogging it out *with* their people when the day came. The mood in the army shifted imperceptibly and took on a focus. *That* was what he wanted; Selenay had helped to make it happen. Now there was a sense of the rightness of the cause, and a certainty of purpose. *Now* their leaders were not some impersonal images somewhere. The King and Heir had personalities and faces, and were well on the way to becoming "beloved."

"Beloved" was excellent; men (and presumably women too) fought fiercely for something that was "beloved." And should anything happen to Sendar, his daughter stood a fighting chance of being able to take up the reins without a pause or hesitation. Nor, should the worst happen, was there now any chance that another contender could take the throne away from her—not that any Herald would try, but he had to operate on the assumption that there could always be someone willing to attempt a coup. Certainly, the common people, the Guard, and the army would support her without a second thought, should a would-be usurper appear. He hadn't revealed *that* part of his plan to anyone, not even Kantor—though he had the feeling Kantor had guessed it and approved. As Sendar would approve, if he ever learned it himself.

Selenay, of course, would be horrified, which was why she would never hear of it.

Now he sat in Kantor's saddle, under a clear, summer sky, with dew still wet on the grass. The planning was over; it was too late now to wonder if they had overlooked anything.

For now it all came down to this: two massive armies, both rested, facing each other across firm ground. The Tedrels had taken their time getting here, and they seemed unsurprised to find the Valdemaran Guard waiting for them. "Seemed" was the operable word, since there was no way of knowing for certain if they were surprised or not; when the Tedrels began to move, Sendar ordered the spies out and back home.

(And they made it; somehow, they all made it, though not entirely intact. A couple were injured escaping, but escape they did, and the last of them had come over the Border two days ago.)

Alberich hoped that was a good omen. He could use a good

omen, for he was not at all confident about this final confrontation. Of all the times to have some handle on the future, this would have been the best, for the sake of his own spirits, if nothing else—so of course, he got no inklings at all. If the Tedrels, or the Sunpriests, were blocking ForeSight, they were doing a good job of it, if he couldn't even get a *hint* of what this day would bring. All he *felt* was akin to having an enormous wave cresting a furlong above him, about to crash down on him, and the sense that nothing he could do would get him out of the way. Which was, in a figurative sense, exactly what was about to happen. He wouldn't describe the feeling as "impending doom" precisely, but it certainly was a sense that events were about to overwhelm him.

Last night, the Tedrels had camped just over the horizon; the glow of their campfires had been clearly visible from the edge of the Valdemaran camp. It had made for an uneasy night on this side of the Border. Alberich doubted that anyone had gotten very much sleep. There had been scouts of all sorts out all night, and double the usual guards—the Tedrels were not altogether predictable, and a night attack had not been out of the question. A lot of people had slept (or tried to) in their armor.

This morning, there they were, having marched into place in the predawn, deliberately arranging their ranks on the other side of the valley, quite as if they were setting up for a review or a parade, looking as if they'd shown up for an appointed meeting.

It might just as well have been an appointed meeting. Alberich had no doubt that they had known since they began moving in this direction exactly where the Valdemaran army was. There was no reason why the Tedrels should not have spies of their own, and every reason why they should. Alberich had done his best to find them, but he doubted he'd made more than a significant dent in the population.

And, when it all came down to cases, it was rather difficult to hide the movement of the entire Valdemaran army from much of anyone in a country that had as much freedom as Valdemar; the Tedrel spies had no doubt counted most of the Valdemaran troops and reported them on the move. Alberich could only hope that the Tedrels believed those troops were made up of old men and inexperienced boys and girls—basically, the last possible lot of conscripts left out of a depleted population.

Working in Valdemar's favor, of course, there weren't many options open to where the Tedrels came across the Border, given where they had made their base, deep in the hills. The fact that Valdemar had known *where* that base was, and had moved to block the only real access point right at the Border itself, might (he hoped) have come as a slight surprise.

Or not. If the Tedrels really, truly thought they had superior numbers, there was no reason why they should care where the battlefield was as long as neither side had a critical advantage.

Alberich surveyed the Tedrel nation from his place at Selenay's side, and hoped that his sinking heart didn't make itself known in his expression. They filled their side of the battlefield, from one side of the valley to the other, and there seemed no end to them. A hundred thousand? Two hundred thousand? More?

Surely not more. *Sunlord help us if it is.*

Beside him, with Selenay's silver-and-blue battle banner streaming above her, Myste sat stock-still, the mask of her lenses making it impossible to tell what she was thinking, but her skin was nearly as white as her Companion's hide. Myste had volunteered to take Selenay's banner, and Alberich had agreed, given that it was unlikely Selenay's party would see real combat—and if they did, it was because they were fighting their way to retreat.

Talamir had the King's battle banner, much larger than Selenay's; both were affixed in a socket behind the saddle and didn't need a free hand the way Karsite banners did.

It was easy to tell which were the real Tedrels and which the mere recruits. Behind those shock troops, whose mounted officers had to constantly ride their lines to keep them in their places, the *real* Tedrels had formed up, rank on rank of them, unmoving and unmoved, silent, waiting. Their armor glittered in the morning sun, each man a minute scale upon the body of some massive beast, poised to claw and rend its way to Valdemar's heart. So far away as to be just barely visible to the naked eye, fluttering above the heads of the enemy at the top of the next ridge, were the purple battle banners of the Tedrel commanders.

Alberich hoped that the King and Lord Marshal were proud of *their* fighters, who stood rock-steady in the face of so numerous a foe. Two or three moons ago, many of these young people had been following plows, sweating at a forge, or tending beasts—or hauling nets, tending shops, working at a craft. Now they stared at the enemy, knew they were about to fight for their lives against battle-tested and hardened mercenaries, and did not flinch.

There was no sign of Sunpriests. Alberich strained his eyes in every direction to be sure, but they simply weren't there, and his heart, which had sunk down into the soles of his feet, rose as far as his ankles. *Thank you, Lord Vkandis, giver of life, awful in majesty. . . .*

"Sire?" the Lord Marshal said quietly, at Sendar's right. "Your orders?"

"This side of the valley is Valdemar; that side is Karse," said Sendar in a low but clear voice. "We will not provoke this fight. Though they have attacked us every summer for the past three years, we will not provoke them, and we will not cross the Karsite Border. If they insist on having this confrontation, they must break the peace and the Border, for we will not."

Sendar sounded completely calm, quite composed, as if he did not care whether the Tedrels came or not. Alberich glanced at Selenay's Six; all were mounted, surrounding her, the Guards on ordinary horses rather than Companions.

Well, not *quite* ordinary horses; these were the big, ugly, fighting horses out of Ashkevron Manor, trained by horse-talkers who were trained by Shin'a'in, or so it was claimed. Knights of Valdemar dreamed of being able to own a single one of these beasts in a lifetime, and Alberich had never seen more than three in all of the time he'd been in Haven, but Ashkevron Manor had sent enough of their finest to mount every one of the bodyguards that wasn't a Herald. They carried their armor, a set of hinged plates that protected vulnerable head, chest, and flank, as if it weighed no more than a bit of barding. Each of the Guards had been schooled by one of the horse-talkers in how to handle their brutes and had not just learned to ride them, but had bonded in a sense with them; the results were impressive. They were pleasant enough in corral and under saddle, but Alberich pitied the man who met them in a fight. A single touch of the knee and a shouted command, and an enemy would be pulp. And if the horses were attacked first, their attacker would be pulp *without* the signal or the command.

Those horses were much heavier than any Companion save Kantor. So the Guards (and Crathach, the Healer) were in the point position for both the King and Heir, carrying wide shields to ward off missiles coming from the front. The Companions wore lighter armor of chain and leather, probably proof against arrows, probably not against axes. Everyone was armored, even lean Jadus; everyone had a shield, even though Jadus wouldn't use one in a fight. If—no, say *when*—arrow storms fell, they'd all trained in locking those shields overhead in the formation called "the turtle," to protect Selenay and Sendar. The archers would have to be in range first, though—that was what the Heralds, used to judging their firing distance, would be watching for.

Where's their cavalry? he wondered suddenly, as he

realized that the *only* mounted troops in sight were the officers commanding the front ranks. *I know they have cavalry; they've had them before. So where are they?*

No time to say anything about his sudden thought; at that moment, a far-off trumpet sounded, and with a roar, the Tedrel shock troops flowed down the side of the hill carrying with them a wall of sound, their running feet making the ground shake. In a moment, they had crossed the little stream at the bottom, and so—broke the peace, and began the war.

As they pounded toward the waiting lines, the Valdemaran front ranks braced; spearmen butting their weapons on the ground and kneeling. Behind them, the pikemen also braced their longer weapons and stood fast. And behind *them,* the archers waited, arrows to bow, for their officers to call the first volley.

"Hoi!" The call came, a little ragged, as the first line of shouting men, their running feet pounding the meadow grass flat, set foot on Valdemaran soil. The sound of a thousand bows snapping, a thousand arrows swishing into the air was like a wind, a perilous wind; the archers aimed up, so as to clear their own ranks, and not at any specific targets, for with the enemy so thick, enough arrows would hit to make a difference—

The wind went up, the deadly rain came down, and hoarse battle cries turned to screams of pain as arrows found seams in plate, or chain-mail insufficiently fitted or tended, heads without helms or helms without visors. And some men went down, and the ranks behind them stumbled over their bodies, but it wasn't enough to blunt the charge. Screams of pain joined the sound of battle cries and pounding feet.

Now Alberich entered that singular state of hyperawareness that a fight put him into; he saw *everything,* but was affected emotionally by nothing. His feelings just vanished for the moment, leaving his mind clear and his body ready to act or react. He knew he would pay for this later, when all of that suppressed emotion hit him, but for now, he tightened his hands on his weapons, and watched, and waited—and, in a terrible sense, *enjoyed.*

The noise was incredible; it battered the senses, and it had a strange effect on the mind. He knew this of old, knew that the quickening of his pulse and the sudden surge of blood-thirstiness was due to the very noises that assailed his ears. Whether any of the others were affected in the same way, he didn't know for certain, but he suspected they were, more or less. Certainly the men of his company had been, some more than others. At the first sound of battle, some of them had nearly gone mad with blood-lust—but those did not last very long. They were first into the fight, charging in with no care for themselves. "Spear catchers," was what seasoned commanders called that sort.

"Hoi!" The best archers of Valdemar were good, none better; they could, if need be, get off two more volleys while the first was hitting the enemy. Again, the whirring, as much like the sound of an immense flock of birds as a wind, again the death-dealing rain rattled down—and still they fell, and still they came. Behind the ranks of charging men *their* archers walked in, slowly, and now it was *their* turn to come into play.

The spearmen and pikemen were protected by their armor and helms and stood fast; the Valdemaran archers dropped back beneath shields on orders from their officers, and the first of the Tedrel troops hit the line of spears and pikes with a shock.

The avalanche of sound as the two lines met was indescribable, and even Alberich winced. Screaming, shouting, the clash of weapon on weapon; there was nothing as dreadful as the sound of army meeting army. Some of the Tedrel fighters ran right up on the spears like maddened boars, screeching as they died; the rest hacked at the shafts with heavy broad-swords and axes, shouting furiously, while more pikemen came up from the rear to take the place of those who'd lost their weapons.

A rain of Tedrel arrows fell on the pikemen and the archers behind them, but the pikemen had good armor and helms meant to defend against arrows, and the archers were under their shields. And the moment the hail of arrows stopped, the archers popped out from under cover and let fly a volley of their own. This volley fell on the Tedrel archers, who were lightly armored and not as fast as their Valdemaran counterparts. This time, the hail of arrows took a higher toll; more screaming, and louder now.

Men of both sides fell and died, or fell wounded, crying out in agony. The innocent little rill that marked the Border went from muddy to bloody.

Though Sendar watched it all, it would be up to the Lord Marshal to issue orders. Wise man, was Sendar; he knew he was no more than a fraction of the strategist under actual battle conditions that his underlings were. The Lord Marshal had faced these troops in his own person for the past three years, while Sendar had only gotten his reports. The Lord Marshal had the direct experience of the battlefield that the King did not, and Sendar knew it.

And at the moment, as the sun climbed into the sky and then reached its zenith, the Lord Marshal was looking for something, peering down at the battlefield with a frown on his heavily-bearded face.

"The cavalry," Alberich heard him saying, as if he was thinking aloud. "Where are their *cavalry?*"

And in the same moment, he turned to his Herald, and there was urgency in his voice. Alberich felt both relief that the Lord Marshal had noted the same thing *he* had, and a heart-sinking moment of dread. "MindSpeak the flanks," the Lord Marshal ordered, "And ask the ones with the birds. Find out if the cavalry is behind their lines, still, or if they're trying to get us in a pincer."

Alberich strained to hear the answer, which came within the instant. "No and no, my Lord," the Herald replied. "There is no sign of mounted troops of any sort."

Now Sendar turned his head, to fix the Lord Marshal with a look of surprise. "Then where *are* they?" he demanded. "Surely they haven't put all of their mounted troops afoot!"

The hair on the back of Alberich's neck stood up, and he got a sick feeling in the pit of his stomach. It traveled rapidly over his entire body, and at that moment, he *knew* his Gift hadn't deserted him. In fact, it was about to come down upon him with a vengeance. He slid down out of his saddle as dizziness engulfed him, so that he wouldn't have as far to fall when it hit him—which it was going to, in less than a heartbeat—

He clutched Kantor's saddle, as his Companion turned his head to look at him. A flash of blue came between him and the rest of the world—

A woman, barefoot, bareheaded, running, but she couldn't outrun the horseman behind her—

Another flash—

A man, looking up from his weeding, eyes wide, then unseeing, as the lance took him through the heart—

—like blue lightning—

Children, screaming, being herded into a pen by a dozen horsemen, while the rest set fire to the village—

"Sunlord save us—" he muttered in Karsite, automatically reverting to the language he knew best. The visions, thank the God, were silent, silent, and he could still hear, dimly, the sounds of the battlefield and the people around him.

"What?" Myste snapped behind him, in the same tongue. Thank the God she did—he wasn't sure he could even understand Valdemaran at this moment, much less respond in it. The visions shook him like a terrier with a rat.

The visions caught him up again and threatened to pull him in so far he would not be able to tell the others what he Saw; he struggled against them, against a Gift that was running away with him. *:Kantor!:* he cried, and a steadying presence held him out of the chaos of a hundred, a thousand disasters playing out at once inside his head. He could still *see* them, but at least he could manage to get a few words out.

"The cavalry has flanked us on either side, but not to attack *us,*" he babbled in Karsite, thanking Vkandis yet again that Myste was there. Myste, who knew Karsite, who could tell the King, tell the Lord Marshal— "They're clearing the countryside—burning the villages, killing the adults, rounding up the children—"

He knew why, but he didn't have time to explain; the visions took him again, despite all of Kantor's help. *A man pinned to the door of his own house by a spear. A child being wrenched from its mother's arms, and the woman tossed into the flames of her burning barn. The Tedrel cavalry, riding across the land like a wave of locusts, clearing it for its new masters, keeping only the young children, whom they would then take into their own ranks and turn into Tedrels—*

He struggled to speak, but his throat and mouth were not his own, not now while the visions held him. He knew dimly that he had gone rigid as a plank, jaw clenched, unable even to whimper.

Fire. Murder. Fear. Death. It went on forever. He was the helpless observer, unable to do anything save—sometimes, in brief moments when the visions released him—babble a report of what he saw, and *where* it was. Names came to him, the names of villages? Villages that were not going to exist shortly—but he called them out anyway. How much was *now* and how much *soon?* How many places were far enough distant that help *might* come in time?

He was engulfed in a sea of horror, until, without warning, the visions let go of him entirely, and he dropped back into his own time and place.

Head swimming, he looked up through streaming eyes to find that he was clinging with both hands to Kantor's stirrup and the pommel of the saddle, that he had buried his face in Kantor's shoulder.

Sendar and the Lord Marshal were arguing at the tops of their lungs, while Selenay's gaze switched from one to the other. *Her* face was white and pinched, and her hands in their armored gauntlets shook.

"But then, we'll *have* no reserves!" the Lord Marshal shouted.

"And what good will reserves do us if every creature older than a child on this side of the Border is dead?" Sendar shouted back. He whirled and turned to Talamir. "This is a royal command, King's Own. You *heard* where the attackers are, now deploy the reserves and every Herald not in combat to the rescue!"

Talamir bowed his head and closed his eyes for a moment, while Taver stood as steady as a statue. "Done, Majesty," the Herald said in a perfectly calm and slightly distant voice. "But you do realize that this will leave us seriously outnumbered on this field?"

Alberich was aware of movement, massive movement, behind them. The reserve troops were moving out, to the right and the left, the cavalry first. Ahead of them, on the swiftest steeds of all, two wings of Heralds, already speeding out of sight over the crest of the ridge, like a flock of swift, white birds. Behind them, the troops pulled out, leaving their rear unprotected.

"Of course I realize it," Sendar growled, and drew his sword, with a bright metallic *scrape.* It glittered wickedly in the sun, matching the hard gleam in the King's eyes. "We need to end this—*now.* Or we won't have a country left when we win the war." There was something wild in the King's eyes that Alberich recognized; something he had felt himself, down in the taverns of Haven. . . .

That feral look matched the savageness that *he* felt, when he let himself work out his frustration on the bodies of those two-legged beasts that populated Haven's criminal underground.

But he was only one Karsite Herald, and replaceable—not easily, perhaps, but replaceable. He could—marginally—rationalize risking himself. *This* was the King of Valdemar.

He's not— Alberich thought with sudden terror.

:He is!: said Kantor, grimly.

No— Sendar couldn't— Someone had to *stop* him!

And as Alberich struggled to pull himself up, the Companion gave a kind of twist and a shove with his nose just under Alberich's rump. That got Alberich most of the way into the saddle, and a gut-wrenching effort of arms and legs got him seated securely enough to turn and try to stop Sendar before he could move—

But the King was already gone, halfway down the hill, though Alberich had no idea how he could have gotten that far in so short a time.

Too late— He could do nothing for Sendar. But *Sendar* was Talamir's responsibility. Alberich had another.

"Stay here!" he roared to Selenay and her bodyguards, who were only just starting to react. The King's Six had—*Vkandis be thanked*—acted in concert with the King. They must have realized the moment he drew his blade what he intended to do; they rode with him, knee and knee, with Talamir at Sendar's right and Jadus at his left, a flying wedge that penetrated the ranks of those between them and the struggling front lines. A roar went up as the King, his banner bearer, and his escort of Heralds and Guards (and Healer!) entered the zone of fighting.

Alberich and Myste imposed themselves as a barrier between Selenay and the path to her father's side; the rest of her escort crowded in, hemming her and Caryo in among them. "Stay *here!*" he bellowed at her, trying to get her attention. "Selenay! Heed me!"

She had no intention of doing any such thing. He could see

it in her eyes, wild with fear and grief beneath her light helm. She hit out at them with mailed fists, flailing at them as she sobbed and cursed; she sawed at Caryo's reins, she even tried to fling herself off Caryo's back and follow on foot. But there were no divided loyalties among those who were protecting *her*. However suicidal Sendar's action might be, however much their hearts and minds cried out to follow him and protect him, their *duty* was with Selenay. To keep her safe. And if there was one thing that a Herald understood—or a Guardsman—

—or the Sunsguard—

—it was duty.

She wept and fought their restraining hands; she hit and screeched at them, with the background of the chaos of battle nearly drowning out her screams. She actually caught Alberich a glancing blow across his chin, and Herald Keren a direct hit that would leave her with a black eye soon. She called them cowards, traitors, and worse. She ordered them to let her go, pleaded with them, threatened them with imprisonment, whipping, death. He paid no attention to what she said, not because she didn't mean it, because of course, she *did,* but because it was irrelevant. No matter how much she cursed them now or hated them later, they *would* keep her here, out of the fighting.

Satisfied that her bodyguards had her pinned, if not under control, he edged Kantor out of the tangle and let Myste take his place. The danger to *her* was not less with Sendar down on the battlefield. If anything, it was greater.

He pulled his own sword and stood lone guardian for a moment over the group, his eyes raking over the hilltop, looking for help. He was in luck; there were still a few of the Royal Guard who stood hesitantly nearby, milling a little in confusion. *They* were not mounted, not swift enough to follow Sendar on his headlong plunge toward the fighting-zone; they were torn between trying to battle their way toward him and staying to guard the Heir. Alberich solved their hesitation for them.

"To Selenay!" he roared at them; given clear orders, they gratefully obeyed, and made a second line of defense in a half-circle around her, weapons at the ready, a line of four archers kneeling in front of another five swordsmen.

He turned back to the group around Selenay; she was still in danger, if the enemy archers took it into their heads to shoot. Perhaps only the fact that the Tedrel commanders wanted her alive had kept them safe so far, for they were the *only* members of the command group still on the ridge. Everyone else, the Lord Marshal included, had followed Sendar. He wanted to look—but Selenay's safety came first.

"Get her *down!*" he shouted, "On the *ground!*" and enforced his order with Mindspeech. No telling which of them would hear—but the Companions would. *Caryo* would. *"On the ground, unhorsed, get her down! Form the turtle!"*

The others fell back a little, as Myste half-lunged and half-fell off her Companion, taking Selenay and the banner with her, while Caryo helped by giving a buck and a twist to dislodge her rider. Myste and Selenay disappeared as Keren and Ylsa spilled off their mounts and formed the turtle over them with their shields. The Guardswomen looked uncertain for a moment. "You four, ahorse stay—help me!" he shouted at them, and they stayed mounted. *:Kantor, I want the Companions and us between the enemy and Selenay, but behind the Royal Guard. Make a circle.:*

:Right.: The Companions, now without riders, made a square of their bodies around the turtle. "Yourselves space out," Alberich ordered. "Bunch not, but knee to flank go—Companion, Guard, Companion."

Garbled and heavily accented as his words were, they evidently figured out what he wanted; with riderless Companions between them, they wedged themselves into the circle, facing outward. Under the turtle of shields, there was still a lot of movement and raised voices, but nothing was coming out, so Alberich dismissed the struggle from his mind.

He looked sharply toward the battlefield; in the middle of the fighting, where it was at its most heated, the King's banner still waved. But—but *their* lines were now on the verge of the little stream, not behind it. Sendar's charge had carried the entire line of battle forward; insane as the move had been, it looked as if it might have had the desired effect.

He saw the faint movement above the heads of the milling fighters on the other side of the stream, behind the Tedrel lines, and acted on instinct.

"Shields up!" he shouted, and put his over his head as example. The others did the same.

Just in time; arrows clattered down on them, force in nowise spent by their long journey. The movement he'd seen *had* been the arrows arcing up to clear the battle lines from the Tedrel side.

The arrows fell harmlessly, thanks to his instincts; the shields, their armor, their mounts' armor, kept anyone from being hurt, and under the turtle, Selenay was completely safe. It sounded like being caught in a terrible hailstorm, however, and the first volley was followed within a moment by a second, a third—

:She's stopped fighting. I think the arrows have scared her.: said Kantor.

Good. One less thing to worry about.

"The turtle stay under! Shields up!" he ordered, as another rain of arrows clattered onto the upheld shields. He did not look behind him to see if he was being obeyed; he knew that even if Selenay rebelled, the Heralds would make sure she stayed put. *Myste* would sit on her to make certain of that.

An unfamiliar mind-voice touched his inward "ear." *:For once being clumsy paid off; if I'd tried to hang onto her and pull her onto my saddle, she'd probably have gotten away from* *me, but she couldn't do anything about my falling off with her.:*

:Myste?: He was astonished. She'd never tried to Mindspeak to him before.

:Don't worry, she can't get away from me now; I outweigh her by quite a bit. She might be a little squashed, but she can't get me off of her.: Although he was nothing like an Empath, he was astonished by the complex emotional overtones that came with her words. Amusement at her own expense, pain, anger, grief, frantic worry for herself, more worry about Selenay and Sendar, and over all, terror held rigidly in check. And yet, her thoughts were so clear, he could hardly believe it. *:Even if they get this far, they'll have to get through me to touch her, and there's a lot of me to act as a shield.:*

He didn't ask if she was all right; she wasn't, none of them were. *:Are you hurt?:*

:My lenses are broken, and I think I broke my ankle, but that's the least of our worries. Don't call anyone, and don't try and get me out of here for now. I won't be moving anyway until this is over, or unless you have to haul her out of here and run for it. Promise me, though, if that happens, make sure I get back in my saddle? I'm curious about these Tedrels, but not that *curious.:*

:You have my word.: He wanted to try and summon a Healer for her, for she must be in excruciating pain, but she was right, and with luck her armored boot would hold her ankle well enough in place that no further damage would occur until they had the luxury of worrying about it. Given the kinds of terrible wounds being inflicted out there in the zone of fighting, a broken ankle counted as "minor." There was no doubt that Myste *knew* what the right answers were, and was giving them, even though she probably was howling inside with terror and the "right" answers were the last thing she wanted to supply.

Probably? Given the level of terror and pain he sensed, she

was howling deep in her own heart, all right. Years ago, when she refused to learn weapons' work, this was the *last* thing he would have expected out of Trainee Myste.

And in that, he had done her a tremendous disservice. . . .

And I'll make it up if we live.

He turned his attention back to the battlefield, and for the first time, felt his heart rise, just a little.

The tide of battle was turning.

Sendar's charge had paid off in unexpected ways. The Tedrels had given up whatever battle plan they'd originally had, and were concentrating on trying to take him down. This had the effect of concentrating all of their attention on the center of the line, and gathering in fighters from the rest of the field as they *all* tried to be the one to take the King. Those who had been hired or recruited were the worst, for their motive was profit, not the gain of a new homeland. Even if the true Tedrel commanders had not put a price on King Sendar's head, these men would *think* there was, and anticipate a golden reward for killing him.

In the meantime, pulling away toward the center meant that the Valdemaran forces were able to draw in to enclose the Tedrels on three sides. The thick press of Tedrels toward the King gave the Valdemaran archers somewhere to aim for, and they were taking advantage of that—those that were not already aiming for the *Tedrel* archers.

When the enemy is in range, so are you. . . . And there was only so much room in the King's immediate vicinity. The vast majority of those struggling to get at him could not actually fight *anyone* because of the press of their fellow fighters; they were tied up without being of any use. But the long Valdemaran pikes could reach *them,* and so could the spearmen, the archers, and the warhammers.

The sight of their King in danger was enough to put extra strength in the arms of Valdemaran fighters. The sight of the

King within reach had drawn the Tedrel leaders down off *their* hill.

And when you are in range, so is the enemy!

The Lord Marshal was in the thick of the fighting, and so was Talamir; there was no one to ask permission of.

He hesitated. But only for a moment.

To the Hells with permission. I'll apologize later.

:Are there any Heralds with bows and *the Fetching Gift left here?:* he asked Kantor, with an idea so impossible, it just might be able to work.

:Ah—: Kantor paused; it was going to take a lot longer for Companion to speak to Companion in all of this mess. And he didn't want to distract anyone who was right in the middle of the melee either. He waited, watching the line of fighting swaying, slowly, like a sluggish snake. Retreating a little *there,* bulging a little *there—*

:Four. And they've pulled out of combat for the moment.:

:Have them shoot for the Tedrel commanders, and put Fetching Gift behind it.: Whether they could even *do* that, he had no idea, but if they could, it would be something no Sunpriest would think of guarding against, if it even *could* be guarded against.

If there are any Sunpriests still helping them. He had to wonder, in the back of his mind, if the reason his Gift had suddenly broken through was because the Karsite Sunpriests had abandoned their erstwhile allies as soon as the Tedrels were fully occupied with Valdemar. . . .

He hoped so. If the priests decided to mix in with this, it would make things so much worse.

At this distance, he couldn't see anything other than the dark purple blot under the purple Tedrel battle banners; he couldn't make out individual arrows, and he *wouldn't* see anyone fall if they were hit, so he didn't even trouble to try to watch for it. He would know if anything happened by the tide of battle. *:If there are any Animal Mindspeakers still here, ask* *if they can spook the Tedrel horses.:* One more bit of damage; the officers were all ahorse, and even if his arrow trick didn't work, if he could drive them off, there would be less control on the battlefield.

He didn't want to interfere any more; the rest of the Heralds were the only way the various parts of the Valdemaran Army had to communicate with one another. Things were falling apart on their side badly enough as it was.

Instead, he kept his shield above his head, although there were no more hails of arrows. The Valdemaran archers were doing that much, forcing the Tedrel archers to duck under cover, or even into a full retreat. And he kept Kantor turning in a slow circle, watching not only to the front, but to the rear and the sides, looking for a suicidal charge into *their* ranks, assuming that there could still be an attempt to capture or kill Selenay. Of course, the Tedrels might not realize Selenay was still here; her battle banner was on the ground, dropped when Myste lunged for her, and the only white uniform on this hilltop was Alberich's.

All the more reason to keep the four of them on the ground.

Then it came—

A flash of blue.

On the left; attackers, fresh, unwounded, and seasoned, hidden in a ditch full of bushes and about to emerge.

It wasn't *much* warning, but it was enough; he turned to the left, spotted movement and shouted, pointing with his sword to get the attention of Selenay's guards.

And they just popped up out of nowhere, a band of twenty, thirty—forty?—more?—suddenly *materializing* as if conjured—but they hadn't been, of course; they'd found cover and slipped through the lines, avoiding detection by avoiding fighting. It was a trick he'd used himself, and so had the bandits he'd fought.

And now, at last, he had something he could vent his own anger and fear against.

His blood pounding in his ears, he howled a curse at them; Kantor didn't need the touch of a heel. Kantor was just as eager for blood as *he* was. What Sendar could do, *he* could do, and for as good a cause—keeping Selenay safe.

Buying some time for her guards to react.

Before the Guardsmen on foot could rearrange their line of defense to meet the attackers, *he* was racing toward the ambushers. Not so far to go, after all; ten of Kantor's long strides at most before he crashed into the first knot of them.

Lightly armored, of course, *much* more lightly than he, to facilitate slipping through cover.

First mistake.

He got a brief glimpse of a swarthy face beneath a light cap helm—a true Tedrel, then. This *was* a group sent to capture the Heir. He swung his blade at the same time as he got that glimpse of *target,* and he felt the shock of his sword meeting flesh as he slashed across the line of the eyes. The man fell; Kantor made a ferret-quick turn to trample him. Then he and Kantor were among them, and for the first time, he learned what it was like to fight with a Companion as a partner.

He gave himself up to it. In fact, he gave himself up *totally* to it, to the terrible joy of killing, for the first time in his life. He would probably be sick later, but now—

Now, these beasts, these fiends, were here to murder his friends, his brothers and sisters, to enslave his country. They were going to take or murder that sweet, cheerful girl he'd come to admire so much, who was so very old for her few years, and yet so charmingly young. They, and others like them, were killing innocent, ordinary farmers like those boys and girls he and Selenay had met around the fires, old men like Dethor and women like Myste, mothers like his—

Now he and Kantor would kill *them.*

He felt Kantor's rage along with his own; Kantor reveled in the shock that traveled up his arm with every good blow—he rejoiced in the impact of Kantor's hooves on flesh. They moved as one in an awful and glorious dance of death, as Kantor's white hide and his white uniform and armor were spattered, splattered, drenched in red, as red blood ran down his sword arm and soaked into Kantor's legs. Kantor danced on bodies that *crunched* and screamed; he reared and kicked, hooves connecting with heads and bodies, before and behind. They were surrounded; Alberich didn't care. *Let* them waste their force on him! *He* was expendable; Selenay was not.

He used his shield as a weapon as well as protection, the heavy metal frame as a club.

And his sword made short work of those too-light cap helms, when he struck them at all. Mostly he went for the faces—the eyes, those dark and fierce eyes that held no pity and no remorse, only a flicker of terror when the blade came at them. He reveled in the terror. He wanted more of it.

He howled in protest when they slashed at Kantor's rump; Kantor screamed in rage as they cut through his armor into his leg.

They fought as he had never before fought in his life, without effort, with endless strength and energy, and in a white heat of rage that slowed time and sped his reactions.

And still they fought—and continued to fight—

The briefest possible flicker of blue hazed his vision for a moment, but not even his Gift could conquer *this* unbridled rage.

But something was going to happen—

Something *awful* was going to happen—

Then a sickening blow to the soul—

—that should have sent him to his knees—

—told them both that Sendar—

—Sendar, his patron—Sendar, his King—

For a moment, just a moment, *he* leaped skyward, out of his body, and found himself looking down on the field of battle where tiny creatures fought and died. There *he* was, the sole target of a circle of Tedrel elite, who had forgotten their primary mission in the face of *his* attack. He continued to fight like a night-fiend, despite the fact that *he* wasn't "there" anymore.

Another blow, nauseating and disorienting, struck him; his attention snapped to the battle line.

Sendar was cut off from the rest of the Valdemaran forces, with only his bodyguards for protection. *He* fought like a demon, and so did they, but even as Alberich realized what peril they were in, three of the bodyguards went down, leaving only Crathach, Jadus, and Talamir to fight with him. There was a blur of motion just *under* the noses of the Companions. A shriek of pain that came from the soul of Taver as well as the body, and Taver flung up his head.

Then a burly hulk with an ax swung at Talamir.

No—*not* at Talamir—at Taver! At the exposed neck—

—of the King's Own Companion—

Nothing could have survived that blow to the neck, no matter how heavily armored. Taver went down, blood gushing from the severed throat, neck snapped, Talamir with him, leaving the King's right flank open.

No!

Alberich howled in protest, uselessly, silently—but suddenly Jadus was there, between the King and the axman, and the ax came down—

This time, not across a Companion's neck, but across Jadus' leg. The Companion, reacting to his Chosen's agony, shied sideways, leaving Sendar unprotected.

As if in a nightmare where time slowed to a crawl, yet nothing could be done to stop what was happening, Alberich saw a hundred fighters moving at the same time. Saw the mob close in, like a pack of rabid dogs, shoving Crathach into Sendar's side, hemming in the horse and Companion so that neither could move.

Watched as too many weapons to count pieced first Sendar's Companion, then Sendar.

Flicker of blue— and a wave of sickening horror *smashed* him back into his body. But he knew what he had seen was real.

Sendar, the King of Valdemar—

—was dead.

That was when a shriek of berserk rage tore the throat of every man and woman in the army, and sent them against their foes in a killing frenzy such as no Valdemaran had experienced in three centuries or more. He and Kantor rode that wave of bitter, mindless hatred, rode it and used it and let it use them, until it ran out—

—and the foes ran out—

—and left them, like every other surviving fighter on the Valdemar side, exhausted and sickened; blinking at the carnage around them, peering at death through eyes that streamed with agonized tears, in grief and mourning that would never entirely be healed.

THE taste of blood was in his mouth; the sweet-sickly stench of it in his throat. His nostrils felt choked with it.

He thought, vaguely, that he *should* be on his knees, throwing up what little there was in his stomach. But instead, all he could feel was grief and numbness.

:Selenay—: prompted Kantor, with unutterable weariness, turning his head in the direction of the Heir.

No, not the Heir, he reminded himself, with a stabbing sensation in his heart. *The Queen.*

He wiped blood and sweat away from his eyes, and peered though a haze of exhaustion toward her circle of protection. He hadn't prevented all of the Tedrels from getting to her and her guardians, after all—just a great many of them. Another clot of bodies marked where the Royal Guardsmen and her bodyguards had taken care of the ones that had gotten by him. Four of the Royal Guardsmen were dead, the rest wounded, two of the four mounted bodyguards were down.

Kantor stumbled to them; he half fell out of the saddle. His leg slash and half a dozen other wounds burned with a fire of their own, but he knew from the way they felt that though they hurt like demons were poking him, they were relatively minor. He wasn't going to bleed to death any time soon, and his injuries weren't going to incapacitate him. Therefore, as he had countless times when he was injured, he would carry on, if need be, until he dropped.

Berda and Locasti were on the ground with their great-hearted horses standing over them like guard dogs. Locasti sat up just as he got there, holding her head in both hands; a dented helm told him what had happened to her. It was a *good* helm, that, double-walled, with extra space between the inner and outer wall on the top of the head—a helm inside a helm, so to speak. Good job it was built that well; it had saved her from a cracked skull or worse.

Berda rolled over on her side, moaning, and Lotte slid down off her mount to help her; blood spewed from the knee joint of her armor. But she was still alive, and Lotte was down beside her, tearing off the thigh armor to get a belt around the leg even as he reached them. Lotte had a slash of her own down her arm that she didn't seem to notice—or else she didn't care, knowing that it was minor compared to that leg wound.

She's going to lose that leg, he thought dispassionately, looking at the joint laid half-open. *Better that than her life. Much better that than losing Selenay. . . .*

:They're telling me all over the field that what's left of the Tedrels are routed,: said Myste into his mind, with a deceptive calm that overlaid hysteria. *:The others are telling me that they're disengaging and scattering to the four winds. And our reserves have caught up with their cavalry and they're cutting them to finely-chopped bits. I think we can get up now.:*

That was when he realized that she was Mindspeaking Keren and Ylsa—and the Companions—as well as himself. The Companions spread out, and the little armored shell at the heart of their circle opened up.

"Your guard drop not," he croaked, as Keren and Ylsa stood up, Ylsa hauling a weeping Selenay up by main force. Myste stayed where she was.

"We don't intend to," Keren said grimly, and put her back to Selenay, shield up, facing out.

Alberich dropped heavily to one knee before the Queen, who stared at him without comprehension, her face contorted with grief, tears pouring down her cheeks. Perhaps it was without recognition as well; his Whites were saturated with drying blood, the white leather-and-plate armor over it blood-streaked and crusting. He must look like something out of a nightmare.

"Majesty," he said in a harsh voice from a throat made raw with screaming. "To your people, you must show yourself. *Now.* Your banner must fly. Know they have a Queen, they must."

He really, truly didn't expect her to understand him. He didn't think she would even *hear* him, much less realize what he had just said.

But as Ylsa's armored hand fell on her shoulder in a gesture as much of comfort as a hand in a gauntlet could convey, he watched sense come into her eyes, watched with awe and wonder as she somehow—out of what reserves, he could not even begin to imagine—pulled herself together. She pulled off her gauntlet and wiped her streaming eyes with the back of her hand, then straightened. "You're right, of course," she said, in a flat voice. "Myste?"

"Working on it." He saw that Myste had hauled herself to her feet—

—no, *foot,* for the other one was held clear off the ground—

—and her Companion was lying down on the ground so she could get into the saddle. She did so with a grunt of pain, leaned over and picked up the bloody, muddy battle banner by a corner of the fabric. Her Companion heaved herself to her feet, rider and all, and Myste manhandled the banner back into its socket. In the next moment, Selenay mounted Caryo, and pulled off her helm so that her golden hair shone in the westering sunlight.

:Heralds of Valdemar—: Myste Mindcalled, the voice echoing painfully in Alberich's skull. That was a *strong* Mindcall. *:Behold your Queen.:*

"Alert remain!" Alberich growled to the remaining bodyguards, and dragged himself back up into the saddle, though a gray film of exhaustion seemed to fog everything.

He made a trumpet of his hands, and shouted what Myste had called out to those with Mindspeech. He was used to bellowing battlefield orders—he put every bit of that into his shout.

"Valdemar! Behold your Queen!"

From that vantage, he watched as slowly, slowly, heads turned toward them, in a wave of motion starting from those nearest the group on the hill until it reached even to where there were knots of fighting still going on.

Myste was right, though; from where he sat, there was more fleeing than fighting, and as combat broke off, those who could still move took advantage of the momentary distraction of their opponents to escape.

There was still a pool of purple between the Valdemaran lines and the hilltop, but it wasn't moving, and the battle banners were nowhere to be seen. Could the Tedrel High Command actually be *dead?*

:I think so—: Kantor told him, after a moment. *:Yes. Your idea worked. The Fetching-Heralds did it, when Sendar died.:*

He winced; for a moment he had difficulty breathing. *If only they could have done it before—*

So many "if onlys." Never had a victory felt so much like a defeat.

:The Lord Marshal?: he asked Kantor.

:Coming.:

A strange silence fell over the battlefield; the sunlight

glittered on helms, but there wasn't a single raised sword or spearpoint to be seen. The pressure of thousands of eyes was a palpable force that even Alberich, in his exhaustion, felt.

Then it began, weakly at first, but gathering strength, a sound—

—a cheer—

Wordless, inarticulate, torn from the throats of exhausted men and women, grew and grew from a thread to a river, from a river to a torrent, to a wall of sound that surrounded them.

They came, walking, then running, sometimes dropping weapons, but all, all cheering; some weeping while they cheered, but all of them saluting her, their Queen—Valdemar incarnate.

And when they reached her, they reached for her, hands outstretched to touch her, touch Caryo, assure themselves that she *was* alive, was real. She reached out to them, touching hands, faces, and as each one of them got that assurance, he made way so that others could discover for themselves that their hope still lived.

Caryo began to move forward, one slow and infinitely careful step at a time, taking her through the sea of upturned faces and reaching hands. Alberich and her remaining four bodyguards followed, though what they could do in this press of bodies if anything happened—

:Let anyone so much as breathe harm on her and the army will tear him to pieces,: Kantor said. *:She's safer now than she has ever been.:*

The Lord Marshal's horse swam through the river of humanity to meet them, and Alberich was immensely grateful to see him. Alberich knew *nothing* of Courts and politics, and without missing a beat, he and Kantor dropped back to ride just behind and to her right, as the Lord Marshal took the place on her left. He wasn't sure where they were going, except farther into the battlefield, until they got there—and he was having enough trouble staying alert and concentrating on Selenay's back to think about it.

It was slow going, wading through that surging sea of humanity. It must have taken at least a candlemark to get from where they'd been to where they were going. And by that time, the handful of men and women who had not been pressing toward the young Queen had accomplished a great deal. . . .

They passed through a protective ring of Guardsmen into a clear space; the men working there among the fallen stopped what they were doing and respectfully dropped to their knees. There was another pile of Tedrel bodies laid to one side—a very large pile. The bodies of several Guardsmen had been laid out respectfully in a neat row, their weapons in their dead hands clasped on their chests. And the blood-drenched, white bodies of two Companions— *Idiot. Of course she'd come here first.*

Selenay slid from Caryo's back to kneel at her dead father's side.

They'd already laid him on a stretcher, with his banner draped as a pall across his body. She pulled the fabric down to reveal his face.

Alberich couldn't watch; he felt as if he was intruding on what should have been a private moment. He wondered if she hated him for keeping her away from her father's side; if she would ever forgive him for keeping her "safe" at the moment. But as he turned away, he caught sight of Healer Crathach sitting on the churned-up, bloody ground with Talamir's head in his lap, both hands resting on the Herald's forehead.

Kantor stepped carefully to the side, to stand over them. Crathach looked up as if he had felt Alberich's gaze on him. His eyes were haunted, but fierce.

"He wants to die," Crathach said, in a low voice, hoarse with shouting, screaming, and weeping. "He wants to follow Taver. But I won't let him, not now. Selenay needs him. We can't afford an untrained Queen's Own, not now; she needs someone with every bit of international, Court, and political experience possible."

"Hold to him, then," Alberich agreed. "Jadus?"

"They've already taken him to the Healers' tent. There's nothing left of his leg to save, but he'll live." Crathach growled. "Bloody hell. Those bastards knew *exactly* what to do at the worst possible time. We were holding our own until they got us too crowded together for the hooves to come into play, then sent a man in to hamstring the Companions."

Alberich bit back an oath. No wonder the two Companions had gone down so easily! And no wonder Sendar had faltered just long enough for the fatal blow to fall. "Stand fast, can you?" he asked.

"As long as I have to—the new Grove-Born should be coming as fast as he can; I just have to hold until he comes." What he was saying made no sense to Alberich's weary mind, but it was too much to try and think about. Jadus and Talamir were going to live; that was all that counted. A pair of stretcher carriers came up, then, and Crathach let them take Talamir up, though he kept one hand on the Herald's head the whole time. They carried the Herald away, with Crathach, as it were, attached.

Alberich found himself swaying in the saddle, and dragged his attention back to Selenay. She had drawn the fabric over her father's face again, and now she stood up.

"Gently bear him away, and prepare him for his journey," was all she said, but there was a rush of volunteers, most of them still weeping, and when the stretcher was picked up there was not a finger's width of it that did not have an eager hand supporting it.

As the body was taken through the crowd, men fell silent, removing their helms and standing with heads bowed until it had passed them. Selenay stood looking after it, with the last scarlet rays of the sun turning her golden hair to a red-gold crown.

Then she mounted Caryo again, summoned Alberich and the Lord Marshal with a glance, and rode from the silent field back to the encampment. For a moment, a curtain of gray haze came between Alberich and the world; it cleared up in the next heartbeat, but it was a sign he couldn't ignore.

Alberich signaled Kantor to drop back a pace, putting him even with Ylsa. "You and Keren—" he began

"We've already figured *you're* in no shape to protect anything," the rangy Herald told him bluntly. "We're on it. And what's more, the minute she dismisses you, there'll be a Healer waiting to take *you* off."

"Ah—my thanks," he managed. Let them decide for themselves what he was thanking them for. He urged Kantor up again. They passed through the camp, and as they did, it was through another corridor of battered fighters. Some wanted to touch her or Caryo, some just saluted her respectfully. Some murmured things like "The Gods bless you, Majesty," and others gazed in worshipful silence. A tiny shard of Alberich's mind that was still able to think was both pleased and sorrowful at these demonstrations. Pleased, because his work with her among the fighters had born such fruit—and full of remorse because the harvest had been gathered too soon.

They moved now through a blue haze of twilight; he was grateful, for it cloaked the injuries, hid the wounds of men and beasts in soft shadows from which the color had been leeched. And he was grateful, too, for the fact that he needed only to sit Kantor's saddle for the moment. He wasn't certain he was up to much else. When they reached the command tent, she paused, and did not dismount as he had expected she would. Instead she turned Caryo so that they faced the crowd of quiet men and women who had followed her.

Someone brought torches and stood to either side of her, so that she was clearly illuminated. Her young face looked years older than it had this morning; her cheeks smudged and armor and surcoat dirtied from the struggle to escape from Myste,

Keren, and Ylsa. And still she looked, he thought, every inch a Queen. "We have fought a terrible foe today, and we have won," she said to all of them, her voice carrying across the stillness. "And it has been at a cost that none of us would willingly have paid. I do not speak of the loss of my—my father only; I do not speak of your gallant friends and comrades only. But many, if not all of you, know that our battle plans changed without warning, and that King Sendar made a strange and some might say, suicidal charge toward the enemy that ended in his death and that of many, many others. There was a reason for that, and I believe that you should all hear *why* my father acted as he did today."

She told them all then what had happened up there on the hillside; why Sendar had sent away the reinforcements, and why he had subsequently made of himself such tempting bait that the main Tedrel army threw away their own plans and strategy, and were lured into defeat. All this was new to those straining to catch her every word—and there was one telling omission. She did not say it was Alberich who'd had the visions; she let them think it had been Sendar himself.

He was astonished, amazed—it was a brilliant stroke, for it made Sendar just that little bit larger than life, that more of a hero, while at the same time it kept Alberich's Gift a secret among the very few that he knew could be trusted with it. If he'd thought of it himself, it was exactly what he'd have asked her to say. Since *she* thought of it, he could not have been more proud of her.

"We have lost a great King this day," she said, when the murmurs of wonder had died away. "We have lost a King who cared so deeply for the lives of his people that he flung his own down to save them; we have lost a wise and compassionate leader, and a great-hearted man as well. And I have lost, not only a father, but my best and truest friend."

Her voice caught on a sob, but she stopped for a moment, wiped her eyes, and went on. "But Valdemar lives, and I live, and together, we will make certain to be worthy of his sacrifice. There is much to do now, and much that will need to be done in the future, but we have proved today that together there *is* no foe that can stand against us, and no matter the odds, we *will* prevail!"

A great roar went up as she dismounted and gave Caryo into the willing hands of waiting aides. Keren and Ylsa were a fraction of a moment behind her, flanking her as she walked into the command tent.

Alberich did not so much dismount as fall out of the saddle, and he had to cling to it for a moment before his head cleared. Kantor swiveled his head to peer at him, but before the Companion could say anything, more aides came to take Kantor away with the other three Companions. Alberich set his jaw, swayed for a moment, and followed Selenay into the tent, intending to stay discreetly on the sidelines. That gray haze clouded his vision, but he had fought it away before, and he would fight it away now.

That was his intention, anyway—

What *happened* was that he got three paces inside the door flap, that grayness turned to blackness, and he passed out cold at Selenay's feet.

He came awake all at once, and blinked up at white, sunwashed canvas.

"It's about time," Myste said dryly, as he realized he was not alone and this was not his tent. "Layabout. Come on, get up and get out of that cot; they need it for someone who's *really* hurt."

He sat up; it was a *big* tent, and it was full of more cots like his. He had been put in one right beside the tent wall; his nearest neighbor was—

"Jadus—" he said.

The lean Herald turned to face them without raising his head from the pillow, and grimaced. "In the flesh, most of it. They had to take the leg."

Jadus' eyes had that half-focused look of someone powerfully drugged; Alberich was surprised he could speak at all. "The saying should be, better the leg than the life."

He shouldn't have said that; he knew it as soon as the words were out of his mouth. Too late. "Better mine than *his,*" Jadus replied, voice thick with sorrow. "But I didn't get to make a choice."

"Seldom does anyone." Alberich reached across and put one hand on Jadus' arm. He didn't have the words of comfort he wanted, not even in his own language, but Jadus seemed to understand that he meant to offer whatever support he had without words.

"Thank you," Jadus told him, in a tone that said he meant the words. "You know—they just dosed me. I believe I need to sleep . . . now. . . ."

His eyelids dropped, and in a moment, he *was* asleep.

"Poor man. I hope we can find something he can teach at the Collegium—" Myste began, but Alberich interrupted her.

"Bah! A sad day indeed it will be, the day a Herald needs two legs to do his duty!" He would not hear of it, a healthy man, certainly no older than the late King, being given make-work, just because he lacked half a limb. "And of legs speaking—"

He looked down at hers; one of them was in a rather odd boot. A very *thick* boot. "I note that *you* manage, having not quite a whole leg. Unless a phalanx of slave boys you have, to carry you a litter upon."

She smiled faintly. "Yes, I broke my ankle. No, I'm not letting it stop me, though let me tell you, it *still* hurts like seven hells, and it's only because the Healers are very good that I'm not screaming now. Between their off-and-on magics and some truly vile concoctions, even if it hurts, I tend not to care, if that makes sense. And this plaster boot they've granted me lets me get around." She looked wistful for a moment. "Though, come to think of it, I wouldn't *mind* a squad of litter-carrying slave boys . . . ah, never mind. I'm supposed to tell you that Selenay sent me for you."

"Me?" He stared at her; he wasn't certain he'd heard her correctly. One of his last thoughts before he passed out, after all, was how long she would hate him—

"Of course, you. You saved her life, she knows that. *Everyone* knows that. You did it twice over, in fact, once by keeping her from following Sendar, and again, when that lot of infiltrators popped up." She spoke matter-of-factly, in such a way that he could not doubt her. "And you did more than that, although there aren't too many who know it was you that caused Sendar to send the reinforcements out to save the countryside. Ah—" She hesitated. "Just so you know, Selenay wants to keep it that way, except for those of us who were there."

He didn't feel up to stumbling his way through Valdemaran anymore, and reverted to Karsite. "Myste, I have *no* objection to that. He might just as well have had the visions as I; what did or could *I* do about them? I just blurted them out to you, and not even in a tongue he could understand. *He* understood what they meant, and in his greatheartedness, elected to save his land rather than his own life. He charged the front line, knowing what he was doing, and knowing full well that he had less chance of surviving that charge than a rabbit charging a pack of foxes. Let his people think whatever they want; he deserves all of it."

"I told her you'd feel that way." She nodded. "Anyway, Selenay did indeed send me this morning to stay here with you until you woke, and tell you to come to her when you did. A bit melodramatic, that, passing out at her feet, wasn't it?"

He winced. "I hope I was discreet about it."

"You weren't, but I don't think anybody cared; actually,

those of us who were still able to think were trying to figure out if we'd have to get Crathach to mind-blast you to get you to stop being so infernally noble and self-sacrificing." She lifted an eyebrow at him. "You saved us from that by neatly falling over."

Well, he was cleaned up, at least; *someone* had done him that tremendous favor, and left him to sleep off his exhaustion in a clean white shirt and trews. The rest of his Whites were beside him on a chair. He started to reach for them—

"No," he said aloud. "I put them on for Sendar, but I do not think I will wear Whites again. Not unless there is a pressing reason."

Myste pursed her lips, but looked curiously satisfied, as if she thought she had been particularly clever. "I thought you might say that. So I stopped by your tent, and brought these."

She pulled a basket out from under his cot—and there were *his* form of the Heraldic uniform; the dark gray leathers he had worn up until they had left Haven.

"Are you certain you are not an Empath?" he asked,

"No, I'm a Herald with work to do, and now that you've been informed that Her Majesty wants you, I need to go do it." She softened her words with a slight smile, then suddenly reached out and took his hand.

"But I won't always have work to do," she said, giving it a slight squeeze. "And I find you excellent company because I don't have to pretend or mince words around you."

Then she picked up a crutch from beside her stool, stood up, and hobbled off.

He stared after her with bemusement.

:You really don't *know what to do with a woman who isn't either untouchable or a whore, do you?:* said that familiar, faintly mocking voice in his mind.

:Well, why don't you *teach me?:* he shot back, stung, and reached for his familiar gray leathers.

:I might. But you'll have to ask me nicely.:

His ears burned.

Changing swiftly, he headed out of the tent, intending to pause only long enough to tell one of the Healers that he would not be needing that cot beside Jadus anymore.

But the first Healer he ran into was a very familiar face, and one he had not expected to see tending to the wounded.

"Crathach!" he exclaimed, and seized the man's arms, grasping him by the elbows with both hands. "But—Talamir—"

"Come see for yourself," the Healer said, taking *him* by the elbow. Crathach led him out of the ranks of the Healers' tents, and into the ring of command tents. Alberich could not help but notice some gaps, where tents *had* been—and felt a stab in his heart.

But one tent still stood. Crathach led him to it. As with many tents used by Heralds, it was fully large enough for a Companion to fit inside, for Heralds sometimes preferred to know that their partners were as comfortable as *they* were. Inside, Talamir lay quietly in his cot, and lying beside him on a worn, rag rug was a Companion.

For one moment, Alberich's heart stopped. There was only *one* Companion that had that special look, that faint aura of otherworldliness—

Taver?

He stopped himself from blurting it just in time. The Companion lifted his noble head, and looked into his eyes.

:Not Taver, Weaponsmaster. I am Rolan.:

"Your pardon," Alberich murmured, a little unnerved.

The Queen's Own's new Companion nodded his acceptance of the apology. *:It was a natural thought, and no harm was done. I am pleased to see you. We will probably be seeing a great deal of each other in the future, but if you will forgive me, I have* my *charge to tend for now.:* The Companion turned his gaze back toward the quiet figure on the cot.

Talamir no longer looked like a corpse, but he had aged,

and aged greatly, in—what? Less than two days? He had looked no older than Sendar, middle-aged at worst, before the battle; now he looked *old,* thin and worn-out with long struggle, his face etched with lines of pain. And he looked fragile. Alberich felt his heart wring with pity, and wondered if, perhaps, it *would* have been better for him if he'd been allowed to die.

But that was not his decision to make—

Vkandis be thanked.

Crathach tugged at his sleeve, and they left the tent to the Companion and his charge. "He did what I could not," Crathach said. "How he got here in so little time—well, I can't guess. But he did what I couldn't. I could only hold him just out of reach of death's gate; Rolan dragged him back to life, then full awareness, and made him stay."

"He has awakened, then?" Alberich asked, still in a murmur, with a glance back at the tent.

"Several times. He's quite sane, now, and he doesn't seem to want to die, but he's fragile, Alberich, very fragile. I've told the Queen that he's not to do much for a while, and she agrees." Crathach tilted his head to one side, and gave him a penetrating look.

"Hmph." Alberich traded him look for look. "Then, until you say, so shall I *sit* upon him, if need be."

"I knew I could count on you." Crathach slapped him on the back. "Now, I think the Queen wants you."

"So I believe, and I shall my leave take of you." He hoped Crathach would say something that might give him a clue to the Queen's mood.

But Crathach didn't seem to have any more idea than he did. "Ever since Rolan arrived, I've been too busy to go near the command tent," he replied and sighed. "And at the moment, my services as a Healer are in far more demand than those as a bodyguard."

Alberich grimaced. "Wish I could, that otherwise it were."

Crathach nodded. "And I. It is good to be able to use one's Gifts, but—" He could only shrug helplessly.

They parted then, but having seen Talamir alive, if not exactly *well,* Alberich's heart felt a little lighter.

But now it was time to face the Queen. And he was not looking forward to that. For no matter what Myste said, *he* was not at all sanguine about his reception. Surely Selenay would never want to see his face again, after what he'd done to her. If nothing else, she would never forgive him from keeping her away from her father's side, and who could blame her?

Probably she wanted to see him only so that she could tell him she wanted him to return immediately to Haven and confine himself to the salle from now on. . . .

It was in this mood that he presented himself at the command tent.

The guards—*his* choice, he saw, with pride—let him past. He tried to slip in unnoticed, but Keren spotted him, and bent down to whisper in Selenay's ear. She looked up sharply.

"Herald Alberich—" she said.

Silence descended like a warhammer.

He cleared his throat awkwardly. "You summoned me, Majesty."

"I did. Come here, Herald Alberich." Queens did not say "if you please." Queens issued orders, and their subjects obeyed. As did he. He made his way between two ranks of officials and highborn who parted to let him pass, thanking his luck that the tent was not all *that* large, for to have to pass a gauntlet of only a double-handful of watchers was bad enough. She was sitting in her father's chair, at his table, and she watched him with a measuring gaze as he approached.

"Don't kneel," she said sharply, as he started to bend. "And look at me." She tilted her head to one side and looked him up and down. "You've gone back to your shadow-Grays, I see. Good; if you've no objection, except when we need you in Whites for—ah—*formal* occasions, I should like you to keep to them. It will serve very well to make it clear that while you are taking Talamir's place for some little while, you are not the Queen's Own."

He blinked. Surely he had not heard that correctly. "Majesty?" he faltered. "I am—what?"

"Crathach tells me that Talamir will not be fit for duty for a while. Until he is, I wish you to take his place, here, at my side." She smiled wanly. "At least until you resume your duties at the Collegium, that is. Crathach thinks Talamir will be ready by the time we reach Haven. I should like Keren to go back to what *she* does best in my bodyguard; meanwhile I need someone here beside me in the capacity of adviser as well as guard, someone with a level head who knows when his Queen needs to be dragged out of her saddle and sat upon."

"Yes, Majesty," he managed, and changed places with Keren, who looked only too happy to relinquish her position.

She resumed the business that he had interrupted, which seemed to concern those enemy fighters who had thrown down their weapons and scattered. Some of them, it was thought, had come north rather than south, and were trying to hide themselves in Valdemar.

There were several arguments ongoing as to the best way to hunt them down; brutal, savage plans, most of them. Apparently it was not enough that the entire command structure had been wiped out. There were plenty who wanted every single person who had so much as carried a bucket for the Tedrels hunted out and strung up on the nearest branch high enough to haul them off the ground, and the corpses left to hang there until they rotted away.

Selenay listened impassively until the various angry speeches had been made, then looked at Alberich.

"Well?" she asked. "Have you any suggestions?"

He supposed that, by all rights, he *should* have been just as full of righteous anger, but he wasn't. He was just—tired.

Tired of death, sick of the stench of it in his nostrils. He didn't want any more deaths, not if he could help it.

"Real Tedrels—if any live—dare not the Border to cross," he said slowly. "And I think the Sunpriests a most—unpleasant—fate will accord them, should they foolish enough be, in Karse for to stay, for heretics by the measurement of the Sunpriests the Tedrels most surely are. Say I would, that their welcome will *not* be warm, except, of course, that it rather *too* warm will be."

It took a moment for the others to realize what he had said, and more to figure out what he had *meant*. The Fires, of course; there wasn't a chance that any real Tedrels would be spared the Fires. Someone in the back snickered, although he had not meant it as a joke.

"As for the rest—" he shrugged. "The worst of mercenaries, and the most foolish of fortune hunters they are. Perhaps some are here, in Valdemar. The first—will swiftly run afoul of constables and Guards, or even of farm folk, and in trouble they soon will be, and have them you will. Now, how to tell are we *which* are those that fought here, and which mere outlanders? Arrest all, who with an accent speak?" He raised his eyebrow. "Then, without acting Queen's Own you will be—"

She blinked, but nodded, and some of the muttering stopped. He had to say this much for most of the people she had about her now, they weren't stupid.

"What is Valdemar if not just?" he asked rhetorically. "Leave some Guards, perhaps, to deal with them as found they are, but I think you need not hunt them. Live off the land, they cannot; when their swords they cannot hire out, leave they shall, or break the law, and so you have them, as *lawbreakers,* which can be proved. The second, either a lesson will have learned, or will not, and thus also—" He spread his hands.

"So you're saying we shouldn't track them down?" Lord Orthallen asked smoothly, as if the question was of no matter to him. "Just leave them as a menace to the countryside?"

"I say find them you will, without hunting. Hide, they cannot, and with nothing more than what on their bodies they have, little have they to live on, and only one trade they know."

"But what if they try and pass themselves off as laborers?" someone asked angrily.

Alberich raised an eyebrow. "To *escape* labor it was, that most turned to sell-swording. Wish them joy of it, I do—and find may they, only the hardhearted as masters."

"Please," said Selenay in an exasperated tone of voice, "Do *think* this through! Do any of you *want* to keep this army together, spending the treasury dry to feed them and keep them in wages, just to frighten the locals by riding over their fields and interrogating anyone who looks the least bit out of place? And how do you propose to tell one of these Tedrels from—oh, say a hillman out of Rethwellan looking for work? Or a poor brute of a Karsite who's taken advantage of this to cross into Valdemar for sanctuary? Or *are* you actually proposing, as Alberich said, to string up every man with a foreign accent from the nearest tree?"

"I repeat, begin with me, you would have to," Alberich pointed out gently.

There were some embarrassed coughs.

"I won't even *begin* to point out how my father would have responded to such an idea," she continued, looking at all of them and making a point of staring each in the eyes until he either dropped his gaze or met hers with agreement. "It is so totally foreign to *everything* Valdemar has always stood for! I agree with Alberich; if anyone *has* crossed to our side of the Border, the likeliest thing is that they'll try to get over to Rethwellan and be of no concern to us. If any stay, they will either settle and fit in, or *not* and break the law, and we can deal with them on that basis."

"Well, Majesty—" Lord Orthallen began.

But he was interrupted.

"Dammit, I *will* see Her Majesty!" snapped a querulous, aged, female voice that he knew and had *not* expected to hear. And a moment later, the owner of that voice, someone he knew—as well as he knew himself—

—pushed her way in past everyone.

He *should* know Herald Laika, though he'd last seen her just before she left to infiltrate the Tedrels in her guise of an old washerwoman. After all, he'd helped form half of the "memories" that now made her what she was.

:And given that fact, you shouldn't be surprised that she's as stubborn as a mule and as intractable as a goat,: Kantor put in, as she bullied her way right past the Lord Marshal, made a pretense at a courtly curtsy, then stood glaring at Selenay with her hands on her hips.

Selenay stared at her blankly and without recognition; well, she *wouldn't* recognize Laika, though she might know the name, for as far as Alberich knew, neither she nor Caryo would have seen Laika before.

"Herald Laika, Majesty," Alberich said carefully. "One of our four Herald-agents, behind Tedrel lines, she was. Within the camp; infiltrated, was she, as a washerwoman. And very valuable."

"Damn right," the old woman grunted. "And that's why I'm here. I want to know what the *hell* you're going to do about the children?"

Selenay blinked. "I beg your pardon, Herald Laika, but we do already have people—Healers and others—out trying to find the children whose parents were killed by the Tedrel cav—"

"Not *those* children!" Laika exclaimed. "Not the children of *Valdemar!* I'm talking about the Tedrel children! What are you going to do about the *Tedrel* children?"

"WHAT Tedrel children?" Selenay asked, blankly.

Alberich was going to explain, but Laika saved him the effort. "This wasn't just a mercenary company, this was a *nation,*" she said, with the irritation of a teacher whose student hasn't studied her subject sufficiently. "Granted, they'd made a vow never to wed or have families until they had a land of their own again, but that sure as hellfires didn't stop them from *breeding.*"

Selenay's eyes widened, and her mouth made a silent, "oh" shape.

"What's more, they used to pick up every stray boy-chick they could get their hands on and throw him in with the rest!" Laika continued. "Not to mention the ones they kidnapped, not a few of 'em from our own people. They didn't have much use for girls until they were of breeding age, but boys—oh, my, yes! *That's* why they were taking such pains to keep *our* littles alive, so they could turn *them* into Tedrels. Now you've got a camp full of orphans and other youngsters over there that the Karsites are *not* going to want. You've killed off their fathers and protectors, if they even *have* mothers, their mothers are probably halfway to Rethwellan by now and might not have waited about for them, and what are you going to do about it?"

"Won't the Karsites just take them?" Selenay asked, looking to Alberich.

"Probably—no," he said, reluctantly. "Karse needs no extra mouths that come not with hands that can work. And—they are heretics, and the children of heretics, and what is more, even their own blood, to the Sunpriests' eyes, they are *not*—or no longer are—Karsite."

He did not elaborate on what that meant, but there was something very unpleasant stirring in the back of his mind; something like a—protovision. An intimation, not of what *would* be or what was *about* to be, but what *might* be.

A vision of the Fires of Cleansing. And the fuel that fed them.

"I don't want to sound utterly callous and hardhearted, Herald, but—not to put too fine a point upon it, what *can* we do?" the Lord Marshal asked. "They're on Karsite land, in Karsite hands."

She looked at him as if he was an idiot. "And this stopped Vanyel? This stopped Lavan Firestorm?"

The Lord Marshal wasn't about to back down. "That was in another situation entirely," he retorted. "And if you're referring to the 'Demonsbane' legend, Vanyel was on *Hardorn* land, not Karsite."

Alberich cleared his throat. "Ah—Herald Laika—a question. Suppose I must, that *you* have these children been among. Think you, they can *be* anything but Tedrel?"

"Most of 'em aren't now," she replied, and shook her head. "Some of 'em, in fact, a lot of 'em, are Karsite orphans—some of 'em are camp followers' children. And, dare I repeat myself, *some* of 'em are ours, grabbed every time they hit Valdemar in the past three years! But like I said, they don't have much use for girls that aren't breeding age, so they don't pay any attention to 'em, and boys aren't useful until they're thirteen and old enough to take into a Tedrel lodge for training, so they're all right up until then. Basically, they're not Tedrel, they're not Karsite, they're not anything, really. When I was in there, they had a lot of the camp followers that were tending to all of them, and most of *those* were girls out of Rethwellan, Seejay, and Ruvan, with a couple of Karsites. So that's what they've been raised as."

"Raised as nothing, then," Selenay ventured.

"Pretty much. A pretty weird mix, they all speak a kind of Tedrel-pidgin with words from all over. The girls don't *ever* get taught pure Tedrel tongue; that's a man's mystery. The kiddies have got some little religious cult they've made up on their own that isn't like anything I've ever heard of. Like I said, they aren't Tedrel, they aren't anything." She sighed. "What they are, is dead needy for adult attention. Even an old hag like me, they swarmed over."

"But babies—without mothers—" someone put in doubtfully.

"Babes in arms—" she shrugged. "That little, the Tedrels don't take. The ones born to the camp followers, well, they may be whores, but they're still mothers; the ones that'll bolt, they'll take the children they can manage to carry and run for Rethwellan. That leaves the orphans, or ones whose mothers don't care, and there's a couple hundred, anyway, of an age we *could* rescue. No more than a thousand. . . ."

Selenay glanced at Alberich, who was thinking furiously. "Karse—I think *might* be busy—elsewhere—"

Elsewhere hunting down all the escapees on their *side of the Border and either conscripting them as bound slaves or making sure no one else ever does—*

"—and," he continued, "If the rescue and evacuation were made quickly, might not know it had been entered at all."

"And a thousand children?" Selenay gulped.

"It's not an *unmanageable* number," the Lord Marshal put in. "It's not as if it would be a thousand captives; most of them couldn't run far."

Laika snorted. "Show 'em food and smiles, and most of 'em won't run at all. And don't forget—*some of them are ours.* And if word gets out that we left *Valdemaran* children to starve or hope for the mercy of the Sunpriests. . . ." she let that particular statement sink in without elaborating. "What's more, they aren't more than a day's march inside Karse! When the Tedrels moved this time, they were preparing the full-on invasion, remember. They thought we were going to go over with just a push, and they had everything and everyone set to move straight across the Border."

"Surely not," Lord Orthallen said skeptically. "Surely they were not going to put all of *that* so close to the battle lines."

Laika smiled grimly. "And what makes you think they were unaware that the moment the fighters left the base camp, the Karsites were likely to grab everything? Believe me, that was the talk all over the camp—everyone wanted to be sure that *they* didn't get left behind. The last camp they made would be where they left all the non-combatants and the baggage and all. In fact, there was talk about setting it less than a half-day's march from the Border, figuring that the closer it was to Valdemar, the less likely it was that the Karsites would come calling. The campfire glow we saw in the farther sky last night was probably from their *full* camp, not their battle camp."

"I thought they looked rather too well-rested," murmured the Lord Marshal.

"Then that means we won't have to break the Border so much as—bend it a little," Selenay said speculatively. "I suppose one *could* consider what is in that camp to be legitimate war loot?"

Now it was the Lord Marshal's turn to smile grimly. "One could, Majesty," the Lord Marshal said, "And in fact, one *should.* Why, after all, should the Karsites have the benefit of this—war booty—when it is Valdemar that suffered?"

Alberich merely raised an eyebrow. "How can we, calling ourselves civilized, leave children to suffer? And welcome in Karse, they will *not* be."

Now Selenay looked to the rest of her advisers and commanders. "I—honestly, gentlemen, ladies—I think we should do this. I know we *can;* I think we should."

"Bringing life out of death?" asked the Chief Healer. "I don't think there is any doubt. *Sendar* would."

Selenay smiled wanly. "My father would have been at the head of the expedition," she said softly.

That seemed to decide them all, and the prospect of having a positive task to organize also seemed to galvanize them, lifting them somewhat out of the slough of depression that most of the encampment had sunk into.

The mood in the tent suddenly lifted, and even Selenay's voice took on more life than it had held since before the battle.

"We'll need wagons to carry the children, won't we?" she asked, breathlessly. "How many? Where will we get them?"

"We already have them, Majesty," said the Chief Healer, catching fire from her enthusiasm. "We were going to send some of the wounded north—leg injuries, not so serious, but needing some recovery—but they'll gladly wait for a little to save these children! The horses are harnessed right now, the wagons are provisioned, we haven't loaded the wounded yet—why, we can be ready to go on the instant!"

She turned to Alberich. "Would—you—"

"Of course he would!" the Lord Marshal exclaimed. "Great good gods, who else! You used to patrol here, didn't you, man? And you won't be doing without him for more than a day or two—"

"What about us?" Laika interjected. "Oh, good gods, not as leaders, but we know the Karsite language and we came across here to get out, and the children know *me,* at least."

"Give me a moment, and I'll send a messenger about the wagons," the Chief Healer put in, and they were off with the bit between their teeth. Alberich simply stood there, while all the decisions were made for him. They seemed to accept without question that Alberich should serve as the leader, and that Laika and the other three spies should be in the rescue party, and that it would consist of Heralds, Healers, and wagons. Heralds to act as eyes, ears, and if need be, guards, Healers to soothe the children, and wagons to carry them. The decision to go was made so swiftly that if—as Laika asserted, the camp was no farther than a half-day's march away—Alberich reckoned that they *might* get there and back by this same time on the morrow.

And it slowly dawned on him that no one, no one at all, even *thought* about the question of his loyalty. *Of course* he would lead the rescue; he was the best person for the job. *Of course* he would bring these children—some of them Karsite—back to Valdemar. And *of course* he wouldn't even consider taking the opportunity to defect back to his homeland. He was a Herald, wasn't he? Divided loyalties didn't even come into it.

Perhaps there were a few who thought differently, but there always would be. There would have been had he come from Hardorn, or Menmellith, or Rethwellan, or anywhere else other than Valdemar.

Within a candlemark, the whole thing was organized and ready to go, with plenty of volunteers. He hadn't been surprised by the ones among the Heralds or even the Healers, but the fact that the teamsters had lined up to a man had come as a bit of a surprise.

He was a little uneasy about leaving Selenay on her own, though. Still—

She was essentially on her own from the moment her father died. She has trained for this for years, hasn't she? If she couldn't handle the reduced Council *now,* when there was so little opposition and she was the darling of the army, what would she do back in Haven?

And as for her bodyguards—they were taking their job just as seriously now as they had before the battle. If any true Tedrels had survived, *now* would be the time for an assassination attempt, for now, whoever still lived had nothing to lose, and such men were the most dangerous of all.

Selenay saw them off, but she kept things brief. "Go safely and swiftly," she said, and impatient to be off, they took her at her word. She didn't linger to watch them rattle across the little stream at the Border either; when he looked back, she was gone.

Not only was he not surprised, he was pleased. It wasn't as if she didn't have more than enough on her hands, for the aftermath of a war generally left both sides in shambles. There were hundreds of decisions to be made, and in the end, only the Queen could make them. Then, when one factored in all of the messages and dispatches arriving from Haven moment by moment, every one of them requiring *her* attention, he was certain she would be getting very little rest between now and when he returned.

Which might be just as well. It would give her very little time to brood, and might exhaust her enough that she would actually sleep instead of lying awake, staring at the darkness behind her eyelids.

It was a strange sensation, crossing onto the Karsite lands of the hills, where he had once ridden at the head of a troop of Sunsguard. "A close watch keep, for bandits," he warned everyone when they first set out. "Driven away by the battle, they were perhaps—but like vultures, return to feast upon the slain they shall." He had to wonder, though, as they rode through empty valleys, and over hills bare of the usual flocks of sheep and goats, if the Sunsguard had actually sealed off this area. If that was the case, and bandits *had* fled the coming conflict, they could easily have run right into the Sunsguard.

He hoped so. He truly hoped so. Not only because it meant that *they* would not encounter any trouble going there and back, but because the scum that had fattened on the misery of the shepherds of these hills for so long well *deserved* to be cut down like the plague rats they were.

It was easy enough to know where to go, despite the fact that there was no road to follow. The marching feet of so many thousands of men had *left* a road across the landscape, the tough and wiry vegetation hereabouts pounded flat, then into dust. This was a tough country, of scrubby vegetation and endless hilly moors, punctuated (as he used to tell Dethor) by endless rocky hills, yet it had its own beauty. The gorse was in bloom, and the heather, and drifts of purple, white, and yellow spread hazy blotches of color across the face of those hills. The weather elected to smile upon them today—or the Sunlord Himself did—for the sun beamed down upon them, neither too brazenly hot, nor thin and chill, out of a sky whose blue was interrupted only by the occasional white, fluffy cloud like one of those missing sheep. Once or twice, they caught sight of wild goats on the ridges, or heard the bray of an equally wild donkey, but otherwise it was nothing but wind and birdsong.

He had no idea how low his spirits had been in the wake of the battle until they were well away from the battlefield, and he could allow himself to pretend it had never happened. But the clean wind swept through his heart and soul; he was going to a *rescue,* not a battle, and he felt as if the wind was carrying away his sadness, a little at a time.

And this was home . . . the breeze felt right, the hills *smelled* right, they were the right color of gray-green, and the right sort of rocks poked up through the thin soil. He might never see these hills again, so he absorbed the changing landscape, stowing it away in his memory to take out on those nights that would surely come, when he felt himself to be entirely alien in an alien land.

Finally, he had to remind *himself* to stay alert; this was no pleasure jaunt. Things could still go wrong at any moment. If the Sunsguard wasn't busy picking off former Tedrels, they could be here at any moment. . . .

:This is a handsome land,: Kantor observed, ears pricked forward to catch every sound. *:Hard, but handsome.:*

:I think so,: he agreed, secretly pleased by Kantor's compliment. *:Ah—we'll be coming up to a spring here shortly, if my memory of this area is any good. There aren't a lot of good watering places here; warn the others that we'll be stopping for a moment.:*

His memory *was* good—and interestingly enough, the Tedrels had not made use of the spring he recalled, for they had to deviate from the track and go over a hill to the east to get to the half-hidden water source. When they did, they found no sign that anyone had been there, and the Tedrels would surely have trampled the bank of the stream that the spring fed, and muddied the basin.

But Alberich was taking no chances. Just to be sure that they *hadn't* been here and tampered with the water (which would have been entirely like them) he called over one of the Healers.

"Test this, for fouling or poison, can you?" he asked the green-clad woman.

"Hmm." She gave him a sidelong glance, but bent to test the water, taking up a single drop on the end of her finger and touching it to her tongue. "That would have been like those bastards, wouldn't it?" she said absently. "Spoil what's behind them so the Karsites couldn't follow."

"My thought," he agreed gravely.

"Well, it's clean; you can bring them all in." She stood up; he waved at the wagons, and the teamsters brought their charges in to drink at the stream fed by the spring, while the humans drank at the source. Tooth-achingly cold, the water tasted of minerals. The horses adored it. Fortunately, they were not so thirsty that they were in any danger of hurting themselves by drinking too much, too fast.

He kept an eye on the crests of the hills around them; the disadvantage of stopping here (or anywhere) for a drink was that doing so made them very vulnerable. But this spring, flowing as it did out of the side of a hill, at least was not as exposed as the stream it fed, that ran along the bottom of the valley. He put a lookout on the crest of the hill, which was all anyone could reasonably do, and trusted also to his Gift and that of the FarSeer that was with them to warn of any danger approaching.

But all that appeared was a herd of sheep and a dog—and a very brief glimpse of the shepherd, who turned his flock aside and back over the hill when he saw them.

:At least he'll know the water's safe,: Kantor pointed out, as he rounded everyone up, anxious to be gone now that they had been spotted. *:I don't think he's likely to say anything to anyone for a while. Days, probably.:*

Considering the taciturn nature of the lone shepherds here, Alberich was inclined to agree. The Sunpriests hated them, for they could not be controlled as easily as villagers. They thought their own long thoughts alone out here, for moons at a time, and could not be compelled to come for the regular temple services. You could not leave sheep to tend themselves while you hiked to the nearest village for SunDescending, Sun-Rising, Solstice and Equinox, after all, and sheep tended to run astray when *they* felt like doing so, not on any schedule. If there was to be wool for the wheel and the loom, and mutton and lamb for the table, the shepherds had to be left to their own ways and thoughts. The priests were not amused, but they could do nothing about it.

On a rock beside the mouth of the spring, he left the thank-token for whoever actually owned the resource. It might even be that shepherd—but whoever laid claim to the water rights would find the proper toll for the use of his water. Alberich had packed several such needful things in Kantor's saddlebags before they'd left. In this case, it was something virtually every hillman would find useful, the more especially since the confiscation of so many weapons by the Sunpriests; a Tedrel crossbow and a quiver of quarrels for it, all wrapped in oiled canvas to keep them safe. There was nothing about any of the tokens Alberich had brought that said "Valdemar" and nothing—such as, for instance, a bit of gold—that would be difficult for a poor hillman to explain.

These were, after all, *his* people still. He would have a care to what happened to them when he was gone again.

And on they went, taking to the pounded track once again, as the sun sank on their right and the light edged into gold, and golden-orange and the shadows of the hills grew long and stretched across their path.

That was when he sent Laika and a younger Herald out on a long scout ahead. If Laika was right, they should be getting near to the camp. And *he* began the usual futile attempt to probe at the near-future, like a man probing at an old wound to see if it still hurt. As usual, his Gift was silent.

Which was, in a way, a good thing, since it wasn't *warning* him about anything.

The sun was dropping nearer the horizon now, and the sky to the left had turned a deeper blue, while the sky to the right, with long banks of cloud across the path of the sun, was turning red. It would be sunset soon, and they still hadn't found that camp. He was beginning to be concerned. They would have to decide very shortly whether to go on under the full moon, able to see all right, but risking ambush, or make camp themselves—

:Alberich!: came a Mindcall; it jerked him out of his preoccupation with scanning the hilltops for trouble, and made his heart race in sudden alarm.

:Steady on, Chosen. That wasn't trouble—: Kantor said. And in the next moment, he knew that his Companion was

right, of course. If it had been *trouble,* there would have been warning and alarm in that mind-voice.

It was from the youngster who had gone out with Laika. And the next words that came were excited, not fearful. *:Alberich, get up here—you have to see this to believe it!:*

The excitement communicated itself to Kantor, who tossed his head in sudden impatience to be gone, ears pricked forward, muscles tensing.

"Laika and Kulen, something have seen!" he called to the rest. "Keep to the track—summoned I have been."

Kantor evidently felt that was enough; he launched from a swift walk into a flat gallop, speeding over the top of the hill, down across the next valley, and over the next hill, and the next, and the next—

And that was when Alberich saw *why* there had been so much excitement in Kulen's mind-voice. Because, coming slowly toward them, flowing over the hill like a dusty, moving carpet, was an army.

An army of children.

Not just children, he saw, after his first astonished look. There were some adult women among them. But not many, and *they* were burdened with infants, slung across their backs *and* their chests, carried in baskets, even.

It was clearly the children themselves who were in charge here—and it made Alberich's heart leap into his throat to see how carefully they were tending to each other. There were carts pulled by donkeys and ponies full of the very smallest, led by those old enough to control a beast. There were more carts that the tallest and strongest were towing *themselves.* And those old and strong enough to walk by themselves were doing so, in little groups, each shepherded by one older child.

And now that Alberich was here, Laika was not going to wait any longer; she and her Companion raced toward the oncoming horde, and after an initial reaction of alarm, several of the children recognized her, and dropped the bundles they were carrying to race toward *her,* cheering as they went.

:Kantor—:

:I've told them,: Kantor replied joyfully. *:They're putting on some speed.:*

By the time Alberich and Kantor got to the front of the mob, Laika was engulfed in children, all babbling in that strange polyglot tongue she had told him about. He remembered what else she had told him as they rode on the way—that these poor children were starved for adult attention, that she used to tell them stories, and had made herself a kind of extended grandmother to a great many of them. The dry, bare bones of her narrative did not prepare him for seeing this, and he felt his eyes stinging with tears. At least *he* had had his mother, lonely though his childhood had been—

He felt a tugging at his sleeve, and looked down at a little girl who had the features of one of his own hill folk. "Aunty Laika says you were of the people of the Sunlord," the child whispered in Karsite, peering up at him hopefully. "And that you are of the White Riders of the Ghost-Horses now—"

"I am both," he told her, immediately dropping to the ground to put his eyes on a level with hers. "This is my Ghost-Horse; his name is Kantor."

:Ghost-Horse? Where did she come up with that? I like that a great deal better than "White-Demon" or "Hellhorse,": Kantor said, lowering his nose to touch the hand she stretched out to him.

"Have you really come to take us somewhere safe?" she asked, as he marveled that a child of *Karse* should ever reach toward a Companion without fear.

"We have—but who told you of all this?" he asked, trying to make sense of the puzzle. "Who told you about Ghost-Horses and White Riders?"

If it was Laika, he was going to have a few choice words

with her. That sort of story could have gotten her killed and the other three Heralds exposed.

"Oh, it was Kantis, of course," the child told him blandly, in a tone that put the emphasis on *of course.* "Kantis has told us about the White Riders *forever,* and he promised us that some day they would come and take us where there are always good things to eat and a soft bed to sleep in, and no one would make us walk when we're tired, and that we'd all have a mum and a da, though we'd have to share—"

Before he could ask her *who* Kantis was, much less *where* he was and how he had come up with this unlikely tale and convinced them it was going to be true, she caught sight of something past his shoulder, and with a squeal of glee, ran off.

He looked around; what she had seen, and what had set the rest of the children running, was the first lot of Heralds and wagons topping the hill, brushed by the scarlet and gold of sunset. And in a moment, he was nothing more than a rock in a flood of children who found a little more energy in their weary bodies to run. They flowed around him like the largest flock of sheep in the world, faces transmuted by hope—and it was all he could do to hold back his tears.

And of course, faced with this oncoming flood of children screaming, not in fear, but with delight, the Heralds and Healers and teamsters reacted just as any decent human beings would—tumbling out of the seats and off their mounts to open their arms and their hearts, to open the boxes and bags of provisions they had brought, to stuff little hands and mouths with food and drink and toss little bodies into wagons padded with blankets, even as more little bodies were helping even littler ones to climb up as well. They couldn't understand what the children were saying, but they didn't need to know to understand what was needed.

And many of *them* were smiling with tears in their eyes. How could they not? After leaving that grim scene of battle aftermath behind them, how could they *not* want to ease their own aching hearts with the warmth of a joyful child?

And it was all sorted out in a remarkably short period of time. Those carts that *had* been drawn by children were fastened to the backs of the wagons. With the children themselves sharing out the provisions in a generous way that made Alberich marvel, *everyone* got enough to fill his empty belly. The few camp followers who had come with the children rather than fleeing, burdened with abandoned infants, were provided with seats and clean linens for the babies, and in lieu of milk, sugar-water for them to suck to at least stop their crying and ease their hunger. The last of the teamsters, finding no need for their empty wagons, asked permission to go on under guard and see what they could get out of the abandoned camp. After a moment of thought, Alberich gave his permission—although, with unchildlike forethought, the little ones were *all* carrying loot in their bundles: whatever was small, valuable, and light.

They gave it up to the Heralds without a second thought, and that pained him. Did they think they would have to *pay* for their rescue?

"No," Laika said, when he asked her that. "No, this is just something that this mysterious Kantis told them to do."

He relayed that information back to the army via Kantor, along with his recommendation that at least a portion of it be kept in trust for the children themselves. That was all he could do about it, but they seemed far more interested in eating and sleeping than in the jewelry and coins they'd lugged along, so he dismissed it from his mind.

As if the One God had decided to ease their way further, the full moon rose before the last light of twilight faded. With the broad track to follow, there was no chance of getting lost, and not much chance that a horse would make a misstep and hurt himself; accordingly there was never even a *thought* but that they would turn around and head back to the Border.

Bit by bit, as Laika and the other three talked to the older children, a broad picture began to form of what had happened.

One of the first Karsite orphans scooped up by the Tedrels when they first made their alliance and moved into Karse was a boy they all called Kantis. It was *he* who had somehow concocted the odd "cult" that Laika had noticed among the children—a cult that admitted no adult members, and whose members were sworn to secrecy with a solemn oath that, apparently, not even the boys who were later initiated into the Tedrel lodges ever broke.

Most of the cult that Kantis had created had a very familiar ring to Alberich, for it was virtually identical to the simple forms of Vkandis' rites that he had learned as a child from his mentor Father Kentroch, even to calling the God by the name of Sunlord. But there were more interesting additions. . . .

Kantis had, from the beginning, it seemed, included a kind of redemption story, told whenever times were particularly hard for the children. He told them all that "some day" the Keepers (as he called the Tedrel adults) would abandon them and never return. And on that day, the White Riders and their Ghost-Horses would come for them and take them all away into a new land. This would *not* be the home of the Sunlord, he had assured those who, out of bitter experience, had feared that this meant they would all have to die. No, this was a very real land, where they would all make families with a shared set of parents, where they would always have enough to eat and a warm, safe place to sleep, and where they would never have to follow the drum again.

The children stolen out of Valdemar only reinforced Kantis' stories, when they identified the White Riders as Heralds.

Somehow, he had impressed upon them the need to keep all of *this* utterly secret, even more so than the redemption story.

And somehow, he had known the very moment when the Tedrels lost their battle, for even before the remnants of the army came running back to the camp to take what they could carry and flee, he was telling the children that *now* was the time. He organized them, told them they should get what they wanted and whatever "shiny things" they could find in the adult camp, hide the ponies and donkeys until the last of the adults were gone, and prepare to march north, themselves, as soon as the last of the Keepers fled away.

Which was exactly what they had done. Those camp followers who had not run off with skirts stuffed full of valuables and some protector or alone had been bewildered by the stubborn insistence of the children on their goal, but had gone along with it, seeing no other options before them. Most of *them* were heartbreakingly young by Alberich's standards, and not yet hardened from "camp follower" to "whore."

They must have set out from the remains of the camp about the same time that Alberich and his group set out from Valdemar. The entire story was mind-boggling. And he wanted, very badly, to meet this boy, this so-clever, so-intelligent boy calling himself "Kantis," and speak with him.

But though he rode up and down the line, he could not actually find the boy. One child after another asserted that yes, Kantis was certainly with them—somewhere—but no one could tell him what group Kantis was with or where he'd last been seen. He might have been a figment of their collective imagination—he might have been a ghost himself—for he had somehow utterly vanished from among them the moment that they spotted Laika and Kulen.

THE wagons loaded with the most portable of the Tedrel wealth caught up with them much sooner than Alberich had anticipated. This was in part because the portable wealth was *very* portable indeed, and in part because the section carrying the children was moving slowly. The poor things were exhausted, and even packed together like so many turnips in a sack, once stuffed with food and water, they fell asleep. So, since the treasure wagons were going to have to catch up with the main part of the group anyway, Alberich took their pace down to a steady walk.

Laika came up beside him; now that night had fallen, he was able to relax his guard. Laika, sharing his memories of Karse, was similarly relaxed. Nighttime held no terrors for Alberich now, not after so many years in Valdemar. *If* the Sunpriests unleashed their demons—and given how quiet the night was, he rather thought that said demons were fully engaged in pursuing stray Tedrels at the moment—he didn't think they would bother to do so here. So far as the Sunpriests knew at this point, there was no one in this part of the hills but the children, and why waste their most dangerous and powerful nighttime weapon on a lot of children?

Children who couldn't escape on their own, and would soon be facing the Fires anyway. . . .

He had to unclench his jaw over that thought. And he sent up a silent prayer—not the first, and he doubted if it would be the last—that one day the Sunpriests would be answering for their transgressions, and one day it would be priests like his old mentor Kentroch, and like Father Henrick and Geri, who would be ruling in Karse again.

One of the other Heralds came riding up, looking nervously over his shoulder. "Herald Alberich, shouldn't we be putting outriders all around?" he asked. "I mean—"

"Peace; at ease be, protected we are by the priests themselves," Alberich said, and exchanged a glance with Laika. She laughed.

"Karsites won't stir out of their doors after dark," she said, with the air of *one who knows.* "Their priests have a habit of sending some sort of creepy-howly thing out at night, to make sure nobody's out doing something they shouldn't."

"Even the Sunsguard stirs not," Alberich added, with sardonic amusement. "So that now, should even a priest order them out, they will not go."

"Caught in their own trap," Laika said. "And serve 'em right. So by the time sun's up, *we'll* be so close to our people that even if they catch on we're here, our folks can mount a big enough rescue to squeak us across without losing so much as a hair."

Alberich considered how much the Tedrels had drained from the country, and sighed with pain. "*If* they scout or FarSee us, we take—so far as they will know—useless mouths only. We leave—think, they will—the camp unplundered." Privately, he doubted that even the Sunpriests would trouble themselves with FarSeeing this part of Karse; they would use their power to track down the Tedrels and Tedrel recruits. They must know that Sendar was dead, but they must also know that now was not the time to attack Valdemar themselves. Valdemar had just fought a terrible battle, and were exhausted, yes, but the Karsite Sunsguard was drained and weakened by the demands of the Tedrels. The current Son of the Sun—

He set bandits against Valdemar, then hired the Tedrels to do his work for him, Alberich thought somberly. *And now, thanks to the drain that the Tedrels put on his resources, the Sunsguard must be even more depleted. He hasn't got the* means *to attack us.*

No, the Sunsguard would be mopping up what was left, with the priests assisting, then they would all descend on the Tedrel base camp with an eye to getting back what had been drained from them.

"Believe me, there is no way the plunder in that camp can be exhausted, even by us and the Tedrels that were left," Laika told them both. "There'll be enough there to satisfy priestly greed even after our wagons come back. It isn't only the Karsite treasury they've been draining; they've got the accumulation of some twenty or thirty years' worth of loot from other campaigns they've fought, and they've been saving it all, waiting for the day when they'd have their own land again." She scratched her head, thinking, and added, "I'll give the bastards this much; they had discipline. Almost a quarter-century of honest pay, extortion, and booty, and they didn't spend a clipped copper coin more than they had to. *Every* fighter had his own store of loot, but beyond that, every true Tedrel war duke had a treasury tent, waiting for the day when he could finance the building of his own fortified keep in the heart of his own principality."

Alberich was greatly pleased to hear *that.* If the wagons sent onward came back so well loaded, then perhaps the children's little hoards could be kept solely for their use when they were older.

If the ride out had been a mixed pleasure, the ride back was an unalloyed—if bittersweet—one. With all worry about encountering Sunsguard gone, under a glorious full moon and a sky full of stars, and buoyed on the energy of the successful rescue, there was nothing in the way of opening themselves up to pure aesthetic enjoyment of a tranquil ride through peaceful countryside. The teamsters, once the situation was explained to them, relaxed and sat easily on the seats of their wagons. Even the babies only whimpered a little, now and then. Timeless and dreamlike, they moved on across ground that seemed enchanted and drunk with peace. It was as if the One God was granting them all a reprieve from their grief, the sorrow that would confront them when they crossed back into Valdemar, giving their hearts a rest so that they could all bear it better when at last it came.

Just about the time when the moon was straight overhead, he heard the wagons coming up behind them, the sound of the wheels echoing a little among the hills. Since they were near to the spring they'd used on the way in, he called a halt there once the whole party was together again. The children didn't even wake up.

"More about these children, tell me," he asked of Laika, when they were on the move again and a comfortable sort of fatigue began to set in. The moon, silvering the grass around them, turned the landscape into a strange sculpture of ebony and argent; with hoofbeats muffled by the soft earth and grass, they seemed to be moving in a dream, and he asked the question more to hear a human voice than for the information itself.

"You'll find they're a funny lot," she replied. "You'd think, being mostly not taught anything, that they'd be wild. But—well, once they got out of babyhood, they pretty much had to teach themselves and take care of each other, and by the gods, that's what they do. Maybe it was because so many of 'em lost their whole families, but they've got a kind of motto—*nobody left behind*—and they stick to it. The older ones see that the little ones get fed and clothed, the little ones do what they can to help the older ones. I think they're the next thing to illiterate, but they'll drink up anything you teach them like thirsty ground. They *all* found out that the Tedrels themselves may not do anything for them, but if they made themselves useful, they got rewards beyond whatever the Tedrels dumped in their section of the camp, so that's another thing they learned to do, how to make themselves useful. Then when that Kantis child showed up, he *really* organized them. Of course—I didn't get to see much of that, since I was an adult." She coughed. "Very secret, that cult was. No grownups were to hear about it."

"So—when into our camp we bring them, they will helpful be?" he hazarded.

"I would be greatly amazed if they didn't swarm the place, doing all sorts of little chores. Anybody expecting a bunch of terrified, wild little beasts is going to get a shock. Having 'em around is a lot like having a tribe of those little house sprites some old stories talk about; they can't do heavy labor, but by the gods, when they get determined to do something, it gets *done.* I had to fish more of 'em out of my wash tubs than I care to think about." She chuckled a little, then sobered. "Listen, *you* have the Queen's ear; make sure no one breaks them up into little groups right away—let 'em sort themselves out. They've made up little family groups of their own, and it's all they've got. Make sure none of us take that away from them."

"I shall," he promised. It wasn't a difficult promise to make.

The caravan moved on, ghosting through the darkness. And even at the slow pace, they reached the Border again a little after sunrise.

The children *were* awake by then, and peering eagerly ahead. Alberich had elected to come into the camp, not from the south directly, but indirectly from the west, saving the children the sight of the battlefield. They might have run tame in the Tedrel camp for most of their lives, and they might be inured to the aftermath of battle, but he didn't think they had ever seen a *battlefield.* Even now, there would still be much of horror about it. The result of so great a conflict was not cleaned up in a day or two . . . and it was no sight for these little ones.

So they actually made a detour upcountry, leaving the trampled "road" that the Tedrels had left until they struck an old track that crossed the Border at a ford, and joined up with one of the Valdemaran roads used by Border patrols. The old track showed some wear, so *someone* was still using it; it was rutted and gave the teamsters some hard times, but they took it in good part, knowing they were nearly home. Whenever a wagon got stuck, the children (if it was one that was carrying children) all piled out and the largest children mobbed it, put their young shoulders to it, and helped in the front by hauling on the horse's harness. No wagon remained stuck for long, with that kind of help.

For Alberich, crossing the Border brought on a mood of melancholy and depression. Not despair—but his heart sank with every pace they came nearer the camp. For a little, he had been allowed to forget, but only for a little and now—

They had all lost so much . . . so much.

And yet, just as they approached the camp with what seemed like half the inhabitants waiting for them, and in the very moment that the blackest depression descended on him, the children changed the complexion of everything.

They had been clinging to the sides of the wagons, peering over and around each other, trying to see ahead—when they saw the lines of white-clad Heralds and Companions, they could not hold themselves back. They *boiled* out of the wagons, spilled over the sides, tumbled to the ground, laughing and shouting, and ran to those who waited. "White Riders! White Riders!" they shouted (virtually the only Karsite they knew), pouring into the camp and running up to anyone who looked even halfway friendly, as if these were not strangers, but friends and beloved relations.

There were a great many of these children, he realized, as more of them spilled out of the wagons and carts. More than the "thousand" that Laika had promised. But no one seemed to mind. Certainly no one called him or Selenay to account for it, not then, and not at any time thereafter.

And in the days following, as the bodies were burned or buried, as the wounded were taken north, as the encampment was disassembled and troop after troop of fighters sent north again, it was the children who kept them all sane. They were everywhere, poking their noses into everything, trying to learn Valdemaran, trying to help where they could, and just being children, some for the first time in their short lives.

Not even Selenay was proof against their sheer exuberance at being *here,* a place that they seemed to consider an earthly paradise, and before long she had "adopted" a half dozen (or they adopted her), making them her pages and promising that they would be allowed to join her Royal Household in that capacity once they all reached Haven. Nor was she the only one; every wagon going north seemed to hold a handful of children going to a new home. Fighters, teamsters, Heralds—servants and highborn—everyone who *could* take in two, three, or four children did so.

"I never would have believed it, no matter who had told me, if anyone had claimed that bringing these children here was the best thing we could have done," Selenay told him on the third afternoon of the return, watching a child dash away with a message to be given to the next dispatch rider going out of the camp. Her eyes were still shadowed with sorrow, but her lips curved in a faint, fond smile. "I thought that it was something that had to be done, but truth to tell, I was dreading the mess they'd make for us."

They'd taken down the black felt linings for the tents, and the painted canvas glowed with afternoon light. That, too, was a mixed blessing. More light raised the spirit a little—but the black felt had gone for use as shrouds. . . .

"And I," he agreed. "Most unnaturally helpful, they seem."

She had to smile at that, just a little. "*You* don't see them at their worst. They're still children, they still fight, and get into things they shouldn't and have tantrums. But for all of that, I'm afraid that in years to come, they're going to be held up as the good examples that every naughty child in Valdemar *should* behave like."

"Or perhaps, as children being, a year from now and they will no better nor worse than others become," Alberich suggested.

She flicked a fly away with the feather end of her quill. "Perhaps." She put pen to paper, and signed another order. "Who knows? I'm no ForeSeer."

"And I—See not that far, when I See at all," he admitted ruefully. *If I had been, could I have changed any of this? Or was it all too big for any one man to change?*

"Speaking of the children, I've given some thought to what to do with them, the ones that haven't managed to get themselves adopted already, that is," she said, looking up at him. "And I wanted to ask you what *you* think."

"Keeping them to their own—ah—'families,' you are?" he asked, a little anxiously, because he had seen, just as Laika had told him, how they sorted themselves out into their own little "families," and stayed together. It had been the smallest of those groups of two, three, or four children that were the ones that found homes first.

"Of course," she replied. "It doesn't take an Empath to realize we shouldn't tear apart what few bonds they have! But that's where the problem lies, you see; there aren't too many families or even childless couples prepared to take in six or a dozen children at once, much less ones that don't even speak our language. So my first thought was to—well—send them to school." She folded both hands over the papers on her little desk and looked anxiously at him to see what his reply would be.

He nodded; that made perfect sense. "Like—the Academy?" he hazarded.

She nodded. "Or the Collegia. Oh, obviously, they can't actually go to the Collegia, we haven't nearly enough room for them, but something *like* the Collegia. And there are a lot of Valdemaran orphans to deal with, too—though those are having to go to the Houses of Healing, I'm afraid; they need Mind-Healers right now, not schooling. . . ."

Her face darkened for a moment, but she took a deep breath and went on. "So I've written to all of the major temples, the ones with both day- and boarding-schools, and asked if they would take in some of the 'families' for a year, teach them Valdemaran and some basic reading and writing, until I've got these orphan collegia built." She waited for his response. He pondered what she had told him. "*Your* project, this is?"

She nodded. "If I have to," she said, with some of the same mulish stubbornness of her father, "I'll pay for it out of my own household budget—"

He raised an eyebrow. "Doubt do I, with the current mood of the Council, you will have to."

And now she had the good grace to blush. "Then better to push it through now than wait," she said, raising her chin. "Given that the booty from the Tedrels has furnished the means to restore all the damage they did down here, there isn't a great deal for the Council to complain about."

That was certainly true. Laika had been correct about that, as well.

"So build housing for these children—but *homes?*" he prompted.

"I'm going to look for childless couples, and ask *them* to serve as surrogate parents," she said, warming to her subject. "More than one couple, of course, for each house! It will probably take a year to get that all sorted out, find couples that like each other enough to share that kind of responsibility, get the houses built. But then we can keep them all together, we can probably even put Valdemaran children in *with* them—"

"That," he interjected, "a most good idea is. Help each other, they can. And good it would be, for Valdemaran children to know, Tedrel children are no different than they."

She sighed deeply. "I was hoping you would say that. Then it's settled; I'll put it up to the Council, first thing. Maybe *they* won't think it's as important as some of their other business, but I do."

So the "prophecy" is going to come true after all, that the children of the Tedrels were going to have real homes, though they would share "mothers and fathers." Once again, he wondered about that mysterious child called Kantis; since arriving back in camp, he'd been too busy to look any further for him.

And by now, he could be gone.

"Well, this will be the last one of *these* that I sign here," Selenay said, signing the last of the papers waiting for her signature and seal, and putting it in the pile of completed work. She closed her eyes for a moment, and it cost him to see how worn and tired she looked. "I won't miss this place."

"Nor I." He could not wait to be gone, truth to tell. If this had been Karse, rather than Valdemar, the aftermath would have been left for the locals to clean up. But it wasn't. So now there was a neat cemetery with rows of wooden markers out there where the churned-up ground had been—and a pit full of ashes where everything that wasn't Valdemaran had been disposed of. There had been too many burials for single ceremonies; each day at sunset had ended with a mass ceremony at which the names of the interred fallen for that day had been read. He had come to hate sunset, as each sunset brought fresh pain or the renewal of old, as names of those he hadn't known were gone, and those he had known were dead, were read out. He woke each morning, it seemed, with the scent of death in his nostrils, and went to sleep at night with a heart too heavy for tears.

Only Sendar and a few of the highborn were going north to find burial. It was too bad, but there were not many who could afford the expense to bring their loved ones home—and the horror of transporting *that* many bodies, stacked in the beds of wagons like so much cargo—and in the heat of summer—did not bear thinking about. There wasn't a teamster in the country who could be induced to use his wagon and team for that. But that was always the case in war. . . .

The highborn had already been taken north in their expensive, sealed coffins, by the family retainers, in black-felt-draped wagons bedecked with family crests. Only the King was left, to make his final journey in the company of his daughter and those who had known him best.

It would be an honor guard, and it was an honor to be included in it. And here was the one factor that leavened, just a little, the sadness of the journey for Alberich. No one, *not one person,* had objected to his presence at Selenay's side. Talamir had already been sent north with the wounded, and there was no Queen's Own to ride with her. But she wouldn't need the Queen's Own on the journey, only bodyguards. The Council had gone on ahead, and now that the most urgent needs had been answered, all decisions were being held until Selenay reached Haven. So when it came down to it, Selenay only needed her bodyguards, not Alberich.

Yet no one said a word when she posted the final list of who was to accompany her, and chief on the list was "Herald Alberich, acting Queen's Own."

"Are we on schedule?" she asked, packing up her writing case with greater care than the simple task warranted.

"Ahead, a little," he told her. "In readiness, all will be, for leaving at dawn."

She closed and locked the case, then sighed. "I suppose I'll be expected to make a speech."

"Yes." He did not elaborate on that; he felt horribly sorry for her, but it was *her* duty, and she knew it. But there was another aspect to this journey of grief that he didn't think she had considered. Not only the army mourned its King, but the country. "It is wondered, Majesty, if pausing you will be at each village?" They'd left it to *him* to ask that delicate question, that and any others that might come up. He was acting Queen's Own, after all; delicate questions, it seemed, were a part of the job.

"At each village?" she asked, looking blank.

"A speech to make?" he elaborated.

She frowned, and looked as if she had suddenly developed a headache. "Oh, gods. I don't *want* to . . . but people are going to want to pay their respects, aren't they? But each time we stop, it's just going to make this whole thing drag out longer, and—" The frown turned into a look of despair, and he sensed that if he told her she *should* make all those stops, she'd do it, but it might break her.

He racked his brain for an answer, and finally thought he had a compromise. "Majesty—perhaps not a *stop,* and not a speech. But—spectacle. Something for memory and showing honor. A Herald sent ahead to warn each place that we come, then . . . drop pace to a slow walk? With—ah—muffled drums? Lowered banners? Through each place's center, though a detour we make? No speech, but—" he sought for the word, desperately, "—on your part, to be the icon of grief? You need speak not, only mourn, publicly—"

She looked as if he had taken a huge burden off of her shoulders. "The very thing—would you go see to it for me, get it all organized?"

She must be near the breaking point, or she wouldn't delegate that to me. "At once, Majesty," he promised. "Please—be eating would you? Little have you had since morning."

That got a thin ghost of a smile from her. "Except for the accent, you sound like Talamir. Or my old nurse. All right,

Nanny Alberich, I'll go get something to eat, and I promise I'll get some sleep, too. Maybe I'll have Crathach give me something to make me sleep, and go to bed early."

"That, most wise would be," he said. "And eat you must. Too thin, you are. How are you to get a husband, so thin you are?"

She stared at him for a moment in utter silence as he kept his face completely expressionless. Then, weakly, she began to laugh.

He allowed himself a smile.

She wiped away a tear, but he could see that some of the lines of grief and worry around her eyes had eased. "And they say you have no sense of humor," she said.

"Nor do I. All know this," he assured her. "Go now, and something impossible demand of the cooks."

"Impossible?" That caught her off guard. "Why?"

"First, that a reason they will have, at last to complain. Cooks must complain; in their nature, it is. Second, that injured their pride has been, that you have asked for nothing. Their pride is in that their masters demand much of them. Third, *concerned* they have been, that you have asked for nothing. They fear you need them not. Fourth, they worry *for* you." He raised an eyebrow. "But be certain, though impossible, it is something you *want.* Suspect I do, that they will create it."

"Ah." She blinked. "Do you know *everything* that is going on around here?"

He shook his head at that. "Not I. But Kantor I have, as Caryo *you* have. Our Companions know much, and what they know not, generally, they can discover. Sendar made use of that, often and often."

"I'd better get used to doing the same, then." This time her smile was a little stronger, as she picked up her writing case and stood up. "And I'll think about impossible things to eat on the way to my tent. Can you find Crathach and send him to me, while you're doing all the other things I've asked you to?"

"Without difficulty." He returned her smile. "Ask Kantor, I shall."

They left the tent together. She picked up her escort of Ylsa and Keren at the door of the command tent, and went her own way in the golden light of another perfect evening, while Alberich started off on the last of the errands she had set him.

The last turned out to be the first; Crathach was nearby, and heartily approved of Selenay's wish to sleep early. Most of the rest were trivial and easily discharged. That left the organization of what were essentially funeral corteges through every hamlet, village, and town on the road to Haven. But rather than solve that one himself, he asked Kantor to have all the Heralds that were left in camp—save only Selenay's bodyguards—meet him back at the command tent, and bring with them the remaining highborn, officers, and Bards. The latter because Bards tended to be very good at concocting ceremonies, and he suspected they would have some ideas.

They did. And it didn't take very long either, since this was only going to be a procession. The greatest amount of time was spent in deciding what the order of precedence was going to be, and then, what places in the procession would belong to whom. He left them at it, after about a mark; *his* place would be with Selenay, and if they settled their differences without any interference from him, even if not everyone was happy, they couldn't attach any blame to him *or* the Queen.

And nothing would be required of her except to follow the wagon carrying the coffin on foot, with Caryo walking beside her. Certainly no speeches. The focus of attention wouldn't be on her, but rightfully, on the King's remains, which should be something of a relief. So he hoped, anyway. If she wept, all the better. He hoped she would weep; she hadn't done nearly enough.

By this time, it was full dark, and the camp was quiet; with an early start planned for the morrow, most people had, if their duties allowed, made an early night. He moved down the now-familiar lanes of tents in the light of the torches stuck on either side of his path, thinking that this place would look very odd when all of the canvas had been struck and there was no sign of what had stood here but trampled grass.

:I'm glad to be leaving,: Kantor said.

:So am I.: At least in Haven, there would not be the ever-present reminders that *this* was the place where they had lost a King.

His tent had been moved inside what had been the royal enclosure to adjoin Selenay's, and out of habit, he glanced at hers to see if there was any light showing.

There wasn't, and with a feeling of relief, he nodded to the guards at the tent door, and entered his own. They didn't trouble to leave guards inside the tent anymore; Selenay's little pages all slept in bedrolls spread out across the floor, and anyone trying to get in would probably step on one of them. He certainly wouldn't get in quietly; those children slept lightly and the least little sound sent half a dozen heads shooting up. Any intruder would set off more noise than disturbing a flock of geese.

A lantern had been lit for him, and hung from the center pole, showing that most of his baggage had already been packed up and presumably put on the wagon. There wasn't much left; only a bedroll, a set of clean linen and the towels and soap he'd need in the morning, and Kantor.

Most Heralds' tents were big enough for their Companion, Myste's being an exception, but she had obviously gotten last choice on accommodations. Somewhat to his surprise, it wasn't at all unusual for Heralds to share their tents with their Companions, rather than using the canvas shelters. Kantor took up roughly half the space; that first night in his own tent again, bowed down by grief, he had craved Kantor's company with a need that was almost physical, and Kantor had obliged by leaving the canvas shelter at the side and moving into the tent proper. And at first, despite that craving, it had still seemed unnatural in a way to have a—horse—in his tent. Now it was just as in the old days when he had shared tent space with another Sunsguard; it no longer seemed at all odd to see him there.

:Excuse me. I believe I am far better company than any *of the Sunsguard you ever shared tent space with,:* Kantor said indignantly.

He felt instantly contrite. *:I beg your pardon. Indeed you are. Did anyone leave anything here for me to eat?:*

Selenay's swarm of little ones had adopted him as well, and lately had taken to fetching food for him at the same time that they got meals for her, leaving them in his tent, well-covered and protected against the depredations of insects and other pests.

:As a matter of fact, they did, and—I don't suppose you'll share?: Kantor asked hopefully.

Since his appetite had suffered as much lately as Selenay's, Kantor's hope was well-founded. *:I don't know why not.:* He sat down on the bedroll and saw that the usual covered platter and cup had been left for him, cleverly balanced on two more cups in a pan of water, which prevented insects from crawling into it.

He took them out, and shoved the pan of water over to Kantor's side of the tent. Taking the cover off the platter explained why Kantor had hoped he'd share.

Selenay had asked for the impossible, gotten it, and had seen to it that *he* got some of the cook's largesse. Perfect for the heavy weather and a failing appetite were two sallats, a savory one and a sweet, the former a bed of greens with cheese, bits of chicken, fragrant herbs and spiced vinegar, the latter of chopped fresh fruit and nuts, with honey-sweetened cream. How had she known he'd like such things, too?

:Piff. She asked me via Caryo, of course; she doesn't need being told something twice. I'd like some of that cress, please, and some spinach.:

With the empty platter and cup left outside his tent door, he stretched out along his bedroll, and listened to the sounds of the camp. He had been a soldier for too long not to be able to sleep when he needed to, but he had also been a soldier for too long not to be able to assess the mood of the camp just from the night noises.

Tonight, he sensed mostly weariness and relief. They had been here long enough, and, through work and time, what had been terrible anguish had muted to bearable sorrow. Now it was more than time to go home and take up their lives again. Except, perhaps, for Selenay, the time for grief was over, and the time to move on had come.

And that was as it should be.

When morning came, he was barely able to get dressed and out of his tent before Selenay's servants swarmed all over it. Her tent had already been struck, and she was finishing a strong cup of *chava* and a buttered roll while in her saddle, as he escaped from the collapsing tent still tying the laces at the collar and cuffs of his shirt.

One of the "pages" handed him a similar cup and roll and waited, impatiently, for the empty cup. Another brought Kantor a bucket of grain; the Companion immediately plunged his nose into it and began his own breakfast. Prudently, Alberich ate and drank *before* getting into the saddle; there wasn't a chance he'd be given a chance to finish unless he did.

The *chava* wasn't scalding hot, as he had feared it might be, but the heavy admixture of cream and sugar, and the color, like thin mud, warned him that it was probably from the bottom of the pot.

It was; even with the help of cream and sweetening, it nearly made his hair stand on end. But it certainly woke him up. He handed the empty cup to the page, who took it and vanished; the second whisked off the bucket the moment Kantor lifted his head from it.

All around them, tents were falling in the thin gray light of predawn. Selenay gave her cup to a page just as Ylsa and Keren walked their Companions into what had been the royal enclosure. Alberich was in the saddle a moment later.

Selenay looked around at the vanishing camp. "Is breaking camp always like this?" she asked, a little dazed.

"A camp, we Sunsguard seldom had," Alberich admitted.

"I got the impression last night that everyone was pretty impatient to be out of here. But don't take my word for it," Keren shrugged. "I don't usually serve with the army."

"That speech you should make before we leave, I fear," Alberich told Selenay in an undertone. "But it will be the last, until Haven we reach. This, I can promise."

She grimaced, but nodded. "I hope you two know where I'm supposed to be?" she asked the other two.

"That's why we're here," Ylsa told her. "They sent us to fetch you."

Selenay gestured broadly with one hand. "Well, lead on, since you know where we're going."

The procession—for procession it would be, even when it wasn't going through a village—had already begun to form up on the road. Keren and Ylsa went straight to the front of it, where the rest of Selenay's guards were waiting. The funeral wagon would *not* be immediately behind her, but would be the first of the string of wagons.

Bard Lellian, in charge of the ceremonial part of the journey, came up and introduced himself.

"Majesty, I have devised something I hope will meet with your approval," he told Selenay, ignoring the rest of them in a way that told Alberich that his single-minded focus was due to anxiety, not an intention to slight them. "It will not be the ordeal that stopping for speeches would have been. You will merely have to drop back and take your place on foot behind the coffin when we reach any sort of town, along with the rest of the notables who have been deemed of high enough rank to follow you afoot. That is all; simply follow afoot, and—do whatever you feel impelled to do."

Selenay's relief at the simplicity of the arrangements was obvious.

"Then, when you have dropped back, the riders here at the front will all divide to either side of the road, let the wagon and the walkers pass, and fall in behind the last of the walkers, except for two Bards with muffled drums," the Bard finished. "Those will ride in front of the wagon." He peered anxiously at her; he was not a young man, but he didn't seem to know Selenay very well. "I hope that meets with your approval?"

:He's a specialist in this sort of thing,: Kantor confided. *:Funeral dirges, memorial ballads, funerary rituals—rather a melancholy profession, I would think, but apparently it suits him. This is the first time he's had anything to do with the Royals, though, and he's nervous.:*

"I think it is very fine," she told him, and he smiled with relief. "You must have worked terribly hard to come up with something this—appropriate—at such short notice."

Now he blushed with pleasure, and murmured a disclaimer. She raised her head to assess the state of preparations even as he thanked her.

:We seem to be ready to move out,: Kantor told his Chosen.

"Would you sound a call for silence, please?" Selenay asked the Bard, who snatched up the trumpet at his saddle bow, and played a four-note flourish.

Silence fell immediately, and Selenay rode Caryo up onto the bank beside the road so that everyone could see her.

"This seems to be a moment that requires a speech," she said, into the waiting silence. "But a speech, to me, means something that has been prepared for the ears of strangers, and after all that we have been through together, I think that none of us are strangers now." She paused and looked up and down the road, and Alberich knew that she was making certain each and every one of those in this cortege felt she had made eye contact with *him.* "Perhaps some day, when our losses are not so fresh, our wounds are not so raw, we will be able to look back on our victory *as* a victory, with more pride than sorrow. And we *should.* It was not only my father's sacrifice that won the day, it was the sacrifice of every single person who perished or was wounded, and every one of you who held a weapon, who wielded your Gifts, who tended a beast, kept us fed, or served any other task here. The victory belongs to all of you, and never, ever let anyone tell you differently."

She took a breath, blinked hard, and continued. "And even if the enemy had won here, he would never have taken Valdemar, for Valdemar is more than land; Valdemar is the people, and the spirit that lives in those people, and that spirit can never be conquered." Now she looked at the sealed coffin, draped in black, and covered with a pall upon which the arms of Valdemar were embroidered—a pall that had once been Sendar and Selenay's battle banners, and which were still stained with blood. Not just Sendar's blood either, but that of all those who had been with him, whether wounded, or fallen. "He knew that, and he trusted to that spirit to carry on, no matter what happened to him. You have shown that spirit is alive in all of you, and he could have no better tribute than that, nor would he have asked for anything more." Another pause. "And I do not ask for anything *less.*"

:Well said, my Queen,: he Mindspoke to her, and was rewarded by a brief flicker of her eyes in his direction.

"Now it is time for all of us to tender him our final service," she finished. "Now—let us bear him gently home."

And she rode down the bank to her place at the head of the procession, and lifted her hand in signal.

Alberich took his place at her side, with Keren and Ylsa to the right and left. She dropped her hand, and they moved forward on the road to Haven.

And though there had not yet been a ceremony, or a

coronation, everyone in that procession knew that *this* was the moment when the Heir truly took up the reins of power. And so, in silence but for the sound of hooves and feet and wheels on the road, the reign of King Sendar ended, and the reign of Queen Selenay began.

THE journey north accomplished for Selenay what the cleanup of the battlefield had done for everyone else; it allowed her to indulge in the full expression of her mourning—in public. Until the moment of departure, she had held her grief firmly in check, perhaps feeling that with so many others suffering, she should not further burden them with her own grief. If she wept, she did so only in private; everyone knew she mourned, but she did so quietly. But on this journey, her *public duty* was to mourn, to be the symbol of Valdemar's grief, and at last she could give free rein to all of the anguish she had held inside.

It seemed that everyone along their route wished to pay their final respects to the King; farmers left their fields, shepherds their flocks, tradesmen their crafts. Villagers and townsfolk lined both sides of the road, and the road itself was carpeted with rushes, flowers and herbs whenever they entered a town, so much so that the wheels of the wagons were muffled and cushioned against bumps. People carrying baskets and great bouquets of blossoms, and even hand-woven garlands and blankets of flowers, brought them up and placed them on the wagon as it crept past them at a slow walk, until it overflowed with blooms and foliage, and nothing of the black-draped coffin could be seen. And *they* wept, which had the effect of freeing Selenay's tears.

It was exhausting for her, but at the same time, it was exactly what she needed. Alberich and Crathach saw to it that she got plenty to drink, plenty of clean handkerchiefs, and the occasional arm about her shoulders. The Healer concocted soothing eyewashes to rinse her sore eyes and face with whenever they stopped. She ate with growing appetite, which was no bad thing, and was so emotionally exhausted by the time they camped for the night that she slept soundly and without waking. Her little pages saw to it that she had everything she needed, faithful as hounds. And each day that passed saw a little easing of the tension within her that had kept her so near to the breaking point.

It was not that she ceased to care, or became numb, as the days passed. It was more as if the worst of her grief was a finite thing, a barrel that had only *seemed* bottomless until she began allowing it to flow freely.

By the time they reached Haven, and the procession made its slow and solemn way through the city to the Palace, that pinched and overstrained look had left her. She wore her sorrow and her loss like a cloak, with grave dignity, rather than being bowed down beneath their intolerable burden.

She needed that release, for as the journey reached its end, she was about to undertake her final ordeal; the entrance to Haven marked the day of Sendar's official funeral. Haven had been waiting too long to put it off for even one more day—and that wasn't a bad thing. The funeral, though it would be exhausting for all concerned, especially Selenay, would put closure to everything.

They all camped overnight just outside the walls at the

Royal and Home Farms, and servants from the Palace brought them all formal mourning garments, Formal Whites, Greens, and Scarlets. The line for the bathing facilities and even to use the horse troughs and pumps for a bath, was a long one, and Alberich (as did many others) elected to bathe in the river instead; the faint, weedy fragrance of the river water was no match for the strong horse soap they used on themselves as well as their mounts. When they arrived at the gate of the city in the early morning, they looked as if they had all come straight from the Palace itself, and the wagons carrying tents, belongings, and a small mountain of dirty clothing had already gone up the hill, leaving only one single wagon, the one that had carried Sendar to his final rest.

The Court joined them at the first gate; the Lord Marshal, the Seneschal, and the heads of Bardic, Healers' and Heralds' Circles all walked with her behind the coffin, while the rest joined the riders. The coffin itself was transferred by a handpicked group of the Guard, with great solemnity and ceremony, to a more ornate carriage used solely for state funerals before Sendar made his last journey through the streets of his capitol.

And Talamir joined them as well; Alberich was glad enough to relinquish his place at the young Queen's side and join the rest of her bodyguards.

But Talamir did not so much ride to meet Selenay as *appear.* It was a very strange moment for Alberich, when the official greetings were over and suddenly, in a pause and a pocket of silence that seemed created for him, there was Talamir.

And Talamir was changed, vastly changed.

It was more than just the twenty years that had been added, overnight, to his appearance. It was more than just that his hair had gone silver-white, like the mane of a Companion. After all, Alberich had found gray roots to the hair at his temples this very morning, when he had stolen a moment at an unoccupied mirror. It was much, much more than that. There was an otherworldly *stillness* about the Queen's Own, a distant look in his eyes as if he was always *listening* to something no one else could hear, and a faint translucency about him, as if his flesh was not quite solid enough to contain all of the light of his spirit. And a sadness that had nothing to do with the all-too-mortal grief he displayed so openly for his King.

It made Alberich shiver a little, and he sensed he wasn't the only one—but not everyone seemed to notice the change. Selenay didn't, for one. But perhaps she was too young, too involved with her own grief, or both—

Alberich was just glad to acknowledge Talamir's thanks, and drop back farther into the procession, selfishly grateful to Talamir for having recovered quickly enough to take his proper place back; it hadn't been a position *he* had been comfortable with. He hated being in the public eye, on show. Now, in the Formal Whites that the young Queen had asked him to don for the funeral, he was just one Herald among many.

Besides, now we're into Haven, we come into Court protocols and precedence, all the pomp and ceremony that I know nothing about. The arrival of the state funeral coach had been the first sign that he was rapidly getting out of his depth of experience.

He and the other Heralds—and the Royal Guards that were left—rode alongside the walkers, between them and the crowds of onlookers and mourners. Here, as out in the country, the streets were carpeted with flowers and the green herbs of mourning, rue and rosemary, but there were far, far too many people here to allow folk to pile more flowers on the carriage; it would have been covered within a single block. That was all right; they seemed content enough to strew their blossoms in the path of the carriage and the procession.

The muffled drums, augmented now by more mounted and walking musicians, made a dull throbbing through the too-quiet streets. That was the strangest part of all, the *quiet* in the city. Alberich was used to the noise of Haven, but today, the silence was broken only by the sound of people sobbing, and even that was muffled, as if the mourners did not want to spoil the solemnity of the occasion by being too vocal.

They stopped three times in the course of the morning, at three of Sendar's favorite temples, for memorial services that were mercifully brief—just long enough that the walkers could rest before carrying on. Similar services were being held all over the city, and would be all day, and well into the night, but *these* comprised the official funeral for the citizens of Haven.

And it took most of the day to get from the city gates to the Palace Gates. They took one break at noon, at one of the huge Guildhouse Squares; Selenay and her entourage retired to the Needleworkers' Guildhouse for rest and a meal, while Sendar's coffin lay in state in the enormous Guildhall of the Woolmerchants' Guildhouse, and lines of folk, some of whom had traveled for a day to be here, filed past.

Then the procession began again after two candlemarks, stopping twice more for two more memorial ceremonies. And at long last, they entered the Gates of the Palace. By then, they were all exhausted, even those who had only joined the procession when it entered Haven.

Sendar was to be interred in the crypt beneath the floor of the Palace Chapel, along with the rest of his line; all was in readiness there, and had been, presumably, for days. The Guard now marched off to their barracks, leaving a much shrunken company to enter the chapel behind the coffin. They all filed inside, where at least it was possible for those who had been walking for so long to sit down.

Candles had already been lit all over the chapel although the last light penetrated the western windows, and the interior was overly warm, with the golden and reddish light making it appear warmer still. Incense warred with the scent of lilies for supremacy. The chapel was packed solid, shoulder to shoulder; Alberich, who had been riding all day rather than walking, took a standing position up against the wall beside the Royal pew. He was glad to be *there,* truth to tell; the stone wall felt cool against his back.

It *could* have been awful; speaker after interminable speaker eulogizing the King, until grief turned to benumbed boredom. And that would have been a terrible thing to do to Selenay. But someone had been wise; there were no interminable eulogies, only a few, brief speeches by those who had known and loved Sendar the best, punctuated by some of the most glorious music that Alberich had ever heard. Not for nothing was this also the site of Bardic Collegium; the Bards had exerted themselves to the utmost, and even though he had thought that the depths of his grief had been plumbed and exhausted, it was the music that brought tears again to his eyes. Anyone who could have listened to such music and not wept must have had a heart of stone.

Needless to say, when it came time for the last of the speakers—Selenay—she mounted the podium with reddened eyes and tear-streaked cheeks. But her voice was clear and steady as she spoke.

"Sendar was my King as well as my father," she said simply. "He was outstanding at both tasks. It can't have been easy to rule this unruly land of ours, and at the same time govern an ungovernable child, being father *and* mother to her—but he did it, and did it well. I will spend the rest of my life missing him; wishing he could be here to see—so many things. I suspect Valdemar will miss his steady hands on the reins, too. I can only pray that I can be as wise and compassionate a ruler as he was; I doubt very much if I can ever equal him as a parent. And I would gladly give my own life to have our positions reversed." She raised her head a little. "Nevertheless, such a sacrifice demands more than just words; it demands deeds. It demands that we *be* worthy of it; it demands that we all go beyond what we think is enough, making our own sacrifices in the name of a better life for all of Valdemar.

That, in the truest essence, is what *he* did. That is what *I* will do. That is what he would expect of all of us; he deserves, and should have, nothing less than excellence as a fitting tribute to his memory. Only then can we be worthy of such a great and terrible gift—the life of a King."

She sat down in silence. And it seemed to Alberich that she had surprised many of her listeners—nonplussed some—and actually startled others. They were not sure how to react to her. This was *not* the speech of a young woman, overwhelmed with grief, that they had expected to hear. . . .

More music filled the silence, then, a final prayer, and the service was over. A small and very intimate party followed the coffin down into the crypt for the final interment; Alberich was not part of that procession, nor did he wish to be. He had been an integral part of a funeral that had stretched on for far too long, from the Border to Haven, and—meaning no disrespect to Sendar's memory—he was weary of it, and wanted only to rest.

:Believe me, Selenay feels the same,: Kantor told him, the weariness in *his* mind-voice clear as cut crystal. *:She's going straight to bed, and she told Caryo that she is going to sleep for a week. We're already bedded down, and Caryo and I intend to stay here and rest. I told Caryo to stay as long as Selenay stays asleep.:*

:Good,: he said, and meant it. He remained where he was only long enough to see them all emerge from the crypt, see that the Seneschal cut short the line of those wishing to offer condolences, and watch Selenay vanish through the private door at the rear of the chapel that led straight into the Royal Suite with Talamir, Crathach, and the Seneschal in close attendance. Then he made good his own escape. Perhaps he should have stayed to listen to the Court gossip and read what he could out of expressions and what was *not* said, but—

—but that, frankly, was Talamir's job.

Then he recalled what Talamir had looked like, and wondered if Talamir was even capable of descending to such mundane and petty depths now. *All right. I had better start to learn it. But not tonight.*

The air in the chapel had been warm, and now it felt stifling; too hot, too heavy with the mingled scents of candle wax, incense, and lilies. He was only too glad to get out into the night. It was sultry and humid out there, but not as suffocating as the Chapel had been.

And he was unsurprised to be intercepted at the door by Dethor, who must have stationed himself right at the exit. He'd sensed the old Weaponsmaster lurking somewhere about, but he figured that Dethor would wait until *he* was free before greeting him.

"By your Sunlord, boy, it is *good* to see you," was all the old man said, but Alberich felt something inside him warm at the welcome. He seized Alberich's shoulders in both hands, and stared into his eyes, while the last few mourners filed out of the chapel door behind them. "I wish I could tell you just how good it is."

"I think that I may know, for as good it is to see you," he replied quietly, and sighed. "A thousand things, I wish to tell you—"

"And all of them can wait. A good cleanup for you, and then your own bed," Dethor told him firmly. "That's why I came here to get you. Falling on your nose won't honor Sendar or help his daughter, and besides, she's got all of the Collegium and every Herald that could get here to keep an eye on her tonight."

He felt compelled to protest weakly. "But—duties I have—"

"Which are in Talamir's hands, at least as far as Selenay is concerned. Do him good." Dethor gave him a little push to send him on the path down toward the salle. "As for your duties as Weaponsmaster, the Court and Collegia are in a week of official mourning. No Council meetings unless there's an emergency, no Court functions, no classes, no lessons. The only thing on anyone's plate is planning the coronation, and *that* is for the Seneschal and Bardic Collegium, not us. Not even Selenay, actually; all *she* has to do is go through what they plan out for her. For you lot, this is a week of rest."

"Ah." He absorbed that with relief—when something that Dethor had said at the beginning of the explanation struck him as odd. "Dethor—Weaponsmaster's Second, I am, not Weaponsmaster—"

"Not as of today, you're not," Dethor said smugly. "With the Dean's approval, *I* just retired, and *you* are Weaponsmaster."

"Ah—" he said. It was all he could say. He felt completely stunned and utterly blindsided. This, he had *not* expected!

"Glad you agree," said Dethor with satisfaction. "Which is just as well, since it's too late for you to back out. Come along. It's a shower bath for you, and then bed. Worry about whatever it is you're going to worry about *tomorrow.*"

:You might as well surrender now,: Kantor said sleepily. *:He still outranks you. Retired Weaponsmaster outranks the current Weaponsmaster.:*

And in fact, there was a sweet relief in doing just that, surrendering and letting someone else give the orders. He had *never* thought he would be comfortable in doing that—but he had never trusted anyone the way he now trusted these friends—these brothers—his fellow Heralds. As *they* trusted him; had trusted him with the safety and life of their Queen, and their own.

As they had trusted him to go home to Karse—and come out again.

"In your hands, I put myself," he said, and gave in gracefully to the inevitable.

"I find it somewhat ironic," Selenay said, a good two weeks and a bit later, as Alberich stood beside her, on her left. "That one of the first things I do is ask you to keep to your shadow-Grays, and yet circumstances keep forcing you into Whites."

They stood outside the doors of the Great Hall, and from the other side came a hum of voices and a sense of expectation. On her right was Talamir, in that same set of Formal Whites Alberich recalled from the first moment he'd actually *seen* the Queen's Own. Now he wore a set of Whites every bit as elaborate as Talamir's, and very uncomfortable he felt in them, too. It wasn't as if they were ill-fitting; quite the contrary, they fit him better than any clothing he'd ever worn. They should. It had taken two cobblers, three tailors, and five fittings to ensure that they did, and the wonder was, it had all been done in just under a fortnight. No, it was that same reaction he'd had to Talamir's Whites; this was a set of clothing for a highborn courtier, not a common man like him.

:I believe at the time you were thinking, "a foppish highborn courtier," or something of the sort,: Kantor observed.

:So I was. I still think so. And the moment all this is over, I am changing out of these ridiculous garments as quickly as humanly possible:

He refrained from tugging at his high collar. It wasn't tight; he only felt as if it *should* be. "Only for one day, it is," he replied. "Tomorrow, Alberich the Grim I shall again be." He did *not* add how much it would take to induce him back into the cursed Whites.

"Is that what the Trainees call you?" Talamir asked with interest. Talamir's health had improved vastly, and continued to do so, but there was still something that was other-worldly about him—more so at some times than others—as if only part of him was still here, among the living. And it wasn't as if he was absentminded, or that his mind wandered; actually, he was, if anything, sharper than ever. He noticed *everything* but said very little. Perhaps that was part of it; he stood aside from life, an observer rather than a participant. The things that irritated and annoyed other people, Talamir did not even comment upon; Alberich wondered if there was even anything he was afraid of anymore.

There were times when he seemed so distant and remote that he didn't quite seem human. . . .

Fortunately, today he was very much in the moment, and the most like his old self that he'd been since before the last battle.

"Oh, that they call me, other things among," Alberich replied. "And 'Great Stone-Face,' or 'Herald Stone-Heart.'" He permitted himself a sardonic little smile. "They take me, perhaps, for granite."

Talamir and Selenay both blinked at him. "Was that a *joke* I just heard?" Talamir asked, in utter disbelief. "A *pun?*"

"Not possible," he replied blandly. "No sense of humor have I. All know this."

It was too late for any retort, for the trumpets sounded just beyond the double doors of the Great Hall. The doors themselves were opened from inside, and Selenay stepped forward, followed closely by her two escorting Heralds.

The Great Hall was crowded as full as it could be with every highborn and notable who had been able to get here in time for the funeral and subsequent coronation. All six of Selenay's little Tedrel pages, decked out in the dark blue of the Royal livery, preceded her as she paced up the narrow path between the two halves of the audience, in time to the music. Each of them had a basket of fragrant herbs, which they scattered in her path with meticulous care. Initial rehearsals had them either dumping handfuls and running out halfway up to the dais, or being so stingy with each leaf that they still had full baskets when they got there, so they were taking immense care to do it *right* this time. The looks of fierce concentration on their little faces were quite endearing.

All of the doors and windows were flung open to the summer day outside the Hall, so at least it wasn't as close in here as it could have been. But the crowd glittered like the contents of an overturned jewel chest, garbed in so many colors that, after a fortnight of the stark blacks and whites of mourning, it hurt Alberich's eyes to look at them. The sunshine pouring in the windows glanced off gold and jewels, and the crowd glittered with every tiny movement.

Selenay set the pace, they only had to follow her; she looked meditative, as if she was taking a stroll in the gardens, not walking up to the throne that she would officially take in a few moments. Alberich thought that *she* looked as beautiful and fragile as a snow spirit in the gown that had been made for this moment, a gown of some soft, silky, draping stuff based on Herald's Whites, but with winglike sleeves and a train that trailed out behind her, glittering with tiny moonstones and gold beads, and a chaplet of moonstones and beads in her unbound hair. He would much rather that she had worn her armor, truth to be told. He would have preferred to see her marching up to the throne like a conquering battle maiden. Who would take this sweet young *girl* seriously as a monarch?

The army. Anyone who was with us on the battlefield. Perhaps those who heard her eulogy for her father. But the others? Highborn and notables from across the land? They knew only what they saw—a girl, a mere girl, come to govern.

Well, she'd better learn how to handle them. It was her job to *make* them take her seriously.

With perfect timing, they reached the dais just as the music ended. And in a silence remarkable for a room holding so many people, the three of them ascended it.

Waiting for them there were the chief members of the Council, ranged in a half circle behind the throne—the Seneschal, the Lord of the Treasury, the Lord Marshal, and the chiefs of the Heraldic, Bardic, and Healer's Circle. Representing all of the various and varied religions of Haven was the Patriarch Pellion d'Genrayes; Alberich didn't know which sect and temple he represented, but he *looked* every inch the part—white-haired, bearded, in robes of purple and white that were absolutely stiff with white embroidery, and an imposing staff capped with a huge globe of amber.

"Who comes before the throne of Valdemar?" the Lord Marshal thundered, placing his hand on the hilt of his purely ornamental sword.

"I, Selenay, daughter of Sendar, and rightful Queen of Valdemar," she replied, in a voice as cool as mountain snow. "In the name of the gods, I lay claim to the throne of Valdemar."

"By what tokens do you claim the throne?" asked the Seneschal, who looked nothing near as imposing as the Lord Marshal. Truth be told, he *looked* as if he should be asking, "Have we got the order of precedence right?"

Selenay answered the challenge as her father's daughter should. "By the token of my blood, of the line of Valdemar, first King of this land. By the token of my Choosing, by the Companion Caryo. By the token of my mind, trained to rule this land as wisely as the first King. By the token of my heart, that is given to the service of the people of this land. And by the token of my right hand, that will wield the sword of war or the staff of peace over it as need be." She held her head high, and her voice remained steady and clear.

"And who vouches for these things?" the Lord Treasurer asked.

"I vouch for her blood, of the line of Valdemar, for my Healers saw her born of Sendar's consort," said the Chief Healer.

It was the Chief Herald's turn. "And I, that she is Chosen by the Companion Caryo, for my Heralds saw her trained and granted Whites."

"I," the chief Bard said, somehow putting far more theatrical flourish into the words than anyone else, "vouch for her mind, for my Bards have tested her training, and found it complete."

Now it was Talamir's turn; his voice trembled a little, but only a little, and Alberich didn't think that anyone noticed but him. "I vouch for her heart, for I am the Queen's Own, and her heart is open to me."

Now, tradition said that the last lines were to be spoken by the Lord Marshal himself, but Selenay had asked for Alberich to take the final part. "Who else could *but* you?" she had asked, and he could not find it in him to deny her. He had drummed his response into his brain until he woke to find himself reciting it in his sleep; this was *no* time to let his Karsite syntax mangle what he was going to say.

"And I," he said, in a voice that sounded harsh to his own ears, "vouch for her hand, strong in defense, gentle to nurture, for I am the Queen's Champion, and I have tested her will and her spirit in the fires of adversity."

The Lord Marshal nodded, and stepped back. "Then come, Selenay, daughter of Sendar. Come and assume your rightful place, Queen of Valdemar."

Selenay took the last few paces until she was within touching distance of the throne, then turned, and faced the gathering. Her pages scrambled to gather up the train of her gown and arrange it at her feet. Alberich moved farther to her left and took the gold wand that served as the seldom-used scepter from the hands of the Seneschal, as Talamir did the same on the right and took the crown from the Seneschal. Selenay removed the bejeweled chaplet with her own hands, and gave it to the Treasurer.

With infinite care, Talamir placed the simple gold crown, hardly more than an engraved circlet, on her golden head, and stepped back to take his place behind the throne. Alberich gave the scepter into her hands, and looked for a moment deeply into her eyes.

She looked back at him fearlessly. A world of question and reassurance passed between them in that look, and he could not have told which of them comforted the other more. But he knew then, in that moment, that no matter what hardships, what trials came in the future, she would not break under them. He *had* seen her tested in the fires of adversity, tested and tried and tempered, and she had come out of it full of strength, true as steel, and as tough and flexible.

:As have you,: Kantor said, a universe of love and pride coloring the words. *:And those who don't see it, haven't eyes. The rest are proud that you are one of us, Herald Alberich.:*

He stepped back and took *his* place, next to Talamir, and the Lord Marshal called out the very same words that *he* had used, all those many days ago, on the road to Haven.

"Valdemar—behold your Queen!"

And the cheer that erupted from those gathered below her held nothing feigned or uncertain.

EPILOGUE

ALBERICH had wanted to come to the Temple of the Lord of Light and visit Geri for nearly a moon, but there had just been too much to do. It wasn't just his full duties as Weaponsmaster, although that was a time-devouring job in and of itself. When you added his continued forays into the darker streets of Haven, *then* his informal, but very necessary lessons with Talamir, lessons detailing the intricacies of the life of the Court and the highborn courtiers that made it the very hub of their existence, as well as all the eddies and swirls of intrigue within it—

There just hadn't been enough marks in a day.

Working with Talamir had been the hardest, although Talamir was, during these sessions, the *most* like his former self that he ever was these days. Alberich walked into the lessons with a shiver, and out of them with a feeling of relief and the strong sense that he'd been in the naked presence of someone who'd been done no favors by being brought back to life, and who lived each moment longing to return to the path he'd been taken from so that he could finish the journey.

But Crathach had been right; there *was* no one else that could serve as the Queen's Own that Selenay needed right now. And Talamir knew that.

Perhaps that was why he was driving Alberich so hard. Transferring the full weight of the job of—intelligence master, for lack of a better title—onto Alberich's shoulders meant there was one less thing holding Talamir back from that delayed journey.

Finally it had been the fact that he *hadn't* been to the temple in far too long that had decided him. Talamir was busy with some delegation or other paying respects to Selenay, and the scum of Haven could stew without him for one night.

Kantor heartily approved, which eased his conscience somewhat. And truth to tell, it felt very good to ride down into the city *without* wondering which persona he should don, if there was going to be any trouble that night, or whether he was going to have to explain himself to the constables and City Guard *again.* He felt relaxed, as he seldom did, as Kantor stopped inside the walls of the temple's outer court and waited for him to dismount.

On a pleasant evening like this one, he had expected the court to be full of the Sunlord's worshipers, and indeed it was. As the priests intended, the court was serving its function as the neighborhood gathering place. Older children who had not yet gone to bed played games along one wall, a number of folk were using the "free" lantern and torchlight to read by, sitting at the benches on the opposite wall to where the children played. There were little knots of gossip and courtship, awkward flirtation and some friendly rivalry, and even a pair of old men playing a game of castles on a portable board. Alberich wouldn't have been surprised to see a hot pie seller there, though no doubt, if one had appeared, Geri would have run him off. There were *some* things that were just a shade too undignified for the forecourt of a temple.

None of them paid any attention to Alberich. He was now a fixture at the temple—though he doubted that anyone knew him for the Queen's Champion, in his dark gray leathers. They probably thought he was just someone's private guard. Anyone could have a white horse, after all, and what would the Weaponsmaster of Herald's Collegium be doing down here, in this little neighborhood temple, anyway? Those with Karsite blood took great pride in the fact that one of their own was a Herald, but no one would ever dream that a Herald would come here to worship the Sunlord, however devout he was.

People, he was coming to think, mostly saw what they *expected* to see. And if they saw something that ran counter to their expectations, they tended to rationalize it away.

Useful, that, for a man in his position, though he would never trust his life to that principle. People were *also* likely to figure out the one thing you wanted to keep hidden from them at the worst possible moment.

The door to the temple lay open to catch the coolness of the night breezes, and he simply walked in. And stopped to stare.

For there was Geri, and around him was a gaggle of children, one of which he *recognized* as the little Karsite girl who had talked to him on the night of the rescue. They were all wearing a version of the warm yellow tunics and trews worn by novices in the service of Vkandis, brand new, and a bit oversized. And they all acted as if they were completely at home here.

Geri was giving them a Valdemaran lesson, with the flock of them tucked out of the way in the side chapel used for long vigils and private meditations. Alberich realized after a moment of complete blankness, that this little temple had taken in all of the *Karsite* children that had been taken by the Tedrels. And if the hour seemed rather late for lessons, well, that might be the case for anyone other than a Temple of Vkandis—

the Sunlord had rites and rituals going on from the dawn to sunset, and only after darkness fell was Geri going to be free to give these little ones the language class they needed before they could hope to learn anything else.

I'll have to ask Myste if she can get down here and give him a hand, he thought, watching them all. *I wonder if there are any other Karsite exiles who've got the time to help? Geri won't push it, but* Myste *will.*

He quickly moved back into the shadows, lest he disturb them, and watched. And felt something extraordinary unfold inside him. Something so extraordinary, that at first, he didn't recognize it for what it was.

Happiness. Pure, unalloyed happiness. Of *all* of the things he had done or had a hand in doing, this was the one that had brought nothing but good for all concerned, with nothing whatsoever to regret or wish he had done differently.

The children responded to Geri with all of the warmth that he would have expected; Geri was one of the kindest souls in the world, and children liked him even when he had to discipline them for something. But these children in particular were blossoming for the young priest like flowers in the sun—already he could tell a vast difference between the too-eager, too-helpful, anxious, pinch-faced little things they had been, and the bright-faced creatures they were now. It was wonderful. This was how Karsite children *should* look. And even as he reveled in the pleasure of knowing that *he* had had a key hand in making it possible for them to be here, he also knew a moment of sadness at the fact that even in Karse, most Karsite children were not this free, not this happy. . . .

Sunlord, gentle giver of light, make it possible for them, too—

A small hand tugged at his sleeve, and he turned and looked down.

"I heard you were looking for me?" said a very small, *very* red-haired boy, with amazing blue eyes that looked oddly old in such a young face.

For a moment, Alberich stared at him, trying to work out what on earth the child could mean. Then it struck him.

"You are the boy they called Kantis?" he asked.

The child nodded. "And you're Alberich, the White Rider, the one who was promised to us. Right?"

"Well—" he squatted down on his heels, so that he could look the boy straight in the eye. "I would say that it depends on just who was doing the promising. And where he got his information."

The child grinned at him. "It would be me that was doing the promising, but the promise wasn't *mine,* it was the Prophecy. And it all came out of the Writ, of course. I know the Writ very well!" He struck a pose, and began to recite. "Alcar, Canto Seven, Verse Nine—*And the children shall be reft from the people, and they shall suffer in the hands of the infidel, but those that keep faith shall endure and the riders of light shall redeem them.* Porphyr, Canto Twelve, Verse Twenty-two—*And lo! in the moment of despair, I shall be with you, I shall guide you, as you were a child, out of the camp of iniquity and into the hands of the saviors, and great spirits of white shall succor you.* Werthe, Canto Fifteen, Verse Forty-nine—*And a rider of the purest white spirit shall—*"

Alberich held up his hand to stop the flow of words. "I would say that you do, indeed, know the Writ very well," he admitted gravely. "But I am not at all certain that there is anything in those verses that *I* would recognize as being part of the—the Prophecy."

He was going to add, *if there ever was a Prophecy,* except that what this child had done, and the hope he had given the others, the way he had organized them and kept them going—how had that been so wrong? Even if it had all been a childish tale concocted out of the scraps of Writ he knew, the tales the

Valdemaran children babbled, and his fertile imagination, it had essentially saved them.

"But I suppose it depends on how you interpret them," he finished instead. And smiled. "I wanted to meet you primarily because I wanted to thank you for helping all of the others so much."

The boy looked at him unblinking, but with a smile playing about his lips. "Isn't that what we're all supposed to do? Help each other? No matter who we are and where we come from? That's what the Writ says, in the Great Laws."

Where had the child learned *that?* Not from any of the Sun-priests that Alberich had served. . . . "Absolutely right." He stood up, and gazed down at the child. "You are a very remarkable fellow."

"And so are you, Alberich of Karse, Herald of Valdemar." The child's voice suddenly deepened, and seemed to fill his ears, his mind, and his world shrank to the boy's young face and the voice that resonated all through him. He couldn't move. And he didn't want to. . . . "A man of such conscience and honor is a remarkable man indeed; so remarkable, that it would seem that his prayers reach a little farther than most."

Alberich could not look away from those blue eyes, eyes which held an impossible golden flame in their depths. He wasn't afraid, though. Far from it. He had never felt such peace before in his life.

"A man of conscience and honor—who has found a fitting place in his exile, among those who value that honor, and honor the conscience." The boy nodded. "It is written that exiles do not last forever, for those who are true to their word, their family, and their home. But remember, always, that the Writ tells us that a man's home is where his family is, Herald Alberich. And also, that friends are the family one can choose. . . ."

The child backed away a few paces, as Alberich felt his pulse hammering in his throat, as if he had run a very long distance. He hardly knew what to think; he couldn't have actually *said* anything if his life had depended on speaking.

The boy turned, and walked a few more steps away in the direction of the door, then looked back over his shoulder.

"And if you think what *I* am is remarkable, wait some few years. And you will see what my daughter can do. Or should I say, my daughter who will be my Son?" Then he laughed and ran off, a high, utterly childlike laugh that broke the spell that had held Alberich motionless.

He still couldn't think; his thoughts moved as if they were flowing through thick honey. But—he needed to run after that boy—

"Alberich!" Geri called, and he turned—

The priest had broken up the class, and apparently had spotted Alberich in the back of the temple. "I was hoping you'd come to see what we've done! We took *all* of the Karsite children when the Queen's people came to ask if we had room for any. You know, we just couldn't turn them away, and they've been a delight to have here. What's more, they are making remarkable progress!"

"Like—that boy?" he replied, feeling his heart still racing with an emotion that held both excitement and fear. No—not *fear,* but an emotion like fear. It took him a moment to recognize it as hope. . . .

"Boy?" Geri looked puzzled. "What boy?"

"The boy I was—" he gestured, but there was no sign that there had ever been anyone there. "—talking—to—"

They both scanned the now-empty temple, but there was no sign of any children now. "It must have been one of the youngsters from the courtyard," Geri replied, looking puzzled. "All of the Karsite children were with me."

"Are any of the children who come here in the evening named Kantis?" he ventured, not knowing whether he wanted to hear the answer.

But Geri only shrugged. "I haven't a clue, there are so many of them, and they just swarm the place in weather like this. Some of them aren't even worshipers of the Sunlord. They just come to play with our children."

Alberich licked dry lips and thought furiously. It *might* just have been a child playing a prank; it would have been natural for the Karsite children to tell others about Kantis and their peculiar prophecy. Children sometimes played the most elaborate jokes, *especially* on adults, when they thought they could get away with it. Although the families who worshiped here were fluent in Valdemaran, they all spoke Karsite at home, and children picked up languages easily. It would have been *easy* for one to pick out some passages from the Writ that matched that "Prophecy." Wouldn't it?

And who was he, to be the recipient of a visitation from the Sunlord Himself? No one. If anyone should have gotten a visitation, it should be Geri. Not him.

And—no. I won't worry this to death. If it was *the Sunlord in His aspect as Child of the Morning, or if it* wasn't, *it is all the same to how I should continue to act.* That was Free Will again, the Gift of the Sunlord, to choose or not choose a path. He would choose the same path he always had, that of honor. *And in either case, because pearls of wisdom drop from innocent mouths, I shall take the advice to heart, for it comes from the Writ, and I shall take comfort from it for the same reason.*

"It probably was one of the youngsters from outside; if you see him again, make sure to get him to talk to you, for he is remarkably well-spoken," he said, and slapped Geri on the back. "I am dying for a decent glass of tea. Why don't you tell me what you've been doing with these children, and give me some idea of how I can help?"

After all, wasn't that what everyone was supposed to do? Even an exile in a strange land—

Exile? The Writ—and the boy—were right. When he had come here, perhaps, but among these people, he had found those who understood that a man had to hold to his word and his honor. People who were the truest sort of friends—and as the Writ said, the sort of friends who became one's family.

Which meant that he wasn't really an exile after all.

It was good to be home.